"This gripping dystopian thriller grabs you from the very start with subtle details and brilliant descriptions, as well as tension-building prose and believable dialogue that immediately endears readers to the unlikely hero. There are patriotic elements to this story, as well as anarchic ones, action-packed scenes, and thoughtful philosophical moments that take a reader by surprise. Eastwood's talent as a flexible and creative author is on clear display as he unravels this twisted vision of the future."
Self-Publishing Review

Midnight black

A novel by

R. J. Eastwood

To Paul —
all the best
always

ISBN:
Hardback 978-1-64456-258-1
Paperback 978-1-64456-259-8
Mobi 978-1-64456-260-4
ePub 978-1-64456-261-1
AudioBook (downloadable) 978-1-64456-262-8

Library of Congress Control Number: 2021931077

The author of this work is Robert J. Emery who writes fiction under the pen name R. J. Eastwood.
Join him online at: **http://www.robertjemeryauthor.com**
If you enjoyed Midnight Black consider writing a review.

Published by

INDIES UNITED PUBLISHING HOUSE, LLC
P.O. BOX 3071
QUINCY, IL 62305-3071
IndiesUnited.net

This book is dedicated to my parents, Angie and Albert, who taught me to always be involved and engaged, never silent.

To my wife Susanne who patiently read each revision.

To publisher Lisa Orban who is always there to support her authors.
Editor Jennie Rosenblum and cover designer Danielle Johnston.

And finally, a shout out to author Steven King who wrote, **"Description begins in the writer's imagination but should finish in the readers."**

CHAPTERS

"I agree with the Constitution with all its faults... I believe, further, that this is likely to be well administered for a course of years, and can only end in despotism, as other forms have done before it, when the people shall be so corrupted as to need a despotic government, being incapable of any other."

Benjamin Franklin
1706 -1790

MIDNIGHT BLACK

IN THE NEAR FUTURE, THE WORLD
REMAINS IN A STATE FLUX.

INDIES UNITED PUBLISHING HOUSE, LLC

The Year is Wherever Your Imagination Takes You.

CHAPTER 1

The Execution

There's no turning back now from what I came to do... what I am compelled to do... consequences be damned... Lady Justice doesn't get her hands on this one... this one is mine... I've been sitting in my car now for ten minutes staring at the house... I've checked and rechecked the address... this is it, a gray two-story four-unit tenement with three ground floor entry doors... I assume the middle one leads upstairs... the one to the left, that's the correct number... this is it, it's now or never... screwing on the silencer to my Glock-22, I approach the door and knock... no response... I strike the door again... this time a voice responds.

"Who is it?"

"I have a package for Mister Jack Kerfoot. It requires a signature."

"I'm not expecting a package. Who's it from?"

"Amazon, sir."

"I'm not expecting a package from Amazon."

"If you'll just open the door and take a look, Mister Kerfoot."

A couple of seconds pass before a lock is released... the door slowly opens about a foot and Kerfoot peers out. Immediately, I kick at it... it swings open hitting Kerfoot's right shoulder and knocking him back... stepping in, I stick my gun in his face.

"Hey! Who the hell are you?"

"Your worst nightmare."

"Get out of here, I'm calling the cops!"

"Go ahead, piss ant, call them."

The last thing this lying son-of-a-bitch wants is the police to show up... not with what he's done... Jesus, he can't be over twenty-five or twenty-six years old, thin face, dirty-blond hair, blue-green eyes... he's short... five-eight if he's lucky... coming face-to-face with him only increases my rage.

"What the hell do you want, man?"

"You, Jack Kerfoot, you."

"Me? What for? Get the hell out of my house!"

Watch his right hand, Billy... why is it behind his back? His hand whips around... shit, the fool's got a gun... instinctively, my right arm swings up and out the Glock smashing against his left ear just as he pulls his trigger... the bullet whizzing within inches of my left ear slamming into the wall behind me... blood's gushing from his ear... his hand goes to it... he squeals like a wounded animal... his gun slips from his hand to the floor... he turns and quick-steps down the hall through a door slamming it behind him like the repulsive rodent he is... hey, jerk off, that's not gonna save you... kicking the door with a flat right foot, it swings open on the first try... it's an oversized closet... the feral pig is on his ass behind a couple of large boxes and hanging clothes, legs bent to his chest, arms wrapped around his knees, fingers intertwined tight, eyes shut like maybe if he doesn't see me I'm not really here and won't do what I've come to do.

"You know why I'm here, Kerfoot?"

No answer.

"Open your eyes, look at me."

His eyelids slowly open, his gaze going first to my gun then up to meet mine... here it comes, the prick is gonna plead for his miserable life, but I'm not offering options here... forget it creep, they'll be no negotiations on this your last day sucking air.

"Who are you... what do you want!"

"Does the name Russell ring a bell?"

"I don't know no Russell. You got the wrong guy."

The hell I have... aiming for his right knee, I squeeze the trigger... the silencer muffles the sound of the exploding bullet... the shell strikes peeling away his kneecap... he's howling like a squealing pig... his body's oscillating like an electric toothbrush. My second shot is to his left kneecap ripping away flesh, cartilage, and bone... his mouth flaps open wide... out comes another chilling scream. Go ahead, you pussy, make all the noise you want, nobody's coming to your rescue... look at me, asshole, look at me before your lights go out and you come face to face with your maker... whoever the hell that is... Satan, maybe.

"Just in case you didn't know her name, it was Diedre."

"What?"

"Diedre, her name was Diedre."

He's shaking badly, breathing hard, and having trouble putting one word in front of the other.

"I... don't... know... any ... Diedre!"

Enough chitchat... do it, do it now, Billy... I squeeze the trigger... the bullet's racing down the barrel at twenty-five-hundred feet per second striking his forehead just above and between his eyes leaving not a neat hole but tearing away the top of his skull splattering flesh, bone, blood and gray matter over boxes, clothes and walls... Lucifer's bastard son is dead... it felt right and righteous and all the other words in the English lexicon that justifies what I've done in Diedre's name... now get out of here, Billy. Whoa, wait! What the hell was that? An earsplitting horn-blast! Jesus, it sounds like it's coming from inside this closet... there it is again, only louder... a sharp stab to the middle of my back... zap, zap... an electrical charge is surging through me doubling me over... someone's in my face yelling.

"Get up, get your lazy ass up!"

"What?"

"You heard me 556, get your miserable ass out of that bunk now."

That voice... that accent... it can't be... its Quasi.

"What the hell are you doing here?"

"I'm everywhere, 556, always watching and waiting for you to screw up. Now get your goddamn criminal ass up."

3

CHAPTER 2

This Place Sucks

When my earthly expiration date arrives, *I'll be whisked off to heaven because I've already experienced hell. I no longer have a sense of what is real and what is not... the memories that once lifted my spirits when all hope seemed lost are gone... like I'm seeing life through heavy gauze. That's what this hellhole has done to my once-functioning brain... but I will endure, I will survive. Until then, like the missing tab of a thousand-piece puzzle, apocalyptic dreams are in control of my nights... those precious memories that once kept me going when I thought I couldn't are distorted and fragmented... those I wish I could erase forever linger within the deep recesses of my consciousness haunting me night after night after night. When I arrived here, I was twenty-six years old, six-feet-two, weighing in at two-hundred and fifteen pounds... I'm one-hundred and ninety now thanks to six days a week hard labor... my hair remains dark brown except for the streaks of white that have invaded my temples... dark circles live under my light brown eyes, my face has forgotten how to smile. Like everyone back on Earth, I had only heard stories of this place that painted a grim picture... little did I know what I was in for. On the day we landed in this nether world, management had us strip and marched past a line of leering, catcalling inmates... the brass's way of removing any sense of self-esteem we had left... from that moment on time and space was altered... I had descended into a black hole of punishment. We were issued identification numbers... names are not used here... my number is 11349556... I'm addressed only as 556, which is stitched on the front of the two shirts I was issued. We sleep in*

4

four cold, dark and gray cramped spaces called 'bays', fifty men to each... I'm in bay three... the bunks are two-feet apart in earshot of every snort, belch, cough, sneeze, grunt, fart, along with a cacophony of constant distractions coming from some of the scariest men I've had the displeasure of coming into contact with... that's saying a lot considering my profession before being sent here. You have to set bunkmates straight right off or they'll make life a living hell of harassment... I did... they know not to screw with me. Apartheid is alive and well thanks to a complicated mix of races... if you're black, brown, red, or yellow, life is a nightmare of racism that leads to an occasional battle royal nurtured along by the all-white goon squads who watch over us. Each day begins on an elevator that accommodates twenty-five at a time... down we go some thirty-five-feet where the tunnel shafts begin. Except for a half-hour box-lunch break, the rest of the day is spent operating machinery that scrapes loose the precious ore deep under the frozen surface of Europa, the smallest of the four Galilean moons orbiting Jupiter. The ore is called Phostoirore... it's French... it's black like coal and smells like rotting chicken parts, an odor that will forever be embedded in my sinus cavities. None of us would be here if not for an unmanned spacecraft called Clipper that was launched in 2024 by NASA to probe beneath Europa's frozen surface. What the good ship Clipper brought back changed the way the world consumed energy. Scientists turned giddy when they heated a sample and it liquefied into metallic hydrogen, a super energy source that had been researched for years with no positive results. There followed a massive coming together of US space agencies and private space firms to launch a manned flight to Europa... it was a miraculous accomplishment given how quickly it came together... the American flag was planted on Europa's surface and the United States claimed all rights to the ore. Next came the construction of a ship large enough to send manpower, materials, and machinery to build an underground facility. That same ship plus two more shuttled manpower to Europa and brought the ore back. The rest is history. MAXMinerai, the mining conglomerate headquartered in Marseille, France, would oversee the mining operation... they're the ones who named the ore Phostoirore. To ensure a continuous flow of manpower to work the mines, Europa was designated a penal colony since no one in their right mind would volunteer to go there. If a country wanted a share of the liquid gold, they paid a price set by the US Government in addition to providing an agreed upon number of men convicted of heinous crimes to work the mines. Medical assistance is all but non-existent... there's always a fresh supply of unwilling manpower waiting in the wings... since I've been here, I've lost count of the number of men that have died miserable deaths. The guards are a mixed bag of mostly ex-military tough-guys from around the world... the accents are all over the place... half the time you can't decipher what's coming out of their mouths. How do I begin to describe seventeen years living deep underground never seeing the surface, sky, or whatever else might be out there in frozen no man's land beside the landing/launch pad? One day rolls into the next without reference to anything outside the dark, dusty, smelly mines, the clamor of heavy machinery, the brutal Neanderthal guards, the marginal food, and inmates looking to blow off steam, or worse, a carnal roll in the sack in the middle of the night with a willing or unwilling participant... each minute, each hour, each passing day plays out without place, time, meaning or documentation... physical pain and emotional stress have a way of turning you into someone you might not have otherwise become. On my bluest days, I remind myself that if I endure and retain my sanity, my sentence will be up and life will resume where it left off, albeit damaged physically and mentally. We have no contact with the outside world... nothing, nada, zip... a family member could die back home and you'd never know it... there's no existence beyond the spaces we occupy. I recall with relish that my early school years established me as the class clown. To this day, I have no idea why I saw, and continue to see, the humor, if not the absurdity, of life. Unfortunately, my warped sense of humor was never embraced by my teachers, which all too often landed me in hot water. When I entered my first year of high school, I began taking a serious interest in this crazy undefined world... life was all around us abundant and diverse and that interested me. What did it actually mean to be alive, and why for such a short time? How foolish and arrogant of me to think that I, William 'Billy' Evan Russell, would discover the answers to such deep questions. Perhaps one day, I thought, I would meet someone who can... I'm still waiting... my sense of humor remains as perverted as ever. On the other hand, like all clueless youth, I was convinced I would live forever. The seven stages of life that begin with infancy and ended somewhere between dotage and death didn't apply to me... now all these years later, I'm dwelling more and more on that end stage... no longer do I see the light at the end of the tunnel as a ray of hope, but a speeding train coming to squash me like a disease-spreading insect. This morning, like all mornings, a bone-shaking siren shakes us awake at five AM reminding us of the lingering aches and pains of the previous day... we're up and standing by our bunks awaiting the arrival of a sorry excuse of a human, an ill-tempered oaf of a man whose first name is Vladimir... don't know his last... we call him Quasi, short for Quasimodo, because his shoulders hunch forward like maybe his head's too heavy for his fleshy frame. He speaks with a tongue-twisting European accent... the mere sight of him sticks in my throat like the foul-smelling Phostoirore. All the guards carry a two-foot instrument resembling a cattle prod that delivers the same electrical results... Quasi's damn quick to use his for the most minor of infractions... this morning he shows up looking more pissed off than usual.

"Leon Wilson, Christopher Hewitt Henley, William Evan Russell, stall przy lozhach."

Quasi has this irritating habit of slipping in and out of his mother tongue... not sure, but it sounds Slavic.

"Sorry, sir, didn't get that last part."

"You three assholes stood by beds."

The word is 'stand', learn the language, you imbecile... whoa, wait a damn minute... did he just call us by our actual names, not our numbers? Not a good sign... no, not a good sign at all.

"The rest of you know drill. Move it."

In a chorus of disenfranchised voices, forty-seven men drone in unison.

"Yes, sir!"

Quasi follows the men to the door counting heads until the last man files out for their morning latrine break and a bowl of mushy, overcooked oatmeal... why he counts heads only he knows. Where the hell would one go if they did try to escape, ice skating on the surface maybe? Chris Henley, with a shit-eating grin on his lips, leans close and whispers.

"Jesus, man, he called us by our names!"

Chris is a smallish wiry white guy about my age... close cropped dark brown hair with piercing, menacing eyes, and a wisecracking mouth not even a loving mother would tolerate.

Near as I remember he showed up a year after I did... on his left shoulder is a tattoo of a 300 Winchester Magnum M24 sniper rifle. Leon Grover is a tall black guy in his sixties with a thick head of black hair and strong facial features... he arrived a couple of years after Chris... Leon's quiet and mostly keeps to himself... he coughs a lot... there's always a cigarette hanging from his lips... just about everyone smokes since cigs are free... our one and only perk. Now Quasi's strolling back with his usual smug, kick-ass look.

"You three have appointment with Commandant. Get dressed."

The Commandant? No one gets an invitation to the Commandant's office unless they're gonna get their ass handed to them for some infraction of their endless rules. As usual, Chris can't keep his bloody mouth shut.

"What does Herr Commandant want with us?"

Quasi scowls... he scowls a lot... he sticks his cattle prod within an inch of Chris' nose.

"Keep mouth shut. Get dressed."

Chris grabs his crotch with both hands and groans.

"Can we hit the head first, I gotta vacate some water really bad?"

Quasi grunts... he also grunts a lot.

"Make it quick."

CHAPTER 3

Get Out of Jail Card

Sleeping bays, latrines, mess hall, staff quarters, and support facilities are on one level twenty-five-feet deep below Europa's frozen surface... the Commandant's office is located at the extreme West end causing us to trek through a maze of twisting narrow passageways with a few emergency airlocks along the way... the entire operation is a technological marvel, but if heat, oxygen, or water purification's systems ever fail, we're mince-meat. The Commandant's name is Oleg Maksymchak, a former colonel in the Ukrainian army... Colonel Maks, as we call him, is short, five-six maybe, thin face, hollow cheeks, eyes coal black like his hair... in all the years I've been here I've only seen him five or six times during his infrequent inspections of the mines marching around quick-step like Napoleon Bonaparte reincarnated with his entourage of armed security following a few steps behind like animated robots. When we're ushered into his office Little Napoleon Maks is sitting at his desk reading... his chair's been jacked up to make him appear taller... Quasi, like the dim-witted loyal soldier he is, clicks his heels and salutes.

"Commandant, sir, inmates Leon Patrick Grover, William Evan Russell, Christopher Michael Henley."

With his eyelids narrowed to slits, Maks glances up with an austere expression that would melt the planet's surface... he sizing us up... when he's satisfied, he picks up whatever he was reading, holds it above his head, and rattles it.

"This communiqué arrived late last night. For whatever reason—which I am not privy to—it directs me to return you on Europa Two when it departs later today."

The three of us exchange confused glances.

"Whoever pulled your ticket on such short notice believes you would be of more use back home."

Did I hear right? We're leaving this cesspool and returning to Earth? Is that what he said? Maks looks as confused as we do... dropping the communique to the desk, he shakes his head.

"I am left to ponder why anyone would consider you three of any use beyond your duties here."

Chris opens his mouth to speak... Maks stops him with a sharp look.

"Which one are you?"

"678, sir."

"Not your number, your name."

"Oh, yeah, sure... Christopher Henley, sir."

"Inmate Henley, just stand there and listen."

"Yes, sir, just wondering—"

"Don't. Further instructions will be provided upon your arrival at Base-Arizona. You do remember Base-Arizona?"

Leon and I nod... Chris, well, Chris is Chris.

"It's in Arizona, sir."

Maks' left eyebrow shoots up... here is comes... Chris is about to get his ass handed to him.

"Was that meant to amuse, Inmate Henley?"

"No, sir, I just—"

"Be quiet. Officer Sokolov will see you are prepared for departure."

Sokolov... so that's Quasi's last name.

"Now you may ask questions. Inmate Russell?"

Think fast, Billy, make it mundane.

"This is welcome news, Commandant, sir."

Maks chuckles low.

"I would think it would be. Inmate Grover, you look unwell?"

"A bug, sir. It's getting better."

"Do you have a question?"

"I have none, sir."

"Inmate Henley?"

"No, sir."

"Very well. Sign your transfer papers on your way out."

"Thank you, sir."

"For what, Inmate Henley?"

"I, uh… well, sir, we're going home and—"

"Be forewarned, much has changed back on Earth. Perhaps you will not find it to your liking."

What's that supposed to mean… what could possibly be worse than remaining here? We're going home, period, full stop.

"I caution you to be on your best behavior during your voyage or you'll find yourselves on the next transport back."

In unison, we answer, "Yes, sir." *Maks swipes a hand through the air.*

"Leave now."

Oh hell, Henley's raising his hand… for Christ's sake, Chris, for once keep your trap shut.

"Inmate Henley, are you hearing impaired?"

"Not that I'm aware of, Commandant."

"Then lower your hand and remove yourself from my presence."

"Yes, Commandant, sir."

Quasi clicks his heels, straightens his hunched back as best he can, and salutes… we file out behind him… with luck this was the last time we'll encounter Bonaparte Maks… on our way out, his aide has us sign our discharge papers, which I sign without reading. As we follow Quasi back through the passageways, there's a renewed spring in my step, but as elated as I am, my emotions are conflicted… who wants us back on short notice and why and what for in a world I barely remember? Why would that even cross your mind, Billy Boy, it's enough that you're going home. So, for reasons yet to be revealed, I bid you goodbye Europa… may your permafrost one day melt, knock you off your axis, and suck you into a black hole. And yet, I have this dreaded feeling the other shoe has yet to drop.

"Guys, this doesn't pass the smell test."

Leon shoots me a stern look.

"Who cares what it smells like, we're going home."

"Aren't you the least bit curious who wants us back so badly they'd cut our sentences short and ship us out hours later?"

"Billy, my boy, who gives a damn?"

"I do, Chris, I do."

Leon lets out a long sigh.

"Will you two get your act together, please, just this once?"

Henley, smiling from ear-to-ear, whispers the same stale joke he repeats at the end of every mine shift.

"What did the Shepherd say when he saw the storm coming?"

Leon's trying to stifle a laugh... Like me, he knows the answer all too well.

"When the storm came, the shepherd said... 'let's get the flock out of here.'"

"Thank you, Leon... drum roll please."

Forty-minutes later, the three of us are in the shower washing off the stink and grime of this insufferable planet followed by our last bowl of overcooked, mushy oatmeal... for as long as I live I will never again eat oatmeal... nor will I trust anyone who does. We're issued black jumpsuits, five pair of new socks, underwear, and a small pouch containing a toothbrush, toothpaste, shaving cream, razor, a bar of soap, a comb, a laminated credit-sized card bearing our photo and ID number, and a green pin-on badge with nothing more than a black barcode running along the bottom... that's it, that's all I have to show for the past seventeen years... not much of a resumé. Now Quasi's growling like the attack dog he's been trained to be.

"ID card and badge only proof you exist. Lose it, you become non-entity."

Thanks, you jelly-faced prick, rabid dogs are treated with more dignity. Before this day is over, we'll be free of the isolation, mines, bad food, inmates, grizzly guards, and you, Quasi, will still be here. Amen, amen, and one hell-of-a joyful

MIDNIGHT BLACK

hallelujah.

CHAPTER 4

The Long Trip Home

Europa Two is a faster, bigger version of the ship that brought me here... we're strapped in ready to be launched into space at frightening speeds for the six months one week and a day it'll take to reach good old Mother Earth. Considering the six months I was jailed, tried, convicted and sentenced, and the time coming and going, I've been missing in action far too long. Toss a match and burn this bridge, Billy Boy, and never look back. Eighteen of us from the four bays are stacked on double bunks in a tight, foul-smelling gray steel box within range of the wafting odors of each other and the nearby latrine... eleven of us are wearing green badges, the rest red. Early on we learn those with red are rotating to other prisons on Earth. Grover's in the bunk above me, Henley's in the lower bunk to my right. Beside the cargo-hold emitting the foul-smelling Phostoirore, there's a mess hall we share with three guards and the flight crew of nine... aside from the boredom of washing our clothes and bedding once a week, reading books, outdated magazines, and watching old movies in what passes for a dining room, boredom rules. There is, however, two highlights to cheer... we're served the same food as the crew... a major improvement. On the port side of the dining area, there's an eight-foot wide, three-foot high portal providing unbelievable majestic vistas of space, which we didn't have on the ship the brought us to Europa. When I peered out that portal for the first time, I stood in awed silence... my eyes welled up... the views were beyond spectacular, beyond belief, beyond anything I could have imagined in my wildest dreams. If every living soul on Earth could spend just a few minutes *gazing out that portal, all mankind would come to the same conclusions I have... how inconsequential our lives are in the grand scheme of the vast, endless, unexplainable universe... there are no words to describe what I've been privileged to see each day... there are no words to express the spiritual effect it has had on me, not in a religious way, but a life-changing way that forces me to question it all more than I already do.*

On the fifty-first day out, things take an ominous turn... *Leon's persistent cough is getting worse and he's having difficulty breathing... by that evening he's spitting up yellow-green stuff mixed with flecks of blood. He was always hacking back on Europa, but never this bad. Unfortunately, we've witnessed this all too often... excessive mine dust and cigarettes resulting in deadly pulmonary infections that invariably led to agonizing deaths as its victims are robbed of precious air. Chris reports Leon's worsening condition to one of the guards and requests medical assistance, but the guard smirks and waves him off.*

"They'll be no medical help for the black man... one less to take up space."

When Chris returns, he's fuming.

"Racist pricks, every last one of them. I should have beaten the shit out of the bastard."

"Let it go, Chris."

"Let it go? Jesus, Billy, have they no empathy for the man?"

"Apparently not. Let's just help Leon the best we can."

We encourage Leon to drink lots of water, but he's having trouble keeping it down... it's coming back up pink. On the morning of the fifty-sixth day, we discover our friend had died during the night... the front of his shirt is soaked in his blood... as if Leon Patrick Grover was nothing more than a dead animal carcass, they have Chris and me carry him off to a storage closet next to the latrine... for the rest of the trip I have difficulty visiting the latrine without staring at that door wondering if his body is still in there… I tried opening the door once, but it was locked.

Except for daily visits to the portal, *which never gets old because the scenery is constantly changing to new and spectacular sights, each passing day is filled with boredom and sleeping… I've never slept so much in my life. Thankfully, we only have fifteen days to go… we've dubbed the end of the trip 'The Homecoming'… to what, we have no idea. Those of us with green badges have been ordered to gather in the dining area at 10:00 AM for a briefing. We're greeted by the ship's First Officer who begins by making clear he will not be taking questions.*

"In fifteen days, this ship will be landing at Base-Arizona. You are being returned to take up new assignments based on skills you possessed prior to being incarcerated. I caution you, the world you are returning to is not the one you left behind. Time passes, things change, and adjustments required. There is new world order governed by the New World Government that now oversees all sovereign nations."

A world government? What's he talking about? Chris shoots me a quizzical look… I shake my head roll my eyes and shrug.

"If you have any hope of making the transition, follow instructions precisely as you make your way through processing. Consider your return a gift, one that is not to be squandered. That's all, gentleman, return to your quarters."

A guy in the front row raises his hand.

"What's this New World Government thing?"

"Did I not make it clear there would be no questions?"

"Yes, sir."

"Then why are you asking one?"

The inmate shrugs, the First Officer walks out leaving a question mark as to what this new government thing is all about. Chris shoots me another quizzical look.

"It seems we're in for a few surprises, Billy. News at

eleven."

You'd think on homecoming day I'd be juiced up and ready to go, but no, not me, I slip into a deep slumber only to be suddenly shaken awake by loud noise and vibrations... for a few frightening seconds, I have no idea where I am and bound to a sitting position.

"What, what?"

Chris leans over from his bunk and whispers.

"Its engine thrust... we've begun our descent to Planet Freaking Earth."

"Jesus, how long have I been sleeping?"

"Oh, I'd say just over six months now."

Rubbing the sleep from my eyes, my face stretches into a wide grin.

"Is today Sunday, January 27th?"

"It is unless they changed the calendar while we were gone. Why?"

"Tomorrow's my birthday."

"Whoa, happy birthday, dude. How old?"

"Forty-four going on eighty."

"How about we celebrate with a nice bowl of mushy oatmeal?

"Never ever mention oatmeal again, Chris, never, never, ever."

CHAPTER 5

Light at the end of the Tunnel

Once the ship is safely docked, an announcement comes over the PA system instructing passengers and crew to disembark before offloading of the ore begins. My God, is this real, am I really back? I can't wait to set foot on solid ground again. Two new security gorillas, who in a previous life could have been crowd favorites in the Roman Colosseum, enter swinging their ever-present cattle prods... in a raspy, nicotine-soaked voice, one of them bellows.

"Okay, you ground-crawlers, listen up. We've arrived at Base-Arizona. When we disembark, follow me single file to the delousing room to ensure none of you vermin are carrying foreign matter back to our beloved planet."

Ground-crawlers, vermin? I should rip out his rancid tongue and stick it up his ass... not today, Billy Boy, not today... play nice. Once off the ship we're led single file down a narrow hall and into a windowless cement block room where we strip... a green mint-smelling mist is released from overhead nozzles, presumably sanitizing us vermin and lowly ground-crawlers. Raspy Voice is barking orders again.

"When you exit, those with red badges to the left, green to the right."

We're issued new clothes all in brown—we look like UPS delivery men... from there we are led down a long, dark hallway... I'm half way back in the line, Chris is directly behind me. I can't help being apprehensive... no, terror-stricken... of what's about to become my new reality... Chris leans into me and whispers low.

"I wish the hell Leon was with us."

"Yeah, me too, Chris."

The hallway dead-ends at a steel door... on it is a framed poster of an eagle with swooping wings reminiscent of those used by Roman Emperors and Germany's Nazi Party... below the eagle, a slogan reads, **'The Peoples Cooperative Populist Party – One World in Unity.'** *Above the door, a small red-light is flashing on and off... Raspy punches in a series of numbers on a wall-mounted keypad... the light flashes green... the door glides open and bright light spills in. When it's my turn to step through, I hesitate... go on, Billy, there's a welcoming light at the end of this tunnel, not a train coming to squash you... take those last few steps to your future, whatever it might be. Raspy pokes me with his cattle prod.*

"Move it before you get a taste of this."

Drawing in a quick, deep breath, I take that last hesitant step through the doorway to wherever awaits me on the other side of this time-warp... a security officer in a black uniform with an WPF patch on his left shoulder and brandishing an automatic rifle, greets me... his finger's on the trigger no doubt ready to ventilate anyone who dares cause trouble... a second guard is holding back a German shepherd straining at its leash ready to sink his teeth into anyone who might piss him off... the first goon scans my badge with a hand device and waves me through.

"Find the door with the first letter of your last name and line up there."

"Yes, sir."

The processing center is one large open area, the walls pastel green, the floor off-white tile... a major improvement over cold, gray steel... there are twenty-five or so green-badges already lined up at various doors. It's then it hits me... I'm a stranger in a strange land without the slightest clue why I've been sent back, where I'm going, or what's to become of me. The thought that I'll soon be reunited with my parents spurs me on... first chance I get I'll call and let them know I'm back. The doors where we are to line up are painted black standing out against the green walls like a portentous warning... over each door is a white on black sign bearing letters of the alphabet... down the line I go until I find the door with 'P-Q-R' and queue up behind the two guys ahead of me... Chris is in his line... I wave, he waves back.

Forty anxious minutes pass *before the heavyset guy that was in front of me comes out with the grimmest of expressions... for a fleeting moment we make eye contact... he looks like he's going to say something, but doesn't, turns left, hesitates, then wanders off like he's unsure of where he's supposed to go next... the light over the door turns green... okay, Billy Boy, showtime... take a deep breath, put one foot in front of the other, and march with courage, confidence, and conviction to your future... through that black door life is waiting for you to pick up where you left off.*

CHAPTER 6

Welcome to the New World Order

The room is a disorientating white Cyclorama... the walls white on white as is the tiled floor... on the left wall is a large poster of the eagle in flight and that slogan that leaves me wondering... a white chair is positioned in front of a white desk... what the hell is with all the white? The desktop is clear except for a clipboard and a nameplate identifying the guy sitting there as Donald P. Costigan... he's a waif of a man, bald with a pale complexion and hollow cheekbones that give him a pinched, pissed-off look... his eyes are locked on his computer screen... his fingers are pounding hard on the keyboard like he's angry at it... his right hand shoots up.

"Your identification card, give it to me."

The card... which pocket did I put it in?

"Hold on, it's here somewhere."

He snaps his fingers twice.

"I don't have a year and a day—your card."

Hey, don't snap your fingers at me, pinch-face... whoa, calm down, Billy, just find the damn card... uh, here it is in my left pant pocket. I hold it up and out... without making eye contact, pinch-face reaches across the desk, snatches it, and points to the white chair.

"Sit."

What am I, a dog? Costigan inserts the card in a slotted instrument below his monitor... the screen brings up a display at an angle I can't see.

"Yes or no answers. Full name William Evan Russell?"

"Yes, but I go by Billy."

"Bully for you. Age 44?"

"Tomorrow."

"Happy birthday. Parents Alistair and Amelia Russell?

"Yes."

"Born Bristol, Rhode Island?"

"Me or my parents?"

He shoots me a pained sideways glance.

"You."

"Yes."

His attention returns to the monitor.

"Graduated from New England Institute of Technology with a Criminal Justice Associates Degree."

"Yes."

"Four years as a DEA Officer in the Providence regional office."

"Yes."

"Married to the late Diedre Arico Russell."

"Yes."

"Convicted of murdering one Jack Kerfoot?"

I hesitate… his eyes come to me again.

"Did you understand the question?"

"Yes."

"Then please answer it."

"Yes."

"Yes, you understand, yes, you murdered Jack Kerfoot?"

"The latter."

"See how easy that was, Mister Russell?"

He punches a few keys and the screen changes… studies it for several seconds before speaking low.

"Hmm, what have we here? The judge deemed your messy closet misadventure a crime of passion and gave you the minimum sentence. That was extremely magnanimous of him."

"She… the judge was a woman."

"And if the judge had been a man?"

I toss him my best shrug… he's shaking his head as if he finds the whole affair distasteful.

"No matter the circumstances, Mister Russell, you do not get to act as judge, jury, and executioner."

"In that circumstance, I was."

"An imperious decision for which you paid a high price. I hear tell Europa is a most inhospitable place."

"That it is."

With a smug expression, he turns back to the monitor.

"Well, now, seems you get to play policeman again."

"What?"

"With the Drug Enforcement Bureau in Boston."

I'm back working for the DEA? Whoa, I hit the jackpot.

"Your parole begins tomorrow at 10:00 AM when you check in."

"Parole?"

"Yes."

"Parole was never mentioned."

"Did you really believe they'd turn you lose to roam at will?"

If this jerk is looking to get his ass kicked, he's doing a great job of it.

"I wasn't told why, when or where I would be going or what I'd be doing."

"All will be explained when you report in tomorrow. You'll travel to Boston today, check into your assigned housing and report to your work assignment in the morning. Any deviation in your itinerary and you'll be marked AWOL, in which case they'll come looking for you and send you back to Europa to serve out your original sentence with five additional years tacked on. That should be incentive enough to insure you show up."

The damn fool's tossing stuff out way too fast. "None of this was explained."

"That's why you get to spend this precious time with me, Mister Russell."

I don't appreciate the little twerp's condescending tone, but I'll keep my cool long enough to get through this. He taps a few keys and leans into the screen.

"Hmm, what have we here?

He leaves me wondering while he reads the screen.

"Sorry to have to tell you this, but it appears your parents are deceased."

Jesus, what? His words hit me like a hard punch to the stomach.

"That must be a mistake."

"No, it says here they died in an auto accident twenty-eight days ago. These records are all I have to go by—never had one yet that was wrong."

"I was traveling back I had no way of knowing."

"Well, you know now, Mister Russell."

What a heartless thing to say, you son-of-a-bitch... I'm on the verge of rage and tears, rage against this sub-human sitting in front of me, and tears for my parents if the information proves correct. He opens a drawer, withdraws a red covered paperback, sets it on the desk, and places his right hand flat atop it like he's taking an oath.

"This is the RedBook. It will familiarize you with all you need to know about the new world order administered by the New World Government."

"Yeah, that, it was mentioned on the ship, but without any explanation."

"Not long after the Pakistan-India incident the New World Government took over."

"The what incident?"

"I'm not paid to provide history lessons, Mister Russell, just listen. Hand me your badge."

This miserable excuse for a human needs a serious attitude adjustment... removing the green badge, I hand it to him... withdrawing my ID card from the slot, he slices both through with scissors and tosses them in a wastebasket behind him.

"I dare say, Mister Russell, you look confused."

"You're moving fast."

"Then I suggest you pay closer attention."

Screw you and ass you rode in on, Donald P. Costigan. His right hand disappears under the desk... a buzzer sounds... a door opens behind him... another guy enters looking like he was waiting back there in the dark for Mister Pinch Face to buzz him in... this one's tall and lanky with a hangdog expression that suggests he's in need of a decent meal... like maybe a nice bowl of mushy oatmeal... in his right hand is an instrument resembling a miniature hair dryer.

"Harvey is going to insert a GPS tracker in your left forearm. If for any reason it's removed, World Military Police will come looking for you."

What's the World Military Police? Hangdog Harvey taps me on the shoulder.

"Expose your left arm."

I remove my jacket and roll up my shirt sleeve… Harvey swipes a small alcohol pad over my forearm.

"You won't even know it's there."

He presses the instrument down on my arm and pulls the trigger… I feel a slight sting… he slaps a band-aid over the spot as if he's given me nothing more than my annual flu shot. Costigan finally breaks a smile.

"Thanks, Harvey."

"You're welcome, Donald."

I smile wide.

"Yeah, thanks, Harvey."

He makes a hasty retreat through door number two… from his middle drawer, Costigan removes a stack of oversized tan envelopes and shuffles through them.

"Russell, Russell—here it is."

Slicing the envelope open, he dumps the contents on the desk.

"A travel voucher for the flight to Boston, one for transportation to your housing along with the addresses of your housing and your work assignment."

He holds up what looks like a credit card.

"This is both your identification and debit card. While on parole you are not allowed to use or withdraw paper money, use this card for all purchases. The government will be tracking you two ways, via the GPS in your arm, and purchases and payments posted to your card."

"Why?"

"You'll have to ask them, Mister Russell. Now, a bit of good news. Since a private enterprise oversees the mining operation on Europa, you earned spendable work credits."

"Really? How much?"

"Six-hundred. Each is the equivalent to one dollar. That will support your immediate needs until your salary kicks in."

I quickly do the math in my head... wow, a whole thirty-six or so credits a year for digging smelly ore. He places the ID/debit card and the voucher inside the Redbook cover, slips it in a large manila envelope, and pushes it across the desk.

"Your employer will be notified you have arrived and on your way. That's it, out the door, turn left to the exit. A bus will transport you to Flagstaff Pulliam International Airport. I caution you to be on your best behavior while mingling with the public."

Picking up the clipboard, he extends it.

"Sign this confirming you understand all that has taken place here."

Without reading it, I scribble my name and hand it back.

"We're finished here, Mister Russell. Try not to kill anyone again else unless it's in the line of duty."

Now he's grinning... not a friendly grin, but a sinister one.

"And thank you for your service, Mister Russell."

"For what?"

"For digging that precious Phostoirore that keeps this world humming along."

I'll be damned if I'm gonna let this arrogant son-of-a-bitch have the last word... shooting to my feet, I plant both hands on the front of the desk... Costigan's rolls his chair back a foot like he thinks I'm gonna attack him.

"The next guy coming through that door might not have my patience, so if I were you, Mister Costigan, I'd work on improving my bedside manner."

The little creep feigns a sigh.

"Take some advice, Mister Russell. You are in for a very steep learning curve. What you left behind seventeen years ago bears little resemblance to what's out there now. I suggest you hold your tongue before it gets you into trouble."

"I'll deal with it as it comes."

"Yes, that's what they all say until they come face to face with reality. There is a new world order, one you may have great difficulty adjusting to. Although, as a Caucasian you should find it less intimidating."

"What's my race have to do with it?"

"Everything, Mister Russell, everything. Now then, out the door, turn left, follow the signs to the bus."

Swooping up the envelope, I back my way to the door never taking my eyes from him.

"I question the origins of your mother, Mister Costigan... bovine perhaps."

The apathetic jerk shrugs and returns to pounding on his keyboard as if I was nothing more than an inconvenient interruption in his otherwise niggling existence.

CHAPTER 7

Reality Bites Hard

I slam the door hard hoping it pisses off Donald P. Costigan *more than I already have...* *forget him, Billy, he's just another* *puny dunce you'll never see again... my gaze goes to the next* *guy in line... for sure he's wondering what takes place behind* *the sinister black door... as one ex-prisoner to another, I feel* *an obligation to offer a friendly warning.*

"Enter at your own risk."

He shoots me a glum look, passes me without speaking, *and enters the inner white sanctum of abuse.*

"Okay fella, I tried to warn you."

Scanning the lines of men standing in paralyzed *despondency, it's easy to spot their apprehensive expressions* *as they wait their turn to be humiliated by the vermin behind* *the black doors. I don't see Chris... he's either being processed* *or gone on ahead... standing there like little boy lost, my* *thoughts shift to my parents... the last time I saw them was at* *my sentencing... as the judge read my sentence aloud, I* *clenched my jaw and swallowed back my tears... it remains the* *most traumatic day of my life other than the day my wife was* *raped and murdered by a deranged animal. Okay, Billy, put* *one foot in front of the other and find that bus... there, to your* *left, there's an overhead sign pointing to ground* *transportation... follow it, get the hell off this base. I'm about* *to take that first step when a loud commotion breaks out in the* *opposite direction... someone's shouting.*

"Stop! Stop or we'll shoot!"

There, to my right, a guy is running at breakneck speed *past the front of the lines... he's coming directly at me and he's coming fast... the PA system is blaring.*

"Code red, all officers to the processing area. Code red, all officers to the processing area."

With weapons raised, security officers are hot on the man's heels... the German Shepherd's straining at its leash, teeth gleaming, drool dripping as he drags his handler toward the running man... the remaining men in the lines back away... the loudspeaker's blaring again.

"All returnees, stay in your line, stay in your line!"

The runner is flying fast one leg stretching far in front of the other in a desperate sprint to outrun security... holy crap, if they shoot, I'm in the line of fire... my brain is screaming at me to get out of the way! The runner, who looks Hispanic... is twenty-feet away, then fifteen, ten, five... three deafening bursts of gunfire echo throughout the room as rounds rip into the guy's back... his mouth flaps open, his eyes bulge, his head snaps back, his arms fly up and out toward me, his hands landing squarely on my chest almost knocking me to the floor... he's clawing at me, his bulging eyes locked onto mine, pleading, pleading... his mouth's open, but nothing's coming out... my arms encircle him... too late, he's sliding down, his eyes never leave me as the last seconds of consciousness slip away... he lands flat on his face at my feet... my God, his shirt's ripped away... his spine is exposed... he's bleeding badly... the German Shepherd is set loose... the beast is charging forward... move, Billy, move! The animal leaps over the dead guy slamming into me with the full force of its weight knocking me to the floor... Jesus, he's going for my left leg... his handler's yelling.

"Heel, Charger, heel!"

The animal whines loudly and sits... the barrel of an automatic rifle is thrust within inches of my eyes.

"Roll over, on your belly, do it now!"

"What?"

"Are you deaf? Roll over, put your hands behind you."

I roll over... handcuffs are clamped on my wrists.

"You know that man?"

"No, sir, no!"

"Why was he running to you?"

"He wasn't, I was in his way."

"Bullshit, you were waiting to meet up with him."

"No, no, I wasn't!"

In the midst of commotion, I hear a familiar voice.

"What's going on out here? I heard gunfire."

It's Donald P. Costigan in the flesh.

"Oh my, what happened to that man? Good Lord, his back! Is he dead?"

"He's a red badge, Mister Costigan, he was making a run for it. We have this under control."

"Why is that man handcuffed on the floor?"

"We think he might have been an accomplice."

"Are you people totally incompetent? I processed him out just minutes ago. Get him off the floor. Come on, get him up."

"Really, sir, we have this under control."

"That's debatable. Remove those handcuffs."

Begrudgingly, the officer helps me to my feet and removes the handcuffs.

"Russell, show the man your identification."

"It's in the envelope."

"I didn't ask you where it was, show it to him."

One of the officer's snatches up the envelope from the floor and hands it to me... with trembling hands, I retrieve the card and hand it to him... he examines it and holds it up to Costigan.

"Can you verify this, sir?"

"What did I say that you didn't understand, Officer? Give him his card and let him be on his way."

"Yes, sir, if you say so."

"I say so."

The officer smirks and hands me the card... I stuff it back in the envelope.

"Officer, apologize to this man."

"We're just doing our job, Mister Costigan."

"Badly, it seems. Do it now, please."

The look on the guy's face leaves no doubt... he doesn't want to apologize.

"Ah, it appears there was a misunderstanding."

That's as close to an apology I'm getting... Costigan's takes my arm and pulls me aside and pats me on the shoulder.

"For heaven's sake, Russell, be watchful, it's a perilous world you've returned to. That man was being transferred to another correctional facility. He must have made a run for it."

"Did they have to rip his back open? With all the security around where would he go?"

"Don't bother yourself with that, it's done. Go now, be safe, catch that bus."

Is this the same Donald P. Costigan who moments ago took perverse pleasure in treating me like I was unworthy of being in his presence and now he's taken an interest in my well-being? Okay, Billy, man up, be grateful he intervened and thank the man.

"Thank you."

Damn if he doesn't smile wide and pat me on the shoulder a second time.

"On your way now, and be careful."

He strolls back to his office, but before opening his door, he turns and grins.

"Still think my mother was of bovine origin?"

"Uh, bad choice of words, Mister Costigan."

"Yes, it was. Have a safe life, Mister Russell."

With a satisfied grin, passive-aggressive Donald P. Costigan enters his lily-white office, hopefully gone from my life forever. Two black men in white uniforms show up with a stretcher and place the dead guy face down leaving his mutilated spine exposed.

"Serves the little brown bastard right."

Jesus, what? I look to the white officer who spewed those racist words and frown.

"What the hell are you looking at?"

"Nothing, officer, nothing."

"Then put your feet one in front of the other and move on."

I've seen more than my share of violence in my time, but the sight of that young man's mutilated spine has left me nauseated... to my left, there's a restroom sign, I make a

31

beeline to it.... the officer, who only moments ago had his automatic weapon pointed inches from my head, is taking a wiz at one of the urinals... we make eye contact, he grins, but says nothing... entering a stall, I lock the door, spin around and miss the commode by six-inches as a projectile of greenish-yellow liquid propels from my throat to the floor leaving me coughing and gagging.

"You okay in there?"

"Yeah, yeah, officer, fine."

"Sure? I can call somebody."

"I'm okay, thanks."

"Suit yourself. Damn close call back there, huh?"

"Yeah, close call." *Right, you mentally deficient mole, you were the one itching to blow my brains out a few minutes ago. When I'm sure the jerk has left, I make it to one of the sinks and douse cold water on my face... I'm white as a sheet... pull it together, Billy Boy, find that bus and make your escape from this place. Outside, the dead guy's body's been removed... an older black woman in blue overalls is mopping the blood from the floor... still shaken, I take a deep breath and follow the signs to transportation. When I reach the exit another WPF officer stops me.*

"Where you going?"

I'm tempted to tell him Disneyland... if it's still there.

"I'm supposed to board a bus."

"Through this door."

"Which bus?"

He shoots me a strained look.

"There's only one, it's big and white, can't miss it."

Outside there's only one bus... a big unmarked white one... an WPF guard holding an automatic weapon is standing next to the seated driver... I smile... neither of them does... a dozen men in brown uniforms like mine have taken up most of the seats... Chris is not among them... the back row on the left side is empty... I take the window seat. Minutes later the bus pulls away... glancing out the back window, there's big black Europa-Two perched on its launch pad looming like something out of a bad sci-fi flick... about a half-mile beyond is the

32

sprawling plant complex that processes the raw Phostoirore. Goodbye, Europa Two, thanks for the ride home... give my regards to the frozen planet when you return. Once the bus is clear of the base, the Arizona desert takes over... a beautiful sight to behold indeed... I could easily disappear out there and live off the land... how difficult could it be after all that I've endured? Dumb idea, Billy, they'd come looking for you and that would be the end of the rest of whatever life you might have left.

__An hour and ten minutes after departing Base-Arizona,__ we arrive at Flagstaff Pulliam Airport and offload at the airline's departure entrance... the thought I'll be moving freely among everyday people gets my adrenaline's pumping... I'm more than ready. Two WPF officers armed with automatic rifles greet us at the double-glass door entrance... a large poster of the eagle and slogan, **"The Peoples Cooperative Populist Party – One World in Unity"**, *is prominently displayed on the left door... this one has an added message below...* **"If you see something, say something."** *Inside at the security checkpoint my pouch is searched and I'm waved through... following the signs to my assigned airline, I pass a half dozen more WPF security brandishing automatic weapons... the place looks like an armed camp... I can't but wonder why. Wow, look at me, I found my airline check-in without having to ask for directions... score one for me. An attractive older lady behind the counter informs me a mechanical problem has delayed my flight.*

"Something to do with the ventilation system. We're anticipating an hour or so delay. sir."

Just wonderful... off to a shit start... I hand her my voucher.

"Say, what's going on with all the security?"

She looks at me with an amusing smile.

"Your first time through here, sir?"

The voucher and my standard issue brown outfit are

glaring neon signs that telegraph I've just come from Base-Arizona... she probably uses that insolent line with every parolee that comes through just to amuse herself. Smiling her practiced smile, she hands me a boarding pass and a small brochure.

"Here's a map of terminal amenities."

"Where will I find the nearest food?"

She points past the long row of check-in counters to double-glass doors.

"Through those doors, follow the signs. Listen for the announcement when your flight is available for boarding. Thank you for flying with us, be sure to come visit again."

God, she's milking this for all its worth and loving it.

"Not if I can help it. And if I do, I won't be wearing brown."

She shoots me a priggish look and turns away... same to you, sweetheart. Passing through the glass doors, my smell box catches the aroma of food in the air... ahead is a food court with a smorgasbord of pizza, Chinese, burgers, and sandwiches... settling on the burger joint, I order a double patty with cheese, fries, and a Coke and pay for it with my debit card... there went eight credits. Finding a seat at a nearby table, I dig into a real burger, not that nasty fake meat crap they served on Europa... my mouth alerts whatever part of my brain that deals with pleasurable sensory sensations just how wonderful real food can be... each bite is pure ambrosia. Once my belly is full, I make my way to my concourse and find a quiet corner and watch with amusement the parade of humanity passing by... tall, short, thin, fat, young and old... our own alien race. Shamelessly, I leer at every fetching woman who passes to the point of embarrassment... theirs, not mine. I haven't seen or engaged with the female species for far too long, and dammit, I want one... one lovely young creature realizes I'm seizing her up, acknowledges my chutzpah with a slight nod and a smile before fading into the crowd never to be seen again. The announcement finally comes that my flight is ready for boarding... my assigned seat is the window two-thirds back on the right... when the door closes, no one is seated beside me... any hope for a lively conversation with a fellow human is dashed. Maybe I should get into this RedBook to find out what this World Government is all about, but before I do, my thoughts return to the loss of my parents... it could be a mistake, it could be another Russell family... I'll call as soon as we land. Do what you always did on Europa during cold black nights when your dreams drifted back to my dearest Dierdre and my loving parents... do it now, sleep... let those memories wash over you like a warm blanket.

I don't know how long I've been out *when I'm awakened by sound of the Captain's voice on the intercom.*

"Ladies and gentlemen, we'll be landing at Logan Airport in approximately twenty-minutes with a straight in approach to runway 22-Right. It is a brisk fifty-two degrees and there is a light snow falling, but we're told the roads remain clear. Sit back relax while our very capable cabin crew prepares us for our arrival. Thanks for flying with us and we hope to see you again."

CHAPTER 8

A Slow Ride to Hell

Following the signs to ground transportation*, I pass through the baggage area and spot a public phone… I'm in the booth, the receiver is in my hand… there's a credit card slot where I can use my debit card… I slip my card in the slot, but hesitate. Do I really want to do this in a phone booth in an airport? Maybe there's a phone at my new quarters… I'd rather call from there. I put my card back in my pocket and approach the revolving door to the outside… a WPF officer is giving me the once over.*

"Good flight?"

"Yes, thank you."

"Better change."

"Excuse me, Officer?"

"The clothes."

"What about them?"

"I worked security at Base-Arizona for a couple of years after I got out of the Army."

Oh, lucky you… did you get to shoot anyone in the back?

"Uh, right, my brown outfit."

"Where're you headed?"

"Boston."

"Transportation's right outside."

"Mind if I ask a question?"

"Shoot."

"I see that WPF patch on your arm. Are you part of a special unit?"

"Been in isolation somewhere?"

"Something like that."

"The World Police Force replaced all police departments."

"Everywhere?"

"Yep. We're under the command of the World Police out of Marseille now."

"Okay, thanks."

"Good luck, and be sure to ditch the clothes."

"First thing on my to do list, Officer."

I was sure he was gonna ask where I had served time... I would have lied... don't want to talk about that excuse of a planet ever again. Outside, unlike the stink of human sweat and Phostoirore, the cool night air hits my nose pure and sweet... further down to my left a flurry of activity catches my attention... a WPF patrol car, its light flashing, is parked next to a police van... five men and two women, looking like the walking dead, are being hustled into the van... by the curb directly in front of me are a half-dozen identical red vehicles... on the rear door of each is stenciled in white **'Boston Taxi.'** *Digging out the address to my destination, I approach the vehicle at the head of the line... a bearded driver with dark wavy hair is leaning against the front passenger door... he's young, maybe in his late twenties... he stands erect and smiles when he sees me approaching.*

"Hallooo, you need ride?"

He has a heavy accent that I can't place.

"Yes."

"Where, sir?"

"477 West 4th Street, South Boston?"

"Yes, sir."

"I have a transfer voucher."

"Very good, sir."

Handing him the voucher, he examines it and stuffs it in his shirt pocket.

"Good, thank you, sir. Luggage?"

"No."

"My name Raj Rashmi. We go now."

"What's going on over there with the cops?"

"No panhandlers allowed on airport property. They round them up take them to jail. We go now."

"Hmm, okay, we go now."

I don't see any private vehicles coming or going... that's kind of strange for one of the busiest airports in the country.

"Where's all the private cars?"

"Curfew, only taxis allowed in airport after nine."

I would love to ask why, but I don't. As we depart the covered area, snow has accumulated on the sides of the road, but the road itself is clear... we dip under Boston Harbor via the Ted Williams tunnel... when we emerge, Raj heads South on I-90. It's impossible not to notice the large electronic billboard off to the right displaying a series of numbers that exceed nine billion, but the total is continually going down.

"Impressive billboard, Raj."

Raj's eyes dart to the rear view mirror.

"Population numbers going down—too many people. You have sign where you come from?"

Quick, Billy, lie.

"Yeah, San Francisco, but it wasn't that big or impressive."

Jeez, we're still don't have a solution to the overpopulation problem? Long before I left, we were kicking out babies until we were crawling over one another for space and resources. Nothing ever changes until it becomes a crisis.

"Mind if I ask where you're from, Raj?"

"Sri Lanka, Sir."

"You like living here in America?"

"Good when I arrive, not so much now. Much drugs, crime, not safe."

Let's see if I can engage this character in a conversation about the Pakistan-India event.

"Damn, Pakistan and India screwed everything up but good."

Rashmi's eyes shoot to the rear view mirror... his brow crinkles.

"Yes, terrible."

His eyes go back to the road and he falls silent. Hmm, that's as far as he seems willing to go on that subject... can't press him further. He picks up I-93 South and exits on West 4th

St Street, crosses over 'D' Street, slows, turns off his lights and rolls to a stop in front of a row of tenements... with his engine running, he points to the building directly across from where he has parked.

"This is it, sir."

There's no street light... it's dark as midnight out there... so is the building except for a dim light in a window on the first floor... Raj sits pole-straight swiveling his head from left to right like he's looking for something.

"Is everything all right?"

"Don't be standing around, not safe. Good night, sir."

"Thanks for the lift, Raj."

As soon as I'm out and close the door, Raj turns on his headlights and peels away leaving me standing alone in the middle of this dark, cold street.

"And a good evening to you too, Raj Rashmi from Sri Lanka. What do you know that I don't?"

Turning to the house, I give it a once over wondering what I'll find inside... hell, it has to be a thousand percent improvement over where I've been. Abruptly, the quiet night is interrupted by the sound of feet moving fast across the road... I look to my left, there's no one, then to my right... two shadowy figures are moving quickly in my direction... I take a quick step back.

"Hey, who's there?"

No response.

"What do you want?"

"Whatever you can give, sir."

It's a man's voice, not demanding, more like pleading.

"I have nothing to give, back away."

The two figures are close enough now for one of them to reach out and touch my arm.

"Take your hand off me."

"We mean you no harm, sir. Anything will do, anything you can spare."

"I told you, I have nothing, now back off."

A light comes on over the front door of the tenement casting just enough illumination to make out an elderly Asian couple standing in front of me, their faces gaunt, their eyes dark and sunken... they're covered in gray soiled knee-length overcoats... the man's unshaven, his thinning hair snow-white, as is the women's... the tenement door swings open... a short, balding man in loose-fitting blue jeans, house slippers, and a blue T-shirt, steps out onto the stoop... his right hand is wrapped around the neck of a ball bat... there's the sound of tiny jingling bells as he moves down the three cement steps waving the bat over his head.

"Get the hell away from that man! Go on move it or you'll get a taste of this bat!"

The Asian man waves his arms and yelps.

"No harm meant, sir, no harm meant!"

"I don't give a damn, get the hell out of here."

The anorexic-looking figures quickly slink off into the darkness.

"Damn Streetwalkers. You're lucky there wasn't more of them. Are you William Russell?"

"Yeah."

"About time, I expected you earlier."

"The flight was delayed... a mechanical problem."

"Wonderful, just wonderful, you've kept me up past my bedtime. Come on, come on, it's cold, get in here. Don't trip over the bloody garbage cans."

Whoever the hell he is, he's rude and bossy as hell... I'm barely past the garbage containers lined along the sidewalk before he's up the stairs entering the house... as soon I cross the threshold, he slams the door, locks it, throws the deadbolt, and turns off the outside light... hitting another switch, a light comes on at the top of a flight of stairs giving me my first good look at this guy... he's seventy if he's a day, medium height, overweight by twenty pounds with loose folds of skin beneath his eyes... ah, there's the source of the jingling I heard... a ring of keys hang from his belt.

"Where you coming from, Russell?"

"Uh, San Francisco."

"Streetwalkers as bad out there?"

"Oh yeah."

I have no idea what on earth he's talking about. Now he's bounding up the flight of stairs two at a time like a rabbit scampering for its burrow with me on his heels... impressive for an aging, fat man. Quickstepping down the hall, he stops at the only door on the right... light's spilling from under the door across from this, one and there's a strong odor seeping out... if it's food, it doesn't smell all that appetizing... the mystery man removes a key from his ring, inserts it into the lock, swings the door open, steps inside, and turns on a ceiling light in the center of the room.

"Your home sweet home, Mister Russell."

As I cross the threshold, I'm assaulted by a musty odor like maybe the place hasn't been occupied in a while... Mister Energizer Bunny notices my sour expression and points to the window overlooking the dark street below.

"It'll be fine, open the window. There's some air spray in the bathroom."

I'm not sure what I expected, but this isn't it... the place is small, really small... the walls are powder blue, the doors and trim white, the gray carpet is worn in spots... behind a small glass-topped coffee table is a faded beige sofa... a desk with a 36-inch flat-screen TV is perched on it is off to the right of the door... to the left of the living area is an old wooden dining table and two matching chairs that would make good firewood... next to it is a small kitchen with a refrigerator and flattop electric stove... on the counter is a microwave, toaster, and single cup coffee maker. My presumed landlord... he has yet to introduce himself... points to three doors just beyond and to the left of the dining table.

"Bathroom to the left, clothes closet in the middle, bedroom to the right. The thermostat is on the wall between the bedroom and closet."

"I didn't catch your name."

"Julius Sommers, owner, house mother, and all-around nice guy. Call me Jules."

I stick out my hand to shake his, but he doesn't offer it.

"What's your handle... William, Billy?"

"Billy."

"William it is then."

"Just Billy."

He ignores me.

"No one's lived here in a few months."

"I would have never guessed."

He shoots me a narrow-eyed look as if he's trying to decide if I'm a wise-ass... he smiles.

"Good, a sense of humor, I like that. Everything you need is here—sheets, towels, cooking and eating utensils. There's no cleaning service, you'll have to keep it up yourself. You'll find some cleaning products on the shelf in the closet. Washer and dryer are in the basement. Cable TV comes via satellite to the local relay station from Menwith Hill Station, the old Royal Air Force base near Harrogate, North Yorkshire, England. Way back in World War Two, Menwith provided communications and intelligence support services to the United Kingdom and the United States. When the World Government took over, they restored it with state-of-the art technology. I know, I know, that's more information than you need, but I'm ex-military and it's all about details, details, details."

"Which branch?"

"United States Marines. You?"

"No, entered police work right out of college."

"Uh, a college kid—good for you, knowledge is power. Now for the TV. Whatever your taste in music you'll find it on channels thirteen through thirty-five, entertainment channels follow. Most of the shows these days are written for nitwits. Those who knew how to write like adults have all died replaced by hacks who fill pages with dog-shit ideas, bad dialogue, and government propaganda. Almost makes watching the silly, uncreative commercials enjoyable—almost. There's sports channels and plenty of government news if that's your thing."

After all those years without so much as a weather forecast, a test pattern would be an improvement.

"Ah, I don't see a computer."

"Don't have one. You can buy one if your life's goal is to cruise the Internet reading all that bullshit on social media. One day all the satellites are gonna come crashing down and then what will we do? Take up reading books again, I guess. The fridge is stocked with a few things and there's a box of coffee pods above the sink, all courtesy of your new employer to get you started. Say, did you know a 9th-century Ethiopian goatherder by the name of Kaldi claims to have discovered coffee when his goats became excited after eating the beans from a coffee plant?"

"Can't say that I did."

"I'm full of useless trivia."

"I'll be working at the South Boston Police precinct. Is it far from here?"

"It's an easy ten-minute walk. Out the door, turn right, cross over 'D' Street, then right on Broadway. The precinct is the two-story red brick building on the other side of the street two short blocks down. There's a clothing store on Broadway and few doors down past the alley is a small grocery store. If you need me, I live on the first floor. Doors on the left at the bottom of the stairs."

"The apartment across the hall—someone was cooking over there."

"Conrad Billings, works at the Exelon Mystic Power Plant. I hardly ever run into him, but I hear him and his friends coming and going a lot. A word to the wise. Keep your door locked and stay off the streets after dark unless you're looking for drugs or have a death wish."

"I have neither."

"Good to hear. What time is your check in?"

"Ten in the morning."

He hands me the door key along with a second one.

"The longer one is for the front door. Never come or go without locking it."

"How much is this place costing me?"

"The lease is in the government's name and they pay the rent—twelve-fifty a month. Okay, that's it, you now know all I know. Sleep well."

"Uh, there's a call I need to make, but I don't see a phone."

"There's no landline. Most don't use them anymore since everybody from the age of two on have cell phones"

43

"I left mine somewhere between here and San Francisco."

"Is the call important?"

"I have to let someone know I've arrived."

He digs into his pocket and hands me his cell.

"Give it back to me in the morning before you leave."

"The call's long distance."

"Not to worry, I have plenty of minutes. Sleep well and pray the garbage trucks show up—they're a week overdue now. Oh, almost forget, there's a decent bottle of Bourbon above the sink if you imbibe, also courtesy of your employer. Okay, see you whenever."

Scurrying to the door, he's gone like a sudden gust of wind... I can see this guy is going to take some getting used to. Okay, Billy, meager as these digs are, it's time to get settled... I'm excited about sleeping in a room without forty-nine other men farting and snoring... they'll be no morning siren blast or Quasi marching up and down the aisle swinging his cattle prod like it's his manhood, and no taking the elevator down to hell every morning. Right now, my lips, tongue and throat are in need of that bottle of Bourbon... finding it and a glass in a cabinet above the sink, I down a shot in one gulp... it stings like hell, but it's damn good and damn welcome... pouring a second, I raise the glass in a toast.

"May Europa be invaded by venomous spiders."

Down the second shot goes, tasting better than the first... the contents of the fridge are next... a package of hot dogs, baloney, Swiss cheese, a can of sliced pears, mustard, mayo, ketchup, and a loaf of whole wheat bread... I've died and gone to heaven... wherever the hell that might be. Slapping a slice of baloney and cheese between two slices of bread smeared with mustard, I wolf it down in short order... a third shot of Bourbon and I'm ready to investigate the rest of my second-floor grand palace... the bathroom's first... whoa, it's an oversized closet, but hell, it's all mine... a commode to the left, sink to the right... a mirrored medicine cabinet mounted above... to the right, a small shower stall hides behind a powder blue plastic curtain covered with red and white stars. Door number two is a two-foot-wide closet with a single wall-

to-wall rod for clothes... a mop, vacuum cleaner, and a few cleaning supplies on the shelf above. Entering door number three, I grope around for the light switch and turn on a ceiling light in the middle of a very narrow room... dead center is a single bed covered in a dark blue comforter... damn, there's barely a foot clearance from either wall... I'll have to crawl in from the bottom, scoot along the wall sideways, or move the bed against one wall... that's not an option... I'm used to sleeping with both sides open. There's no nightstand, lamp, closet or window, just the bed. Sitting my myself down on the end of the mattress, my neurons begin spinning with justifiable confusion... there's the little matter of a seventeen-year-plus brain-gap that's in dire need of replenishing. Everything that's happened since my return yesterday feels surreal... what they didn't strip from me on Europa, although they damn well tried, was my humanity and my moral compass, both ingrained in me from early childhood by mom and dad... let that be my criterion going forward... you're beginning a new life, Billy Boy, run with it, turn grapes into wine. Jules's cell is burning a hole in my pocket... I have to make that call, yet I'm dreading it. What if the accident report is correct, what do I do then? I dial my parent's old number and hope they hadn't changed it... two rings and I hear the all too familiar three-tone beeps followed by, **"The number you have dialed is no longer in service. If you feel you have dialed incorrectly, hang up and try again."** *Damn it, damn it! The report must be accurate or that number would still be working. With tears in my eyes, I turn off the light, flop on my back to the mattress fully clothed and cry myself to sleep.*

My eyelids flutter like a butterfly's wings *flapping in a breeze before popping open... it's dark... I can't see a damn thing... I'm confused until my brain decides to cooperate... okay, got it, I'm in my new digs in South Boston, Massachusetts... finding the light switch, I discover I'm still fully dressed. Light spills to the living area casting shadows on my meager*

surroundings... I need to find a good decorator. Dragging myself into the living room, I find the TV remote on the desk next to the initials SKL carved into its surface, not doubt put there by a previous occupant... pressing the power button the TV screen comes alive.

Press 26 for entertainment channels, 10 for news, 13 for music.

Roll the dice, try channel 26... the music is loud and hard driving... a young man's racing toward the camera... hot on his heels is a heavyset tattooed bearded guy swinging a regulation baseball bat... he catches up with the man and beats him senseless... shades of that horrific incident at Base-Arizona, only with a bat... let's try channel 18 for some music... whoa and whoa again... after all these many long years they're still playing Beatles music... Paul McCartney's singing 'Yesterday'... rescuing the Bourbon from its hiding place, I down another shot, remove my clothes, and crawl back into bed while McCartney serenades me back to dreamland.

CHAPTER 9

Welcome to Purgatory

Phantom images bounce around my skull like an errant bullet... I'm working my ass off in one of the cold damp mine shafts covered head to toe in dusty, smelly, Phostoirore... lying in bed way too close to snoring, belching, inmates... Quasi's jack-booting up and down the row of bunks threatening to zap anyone for the slightest infraction... I see my parents... they're laughing and talking, but I can't make out what they're saying... now Dierdre's standing at the foot of the bed... I can see her face clearly...her auburn hair, her matching eyes... she's smiling... God, she's as beautiful as I remember... she extends a hand... I reach for it... Quasi steps in and jerks her hand away... oh hell, now the slug's tugging hard on my left big toe.

"Hey, Russell, wake up!"

Crap, what have I done now?

"Open your eyes!"

Wait, that not Quasi's voice... my eyelids pop open like a soda can... who the hell is this fat, balding man at the foot of my bed?

"Hey, wake up."

Jesus, it's Jules the landlord.

"Yeah, yeah, what?"

"I didn't hear you go out, so I came up to check on you."

"What for?"

"Didn't you say you had a 10:00 AM check in?"

"Yeah."

"It's nine twenty-five, soldier."

"Nine twenty-five! Holy crap!"

"When you didn't answer, I used my key to get in. First day in school, you don't want to be late."

"Jesus, thanks, Jules.

He bounds to the door.

"Hey, wait, your phone. It's next to the TV."

He returns, takes the phone, and moves to the door again.

"A word to the wise. If Streetwalkers bother you, tell them you're a cop and that'll send them sprinting for cover."

What the hell are Streetwalkers? Before I can pursue him for an explanation, he's gone... I skip shaving and a shower... a questionable decision on my first day... settling for a quick face washing, brushing my teeth, and combing my hair, I dress and bolt out the door descending the stairs two at a time... Jules is standing by his open door.

"Don't dilly-dally on the way."

"What?"

"No sightseeing."

Sightseeing? Is he kidding? I reach for my key to unlock the door.

"It's unlocked, William, go."

Outside, there's not a soul in sight... an inch or so of snow covers the sidewalk... the road is wet but clear... it's cold, but the sun, that glorious orb of light and warmth, greets me with a chilly kiss through a light haze... it's gonna take a few days before it sinks in that I can walk about freely again... and on the surface of my own planet yet. Taking a deep breath, my nose is assaulted by the rancid smell rising from snow-covered stacks of garbage bins lining the sidewalks... I'm getting my first look at 4th Street lined with old two and three-story tenements, some painted white with gray trim, others light gray with white trim... nothing like New England conformity. Following Jules's instructions, I make my way up 4th toward Broadway when an older couple approach with outstretched hands... I think they're the same two from last night... not sure they recognize me.

"On your way, I'm a police Officer."

Jesus, Billy, that sounded whinny... they slink away like I have a communicable disease. On the corner of Broadway is

Sully's News Stand... a sign touts fresh brewed coffee... no time for that now... the sidewalk on both sides of Broadway is lined with overflowing garbage containers and black plastic bags... the sidewalk's busy with foot traffic... I'd have to be indifferent not to notice there's two distinct groups... some look quite normal going about their business, others looking downtrodden walking aimlessly or approaching passersby for handouts... some as young as ten and twelve... they must be the Streetwalkers Jules referred to... I've never seen anything like this... what's caused all these souls to be out here? I pass at least a dozen of them and get cold stares, but none approach... maybe I look like a cop. I peer in the window of the clothing store as I pass... I'll stop on my way home and celebrate my birthday with new clothes, shots of Bourbon, and hot dogs. What's going on over there? There's a commotion about a block ahead... a dozen people of mixed races are marching single file carrying large placards... 'EQUALITY FOR EVERYONE—NOW.' *There's a light whirring sound above me... a drone whizzes overhead swooping low over the heads of the protesters before turning and hovering... two patrol cars and a van, lights flashing, siren's blaring, screech to a halt... the protesters are chanting.*

"Equality for everyone now! Equality for everyone now!

The cops are in black uniforms with those WPF patches... Jesus, they're whacking the protesters with their batons, spraying them with pepper spray, and pulling the placards down. One protester, a tall blond white guy, is giving them an argument... he's tasered, howls, and falls to the ground writhing in pain... they handcuff him and drag him into the van. What in the living hell is going on? Move on, Billy, move on, it's none of your business... cross the street and keep moving. I'm no sooner on the other side passing a narrow alley between a pizza joint and a drug store when a young man step's out. He's in his mid-twenties, lean, long hair and he looks nervous.

"Sir, sir."

What now? His eyes whip to the cops busting the protesters then back to me... he's trying to hand me a sheet of paper.

"Whatta you want, kid?"

"Take it, read it, join the movement before it's too late."

He thrusts the paper toward me... take the damn thing, Billy, and get rid of him.

"Read it, man, read it, time's running out, Armageddon is around the corner."

Nervously, he looks to the cops again before trotting off to the back of the alley and disappearing... without looking at the paper, I crunch it up and stuff it into my left pocket and move on at a quick pace. On the corner of E-Street and Broadway I come to a two-story red brick building identified by a black sign with white letters... **'World Military Police, South Boston Precinct'.** *A dozen police vehicles, eight black Chevy Traverse's with tinted windows, and an unmarked military Humvee are parked in an adjoining lot.*

"Okay, Billy Boy, it's show time."

Inside, the first thing that catches my eye is another eagle poster on the wall... nothing like a little hard sell... at the reception desk, a lady in a WPF uniform greets me.

"Yes, sir?"

"Good morning, I'm reporting in."

"Your ID card, please."

I hand it to her... she inserts in a device next to her computer, makes a few quick entries, and hands it back.

"You're assigned to drug enforcement. Second floor, turn left to the last office on the right. The stairs are over there."

"Thank you."

"One heck of a tough bunch of dudes up there. Good luck."

Sounds like an ominous warning at best. At the top of the stairs is a wall sign... **'World Military police'...** *an arrow points to the right,* **'World Military Regional Commander'** *and* **'Regional Drug Enforcement'** *to the left... I head left along a row of windows that overlook Broadway... the sign on the first door reads* **'World Military - Colonel Andrei Chernov, Commander.** *Door two is open... it's a break room, three tables, snack vending machines, and one of those fancy single-cup multiple-choice coffee dispensers... the third door* *sign reads,* **'Regional Drug Enforcement – Lieutenant Frank R, Wilson, Director'**. *Damn, I wish I was clean shaven and dressed in any color other than UPS brown... too late now... taking a deep breath, I enter... a woman is seated at a u-shaped desk with her back to me... the nameplate on the desk says she's* **'Jade Miro'**... *she's typing... beyond her is a large windowless open space... the walls are a soft beige with off-white floor tile... four desks face out... a fifth is positioned against the right back wall between two doors... the first desk is the only one occupied... the man sitting there pays me no attention... the lady rotates in her chair... she's Asian... I'd have to be brain dead not to notice she's pretty damn attractive... flawless olive complexion, high cheekbones, full lips and expressive almond-shaped brown eyes that match her hair that's pulled back in a ponytail... Dierdre often wore hers in a ponytail.*

"Yes, sir?"

The words escape her shapely mouth in a low, smooth, smoky tone... at least that's how it's reaching my ears... put your tongue back in your mouth and focus, Billy, focus.

"Good morning, I'm reporting in."

"Russell?"

"That would be me."

She raises an eyebrow and glances at her watch.

"You're late."

Oh hell, first day and I'm already scolded by the receptionist... strike one.

"Lieutenant Wilson demands promptness."

"Sorry, I was running late."

"We've already established that."

Ouch! Strike two.

"After you pass muster with the effervescent Lieutenant Wilson, I'll get you up to speed. Beside promptness, the Lieutenant demands his boys be clean shaven except for Victor's mustache."

She taps her intercom.

"Lieutenant, Officer Russell's here."

A deep, gravelly voice resonates back.

"He's late."

Crap, strike three... Ms. Miro points over her shoulder to the door on her right.

"Knock first. I advise you listen and speak little."

"Got it, thanks."

I smile, she doesn't and goes back to typing... as instructed, I knock at the Lieutenant's door.

"Come."

Lieutenant Wilson is sitting at his desk. He looks to be in his mid-sixties, average height, receding salt and pepper brown hair, stout build, and a weathered but well-lived-in face. The office is small... two chairs face a brown wooden desk... behind Wilson is a matching credenza, above that a large framed wall map of New England... that's it, no pictures or mementos anywhere. A double-wide window to my right overlooks a row of single-story houses in a middle-class neighborhood... black garbage bags and containers are stacked along both sides of the street. What's with the lack of garbage collection?

"Russell, come in, close the door, you're late."

"Sorry, I was whacked from the trip and overslept. It won't happen again, sir."

"No, it won't."

Ouch and ouch again. ... Wilson spies my unshaven face.

"No facial hair here except for Victor's mustache."

"Yes, sir."

He's up and coming around the desk thrusting out a beefy hand... his grip is firm.

"Settled in okay?"

"Working on it, sir. Thanks for the groceries and the booze."

"You're welcome, take a seat."

As he strolls back to his chair, I notice what I hadn't before... he walks with a limp favoring his right leg.

"You go by William?"

"Billy."

"First things first, Billy. I know where you've been, for how long, and why. That information stays with me and

Colonel Chernov. The rule here is don't ask don't tell regarding anyone's past. Got that?"

"Yes, sir."

"From what I hear, Europa's a hell hole."

"It's that and more, sir."

"Then consider your early release a gift. But buyer beware, seventeen years is a lifetime, a lot has changed. Forgive the pun, but it's going to feel like you've landed on a foreign planet, so take it one day at a time."

How much more foreign can it be than from where I've just returned?

"Marseille chose you for this assignment based on your DEA background as well as how you handled things in that closet."

"Sir?"

"In that closet you delivered justice."

So, I murdered a guy in a closet and that qualifies me as an exemplary candidate for this job?

"I'm not proud of what I did, sir."

"Just the same, he had it coming and you took care of it."

I wouldn't begin to know how to respond to that, so I won't.

"It's been over seventeen years since I worked with the DEA, sir."

"And your point is?"

"Just that it's been a while."

"During that time did you ever lose confidence in yourself?"

"No, sir, I can't say that I did, but I—"

"Then you have your answer. Your performance here is all that counts now. Under the terms of your release, you're on parole for one year from today. At the end of that time—assuming all goes well—your parole ends and your record expunged. Second condition. This is your life's work until you either expire in the line of duty, or retire—for your sake I hope it's the latter."

Since I'm hearing this stuff for the first time, best to just smile and agree.

"Yes, sir."

"I expect you to be where and when you need to be on time, keep your eyes and ears open, and above all trust no one outside this office."

"Yes, sir."

"There's no 'sirs' here. It's Lieutenant."

"Yes, Lieutenant."

"The government has charged us with ferreting out drug lords and their minions from their rat holes. Having served with the old DEA, you know how dangerous this work is."

"There was never a day when it wasn't, Lieutenant."

"The World Government estimates that at least fifty percent of the planet's population is on one drug or another or a combination of several. That's one hell of a lot of junkies out there who will do whatever it takes to get a cheap fix resulting in the highest worldwide crime rate in decades. And then there's the elite crowd who can afford the high-priced designer stuff. Both groups are the problem. Our job is to cut off the flow wherever we find it. Am I going too fast?"

"No, Lieutenant."

Yes, lieutenant, I'm confused as a barrel of pissed off monkeys looking for a way out.

"We're a unit of the World Military. Colonel Andrei Chernov, formally with the Federal Security Service of the Russian Federation, is the regional commander. He reports to the World Military Commander in Marseille, French General Marcel Couture."

He swivels in his chair and points to the wall map of New England.

"This office covers the New England States. Two more units—one in Kansas City, the other in Portland, Oregon— cover the rest. All three units report to Colonel Chernov. There're a number of similar units across the globe. Questions?"

Ask what sounds like a reasonable intelligent question before he gives you an 'F' for your first meeting.

"What's in the supply line?"

"Gray Death, the color of cement, is the drug of choice these days. It's a blend of opioid substances—heroin, fentanyl, and U-47700 better known as 'Pink.' The combination can be lethal and induce an immediate overdose with minimal contact if you don't know what the hell you're dealing with. Other drugs like MDMA, ecstasy, and Oxycodone are also laced with fentanyl. It's a lucrative cash business. We catch one bad guy, two more pop up."

"That must keep the courts jumping."

Wilson's eyes bore into me like maybe I said something utterly stupid.

"The courts play no role in how we conduct business here, Billy. Marseille makes the rules, and those rules dictate how we do things. None of the scum make it in alive unless we decide it's to our advantage to interrogate them first."

Did I hear right? He can't be serious.

"You mean, uh—"

"It means exactly what you think it means."

"I'm not comfortable with—what I mean is, maybe they chose the wrong man for this position."

Wilson's eyes bore into mine like a laser... one of those long hard looks like I said something stupid again.

"If you're uncomfortable with how we do things here, then this is your one and only meeting in this office. What Marseille does with you after is up to them. Most likely it'll be back to some shit hole prison."

My heart skips a beat.... my stomach turns queasy.

"I'm waiting, Russell. What's it to be?"

Quick, Billy, think... he's just given you a choice between evil and evil... I can't go back to prison, I can't. Tell him what he wants to hear... buy time... figure it out later. I lick my lips, swallow hard and nod.

"Look, Billy, this is not the easiest job in the world by any stretch of the imagination. But it's necessary and has to be done. Playing footsies with these bandits in the courts is a waste of time and money. What we do and how we do it is legal by government decree. Understand?"

"Yes, Lieutenant."

"You're sure?"

"Yes."

"Any questions?"

Don't say anything, Billy... nod your head and agree if you know what's good for you.

"Okay, let's wrap this up. We have two teams of two. You'll be partnered with Hank Drummond. We have a fifth man coming. When he shows up, he'll rotate as backup between teams. When you're out on the streets, if you come across anything requiring immediate attention, call for backup before taking action. Got it?"

"Got it."

He pops to his feet, comes around, and pats me on the shoulder like he would a loyal dog.

"Welcome aboard. Life here should be more to your liking."

"That would be an understatement, Lieutenant."

"Damn tragic what happened to your wife. If it's of any comfort, I would have done exactly what you did."

"And you would have paid the price I did. Up there living underground 24/7, seventeen years felt like fifty."

His eyes go to the ceiling... I know where he's going next... I wish he wouldn't, but damn it, he does.

"Just how bad was it up there?"

"Where would I begin?" *He's waiting for more, but a shrug is all I offer.*

"Okay, someday you'll share the gritty details over a beer."

"Yeah, someday."

Like hell I will, Lieutenant.

"Ah, there is one thing. During processing in Arizona there was reference to the Pakistan/India event, but no explanation was offered."

"Jesus, you really don't know?"

"We had no access to any news—it was their way of controlling body and soul."

He falls silent, his head swivels to the window... he's thinking... he blows a hard breath... his expression turns somber.

"Pakistan and India were still fighting their age-old border war. It came to a head nine years ago when Pakistan fired off a nuke at New Delhi."

"What?"

His face tightens, his eyes slowly come to me.

"Unexplainably, the warhead exploded five-miles short of its target— two million on the ground were vaporized instantly."

"My God."

"The world was on the verge of a global nuclear war when the UN negotiated a halt to further escalation. They tried for a nuclear ban, but it never came to a vote—not one country was willing to give up theirs. As for the move to a world government, radical as it was, I personally was for it. In some ways I still am, in others not so much. We're still waiting to see where it's going and if it is the answer to our problems. I'll reserve my opinion since I'm not sure we have the right people in there to get it done. We'll see. All right, that's it, come meet the crew. You're pale as an albino's ass, get some sun."

"Uh, Lieutenant, I hate a favor to ask."

"What is it?"

"My parents died in an auto accident in Bristol, Rhode Island."

"Yeah, it's posted on your records. Just terrible."

"I only learned of it yesterday."

"Oh, jeez, Billy, I'm sorry."

"How can I get a copy of the accident report?"

"Leave your parents' names and address with Jade and I'll take care of it."

He limps his way to the squad room and introduces the guy sitting at the first desk.

"Hank Drummond, meet Billy Russell, Rod's replacement and your new partner."

Drummond's around my age, small in stature, lean and muscled with tight-cropped brown hair and an unsmiling flinty expression that tells me he's all business... he's sizing me up from side-to-side, top-to-bottom.

"Welcome to purgatory, Billy."

After what I just learned from Wilson, pass purgatory and go straight to hell.

"Jade you met—she keeps us on the straight and narrow. Don't make the mistake of treating her as the receptionist or she'll hand you your balls."

Jade raises an eyebrow and smiles.

"For once the Lieutenant's telling the truth."

"Hank, where's Gustav and Victor?"

Drummond swivels in his chair and points to a door to the left of the back wall desk.

"Okay, Billy, get settled in, you'll meet them later."

*Without further comment, Wilson limps back to his office...
Jade waves me over.*

"Billy, take a seat over here."

Happy to, beautiful, happy to. She turns to her computer, taps a few keys, and reads from the monitor.

"William Evan Russell - Age 44 -Residence: 477 4th Street, Boston, MA. Special Officer, Boston Police Department, Drug Enforcement Unit, South Boston Precinct. Weapons Restriction none. Restricted to M-5 Clearance."

At least I'm listed as a living breathing member of the human race again.

"What's an M-5 Clearance."

"Whatever the Lieutenant chooses to share with us."

From her bottom right drawer, she fetches a black leather holster with a Smith and Wesson 9MM 45ACP stuffed in it with an extra slot holding what looks like a silencer along with a shiny gold badge with a big black number 513 in the center.

"When you're out and about keep your weapon and badge visible on your belt. Cops are the last humans Streetwalkers are looking to interact with."

From the same drawer, she withdraws a pair of handcuffs and a cellphone.

"Anytime you need to call in just press 'home'. As for your apartment, while you're on parole, the government pays your landlord to insure you don't spend it on wine, women, and song. The first of each month your salary is electronically posted to your debit account and the rent is automatically deducted.

"And my salary?"

"$3,800.00 a month."

Forty-five thousand six-hundred a year to risk life and limb. Eighteen-years ago, I was making a third more than that as a DEA Officer and I didn't have to kill anyone for it.

"You're in luck, today's the 28th. Your first month's salary gets posted in a few days. Don't spend it all in one place. Oh, just noticed today's your birthday—happy birthday."

"Thanks."

She points to the desk that's pushed up against the far back wall.

"For now, that one's yours. You'll move next to Hank when the fifth guy shows up. You're not wearing a watch."

I roll my eyes and lie through my teeth.

"Stupid me, I left it in the airport restroom."

"Which explains why you were late."

How many times is the lady going to chastise me for being late? From her middle drawer she rescues a cheap watch with a faded dark brown leather strap.

"The guy this belonged to won't be needing it anytime soon. Okay, that's it. If you need anything, come see me."

I slip the watch on, pretend to admire it, then like a smitten schoolboy sit and stare at the lady's dazzling good looks.

"Was there something else, Officer Russell?"

"The Lieutenant said I should leave you a note—a little matter he's taking care of for me."

"Jot it down on this pad."

I print my parents' names and address and hand the pad back to her... she doesn't look at it.

"Go now, you're already late for your meet and greet with Colonel Chernov—first door down the hall past the breakroom."

CHAPTER 10

The Military Rules the Roost

As I make my way down the hallway, I glance out the windows overlooking Broadway... the human misery I don't yet understand remains in plain sight. Was it this Pakistan-India event that brought the world to this, or is there something more going on that's yet to be revealed? Life on the planet was bad enough when I left... we had begun to slide into a vast chasm of political stupidity foisted on us by a polarized two-party system that seemed incapable of getting anything constructive done... hatred, bigotry and intolerance continued to sweep across America and no one knew how to stop it. What happened after I left that bought it to this advanced state? Taking a deep breath, I enter Colonel Chernov's office... sitting at the desk is an attractive redhead who looks to be in her late thirties... on the wall behind her is another one of those Eagle posters... along the back wall are two offices... the doors are closed... to the left of the redhead is another office, its door also closed... the lady's head comes up from whatever she's reading.*

"Can I help you?"

I catch a Russian accent since I heard enough of them on Europa.

"I have an appointment with Colonel Chernov."

"William Russell?"

"Yes."

She glances at her watch... here it comes.

"We expected you fifteen minutes ago."

She gives me a quick once-over inspection before reaching for the intercom.

"Sir, William Russell is here."

A deep voice boom's back.

"Send him in."

"Through the door to my right, Officer Russell. I'm Antonina Lebedev, Colonel Chernov's administrative assistant. See me if you need anything."

"Thank you."

Colonel Chernov's office is larger than Wilson's... a six-seat conference table takes up most of the left side of the room... on the left wall are a series of photos of Chernov posing with military brass along with a half-dozen military citations, all Russian... the double-window to the right of his desk overlooks the same neighborhood I saw from Wilson's office. Chernov, head down, is sitting at his desk reading some papers.

"Russell. I'm up to my ass in alligators, so we'll make this short. Have a seat."

He speaks with a distinct Russian accent in a quick cadence like he's in a hurry... I sit and wait... he scribbles something on one of the sheets of paper and sets them aside, stands and saunters to the photos and citations like he wants to be sure I noticed them. He's lean, in good physical shape for a man that looks to be somewhere north of sixty-five... a full head of light salt and pepper brown hair, eyes to match, with an unsmiling expression that signals he's all business... on the shoulders of his neatly pressed and creased combat fatigues are polished silver Eagles.

"Settled in okay?"

"Working on it, sir."

Hey, Colonel, you going to stand there and talk with your back to me? He finally turns to me slowly giving me a stone-faced once-over before moving to my side... I begin to stand... he places a hand on my shoulder.

"No, sit."

He's so close I have to pitch my head back to look him in the eye.

"I knew a fellow Russian officer who spent time in security on Europa. Alexander Smirnoff—like the gin. Perhaps you knew of him?"

Yeah, I knew the bastard. He was in charge of security the first four years I was there.

"No, sir, can't say that I did."

"He told me if it wasn't for the bloody ore that keeps this failing planet going, no one in their right mind would go to such a place."

"Descriptions don't match the reality of actually being there, sir."

I wish he'd move back a bit... this feels awkward... almost creepy... I can smell his warm breath when he exhales. He removes his hand from my shoulder, but doesn't back away.

"Because you delivered swift justice in that closet, Marseille believes you are our man."

Yet another one who thinks blowing a guy away in a closet makes me a perfect fit for what they really do here.

"Like that man you executed, the world is overrun by human garbage. They all deserve the same fate. Here we accommodate them."

So, Lieutenant Wilson said, Colonel. So glad you confirmed it. Finally, he takes a step back and looks to the window.

"These goddamn Latinos and blacks are clever bastards. Они все злые люди. Нам нужно избавить страну от всех до единого, и мы будем."

Either he's not aware that he slipped into Russian, or I wasn't meant to hear what he said.

"Vicious sub-humans every last one of them. Marseille has given us carte blanche to do whatever it takes to shut them down. Officer Drummond is a good man, he'll show you the ropes. Do you have any questions for me?"

I'm full of them, Colonel, none of which I'm going to ask... not yet, anyway.

"No, sir, can't think of any."

Now blow smoke up his ass.

"I plan to give it my all, sir."

"Excellent. Do things by our book and you'll have no problems."

"Got it, sir."

He offers me his hand I stand and we shake.

"Welcome to the hunting party, Officer Russell."

Hunting party? That's putting an interesting spin on it... this guy is just short of spooky- land... enough to put me on alert.

"Thank you, Colonel."

"I see in your file you blew the top of his head off?"

Oh crap, now he wants the grizzly details.

"Yes, sir."

"At point blank range?"

"Yes, sir."

"Given the circumstances, I would have done the same, Officer Russell."

He places a hand on my shoulder again... was that a chill that just ran through me?

"My only regret is I wasn't there to witness it.

That settles it, this guy is short a few bricks.

"That will be all for now, Officer Russell. Welcome to the team."

I could have gone another seventeen years without that meeting... *Chernov's a cold fish and more than a little threatening in his demeanor ... but, hey, Billy Boy, you're here, not on Europa, so stop your bitching. Whatever comes your way from here on in you're gonna have to deal with one day at a time... that is, once I'm up to speed on what's really going on beyond what I've seen already. Making a quick stop in the break room for a cup of coffee on my way back to the office, I can't help wondering what the rest of this day is going to look like. An unsmiling Jade greets me.*

"You found the breakroom."

"Yeah."

"How goes it with the good Russian Colonel?"

"He was interesting enough."

"Hmm, first time I heard him described as interesting."

Actually, I thought he was a pompous asshole.
"Go now, build your nest."
I know when I've been properly dismissed, but before I do, Wilson calls from his office.
"Billy, a moment please."
He hands me a sheet of paper.
"The accident report you asked for."
"That was quick, thanks."
Folding the report, I slip it into my shirt pocket.
"All's well with you and the Colonel?"
"One-hundred percent."
"Good. Come see me if you need anything."
As I stroll back to my new desk, I smile and nod at Hank... he nods but doesn't smile. My assigned desk is up against the wall between two doors... the one to the right is the men's room... not sure what the one to my left is... settling in, I retrieve the accident report from my shirt pocket. Before I can unfold it, I hear a loud voice coming from the room to my left... someone is shouting, but it's muffled, I can't make out what's being said... then comes what sounds like a hard whack followed by a moan... I look to Hank, then to Jade... neither show any interest... there it is again, only this time it sounded like someone bounced off a wall... I look to Jade and Hank again for a reaction... nothing. Too dumb to mind my own business, I stuff the accident report back in my shirt pocket, pop to my feet, and take the few steps to the door.
"Don't go there, Russell."
It's Hank.
"What's going on in there?"
"Business."
"What kind of business?"
"The kind that's none of yours."
From behind the door, I hear a male voice cursing in a foreign language followed by another loud whack and a thump like this someone hit the floor... my right hand goes to the doorknob.
"Billy!"
This time it's Jade, her strident tone a clear warning not to

64

do what I'm about to do.

"What's going on in there, Jade?"

"Nothing that concerns you."

Hank's calling to me again.

"Hey, turn up your hearing aid, man, I told you it's business, get away from the door."

But no, not me, I don't know when to leave well enough alone or take good advice when freely given... turning the knob, I swing the door open wide... the walls are covered with thick sound padding... a black man is lying face down on the floor with his hands handcuffed behind him... he's bleeding from his nose, mouth, and left ear... a man is down on one knee beside him... fiftyish, black hair, trim body with a twisted, snarling expression that would scare ghosts on Halloween... his right hand is tightly wrapped around a foot-long rubber club... on the inside of his wrist I spot a tattoo of an eagle like the one on those posters... a third individual, heavyset, pale complexion, dark curly hair and mustache, is leaning against the back wall with his arms folded across his chest... the one down on his knee snaps his head in my direction.

"Wer zum Teufel bist du?"

Here we go again with the foreign language crap.

"What did you say?"

The dude leaning against the wall spits out a translation.

"He wants to know who the hell you are?"

He too has an accent, but it's not the same as the other guy... this one sounds French. With a few quick steps he closes the distance between us and slams the door in my face. Now I'm really pissed... I don't appreciate having a door slammed in my face without at least a hug and a friendly hello. Swinging the door open again, I take a step inside.

"Excuse me, but surely you've noticed that man is bleeding badly."

The guy down on one knee waves the club in my direction.

"Get your lily-white-ass out of here!"

Whatever his accent is, it's thick... I'm thinking German.

"You should kiss my lily-white ass and explain why you're beating a handcuffed man."

I step in for a closer look at the black guy... he looks unconscious. In one fluid movement, the one on his knee drops the club to the floor, pops to his feet and lunges, his right arm rising, his fist coming at me like a deadly snake strike. WHACK! His knuckles crunch against the left side of my nose ... my hands fly up to my face.

"Goddamn it!"

I warble back falling to the floor and landing on my tailbone. Jesus Mother of God that hurt!

"Hey, hey, hey! What's going on? Russell, what the hell are you doing on the floor?"

It's Lieutenant Wilson.

"They were beating the hell out of a handcuffed man."

"And what business was that of yours, Russell?"

The one that socked me is pointing a threatening finger.

"Who the hell is this asshole, Lieutenant?"

Wilson's brow crimps down hard.

"Officer's Gustav Heinz, Victor Augier, meet Rod's replacement, Officer Billy Russell. Now, don't the three of you feel just a wee-bit stupid?"

Struggling to my feet, I point to the handcuffed man.

"For Christ's sake, Lieutenant, the man's unconscious and bleeding."

In a flash, Wilson's in my face.

"Be quiet!"

He's shaking a finger at Heinz and Augier.

"Get that guy off the floor and out of here."

Now Wilson's angrily wagging that finger at me.

"Your first day and you're off to a shit-start."

If you know what's good for you, Billy Boy, say something that sounds semi-contrite.

"Sorry, I overreacted before I—"

"Ya' think, Russell? Your nose is bleeding. Jade, take him to the breakroom, get him a cup of strong coffee, educate him before he gets himself killed by one of our own."

Wilson limps off to his office... Jade's at my side with a handful of Kleenex.

"Hold these to your nose, clean up in the restroom."

This Heinz character moves close enough that I can smell his too-sweet cologne.

"Russell is it?"

"Yeah."

The fool sneers.

"I expect an apology."

I sneer back.

"Take a deep breath and hold it until I get back."

Jade places a hand on my arm.

"Okay boys, enough testosterone for one day. Billy, go clean up."

In the restroom, I check to be sure my nose isn't broken... it's not, but I'm getting a shiner around my left eye... a few splashes of cold water and I'm ready to go back to face the music... Jade's waiting.

"Come on macho man. Hank, cover the phones."

Hank smirks and shakes his head from side-to-side.

"Bring him back alive, Jade."

"I make no promises, Hank."

Following a few steps behind Jade as she leads me to the breakroom, I can't help but notice her fetchingly long legs wrapped in tight-fitting black slacks... in the breakroom she points to one of the tables.

"Sit. How do you take your coffee?"

"Black... with a mushy oatmeal."

"What?"

"Sorry... inside joke."

I take a seat at one of the three small tables... Jade fixes two cups, sets mine down, and parks herself across from me and stares.

"Ms. Miro, you're staring?"

"Wondering what motivated you to do something that stupid?"

"Instinct."

"Did Chernov and Wilson not give you the speech?"

"Yeah—so?"

"Either you didn't listen or you have a thick skull, which is it?"

"Pick one."

"Not funny, Billy. In this job you don't win a prize for being mister nice guy. Get with the program or Wilson will ship you off somewhere not so nice. Embed that thought in your memory bank."

With her sexy, expressive eyes trained on me like two bright seal-beams, she stands.

"You were chosen for this position for a specific reason... the sooner you figure out what that is, the better your chances of surviving. Come on, take your coffee."

If you want to stay in this lady's good graces, Billy Boy, convince her you have a working brain.

"Okay, I overreacted."

She shakes her head and rolls her eyes... when we reach her desk, she hands me a sheet of paper with a row of four-digit numbers.

"Remember how to use a computer?"

"Top speed, fifteen words a minute."

"Close enough. When the main screen comes up, click on the case file icon. In the search box, enter one of these file numbers and get educated. And keep your distance from Heinz and Augier until further notice. Go."

The lady would have made an excellent drill sergeant... as I pass his desk, Hank gives me a 'you screwed up' look... whatever you're thinking, Hank, you'd be right... but then again, I've been digging smelly ore for a lot of years, so cut me some slack. Firing up the computer, I find icons for the Internet and case files... I click on the Internet first... a screen pops up asking for a password. "Hey, Jade, what's the password for the Internet?"

"Not until Wilson authorizes it."

"When's that?"

"When he authorizes it. Until then, read case files."

Okay, for now it's case files... I type in the numbers for the first file in the search box... up comes a screen— **'Investigation Complete, Case Closed.'** *I skip it and move on to the next file... this one documents the death of drug dealer by the name of Royal Flush, obviously his pen name... his* *death's attributed to gunshot wounds received during a shootout with officers Hank Drummond and Rod Holbrook. With minor variation, the next file reads the same like someone cut and pasted from one file to the next with the exact results... the suspected drug dealer was DOA this time thanks to the handiwork work of Officers Heinz and Augier. The next file details the raid of a suspected drug factory... two of the five suspects were brought in for questioning... there's no mention of what became of them... the information is limited to date arrested and copies of signed confessions—no charges, no court date. That accounts for two, what happened to the other three? Wilson and Chernov's job description slams through my head like an ax splitting a log... Chernov's words replay like one of my bad dreams...* "Like that man you executed, the world is overrun by human garbage. They all deserve the same fate. Here, we accommodate them." *Without my compliance, I've become the newest member of a government sanctioned assassination squad, authorized to off drug lords and their underlings whenever and wherever we find them, and due process be damned. If it looks like a duck, walks like a duck, quacks like a duck, it's a duck. Damn it, I don't wanna have anything to do with this duck, not now, next week, not ever.*

"Russell?"

Lieutenant Wilson's standing over my shoulder... I'm sure he didn't come over to chit-chat about these case files... why would he, he probably made a few of the entries himself... I smile and nod... the kind of smile and nod that kept me out of trouble on Europa... most of the time, anyway.

"Hey, Lieutenant, I'm just going through old files."

"And?"

"Well, uh, most of them seem to be—"

"Educational?"

"Yes, very."

"Sorry to say your first day has been a bust."

"Uh, sorry, Lieutenant, I should have known better than to stick my nose in like that."

"Go home and ice that eye."

"I'm fine, Lieutenant."

"That wasn't a request, Billy. Go home and take care of that eye."

"Right, got it, ice the eye."

But he's not listening, he's halfway across the room on his way back to his office. You blew it, Billy, so do as he says get out of here. I'm up and making my way to the door just as Heinz and Augier come strolling back without their bloodied prisoner... I can't resist, I gotta get in the last word.

"My compliments, you really know how to beat the hell out of a handcuffed suspect."

Heinz gives me the finger and moves on... as I pass her desk, the lovely miss Jade delivers a warning.

"Let it go, Russell. And keep the gun and badge visible out there. Remember, lots of ice and several acts of contrition for today's faux pas."

"All of the above."

CHAPTER 11

Happy Birthday to Me.

There's a flurry of activity at the end of the hall... four WPFs in riot gear are racing down the stairs where they're joined by six more in their gladiator outfits... out in the parking lot they pile into three patrol vehicles and peel off, light bars flashing, sirens blaring as they speed West on Broadway... nothing like a little excitement to keep the troops on their toes... along Broadway, far too many poor souls stare at me with wanting if not threatening eyes... where do they all come from, how do they get by, where do they huddle through the long cold nights? Answers, I need answers. I duck into the clothing store... the place is on par with Goodwill... a friendly sales lady stares at my bruised nose and black eye, but doesn't ask how they came to be. We wade through what's available in my size... three pairs of khakis, three shirts, dark blue, tan and a pastel yellow... hopefully, it all fits... the total comes to eighty-two credits... at least the price was right. I'm living large with new clothes, food in the fridge, and a bottle of decent booze. What more could an ex-con ask for on his forty-fourth birthday? Another line of work would be a major step in the right direction. I'm home a few minutes past noon, toss the new clothes on the sofa and head for the John... the mirror doesn't lie... I have a first-class shiner on my left eye and my nose is slightly swollen. Whose fault is that, Billy Boy? All that was required was for you to show up and mind your own damn business... problem is, I'm not ready or willing to let their nefarious business brand become mine. Wrapping ice cubes in a washcloth, I flop on the sofa in my loosely referred to living area and apply the cloth to my nose... my neurons are replaying the events of the morning... Wilson and Chernov's in-your-face hold-nothing-back description of the job... it's déjà vu all over again, only this time it'll be me zapping suspects with a cattle prod... no, check that... with rubber clubs... but only if we bring them in alive. They gonna test me sooner than later to confirm they've chosen the right man for the job... that'll be due or die crunch time, Billy Boy. My thoughts are interrupted by a knock at the door.

"Billy, it's Jules."

Oh, crap, bad timing, Mister Landlord, I'm not in the mood... he knows you're here, better let him in.

"It's open."

He sweeps in like a tornado... the man has only one speed.

"Did I not tell you to keep your door locked?"

Who in the hell is this guy to be talking to me like that? Humor him. I slap my chest with an open hand.

"It won't happen again, I promise."

"What's with the washcloth?"

"Ice."

Here he comes, he's moving in for closer inspection... I remove the washcloth.

"Ouch! What's the other guy look like?"

"Better than me."

"Now I know why you're back so early on your first day. Come on, tell me what happened."

"Ran into a big-breasted old lady. Washing machine broken?"

"What?"

"You're wearing the same clothes as yesterday."

"So are you, William."

Smiling, I pat the new clothes resting beside me.

"Yeah, but I got new ones."

"Lucky you. Not gonna tell me what happened to the eye?"

"Nope."

"Hmm, okay, have it your way, soldier."

He strolls to the refrigerator and swings the door open... now what the hell is he doing?

"Looks like you haven't touched anything."

"Baloney and cheese sandwich last night."

"Do you cook?"

"I'm a five-star Michelin chef, but nothing that calls for more than three ingredients."

"Well, William, I can see you're going to be high-maintenance."

Why is this busybody inserting himself in my life like we're blood brothers? I don't know him from the man in the Moon... I'm in no mood for this.

"Don't you have a sick puppy that needs your attention?"

That was a bit aggressive, Billy... tone it down.

"Relax, will ya, be grateful I'm going to fix you lunch."

"You're gonna do what?"

"Fix you lunch."

"Really, Jules, no need to do that."

He's smiling from ear-to-ear like he discovered a stack of hundred-dollar bills stashed in the back of the frig.

"Whoa, Billy, there's hot dogs in here. I love hot dogs. Invite me to lunch and I'll do the cooking?"

"Ah, ha, there's a method to your madness."

Now the old fool's searching through one of the cupboards and finds a box of mac and cheese.

"What have we here? Golden pearls of joy. Hot dog's mac and cheese ala Jules Summers coming up."

It looks like I'm not going to get rid of this pest.

"If you insist, knock yourself out, old man."

Jules tosses his head back and laughs... his belly jiggles like Jell-O, his keychain jangles like chimes swaying in a breeze. While he finishes preparing the meal, I check out my new clothes trying to decide what to wear in the morning... that I even have a choice makes me feel semi-human... almost. I decide on the blue shirt and the newer-looking khakis.

"Hey, fashion king, food's ready in a few minutes, set the table."

Be a good host, offer him a drink.

"Too early for a shot of Bourbon to go with your gourmet meal?'

"Never too early for any liquid containing alcohol."

Retrieving the bottle, I pour two shots and set them on the table and smile wide.

"What are you smiling about?"

"It's my birthday and I'm eating hot dogs and mac and cheese."

"Happy birthday and all those yet to come. How old, William?"

"Forty-four."

"Jesus, you're just a kid."

"I wish."

He raises his glass in a toast.

"Happy birthday, kiddo, now we eat."

After the slop served on glorious Europa, this meal, like that memorable airport cheeseburger, sends my taste buds into overdrive... I dig in with gusto like I haven't eaten in a while.

"Slow down, you'll choke."

"Jules, is there no one you can harass beside me?"

"No one around in as much pain as you, William."

"The nose will heal."

"I wasn't referring to your nose. I sensed right off when you arrived that you were carrying heavy baggage."

"Heavy baggage? So now you're physic?"

"I have eyes, William, I can see."

"Feel free to close them."

I'm not about to let this stranger psychoanalyze me for his amusement. We eat in silence, him stealing glances at me, me at him until it begins to feel awkward.

"So, Jules, what do you do besides play house mother?"

"Read, study, learn."

"Like what?"

"History. If more people paid attention to what took place in the past, the world would be a lot less messy in the present. Go ahead, ask me anything, I'm a walking encyclopedia."

"Okay, uh, here's one. When was Albert Einstein born?"

"That's easy, March 14, 1879."

"I'll take your word for it. Who gets credit for inventing the Internet?"

"It's impossible to credit the internet to a single person.

Dozens of scientists, programmers and engineers contributed, notable among them was Robert E. Kuhn and Vint Cerf. If those guys were around today, I'll bet they'd agree it didn't quite work out as planned. Oh, it's an incredible source of information from A to Z all right, no doubt about. Except of course for social media. They'd have to build a special sewer plant just to flush away all the crap that gets posted."

"Who created ice cream?"

"An ice-cream-like food was first eaten in China in 618-97AD when a milk and rice mixture was frozen by packing it in snow. Are you having fun with this?"

"You said to ask anything."

"I meant serious questions."

"Ice cream is serious, Jules."

He tosses his head back and laughs. Work him, see if you can get him to fill in a few gaps about what in the hell is going on in a world that acts like it's spun off its axis... make it sound like you're aware, but want his opinion.

"Never a day goes by when I don't question how we got to this point."

"That places you in the majority, son."

"Like this out-of-control drug epidemic. How will it ever be brought under control?"

"Remember, the drug problem hit the general population as far back as the nineties when opioids came into fashion. What we have now is just an extension, only this time it's ten-times worse with a bigger selection and cheaper drugs to choose from. Until we find an answer, you guys in drug enforcement are in charge."

How does he know I'm in drug enforcement, I never mentioned it? He pushes back and folds his arms across his chest... he's studying me with narrowed eyes, pursed lips, and a furrowed brow... here it comes.

"What year were you born?"

"On this day two-thousand Twenty."

"Lucky you, you missed all the excitement."

"Not quite, Jules. On my thirteenth birthday, my dad thought it was important I understand what the world was going through the year I was born. He gave me a book that documented all that I missed while I was being potty trained and learning to walk and talk. I was stunned by what I read."

"And after that?"

"I don't recall many conversations of that period, like maybe the subject was taboo and not to be discussed."

"Not surprising. There are events that are so disruptive to our lives, people box 'em up and try to forget. Like the soldier who survived a war and never speaks of it again. That was 2020. And if our crazy politics weren't enough, along came the COVID pandemic that spread across the globe like an out-of-control California fire. The President's response was to play it down by calling it a hoax and telling his supporters to ignore the threat as nothing more than a version of the flu. His faithful believed his every lie. The COVID pandemic was a hoax when in fact it wasn't, and the 2020 election was fraudulent and stolen from him when it wasn't. During his tenure as president, the press counted over."

"All politicians lie at some point, Jules, but that sounds like a record for any president."

"It was, William. As for the pandemic, there was no plan, no strategy, no leadership. Mister President was winging it with off-the-top-of-his-head delusions while failing his most basic obligation, protecting American citizens. His blundering led to rapidly increasing numbers of the sick and dying along with some of the most extreme unemployment and poverty we had seen since the great depression. By the end of 2020, the COVID pandemic had claimed over three-million souls world wide—over six-hundred-thousand here in the U.S. alone, as I recall. It was an incomprehensible loss of life. I lost both my parents."

"Sorry, Jules, it must have been painful."

"No one was prepared to deal with the suddenness and sadness of it all. It wasn't until the end of 2021 when life began its slow return to semi-normal. You do know who was President from 2016-2020?"

"He was called the Twitter President, wasn't he?"

"Yeah, the greatest Twitter insulter of all time, a would-be autocrat who took perverse pleasure in governing via Twitter and berating his perceived enemies there as well. He packed his administration with campaign donors, golfing buddies, grifters, hangers on, and those willing to kneel at his altar of loyalty. Before our very eyes we watched the disintegration of the norms we had come to expect from our government. Four years later, after being impeached twice, but failed to be convicted in the Senate, he left us with uncertainty, fear, division, and a dysfunctional government. We had come awfully damn close to crossing the Rubicon, as the saying goes."

"The what?"

"It refers to Julius Caesar crossing the Rubicon river that precipitated the Roman Civil War, which ultimately led to Caesar's becoming a dictator and the rise of the imperial era of Rome."

"I learn something new every day."

"Happy to oblige, William. Unfortunately for us, Twitter Guy suffered from a severely damaged narcissistic personality. Every crisis—and there were many—was self-induced, but he always found others to blame. His feckless political party was busy sucking up and genuflecting at the altar of an egotistical and inept despot instead of disavowing his constant attacks on democracy."

"Power is a mighty aphrodisiac, Jules—always was, always will be."

"True, but that's no excuse for not using it for good once in a while."

"Jules, you're talking human nature."

"Bullshit, call it what it is, power-hungry greed for personal advancement. Early on, before the election 2020 election even took place, Twitter Guy labeled it a fraud, setting the groundwork for what was to come. They were the words of a demagogue, not a leader. Not sure you know this, but back when this country was writing its future, Benjamin Franklin pushed for a committee rather than a single president, believing that consensus among several would make it near impossible for any one person to become a despot. If only Mister Franklin had won the argument."

"Your history lesson is depressing me, Jules."

"I'm just beginning, son. Smack in the middle of the pandemic, the Black Lives Matter movement exploded. It was the year the phrase 'I can't breathe' became a battle cry for the Black Lives Matter movement when a man black named George Floyd lost his life at the hands of the police. Across the world, both blacks and whites came together in a show of strength to make their voices heard in the name of justice. It played right into the hands of Twitter Guy—he swooped in and pretended to be the law-and-order President. That backfired big time when time and again he praised hate groups, white supremacists, and militia groups as 'good people on both sides.' I'm not remotely surprised that more than a month after he lost, he still refused to concede. Instead, he continued to spout cockamamie conspiracy theories of voter fraud, insisting he won the election by a landslide. He filed endless lawsuits and lobbied Republicans to toss out state election results and appoint electors pledged to him. The courts roundly rejected his claims at every turn.

"He was trying to pull off a coup."

"Exactly, William. But even with the loss of his court appeals, he refused to go quietly into the good night, fighting like a spoiled, petulant little rich boy right up until the end, including encouraging a riot at the United States Capital by an angry, seditious gang of thugs, which accounted for his second impeachment."

"I know all about the invasion of the Capital, Jules, it was thoroughly covered in college as what not to put up with ever again."

"It stands as the blackest day in this country since the American revolution. On that day, people lost their lives including members of the Capital Police who bravely defended the precious symbol of freedom. Many more were hurt, and lots of physical damage was done to the Capital itself. In that moment in time, America wasn't the shining city on a hill. No, it was a great big red flag of darker times to come. Twitter Guy had created a cult of personality that wasn't going to change anytime soon. Enter the PPP and you know the rest. As for

Twitter Guy, on January 20th, 2020, he left in disgrace. Perhaps he should have paid attention to the sayings of Abraham Lincoln, his parties founding member, who in 1862, said, 'In times like the present, men should utter nothing for which they would not willingly be responsible through time and eternity.'"

"Amazing how you remember this stuff, Jules."

"I have a mind like a steel trap, son. After Twitter Guy left, he spent a lot of time and money defending charges against him. Like most, I just wanted to shut it all out and forget him and the whole damn mess. Now you know why not many are willing to speak openly of that painful period in our history."

"You know Jules, all the public really wants is for elected officials to govern efficiently with integrity so we the people can get on with our lives without having to participate any more than necessary. We've always been guilty of a 'Let George do it' mentality."

"Yeah, well boys and girls, like so many times before, George didn't do it. The message should have been clear—don't keep picking losers to solve our problems. Because we do, we've been on a path of unstoppable polarization ever since, the result of which we are now paying the price for in spades."

Make it ring true, Billy, agree with him like you know and understand all that's happening and why.

"I can't imagine anything worse than that what the country is living through now."

"Back when we were enjoying the spoils of America's success, our brains failed to connect the dots that we were on the wrong course that would lead to what we're struggling through today. It's all so totally insane, which proves my theory. When it comes to our mental acuity to sustain and protect our chosen way of life, the distance between sanity and insanity is about an inch—two at the most."

He chuckles softly like that amuses him.

"It falls upon each of us as individuals to recognize the pitfalls along the way and to do our best to avoid them and to use the time we are given wisely. In the end that's the true measure of a man or women."

"Yeah, Billy, you're right, but most us live each day like all is okay as long as we get through it unscathed. That will never change until we accept one simple fact—we are the real power, the real government. We need to step outside our bubbles and understand that elected officials, charged with making decisions that benefit those who put them in power, are nothing more than over-paid employees engaged to do our bidding, not theirs. And therein lies the rub. Why we allow these people to live out their fantasies at our expense remains a mystery. We're great at talking the talk, but terrible at walking the walk—three steps forward, one or two back, and repeat. The irony is, right around Twitter Guy's second impeachment, there were those talking about starting a third party. Whether they knew it or not, it was a foretelling of what was to come—the authoritarian Peoples Populist Party we have today. Okay that's enough history for one day."

He's up on his feet strolling toward the door.

"Where are you going?"

"Gotta' go, things to do. I leave you with these profound thoughts of wisdom. During the pandemic the total net worth of America's billionaires, all 686 of them, jumped by a trillion dollars. Whatever problems they may have had, they didn't come close to those who died, or the millions who were sick and lost their livelihood, had to choose between food and medicine, or had their electricity turned off, or worse, eviction. I am normally an eternal optimist, Billy, but the underlying mentality that allowed 2016 through 2020 and beyond to happen at the level it did is the same mentality that's allowed those rascals in Marseille to seize power. Yet, I have to believe that the good guys win in the end."

He stops, he's thinking again.

"You know what wrong with us, William?"

I never know when this guy is done.

"I do, but you're going to tell me anyway."

"Most of us interpret what we hear they way they want to, not necessary what leads to the truth, but what supports our core beliefs. Our eyes fail to see and our ears fail to accept the truth when it's staring us in the face."

He pauses and taps lightly at his right temple.

"Along with all our fancy technology advancements, we better learn how to use this original computer, or one day there will be no human race, we will have left the Earth to the animals and insects.

Depressing thought. However, everything Jules just told me matches up with that book dad gave me at the tender age of thirteen. Perhaps back then I was too young to understand the impact it would have on future societies. Jules slips his hand in his right pocket, withdraws his money clip, peels off a twenty-dollar bill, and holds it high in the air.

"This, the almighty buck, is what really controls society. It is the bane of our existence and will forever remain so as long as we insist on placing more emphasis on wealth, power, and possessions rather than life itself. To drive that home, in 1973 the Massachusetts Institute of Technology created a computer program to model global sustainability over time. Some years later, it predicted that by 2040, human civilization would have perished. Like so many others that made apocalyptic predictions, the end date failed to materialize. But, here, my boy, is the scary part. What that computer predicted back in the 70's has mostly been coming true. So, just in case the computer is right, we should live our lives the best we can leaving nothing to tomorrow. At the moment the score is Earth one, mankind, zero. To add to our woes, they no longer pick up the garbage on a regular schedule. So, in parting, I remind you keep your gun loaded, your door locked, and keep icing that shiner. Government news comes on the hour, watch if you dare.

"Jules, hold on."

"What is it?"

"Is there a rental car place around here?"

"Yeah, Enterprise on West Broadway. Why?"

"I gotta go down to Rhode Island for a couple of hours on personal business."

"No problem, William, I'll run you over there."

"Um, would you, uh, would you consider renting a car in your name? Like a dummy, I let my California license expire. I have to apply for one here."

He digs into his right pocket and pulls out a keychain and hands it to me.

"What's this?"

"My Mazda, out back in the garage."

"That's very generous, but I couldn't."

"Of course, you can. I won't have to run you to Enterprise and you'll save the cost of the rental. If you get stopped, I'll tell them the vehicle was stolen."

He laughs, then like a fart in a whirlwind, Jules is out the door, leaving me alone with my thoughts. What little I've seen in the short time back, and what Jules generously added, sounds worse than what I left behind... an oppressive World Government, WPF Officers everywhere, what Jules calls Streetwalkers roaming the neighborhoods in large numbers, and a drug enforcement bureau authorized to execute drug lords on sight. Why am I not surprised that we're still struggling with some of the same age-old problems? Time and again we didn't heed history's almanac, failing, like Jules said, to examine the past and learning from it and not simply wishing it had gone differently... a wish is not a plan, never is. Like the caged hamster racing around its wheel only to return to its starting point, we replicated past blunders generation after generation abdicating solutions to less than stellar elected officials present in name only to boost their bank accounts and political fortunes. We sat on our hands with the climate change problem until mass migrations from the most blighted areas began in earnest resulting in heartless immigration policies concocted by politicians who dealt with it inhumanly... white supremacist and hate groups plied their hatred with impunity comparing those of color to animals and insects, warning that hordes of immigrants were bringing disease, crime, and unwanted cultural and ethnic changes to the white man's world. U.S. corporations no longer saluted our flag in the fast-emerging global economy, replacing loyal workers with robotic machines not requiring pay raises, vacations, sick leave, or health benefits... it was all about boosting corporate profits at the expense of workers. Fast moving technology brought us the Internet and social media, swamp fields cluttered with clichés, conspiracy theories, and unfiltered trash talk... ever-active hackers stoked digital warfare between governments, terrorists, and hate groups... must be something in all that crap we can be proud of. Everything changes, nothing changes. Before I head to Bristol, I better read the accident report. I retrieve it from my shirt pocket and begin reading. To my horror, a fifty-eight-year-old man named Donald Malcolm Stevens, driving a late model red pickup truck, swerved and hit dad's car head-on... Steven's blood alcohol level was twice that of the legal limit... he was sentenced to ten years for vehicular manslaughter... ten lousy years in exchange for my parents' lives. The right hand tells us how lucky we are to be alive... the left hand steals it all away in a split second. My emotions rise to my throat... I'm on the verge of tears... ripping the report into small pieces, I fling it to the floor. The report confirms what I've always believed... when our expiration date arrives, often feeble and diseased, only then do we acknowledge that in the end, nothing really mattered beyond human relationships... if we failed those, it was all for naught... everything else... money, stuff, positions... counted for nothing. The heart stops, the brain ceases to function, and that's it... death is the supreme equalizer, and we're soon forgotten—next.

CHAPTER 12

Time to Face the Music

An hour and a half after leaving Boston, *I'm cruising in Jules's Mazda SUV down Hope Street in Bristol, Rhode Island, my home town... the line down the center of the road is still striped red, white, and blue marking the route of the oldest 4th of July parade in the country... nothing's changed, it's still New England small town at its best. My emotions are mixed... I'm happy to be home again, but it's a sad return, not a happy one. Passing through the main downtown area, I take a left on Constitution Street up over the hill and down to Wood Street. Crossing over Wood, I roll onto Catherine Street, pull over to the curb, and turn off the engine. The street hasn't changed... old one and two-story clapboard houses line both sides... down on the right is the house where I grew up... one month... one lousy damn month... if not for that horrible accident, I would be with them again... come on, Billy, you came for a reason, drive on. Starting the engine, I roll slowly down the street, stopping just short of the house, turn off the engine, and sit staring at my family's two-story home... the window blinds are closed tight... the grass needs cutting. As painful as I know it would be, I wish I could go inside to touch and feel things one last time... to let the walls speak to me reminding me of all the good and decent times that filled this house with so much love so many long years ago. It crosses my mind that I have to find out what's become of the estate... maybe Jimmy Oliveri is still around... he'd know, he handled all of Mom and Dad's legal affairs... his office was on Hope Street next to the post office as I recall... I'll drive there and see if it's still there. Ten minutes later I'm there and sure enough, there's a sign...* **Bennington**

& Oliveri, Attorneys... *there's a phone number, great... I have no interest in going in and explaining my sudden return... everyone in town and across the state knows what happened, it was all over the newspapers and the Providence TV stations... if word was to get out that I was back, some aggressive reporter would track me down and hound me for an interview. With nothing to write on, will I remember Jimmy's number when I return home?*

When I arrive back at the house, I return Jules's car key.
"Get your business taken care of okay?"
"Yes, can't thank you enough for the loan of your car."
"Invite me to lunch again sometime."
"That's a deal."
As soon as I enter my place, I jot down Jimmy Oliver's office number hoping I remembered it right and proceed to place the call... his secretary informs me Jimmy's in Denver at a legal conference and won't be back for a week, would I like to leave a message? Yes... yes, I would... she connects me to his answering machine... I explain that I'm back and he should call me on my cell and I end the call. The government news... Jules said it's on every hour... it's about that time... let's see what this World Government has to report that might give me a nickel tour of a world I no longer recognize. Loud brassy rah, rah, patriotic military music is playing... a waving white flag with green edging and an eagle in flight in its center fills the screen... below it reads,

'The Peoples Cooperative Populist Party, One World in Unity. In the name of the Creator, citizens remain loyal and supportive.'

I'll bet they do. A deep, commanding, off-camera voice begins.

"From the World Broadcast center in Marseille, France, this is world news briefs on the hour."

The waving flag changes to a sped-up space-view of the rotating Earth before dissolving to a photo identified as the

President of Turkey.

"A special combat unit of the WPF invaded Turkey and arrested Turkish President, Mirac Demir, along with eleven high-ranking military officials on charges Turkey was secretly developing a short-range missile base near the southern border it shares with Syria. Military activities of any kind outside those of the World Military Command are against international law. All twelve men have been flown to Marseille to face charges."

The video switches to a crowd of several hundred being rounded up by WPF riot squads... the area is thick with smoke from lingering tear gas.

"Earlier today, in sight of World Government headquarters in Marseille, the WPF released tear gas and fired rubber bullets to disperse several hundred protesters claiming to be members of the dissident group, Apostolic Channel, who were protesting government population control policies. Twelve were injured and thirty-seven arrested."

Then comes video of seven men lined up against a cement block wall.

"In Quezon City in the Philippines, seven men were found guilty of selling illegal drugs on the black market. They were sentenced to death and executed by the Philippine government. Viewers are warned the following images may be too graphic for some viewers."

The seven men are lined up against a wall... Jesus, they're actually going to show this? Oh, my God, there're cutting them down with machine guns... I close my eyes... when the shooting stops, I open them... the screen has changed to a head shot of a middle-aged man.

"Shaday Zalat, age 57, Senior editor of the newspaper Egypt Today, was taken into custody for posting articles falsely accusing the World Government of censorship of the media."

Again, the image changes... I recognize it as the big population billboard at the West end of the Ted Williams tunnel, but it's no longer lit up.

"Earlier today in Boston, Massachusetts, in the United States, three men driving a late model blue Chevrolet van and wearing ski-masks appeared at the Western end of the Ted Williams tunnel. They blocked the road while shooting and destroying Boston's population billboard."

Good God, that's why the WPFs were scrambling when I left the precinct this morning.

"Before racing from the scene, the three gunmen scattered leaflets identifying themselves as members of the resistant's group 'Apostolic Channel'. Anyone in the Boston area with information is encouraged to call the local office of the WPF."

What the hell is Apostolic Channel? The screen changes to a full-screen photo of a man identified as Alexandre Boucher... the headshot is reduced to the lower left corner revealing a second photo of a large, ornate conference room... a group of all white men are gathered around an equally ornate conference table.

"This morning, Commissioner Alexandre Boucher addressed the World Council accusing fellow Commissioner Henry Dion of inflammatory rhetoric in his condemnation of the government's population reduction policies calling them barbaric."

Boucher's photo floats up and to the left... a second photo appears on the right identified as Commissioner Henry Dion.

"Quoting a recent worldwide poll expressing support for the government's policies on population control as critical to mankind's survival, Commissioner Boucher accused Commissioner Dion of statements bordering on sedition. Mister Boucher vowed that if Mister Dion's rhetoric continued, he would propose sanctions against him. Such action would require a vote of fifty-one percent of Council members."

A graphic displaying large numerical numbers appears.

"The Central Population Control Commissioner reports that for the previous month, three-hundred and twenty-seven thousand world citizens died of illnesses, accidents, natural causes and illegal drug use reducing the world's population to just over nine billion and moving the total closer to the government mandated goal of eight billion."

They're trying to reduce world population by over a billion people? A billion human beings? Unbelievable. The music changes to a bouncy tune accompanied by cartoon characters dancing across the screen... flashing red text appears at the bottom... 'World Lotto Winners.' *The dancing characters are replaced by happy, smiling families.*

"Seven families are the lucky winners of this week's world lottery population estimate. Each family will receive government subsidies for a period of one year. Congratulations to all the winners. Keep playing Population Lotto."

Jeez, there's a lottery to see who guesses the number of people that bit the dust? Death is cheered on like a reality TV show? Sick. Welcome to happy news hour. Enough of this bullshit, I have my own bag of problems, so unless you have some uplifting news to pass along beside your disgusting world lottery on this my birthday, forgive me if I turn a blind eye to what crap you might add to this less than uplifting newscast.

CHAPTER 13

Reality Returns with a Vengeance

I tossed and turned all damn night, which accounts for my foul mood this morning... at least I have new clothes... hopefully, being free of the color brown will improve my state of mind. Following two cups of coffee, I gather up the accident report from the floor, place the dirty dishes in the sink, gather up my old clothes from where I left them the night before, and dig out my debit card from the left pocket of the pants... it's there along with the crumbled leaflet that guy in the alley stuffed in my hand... I'm betting he was a conman trying to sell me something... when I read the first line, I find I was dead wrong.

We must not be guilty of turning a blind eye to what we know in our hearts to be true. The Fascist state's failing economic policies are directed at the poorest of the poor. If we did not know better, we would have to assume this allows the thugs in Marseille to rid society of those deemed unfit to share 'their' planet. Call it what it is: Genocide. Look at the streets and the crowded camps. Who do you see there? Sacrificial lambs. We must rise up and put an end to the New World Government's hatred, racism, vulgarity, ineptitude and greed. The time is now for each of us to stand tall and be counted. If freedom and democracy are to be restored, then fight we must. Join the movement, join Apostolic Channel now and fight side by side to restore our God given right to life, liberty and the pursuit of happiness free from the demagogues who have imprisoned us.

It's signed 'Apostolic Channel'... the name of the group reported to have shot up the population sign. Right, I'm gonna put my life on the line for some crazy dissident movement that probably won't make it out of the starting gate. Crumpling the flyer, I toss it on the desk... I need to get a move on or I'll be late again. When reach the top of the stairs, I hear Jules's talking to another man by the front door. They're speaking low, I can't make out what's being said... *better wait until they're gone or Jules will engage me in conversation... no time for that this morning.* I hear Jules'ss door close... *I descend the stairs and out the door just as a late model blue Honda sedan pulls away from the curb. At Sully's News Stand, I pick up a copy of the Boston Globe, a cup of black brew, and make my way to the office, passing far too many Streetwalkers who avoid me when they spy my gun and badge... at the office, Jade greets me with a frown.*

"Nice blend of black and blue you have there. And the new clothes, great improvement over brown."

I've yet to decide whether the lady is just direct, arrogant, or a smart ass who enjoys beating up the new guy.

"Your presence is required in the lieutenant's office. Gustav and Victor are in there so watch your tongue."

"I'll be on my best behavior. Hang on to my newspaper until I get back."

I have a pretty good idea what the subject of this meeting will be, so I put on my best smile... Gustav's sitting in one of the chairs, Hank and Victor are standing by the window... Wilson avoids eye contact with me.

"Take a seat, Russell."

Take a seat next to the good German Gustav and play nice, Billy Boy... I sit and glance sideways to Heinz... he doesn't look at me... then I make my first mistake of the morning. "Gustav, where did you dispose of your suspect after you and Victor beat him unconscious and dragged him off?"

He rolls his eyes and leaps to his feet.

"Schwachsinn! Who the hell do you think you are?"

Whatever the hell translation of Schwachsinn, it gets Wilson up out of his chair.

"Hold on, Gustav."

"Screw him, Frank, he has no right to speak to me that

way."

Wilson's wagging a finger at Gustav.

"Goddamn it, Gustav, cool it! And you, Russell, no one gives a damn about your code of ethics. Are you reading me loud and clear?"

"Yes, Lieutenant."

"Good, keep it that way. I'll assume we're all warm and cozy fellow workers again ready to join a bowling league."

"As long as he—"

"Enough, Gustav, I said it's over. See to it that it stays that way. Now, go find something constructive to do. Billy, stay."

Wilson waits until the others leave.

"Close the door."

Here goes, I'm in for another ass chewing.

"For a man who spent seventeen years digging black ore, you're working really hard to toss away the only favorable opportunity that's come your way."

"Sorry, Lieutenant, I—"

"Sorry doesn't cut it. You don't get to change the rules, you carry them out without question. Expect serious consequences if you don't."

I hear it in his voice, I see it in his eyes... it's an unmistakable threat... he's short on details, but I get it.

"Today you get the benefit of the doubt, but you better damn well get up to speed quick. And keep your nose out of everyone's business but your own."

"Yes, Lieutenant."

"And if you run into Colonel Chernov, do not tell him where you got that shiner. The new clothes are an improvement."

"Thanks."

Having been dutifully chastised for yesterday's misbehavior, I make a speedy exit out of there... on my way to my desk, Gustav pops up from his chair.

"Wait a minute, Russell."

Oh crap, this prick is not about to be denied his pound of flesh.

"What now?"

"If you're not part of the team, you are part of the problem."

"I thought we just settled that, Officer Heinz?"

Now the damn fool makes the mistake of wrapping a hand around my left forearm.

"Take your hand off me."

Instead, he tightens his grip... with one swift move my right-hand swings to his crotch cupping his balls and squeezing just hard enough so it hurts... he moans and backs up... I move with him, squeezing a little harder... Hank is on me gripping my shoulders and pulling me back.

"All right, all right, boys and girls, that's enough, recess is over!"

Releasing the Heinz family jewels, I back up a step.

"Explain to Officer Heinz that it's a bad move to put a hand on me."

Gustav sidesteps me, growls and stomps off to his desk, tossing off what I hope are his final words on the subject.

"Fick dich... ich vertrue dir nich."

With a smug smile, Victor sidles up to me.

"He said he doesn't trust you."

"Okay, sure, I can live with that."

Hard to believe I had his testicles in my hand and he walked away without a fight... just goes to prove it pays to squeeze a bully's nuts once in a while... Hank looks my way and rolls his eyes. I'm not sure where I'm going, but I amble off toward the exit... Jade grimaces and shakes her head.

"Bravo, Billy... wonderful display of misplaced male testosterone as usual."

"There's lots more where that came from."

"Where are you going?"

"Breakroom for coffee."

"You're on the street with Hank in ten minutes."

"Be right back."

I quick-pace down to the Breakroom and pour myself a cup of coffee... damn, it would be great if I had a cigarette to go with it... got to get me a pack. Someone enters behind me.

"Coffee, I need coffee."

Oh crap, it's Colonel Chernov. "Good morning, Colonel."

"Dobroye utro, good morning."

He spots my black and blue eye.

"Jesus, Russell, what happened to you?"

"A little tussle with a guy on 4th Street."

"What about?"

"A handout, what else. I told him I had nothing to give, but he insisted I buy him something to eat. When I refused, the fool rushed me. We did a little dance and he caught my nose with a right before I slapped handcuffs on him and hauled him in to the guy's downstairs."

Jeez, even I believe that perfectly delivered lie.

"Good work. Nasty bunch of immigrant bastards out there. The sooner we reduce their numbers, the better for the rest of us. Keep that nose iced."

"Yes, sir, I will."

Right after you explain why you believe other racial groups are inferior to yours. By the way, Mister Russian Colonel, sir, I never said the guy was an immigrant.

CHAPTER 14

Hard Lessons to be Learned

Hank and I are off cruising the mean streets in one of the government Chevy Traverses. It's my real first exposure to South Boston beyond Broadway and 4th... what I see is disturbing and heartbreaking... the homeless walk aimlessly begging for handouts or drugs or crouched in alleys to stave off the cold. This is what it's come to... this is the new world order? It needs serious work.

"Billy, you can't let Gustav get to you. If you do, you'll lose."

"Gustav's a bully—bullies need their nuts squeezed occasionally."

"Proceed at your own risk."

"Duly noted, sir. By the way, this Rod Holbrook I replaced, what happened to him?"

"A snitch told one of Chernov's guy's Rod was on Dominick 'Scaggy' Scaglione's payroll."

"Who?"

"Scaglione, a second-tier drug dealer, but a dangerous one. Every time we thought we had him he'd be gone by the time we showed up. Rod, it seems, was tipping Scaggy off. Chernov received word from this same snitch Scaggy would be at Faneuil Hall in Boston's North End on Thursday afternoon. We were told we'd be going on a bust, but weren't told who, which was highly unusual. At 2:10 Scaggy comes out of Faneuil Hall with his bag of goodies flanked by two of his goombahs. Rod's face turned whitewash when he saw who it was. Scaggy spots Rod, goes bat-shit-nuts, whips out a gun, and yells, "Holbrook, you sold me out!" BANG! Rod takes one in the jugular and hits the pavement a second before we dropped Scaggy and his two goons. All four died there in the street. End of story."

There isn't more to be said on the subject so I drop it. Hank turns on Columbia Road... about a half-mile down, he pulls over to the curb.

"Welcome to Joe Moakley Park."

I'm stunned... as far as I can see there're small tents erected on just about every available space.

"My God, Hank."

"It's shameful—several thousand clinging to life within a few feet of one another."

"I don't know what to say, Hank. How do they survive?"

"If it wasn't for a local charity that provides one hot meal a day, I don't know what those people would do. There's another encampment at Medal of Honor Park just North of here and one in Peter's Park, west of I-93."

It's painful to see human beings living cramped together in a tent city like some far-off refugee camp in a desert war zone... this can't be America... this can't be the country I left behind... and yet there it is in living color right before my eyes.

"Seen enough?"

Unable to take my eyes from the demoralizing sight of the tent city, I nod. We continue to cruise the streets of South Boston aimlessly... we're out killing time and wasting gas is all I can figure. As we roll down Yonkers, Hank's back stiffens, his head whips left, and his foot comes off the gas pedal.

"There, the alley on the left!"

"What?" We passed the alley too fast... I didn't see what he saw... he makes a U-turn cruising back and stopping ten-feet short of the alley's entrance.

"What is it, Hank?"

"A deal's going down in the alley—two in suits, a third in jeans and a windbreaker—go for him."

"You're sure it's a drug deal?"

"As sure as the Pope is still Catholic."

"Wilson said to call for backup before engaging out here."

"We can handle this."

He got his weapon out.

"We should do this by the book, Hank. Let me call for backup."

"Jesus, Billy! All right, all right, call it in. Put it on speaker."

I hit 'home' on my phone... it rings three times before Jade answers.

"Hey, Billy, what's up?"

"Hank spotted a deal going down—two buyers and a deliveryman. We need backup."

"Where are you?"

"Hank, where are we?"

"On Yonkers... the alley between Winston and Thurman. Got that, Jade?"

"Got it. Gustav and Victor are here. Hang tight until they arrive."

The line goes dead. Out my Smith and Wesson comes... the first time I've held a weapon of any kind with the intent of maybe using it in over seventeen years.

"The one in the windbreaker, if he even looks like he's going for a weapon, ventilate him."

Hanks's out the door moving fast toward the alley's entrance.

"Hey, what the hell? What happened to waiting for backup?"

Move, Billy, move... don't leave Hank out there alone... scrambling out the door, my right toe dips in a rut in the sidewalk sending me tumbling head over heels and landing on my back... damn it, damn it! Bounding to my feet, I rush to Hank's side just short of the alley's entrance.

"Stay the hell on your feet, will ya'."

"What happened to waiting for Gustav and Victor?"

No reply from Hank... he's hyped pumping up and down on his toes like a prizefighter... before I can say another word, he takes a long step into the alley's entrance, plants his feet wide, and raises his gun.

"Is this a private party, Gentlemen?"

What the hell is he doing? You need to be out there with him before he gets himself killed... with my gun raised, I step to his side just as the trio spin to us... there's two white thirty-something guys in suits... the tall one in the windbreaker looks Hispanic... he pulls a weapon from his belt, grabs the suit closest to him in a chokehold, and places a gun to the guy's right temple.

"Le volaré los malditos sesos!"

Hank sniggers.

"English, amigo, English."

"I said, I'll blow his goddamn brains out!"

Hank raises his weapon to eye level and takes aim.

"If you do, we'll remove yours."

The third man, shaking like a vibrator, drops to his knees.

"Don't shoot, please, don't shoot!"

"On your stomach, hands behind your head!"

The guy hits the asphalt face down... the one standing with the gun to his head begins to cry.

"Please, please, I have a wife and two young daughters."

The gunman presses his weapon against the man's temple and yells at the other one.

"Shut the hell up."

Hank takes a step forward.

"Hey, Batman, you know how this works, you off him we off you."

"The only way these junkies make it out of here alive is if I do too. You cool with that, Officer whatever the hell your name is?"

"Play nice, put the gun down, live another day."

"Luego me dirás que me vas a cantar una canción de amor."

"No entiendo amigo."

"That's bullshit, Chico blanco. Next, you'll tell me your gonna sing me a love song."

Hank leans to me and whispers low.

"His right leg, it's in the clear. My shot will be to his knee. He'll peel right, the hostage left. That's when you unload on his chest. Don't miss."

"Hank, we can take him alive. He'll go down when you hit his knee."

"And if he begins shooting, Billy, what then?"

I want to diffuse this... I shout to the guy.

"Put the gun down and you get to leave here alive."

"In custody? Forget it, I'm not going to the white man's jail even if you did let me live."

Hank takes another step forward.

"Come on, amigo, whoever you're working for doesn't give a rat's ass about you. Let's talk."

The guy tosses his head back and cackles.

"I'm supposed to trust you?"

Hank's grinning and whispering again.

"Hell no, asshole."

I hear it in his voice... Hank's mind is made up... he's driving this train now, not you, Billy... you're along for the ride. Hank takes two steps forward... I move with him... my eyes flit to Hank's gun... his finger squeezes the trigger ever so slowly—click—BANG! The shot echoes throughout the narrow alley like a cannon shot... the bullet smashes into the gunman's right knee, a guttural cry escapes his throat, his gun slips from his hand to the pavement as he rolls to his right... the hostage breaks to his left... now Billy, now, fire... my shot slams into the gunman's right shoulder... with a wide-eyed stunned expression, his mouth flaps open... he stumbles back two steps and collapses flat on his back... the hostage drops face down to the pavement next to the other guy... it all happened in the blink of an eye just as Hank said it would... except I made a split-second decision not to kill the man.

"Goddammit, Billy, what the hell did you do?"

Hank's hotfooting to the wounded drug dealer, kick's his gun away, holsters his, rolls him over and handcuffs him... the guy's wailing in pain.

"Hurts doesn't it, asshole."

"Jesus, man, I need to get to a hospital."

"And I need to get to lunch."

He rolls him onto his back and unzips his jacket... the inside is lined with pockets... Hank's pulling out the contents.

"Lots of little bags and I'll bet it's not aspirin."

He turns to the two men lying on the ground.

"You two, on your feet, and don't say a word or you'll royally piss me off."

Like frightened children, both men rise.

"From the looks of those suits and expensive shoes, I'd guess you're a couple of business guys regretting you ever entered this alley."

The shorter of the two looks like he's about to cry.

"Lawyers, we're both lawyers, man."

"Dumb ones at that."

Hank turns to me and winks.

"Whatta' think, Billy, should we give these brainless addicts a break?"

I don't know where he's going with this, so I go along. "Sure, sure, why not."

"Your lottery numbers just came up a winner, Gentlemen. Get your dumb asses out of here before we run you in. And do yourselves and us a favor, sign up for rehab. Now beat it."

The men scamper out of the alley like cats being chased by angry dogs... as soon as they're out of site, Hank's on me.

"What the hell was that all about, Billy? Did I not tell you to drop him?"

"You want to kill people, go for it. I don't want any part of it."

"Who the hell gave you a choice?"

The sound of screeching tires and car doors slamming echo into the alley.

"There's your goddamn backup."

Heinz and Augier come racing into the alley weapons drawn... Hank scoffs.

"You're a little late, boys."

Victor shakes his head and mumbles something or other in French.

"Tu aurais du attendre."

"Do you two slip in and out of foreign languages just to piss us off?"

"I said, you're supposed to wait for backup."

"Next time for sure, Victor, I promise."

"How many were there?"

"Three."

"Where's the other two?"

"A couple of lawyers out signing up for rehab. Bad boy over there has a couple of painful wounds. Better get him some medical attention or whatever else you have in mind"

Gustav glances over at the guy on the ground.

"Why is he still alive, Hank?

"He had a hostage. Didn't want to get him killed."

Thanks for that big lie, Hank. He begins to leave.

"Come on, Billy."

"Where the hell are you going?"

"Lunch, Victor, wanna come?"

"What about him over there?"

"We caught him, you deal with him. Billy, let's go."

As we're leaving, Gustav calls out something or other in his mother tongue... Hank smiles and tosses him the finger. Just as we reach the sidewalk and turn to our vehicle, we hear a gunshot. "Oh my God, Hank, they didn't."

"Lesson number one, Officer Russell—they did what we were supposed to."

Not a word passes between us as we travel on William J. Day Blvd., along Boston Harbor. Hanks got a long face on... now doubt he's pissed at me... fine, let him be, I wasn't about to be that man's executioner. Across the harbor from the John F. Kennedy Presidential Library, he stops in front of a small one-story building tucked tightly between two tall office buildings... painted on the picture window in bold red letters is one-word... MAGGIE'S.

"What is Maggie's?"

"Lunch, Billy, lunch."

One of those ever-present eagle posters greets us at the door. The inside is small and in serious need of TLC... there's a lunch counter with six stools and a dozen booths... most are occupied... a sign the food's good... I'm heading for an empty one by the window when Hank waves me over to another.

MIDNIGHT BLACK

"Never sit by the window."

"Why not?"

"Streetwalkers stare at you while you eat."

"Gee, Hank, I can see how that could be traumatizing." *We settle in the booth.* "How has this place survived between two office buildings?"

"When Maggie's husband died, she turned down a shit load of cash from builders who wanted to tear it down and build another tower. Sentiment, I guess, who knows."

A middle-aged unsmiling, short, portly woman with a surly expression and a food-stained white apron comes to our table.

"Hank."

"Hey, Maggie, how're they hanging?"

She raises an eyebrow and cups her sagging left breast.

"Better than your testicles, Hank."

Whoa, what's going on with these two?

"Where's your waitress of the day?"

"Flu bug. Who's the new face?"

"Billy, meet the one and only Maggie Daggerman. Billy's my new partner."

"Sorry to hear that, Billy. Hank's a degenerate. You got a last name?"

"Russell."

"What happened to your eye?"

"Walked into the bathroom door in the middle of the night."

"No lights in your house?"

I chuckle softly.

"Having the special, gentlemen?"

"Should I know what that is, Maggie?"

"Cheeseburger and fries, Billy, guaranteed safe for human consumption. Coffee?"

Hank and I nod.

"Don't trash-talk me while I'm gone."

Maggie waddles off with a smile… apparently these two take perverse pleasure trading insults. "Is this the regular routine, Hank?"

"If I don't yank her chain, she gets depressed. She dishes it back pretty good."

"Listen, Hank, not to change the subject, but what happened back there was—?"

"What happened was you took it upon yourself to change the plan."

"What plan? You bounced into that alley without so much as a 'here's what we're gonna do'."

"Cut the bullshit, Billy, you didn't follow the rules."

"Oh, how brazen of me for not following protocol—execute on sight."

"Get off your high horse, Billy. That guy could have gotten off a couple of shots dropping one or both of us. In those situations, there's no do-overs. Today, you get a C-minus. Next time put your personal principles aside and make it an A-plus or don't plan on riding with me."

"Jesus, we really didn't need to kill him, Hank?"

"I know that, you know that, but if we don't do this by their book, you and me will end up the victims. Get that embedded in your moral brain."

Three haggard looking middle-aged men appear at the window... Hank frowns.

"There, what did I tell you?"

Maggie, still looking like her dog died, returns with our food.

"Eat it up boys before the flies get to it. Call me if you need anything."

She waddles off again her feet spread apart to balance her weight... when she's out of earshot, I lean in and lower my voice to a whisper.

"All I'm saying, Hank, is they didn't have to kill him."

Hank's brow furrows... he leans in as far as he can.

"Look, Officer Russell, before we get too invested in each other's well-being, let's lay our cards face-up."

"What's that supposed to mean?"

"We're both ex-cons. I don't wanna know what you did, nor will I tell you what I did that earned us this once-in-a-lifetime plush assignment. But whatever we did guarantees we do what they want the way they want or settle for another uncomfortable jail cell or worse. Keep reminding yourself what we do is legal by government decree."

"Define legal."

"Whatever the brain trust in Marseille damn well says it is."

"That doesn't make it morally right, Hank."

"Define morality."

"I'm just saying—"

"Yeah, well, don't. We're not paid to bring them in alive, period. And if we do, we beat the hell out of them before delivering the coup de grace. Morality has nothing to do with it, yours and my survival does."

"So, we've sold our souls to the devil to stay alive."

"Considering the alternative, yeah. The bad guys are running this world, Billy. We either play their game or there's no end game for us."

"As long as its cards face up, how many times have you actually—"

"Stop. Don't ever ask me that again or you'll royally piss me off. When your time comes, you'll make your decision and live with the consequences. Until then, this subject is off the table for any further discussion. Got it?"

You've put your foot in your big mouth again, Billy Boy... change the subject. "What's the story with Heinz and Augier?"

"Heinz is a Kraut, Augier's a French Fry. Both are from Central Drug Security out of Marseille, which raises the question, why were they sent to work in a drug enforcement unit in Boston along with Rod and me."

He does a quick scan around the room and leans in again.

"Those two take their orders from Colonel Chernov, not Wilson. I can't prove it, but I suspect the unit is their cover."

"For what?"

"From time-to-time they're missing in action for a couple of days—off on a special assignment for Chernov, so we're told. Each time they're gone someone in the world meets an untimely death—a rogue journalist in London, another in New Delhi, one in Dallas, an outspoken priest in Brazil, a veteran network news anchor who, in the middle of delivering the nightly news, stood up and shouted profanities against the regime, then went home and nosedived off the balcony of his twenty-second floor New York condo. His death was ruled a suicide—suicide my ass. Every time those two are off on an assignment for Chernov, someone the Marseille government wants out of the way gets whacked. If it looks like a duck, walks like a duck, it's a duck."

"What about Wilson and Chernov?"

"Wilson's a retired Marine, divorced, no kids that I know of. As for Chernov, rumor has it he's got a wife back in Russia. His three aides, Antonina Lebedev, Ivan Oblansky, and Boris Tangenev, came as a package with Chernov. That's all I know about them. All four were with Russian Intelligence before joining the World Government. So, you see, there's more going on here than meets the eye. Finish eating, let's get out of here. Lunch is on me."

No sooner do we arrive back at the office, Gustav's mouthing off in German.

"Uh... die amerikanischen Cowboys sind zurück. Warten Sie das nächste Mal, Hank, auf das Backup."

Victor, standing nearby, laughs.

"He said the American cowboys are back. Next time, wait for backup."

"You two make a great ventriloquist act. Next time show up a bit quicker."

Jeez, the conversations around here reverberates like a bunch of high school jocks in a locker room snapping towels at one another. With nothing else on the schedule, I settle at my desk and scan more case files... they're carbon copies of the ones I've already reviewed, so what's the point? Come closing time, Wilson calls me to his office.

"Russell, a minute please?"

Oh crap, what have I done now? When I enter, he eyes me for a moment.

"You lost your cherry today."

Lost my cherry? Terrible metaphor.

"Hank said you worked well together."

He's studying me like he's mulling over how to make his next point.

"The hostage thing, you and Hank made the right call. We don't want lawyers losing their lives over a fix. Bad PR. But if that guy hadn't taken hostages, you would have dropped him, right?"

There it is, that's what he's called me in for... he wants to hear what he wants to hear... nod, Billy, nod, agree with him.

"Good, I'll take that as a yes. Go home, relax, get some rest, see you in the morning."

Move, put one foot in front of the other, Billy Boy, get out of here... except for Jade, I find the squad room empty.

"Where is everybody, Jade?"

"Gone for the day. I'll walk out with you."

Finally, an opportunity to flirt outside the office... she grabs her coat and we're off... out on the street, she motions to her left.

"My apartment's two blocks in the opposite direction."

"Ah, that's close. You walk every day?"

"When the weather's good."

I wish I could throw some light on why I feel the way I do around this woman, but in the two short days I've been here, I'm inexplicably drawn to this lovely creature I know nothing about... sure, she's damn easy on the eyes, and God knows I'm wanting in that department, but that's not what's driving me... there's more going on than my desire to jump her bones.

"Have time for a coffee somewhere close."

"Gee, thanks, Billy, not tonight. Gotta get home to feed my cat. I'll take a raincheck."

"Okay. Be careful going home."

She tosses her head back and laughs, opens her coat revealing her belt-mounted revolver and badge.

"No one messes with Jade Miro."

"I didn't know you carried."

"Always, Billy, always. Till the morning, then."

Good night, Jade Miro, sleep tight, I'll see you in my

dreams... my eyes remain locked on her until she disappears around a corner. Remembering the only real meat in the fridge was the hot dogs and baloney, I duck into the little grocery on Broadway and pick up a ham steak, a pound of hamburger, butter, more coffee pods, and I'm off. As I turn down 4th Street, there's a city squad car and an EMS pulling away from the house... hotfooting the rest of the way, I find the front door's ajar... climbing the steps, I knock on Jules's door... no answer.

"Jules, it's Billy, you in there?"

"Up here."

He's standing at the top of the stairs, legs apart, hands on his hips.

"What's going on, I saw cops and an ambulance leaving."

"Lock the door before you come up."

Upstairs, Jules is standing by the open door to Conrad Billings' apartment.

"What's going on?"

"I heard loud noise like maybe there was a fight going on up here. By the time I came up to investigate it had stopped. I banged on the door, no answer, so I used my key, I found Conrad face down on the kitchen floor over there."

The apartment is a pig pen... dishes piled in the sink, a plate of uneaten Chinese takeout on the table, dirty clothes strewn about on the sofa, and the place reeks... it wasn't cooking I smelled after all.

"Did he have a heart attack?"

"OD'd. Cops found enough Coke, heroin, and Fentanyl to kill a herd of angry Buffalo, a hell of a lot more than Conrad needed to keep himself floating on a cloud, that's for sure. Cops think he might have been a middleman for one of the cartels. Had to be with as much stuff as he had stored here. Now that I think of it, he had a lot of visitors coming and going at all hours."

Jules spins around and stomps off down the hall at his usual quick speed.

"I gotta get somebody to clean up the mess. Close his door, will you?"

I peer into Conrad's apartment again before closing the

door and entering my place... I have a new appreciation for my meager digs after seeing the dump across the hall. Stashing the groceries in the frig, I retrieve the Bourbon, pour a shot, and raise the glass in a toast.

"Here's to the memory of Conrad Billings, who I never met, and to my assist today in taking down a drug pusher who Gustav and Victor saw fit to execute. I'm gonna get very drunk and there isn't a damn thing anyone can do about it. And I'm talking to myself... not a good sign."

Down the first shot goes in one gulp, then a second and third and I'm out for the count on an empty stomach.

CHAPTER 15

Will It Ever End?

My dream's running in an endless loop... we're in the alley, I miss the shot on purpose, rewind, we're in the alley, I miss the shot on purpose... damn it, I'm dreaming... the only way to stop is to wake up! My brain cooperates, my eyes pop open wide... I'm sweating and breathing hard... if I go back to sleep sure as hell it'll be a replay of the same. I gotta take a wiz anyway, good excuse to get up... feeling my way in the dark to my luxurious bathroom, I relieve myself without turning on the light... from the sound of it I'm missing the bowl... a slight shift to the right, and bingo, water on water... I'll clean the floor later. The sound of my cell ringing startles me... I miss the damn bowl again... I don't know anyone outside the office... who could be calling this time of night? Has to be a wrong number... the phone, where did I leave it? Uh, I stashed it under my pillow... dashing back to the bedroom, I rescue it from its hiding place.

"Yeah, hello?"

"Billy, it's Hank."

"Jesus, Hank, what time is it?"

"2:20."

"It's still dark."

"Always is at this hour. Be out front at 3:30."

"What the hell for?"

"Take a shower, shave, brush your teeth, comb your hair and be out front."

"Why?"

"Company business. You wanna chit-chat or you wanna get ready?"

"Okay, okay, mystery man, pick me up at the newsstand."
The line goes dead... what in the bloody hell needs to be dealt with in the middle of the night?

At 3:25, sleep deprived and in a foul mood, *I'm huddled by the closed newsstand under the corner street light and wondering why... it's cold and there's light snow flurries... all I have is this brown jacket issued me when I vacated the preferred vacation spot of the Cosmos... should have gotten a warmer one when I bought the new clothes. I'm scanning both Broadway and 4th from left to right... one or more Streetwalkers could decide I'm easy pickings at this ungodly hour. What would I do if they challenged me? I have a weapon... unless they too have one. Just in the nick of time, Hank arrives driving one of the government vehicles... I slip in the passenger seat... he hands me a cup of hot coffee.*

"You look like crap, Billy."

"Because you jerked me out of bed at 2:20."

"Drink the coffee and be quiet."

"Where are we going and why?"

"Twenty-eight miles South to Marshfield."

"Whatever this is can't wait until daylight?"

"Drug breweries never sleep, Billy."

Oh crap, we're going on a raid? What did you think it was at this hour, Billy Boy, a belated surprise birthday party in the middle of the night? This is what I've been dreading, but I didn't think it would happen this soon... I should have run off to the Arizona desert when I had the chance.

"Fill me in."

"I don't know any more than you do, pal. Wilson said to pick you up and meet them in Marshfield. Drink your coffee and enjoy the ride."

Hank goes quiet as a church mouse, so I don't engage him further... GPS takes us South entering the Marshfield area on two-lane 3A South, then left on Soule Avenue, right on Bay Road and another right on Seabury Point Road... we follow it until it turns into a one lane dirt road... another quarter mile and we approach a thick stand of tall trees ahead... the road swings way to the right around the tree line... Hank turns off his headlights, shifts the car to neutral, and rolls off the road stopping next to two government Chevys and an unmarked Humvee... close to the tree line we can make out six men in black uniforms milling around a large black box van... white lettering on its side identifies it as 'SWAT - World Law Enforcement, Boston.'... an EMS vehicle is parked next to it.

"Jesus, Hank, are we going to war?"

"Today you lose your training wheels, Billy."

"And what pray tell was that action in the alley?"

"A pee-shoot. Be on your toes for this one."

That sends the cold of night deep to my bones... or maybe it's cold fear that today they're going to test me... I'm not a cold-blooded killer despite what I did in that closet... I've justified that a thousand times... an eye for an eye... what I suspect is going to happen here today bears no comparison. We're out of the vehicle, heading to where the others have gathered... the snow is coming down harder now... Gustav and Victor are there along with the two guys in fatigues I've not seen before... Wilson and Chernov, also in fatigues, are talking nearby... Jade and Chernov's lady, Antonina, have their arms wrapped around automatic weapons and wearing communications headsets, as are the others. As we approach, I smile big at Jade, she doesn't smile back.

"Good morning, ladies."

Jade motions to Wilson.

"The Lieutenant's looking for you two."

As we move on to Wilson, I ask Hank what I think is an obvious observation.

"Why are the ladies carrying heavy artillery?"

"In case they have to use them."

"Have they ever?"

"Not yet."

We pass Heinz and Augier... Heinz shoots me one of his poisonous looks, but it's Augier who rags on us.

"Hey, it's Officer's Russell and Drummond, the straight-shootin' American cowboys."

"Give it a rest, will ya' Victor."

I'd like to punch the arrogant French bastard out just once. An unsmiling Colonel Chernov greets us.

"Good morning, welcome to the hunting party."

That has to be his favorite metaphor... he spits it out with a little too much bravado for my liking... maybe this is what he lives for... these 'hunting parties' get his juices flowing... I nod and give him my best Billy Russell smile.

"Any trouble finding us, Hank?"

"No, Lieutenant. This one must have come up fast to haul us out at this hour."

"Around eleven last night, the Colonel got a call about an abandoned warehouse on the other side of this tree line. When he learned there was a nightshift, he decided not to wait and rousted everyone out of bed.

"Do we know how many are in there?"

"The snitch says four guards, Hank. Don't know how many actual workers. Get suited up. You, Gustav and Victor cover the back. Russell, since this is your first real hunting party, you'll go in the front door with the Colonel and me."

Please, Lieutenant, don't feel like you have to treat me special... maybe I could stay here and monitor communications with the ladies. Jesus, I sound like a pansy, but never, ever in my time with the DEA were as cold blooded —never. If any of us ever executed a suspect without justification, we'd be the ones standing before a judge and jury. Our job was to bring them in for trial. The end goal here is to execute them on the spot. One of the men I had not seen before is approaching with two flak jackets, communication devices, rifles, and hands a set to Hank.

"See you when this is over, Billy."

"Stay safe, Hank."

He disappears into the dark tree line with Heinz and Augier... the guy with the equipment approaches me.

"Officer Russell?"

"That's me."

"I'm Ivan Oblansky. The tall one over there is Boris

Tangenev."

He has a pronounced Russian accent.

"Welcome to the hunting party."

Yeah, Ivan, you work for Chernov all right ... he hands me a flak-jacket, headset and an M4 rifle not bothering to ask if I ever handled one before ... I haven't ... how difficult can it be, lock and load, aim, pull trigger, shoot bad guys ... no, don't shoot anyone unless they're shooting at you. I put on the flak jacket and adjust it then slip on the communication headset just as Gustav's calling in.

"Jade, Antonina, we're in position."

"Copy that."

Chernov's prancing around the back of the Humvee like a race horse waiting for permission to go out and kill all the other horses ... the man gives me the cold jitters ... crap, he's coming in my direction.

"Here's how this works, Russell. Boris opens the doors, then SWAT goes in and takes out the banditos leaving the workers for us to interrogate. Questions?"

A million I won't ask, Colonel.

"No, sir."

"Stick close to me and Lieutenant Wilson."

"Yes, sir."

He calls to Boris.

"Okay, Boris, let's do this."

From the back of the Humvee, Boris retrieves a small shoulder-mounted rocket launcher ... so that's what Chernov meant by opening the doors.

"Time to light up the night."

The good Colonel spits that out with a full-on air of arrogance that causes me to be more apprehensive than I already am ... we follow Chernov, Wilson, Boris, Ivan, and SWAT into the dense trees ... a couple of minutes later we break through to a clearing and come upon an old white two-story warehouse about thirty yards away ... light is bleeding from the edges of the boarded-up windows on the first and second-floors ... Chernov holds up a hand.

"We'll hold this position until the fireworks are over."

Boris, Ivan and SWAT are making their way to a position that gives them a clear shot at the building's double sliding wooden doors. From the side road leading to the barn, the EMS vehicle takes up a position. Boris lifts the launcher to his shoulder... a few second later there's a loud boom momentarily lighting up the area around Boris and Ivan, then a whooshing sound as the projectile streaks through the air slamming into the doors splintering them into hundreds of small pieces of shrapnel and leaving a gaping hole... orange-red flames snake up the side of the building dissipating into thick swirls of gray and black smoke... the SWAT team's dashing toward the hole left by the blast... a hail of gunfire begins... it's coming from inside... scattering left and right and taking up position against the barn, SWAT returns fire, bullets whizzing and ripping at what's left of the door frame... two SWAT members make it to the opening and open fire... seconds later they dash to the inside... shots ring out before all goes silent... a call comes from the SWAT team leader.

"First floor's secure, Colonel, two bad actors down. Activity on the second level."

"Your men okay?"

"Everyone accounted for, sir. Moving up now."

A few moments of nerve-wracking silence pass, then a burst of gunfire followed by a second and third... it sounds like it's coming from the second-floor... all goes quiet again before we hear the calm voice of the SWAT leader.

"Building secure, Colonel."

Chernov's face widens in a satisfied grin.

"Damn, you guys never fail me."

Wilson makes the call to Jade and Antonina.

"Jade, Antonina, we're our way to the second floor. You can move up now. Position yourselves by the EMS."

Antonina's voice comes back.

"Copy that, Lieutenant."

Chernov thrusts his right arm forward like he's leading a charge in some long-forgotten skirmish in some far-off hellhole.

"Let's go!"

We enter the barn... two SWAT team members are standing over two bodies at the foot of the stair's bodies... blood pools on the dusty floor from their terminal wounds... without paying them any attention, Chernov steps over their bodies charging up the stair two at a time with Boris and Ivan right behind him and Wilson and me taking up the rear... at the top of the stairs the odor of smoldering wood and gunpowder lingers... the SWAT leader is motioning to the end of the hallway.

"Through that open door, Colonel."

"Thanks, good job as always."

It all went down as planned without any of us firing a shot thanks to SWAT... Chernov takes off down the dimly lit hallway with us close behind... halfway down, Wilson stops and peers into a small room to the right and gasps... the grizzly sight of a man is propped haphazard against the blood-splattered wall... God, the left side of his face has been blown away. We move on to a large open room at the far end of the hall... a SWAT member is standing over a black man and a Hispanic woman down on their knees hands handcuffed behind them... neither looks older than their early thirties... Chernov turns to the SWAT leader.

"I counted three."

"That's all we encountered, Colonel."

"These two the only workers?"

"Yes, sir."

The SWAT leader's motioning to three tables with neat mounds of powder on them.

"There's enough coke here to supply the greater Boston suburbs for a month with whatever crap they mix with it. My guess is caffeine laced with a touch of fentanyl. Gets them hooked every time."

"I can always rely on you and your men."

"Thanks, Colonel, as always, it's been our pleasure."

Chernov tosses him a quick salute.

"Until the next hunting party."

"Until the next hunting party, Sir."

The SWAT leader tosses Chernov a quick salute and leaves... Chernov's attention is now on the two down on their knees.

"You two working the nightshift alone?"

The black man nods, but neither makes eye contact with him.

"Who wants to go first?"

No reply from either.

"Tell me who you work for and we'll go easy on you."

No response... Chernov approaches the man, stares at him for a beat, then swift-kicks him in the ribs with the toe of his right brogan with such force we hear ribs crack... the man cries out and falls behind the women to the dusty wooden floor... she cringes and looks away.

"If I ask a question, Schwarzer Mann, I expect an answer. Russell, pull this black excuse for a human to his knees."

Racist are we, Colonel? Setting my rifle down on the floor, I slip my hands under the guy's armpits and lift him... he cries out in pain... Chernov crouches and gets in his face.

"Let's try this again. Who do you work for?"

"I don't know, honest."

Chernov stands and kicks him in the same spot... he tumbles to the floor again writhing in pain.

"Maybe the lady will be more cooperative, Colonel."

"Ya' think, Lieutenant? Let's give her a try."

The woman's eyelids slowly open her dark eyes telegraphing her fear... Chernov approaches her.

"What do you have to say for yourself, brown Senorita?"

Her eyes come up to him... she hesitates.

"An Ecuadorian kid shows up at the end of the week, pays us in cash, we go home."

She speaks with a distinct Hispanic accent.

"What's your name?"

"Maria."

"Okay, Maria from wherever the hell you're from South of the border, watch and learn. Russell, lift our boy to his knees again."

What the hell is going on here... what is Chernov doing? Reluctantly, I do as he asks and lift the man... he groans loudly.

"Jesus, man, wait, wait, I'll tell you what you want to know!"

Maria whips her head around and bellows.

"Anthony, shut the hell up!"

In a flash, Wilson swings his arm up and across striking the left side of Maria's face with an open hand... her head whips right and she cries out. Jesus, this isn't an interrogation this is sadistic torture... during my time on Europa I witnessed more than my share of violence, both from the inmates and guards, but this isn't violence, this is sadistic torture. There're footsteps in the hallway... in comes Hank, Gustav, and Victor.

"You're just in time for the grand finale, gentleman."

"Whatta we got here, Colonel?"

"Human scum, Victor, human scum."

Chernov turns to Maria... she lifts her head and looks at him with contempt in her eyes.

She spits... saliva splatters on Chernov's left shoe.

"You're a crazed animal."

"You little bitch. Russell, bend her over."

"What?"

"Bend her to my shoe."

Jesus, he's lost it, he's frigging nuts... I look to the others... nothing... not one of them is going to step in and stop this madness.

"Did you hear me, Russell?"

"Sir, I—"

"Then goddamn it, do it."

Reluctantly, I move behind Maria and place my hands on her shoulders and slowly bend her forward.

"Rub her face in it."

"Sir, really, I think—"

"Do not think, Russell, just do as I instructed."

This is not the act of a man in control, this is the act of a psychopath... if I don't do as he asks, the crazed bastard's liable to turn on me... as gently as I can, I bend Maria forward until her face is a couple of inches from his shoe.

"All the way, Russell."

Two inches more and Maria's face is touching the saliva...

she's crying... Chernov, the crazy fool, cackles, turns and points to Wilson's sidearm.

"Lieutenant, a little assistance please."

Wilson sets his M4 down and takes out his Smith and Wesson and crouches in front of Anthony... it's clear he and Chernov have played this game before... he jams the barrel of the weapon into the Anthony's groin... Anthony cries out in pain.

"Tell the Colonel what he wants to know."

The guy is shaking with pain from his broken ribs... his eyes have teared up... his mouth opens slowly.

"We make a deal?"

Chernov takes a step closer and squats next to Wilson and leers at the poor guy.

"Do either of us look like your parish priest?"

Chernov nods to Wilson, Wilson jabs the pistol further into Anthony's crotch... Anthony cries out.

"Jesus, man stop! My ribs, I need help."

"There's two EMS guys outside. Tell the Colonel what he wants to hear and they'll see to your injuries."

"Okay, okay."

Chernov's face lights up like a kid in the fifth grade who just received an 'A' in math class.

"Say his name."

"Alvera."

Maria breathes a hard sigh and looks away... for a moment I think Chernov's going to hit her again, but he doesn't... he turns to Anthony.

"Say his whole name."

"Matias Diego Alvera."

"Louder."

"Matias Diego Alvera!"

"Where might we find the ever-charming Mister Alvera?"

"I don't know. If he walked in here right now, I wouldn't know him from you."

With his right hand, Chernov wiggles his fingers in a 'gimme' motion to Wilson... Wilson hands him his pistol and moves aside... Chernov places the gun in Anthony's crotch.

"You have kids, Anthony?"

"No."

"I hope you weren't planning on having five or six anytime soon?"

Anthony's face turns ashen-white... he's shaking... his eyes go to the pistol, his mouth gapes wide... Chernov pushes the gun in further... Anthony cries out... God Almighty, I think Chernov's going to shoot! Boris moves quickly to Chernov's side and grips his right shoulder.

"Colonel."

Chernov doesn't answer... his eyes are locked on Anthony's.

"Colonel!"

Chernov, eyes wide, turns to Boris.

"What!"

"Time to go, sir."

Okay, something really weird is going on here. Boris leans close to Chernov's right ear... he's whispering something we can't hear... slowly Boris' hand slides down Chernov's arm... his hand grips the barrel of Smith and Wesson... he's whispering in Chernov's ear again... Chernov's grip on the pistol loosens... Boris removes it from Chernov's hand and passes it to Wilson. I look to Hank... this time I catch his eye... ever so slightly he shakes his head from side to side... Wilson is standing there doing nothing... Boris helps Chernov to his feet and he and Ivan lead him from the room. There is no way in hell I can begin to understand what just occurred.

"Gustav, Victor take care of this. Russell, watch and learn."

There isn't going be a next time, Lieutenant... I will find a way out of this madness if it's the last thing I do... knowing full-well what's coming next leaves me sick to my stomach. Once the room is clear, Gustav walks around back of Anthony, Victor behind Maria... I turn my head away.

"Don't you want to watch, Russell?"

No you crazy son of a bitch... those are human being kneeling before you in case you failed to notice. Two shots ring out... every muscle in my body tightens... I feel like I've been stung by a thousand bees. When I look back, Maria and

Anthony are lying face down on the floor, blood seeping from their head wounds. Is this who we are, is this what we've become? Hank grips my arm and pulls me toward the door.

"Come on, Billy."

In the hall, in a small room off to the left, Wilson, Boris, and Ivan are huddled with Chernov... I peer in, but Hank's tugging at my arm.

"Come on."

As we reach the top of the stairs and begin to descend three rapid shots ring out... we both freeze... Hank looks to the busted doors.

"Those shots came from outside!"

Dashing down the stairs, we make it through the bombed-out entrance... Antonina is on lying on the ground about thirty-feet away rolling from side to side, her hands are gripping her upper right thigh... the EMS medics are rushing to her... Jade's a few feet away, smoke's seeping from the barrel of her M4... she's white as a ghost... the rifle slips from her hand to the ground... she's pointing to the right corner of the warehouse... a man is lying face down in the overgrown grass, a handgun within inches of his outstretched right arm...

"Jade!"

"He came out of a side door, Billy, fired one shot and hit Antonina before I put two in him."

Wilson comes running out of the warehouse followed by the others.

"Hank, what happened?"

"That one over there came out a side door and shot Antonina, Jade took him down."

One of the EMS medics is waving a hand.

"The shot went clean through the fleshy part of the right thigh."

My attention is on Jade... she lowers herself to the ground... her hands cup her face and she's crying... rushing to her, I place an arm around her shaking shoulders as Boris, Ivan, and Chernov disappear through the tree line... so much for their concern for Antonina. Wilson's barking orders.

"Gustav, Victor, drag that son of a bitch inside with the

others and torch the goddamn place."

I help Jade to her feet.

"Come on, the EMS guys will take care of Antonina, let's get you out of here."

Hank joins us and we make our way back toward the tree line... before we enter, I turn back, the dead man is gone and building is already ablaze, flames leaping up through the old wooden structure like crepe paper. When we break through the tree line, Boris and Ivan are helping Chernov into the Humvee.

"Hank, what the hell happened back there?"

"Come on, let's get on the road before the locals show up to watch the fire."

The atrocities committed in that warehouse were beyond human cruelty. As we drive back, I'm waiting for Hank or Jade to say something, anything, but neither does... Jade's in the back seat staring vacantly out the window... her arms are wrapped tightly across her chest... I want to console her, to reassure her that in taking that man's life, she saved Antonina's life and possibly hers... but there's no words, not now, maybe never... leaning across the seat I whisper to Hank.

"For Christ's sake, Hank, that was a gangland execution."

"Policy is set by Marseille, today you saw how it's carried out."

"Policy rooted in—" *Hank cuts me off.*

"Enough, Billy. Get past it or it'll scrape at you until you bleed."

I gaze over my shoulder at Jade... she shakes her head and places a finger to her lips signaling I should I drop it.

"At least explain why SWAT and the others left the room?"

Jade leans forward resting her arms on the back of my seat.

"Plausible deniability."

"Plausible what?"

"As crazy as it sounds, they can't be held responsible for what they didn't see or take part in."

"Are you joking, Jade? They ordered it. And why in the hell do they need us, SWAT does just fine on their own."

"You don't get it, Billy."

"Get what, Hank, what am I missing?"

"Ask yourself why we are the ones who do the killing. If this ever blows up, we'll be accused of being rogue cops and we'll take the fall for the executions."

CHAPTER 16

Like A Whipped Dog

When we arrive back at the office, Hank pulls into the parking lot next to his car—an older model Ford Taurus.

"Either of you want a lift home? Jade?"

"Yeah, Hank, thanks."

"Billy?"

"No, I'm gonna walk."

"Okay, suit yourself, but go straight home."

Dispirited, I meander down Broadway through an inch of fresh snow, hands in my pockets, shoulders slumped forward as I weave my way around Streetwalkers and garbage containers. Even though the sun is up, and it feels great on my face, my mood's dark and for damn good reason... I can't erase from my mind the torture that took place before the executions... how can we justify such inhumane behavior under any circumstances? I have to find a way out... I won't be a party to this lawlessness. I better make it to the house without running into anyone who might piss me off... not tonight... nor do I want to run into the Energizer Bunny... not in the mood for him either... thankfully, I run into neither. Dragging myself up the stairs as quietly as I can, I stop at Conrad Billings' door wondering who he was... everyone has a story... I can't help wonder what his was? Entering my place reminds me the dirty dishes are still in the sink and urine on the bathroom floor... they'll wait... what I need is a shot of Bourbon and sleep... lots of sleep... dropping my gun and badge on the table, I retrieve the bottle, pour a shot... down it goes and I'm off to bed.

MIDNIGHT BLACK

By the time I awake its dusk, I had slept the day away... my head is fogged, but the memory of what happened in that barn lingers like a bad nightmare. I'll eat something, then wash the dishes and clean the bathroom floor and try to put it all behind me. I'm rooting around in the frig looking for something easy to fix when I hear what sounds like a knock at the door... someone's moving around in the hall... I wait for another knock... it doesn't come... still hyper from the raid, I sweep up my gun from the kitchen table and clear my throat to let whoever's out there know I'm here... damn, the doorknob's turning... did I lock it? Slowly, the door swings open... Holy Mother of God, it's Jules... he freezes at the sight of my weapon pointed at his head.

"Whoa, put that damn thing away!"

"Good God, Jules, I could have shot you."

"I thought I heard you say come in."

"I coughed."

"Next time cough louder. And keep your door locked. There are sub-humans out there that'll kill you for a Saltine cracker. What's up, you look like you lost your best friend?"

If only you knew, Jules, if you only knew.

"Uh, long day."

Good, he has no idea I've been here sleeping all day.

"Your eye's looking better."

Strolling to the sofa, he plops down like he owns the place... bless the landlord who makes himself at home.

"Heat not working, Jules?"

"What?"

"You're wearing an overcoat."

He ignores me... his attention goes to the bourbon on the kitchen counter.

"It's against the laws of nature to drink alone."

"A myth perpetuated by those in need of a drink."

"Consider me in need, William."

Damn, the bottle's almost empty... okay, be a good host and pour him one and another for yourself and see what's on the old boy's mind... he raises his glass in a toast.

"Success in your new job."

Would you say that if you knew what we really do at Auschwitz West? Downing the shot, I join him on the sofa... he offers me a cigarette.

"I quit."

"Suit yourself, William. Mind if I do?"

"It's your house, go for it."

He sucks in a long, slow drag like maybe it's his last, then blows perfect smoke circles that float up and disperse like an errant cloud... that's it, damn it, I want one.

"Okay, toss one over."

"So much for willpower."

"Willpower's highly overrated, Jules."

Lighting the cigarette, I inhale deeply hoping the poisonous toxins erase the evil I witnessed this lurid day.

"You came up for a reason?"

He downs the rest of his drink and snuffs the cigarette in his glass.

"I was going for a walk. Wanna join me?"

"It's dark and cold out there."

"Jeez, William, a little chill won't kill you."

"I only have this light jacket."

"So, buy a less light jacket."

"All right, all right, Jules, but just a short walk."

"Bring your badge and gun, leave your phone."

When we hit the street, a city dump truck is clearing the sidewalks of garbage... like an alien robot from a sci-fi movie, its mechanical arm noisily swings out, grips a container, sweeps it up, and empties it... Jules lights a cigarette and chuckles low.

"Be still my heart, they finally showed up, and in the dark yet."

"Who cares as long as they remove the stench. Say, why did I leave my phone behind?"

"You know damn why, William. Your phone, along with satellites, drones, and cameras on poles with their facial technology, are tracking our every move, and I'm damn sick of it all."

"Jules, I doubt whoever tracking cares we went for a

walk."

"Says you. That truck's giving me a headache—let's walk the other way."

We stroll slowly over the snow… something's rattling around in Jules's head… he's got me out here for more than just a casual walk in the cold, snow, dark and lingering stench of garbage.

"Jules, something's on your mind, what is it?"

"Not that it's any of my business, but I thought you should know. After you left this morning, this Godzilla shows up flashing an official badge—says he was your parole officer."

Wilson never mentioned anything about a parole officer.

"What did he want?"

"He wouldn't say, just that he'd return later."

"You could have told me this in my nice warm apartment, Jules."

"The walls have ears."

"In the house? Jules, you're paranoid."

"And for good reason. Best watch your back until you know who that guy was. There's lots of government types skulking around pretending to be who they're not. You're not a spy for one of them dissident groups, are you?"

"Huh, me? Not hardly."

We amble on in silence while Jules sucks on his cigarette like it's a stick of candy… I have no idea why he's hovering over me like we're best buds… he doesn't know me, where I've been, or why… but I'm just hungry enough for information to risk exposing my past… let's see if this new-found friendship will shed some light.

"Jeez, Jules, it's like a third-world country out here."

"It's that, all right. Must have been the same out there in San Francisco, huh?"

"Yeah, if not worse."

"Millions around the world are huddling hopeless and scared tonight looking for places to sleep that no human should have to. None believed one day they'd end up begging for food and shelter and taking deadly drugs to make it through another night. Every day, within a mile radius of here, there's at least a dozen overdoses, and they're left to die like diseased animals. There were eight suicides last week in South Boston alone— the youngest was twenty-two. Problem is, we were taught that America was exceptional, the greatest democracy in the world, the land of the free, the land of milk and honey. We bought into that and became complacent and failed to protect our precious democracy. So, son, here we are all these years later and democracy's ashes are stashed away in a Tupperware container somewhere. French philosopher Montesquieu summed it up in 1748 when he wrote, 'The tyranny of a prince is not so dangerous to the public's welfare as the apathy of a citizen in a democracy.' To that I will add, life is short, dead is dead, when your brain runs out of fuel there's no second act, so make the first one count."

The Energizer Bunny is wound up and talking up a storm... let's see if I can get more out of him.

"I have to say, Jules, your knowledge of history is impressive."

"It's no more complicated than paying attention to what came before, son. Study the past as I have, and you begin to see all the wavy little lines coming together in a single thread leading to the day the Bandidos swooped in and skinned us alive. We were facing a mountain of challenges, we always are, not the least of which was climate change and over-population. By the time we got around to accepting climate change as real, it was a crash course keeping up with it. No matter what we did, it stayed one step ahead of us. It's always been that way with all our problems. We think we solved one problem and another comes along. As for over-population, what in the hell were we supposed do with all those bodies taking up space and polluting the planet even more than it already was? Well, friend, take a look around. Looks like the Fascist ninnies in Marseille found a solution—short term pain in exchange for long term gain, and they're betting the average Joe is too stupid to figure it out."

"You think all this was planned?"

"If it wasn't, those jerks in Marseille are dumber than I thought."

If I shift this conversation to recent history, he'll question why my lapse in memory... the hell with it, roll the dice and see where it goes.

"How's your knowledge of current events?"

"What kind of question is that?"

A dumb one... wished I had phrased it better.

"I'm interested in your take on things."

"What time period we talking about?"

"The past seventeen years or so?"

His face compresses... he shoots me a questioning look.

"You'd have to be living on another planet not to know."

Ha, that's a laugh, I have been living on another planet. Jules blows a hard breath, shakes his head, and walks off... I gave it a shot, looks like he doesn't want to go there. We continue on in silence for a long-thirty-seconds while he drags on his cigarette... it's almost down to the filter.

"Seventeen years, huh?"

Okay, great, I have his attention.

"Yeah."

"That's a hell of a big chunk of time, William. What's the real reason you're asking?"

"I want your take on things, that's all."

He goes silent again and continues walking until he stops and turns to me.

"You want my take on things?"

"Yeah."

He's eyeing me suspiciously.

"Hmm. All right, all right, William, I'll play your game, but first a few ground rules."

"Okay, shoot."

"You get an abridged version of my perception of what screwed everything up."

"Why is that?"

"Because it'll take all damn night to fill in the who, what, and why. And you don't get to ask questions."

"Not happy about that."

"Too bad. And this conversation never took place. It's not the kind of truth that's openly talked about unless you have a death wish."

"I don't and my lips are sealed."

He tosses his spent cigarette to the snow, crushes it beneath his foot, and lights another.

"One of our major problems is, we Homo sapiens have been tribal creatures from the beginning of our trek across the planet. You know, my tribe is better than your tribe, bullshit. It's an endless, dangerous, ignorant mindset that causes so many to buy into conspiracy theories and alternative facts to support their worldview, which means they're either too stubborn or too ignorant to put two and two together and come up with four."

"Jules, you're talking about human nature."

He tosses his head back and laughs... his key chain jiggles under his coat.

"Human nature? That's a joke, William. We're nothing more than a video game."

"A video game?"

"Yeah. We're controlled by an unseen force with each of us playing a small transitory role for the short time we're here. That's the only answer that makes any sense. How else do you explain all the craziness? Now ask yourself, was this game created for us by some intelligent entity, or did we create it for ourselves? Either way the world is in the shitter. Did you know more than half of all adults believe in intelligent extraterrestrial life?"

"No, I didn't."

"That statistic rivals belief in God. Think about that for a New York minute. When those little green men do show their faces, where will that leave our sanctimonious religious beliefs? In the toilet, that's where. All right, all right, enough of my babbling. Let's get to your seventeen-year period."

"What about the—"

"No questions, remember?"

"Sorry, professor Sommers, proceed."

"Hopefully, you recall fifteen years ago when millions took to the streets again accusing the aristocracy of being society's money-pariahs scooping up the winnings with both hands while sucking the marrow from the bones of the rest of us. Did the Glitterati care? Hell no. News cycles come and go and protests soon forgotten. Capitalism, however, rolls on protecting the mighty upper-white class while minorities are kept down with a knee on their necks. How many times do we have to get kicked in the balls before we kick back? As Forrest said, 'Stupid is as stupid does.'"

"Who?"

"Forest Gump."

"Never heard of him."

"He was a movie character who said 'Stupid is as...' Oh, never mind, it's just an old movie and a damn good one at that."

"And you remember a line from it all these years later?"

"There're lines from films that become iconic like, "Frankly, my dear, I don't give a damn."

"Not familiar with that one either."

"Clark Gabel, 'Gone with the Wind' 1929."

"You're movie buff too?"

"What else is an aging genius going to do with his free time? Where was I?"

"You were expanding on the elite class and capitalism."

"Right, let's back up a bit. Like I said, climate change kept biting at our asses like a pissed-off pack of wolves. The canary in the coal mine should have been when the mass migrations from the poorest areas began in earnest. Countries began slamming shut their borders in a desperate attempt to stem the flow. Despite their efforts, the undesirables, as they referred to them, kept coming in swarms, leading to increased racism, xenophobia, and violence. Caucasians were determined to remain the dominant race at any cost, not necessarily in numbers—it was too late for that—but in control, and control is always where the money and power is. Am I boring you yet, William?"

"Not at all."

Jules wipes a hand over his face and sighs... he's thinking again.

"It took a disastrous event—a border war between Pakistan

and India—to finally kick our collective neurons into high gear."

Finally, the details of the mysterious Pakistan-India event... don't mention Wilson brought it up in passing... let him roll through his version.

"Why do I get the impression you don't know this stuff?"

"Like I said, I want your take on events."

"Sounds like you're pulling my chain, William."

If he calls me William one more time, I'm gonna return to the apartment without him. "Why do you say that, Jules?"

"You tell me."

"There's nothing to tell, old man."

"All right, all right, have it your way. There was a lot of bad things happening, not just here, but in the whole bloody damn world. People were fed up with the gilded-edged crowd humming along like happy campers as they always did. As for government policies, they've always supported financial markets and whatever else makes the rich richer."

"It will never change, Jules. It's a shell game and it's stacked against us."

"You got that right. The whole world finally got shaken awake ten years ago. Following a contentious border war, Pakistan in all their wisdom, fired a one kiloton nuclear-tipped missile at New Delhi, a city of almost twenty-two-million at the time."

"God Almighty."

"Yeah, well, son, God chose to look the other way on that one. The warhead exploded six miles short of New Delhi's center—to this day no one knows why. It was the height of mankind's propensity for treating one another with unspeakable cruelty, and raising the question, were we the most intelligent species on the planet, or the dumbest?"

My God, how could the brass on Europa have kept that from us?

"The world came to a dead stop. Fear consumed every last person capable of comprehending the consequences if it was ever to happen again. There was an immediate call for the ban of all nuclear weapons, but not surprisingly not a single country was willing to give theirs up. The U.S. had the clout to get it done, but didn't. Say, William, why are we doing this dance?"

"What do you mean?"

"Stop bullshitting me, you don't know any of this stuff."

"I, uh—"

"Never mind. I said I'd play, so I will. Following the Pakistan India debacle, the entire world was on the edge of a major revolt. Protesters around the world took to the streets constantly clashing with authorities—arrests were made and prison filled up fast. Something, had to be done. Here in the U.S. neither political party was delivering the goods—they were way too busy clashing with one another over who was going to be king of the hill. Then came the news a new political party was in the works. They named it The Peoples Cooperative Populist Party—the PPP. Who wouldn't fall in love with a warm, cozy, patriotic, flag-waving moniker like that? The rascals pitched a liberal bent that played like a love song to the fed-up masses—equality and opportunity for everyone regardless of skin pigmentation, their status, or where they came from as long as they were legally here. Suspiciously, there was little push-back from either of the existing two parties. The question was, why, why weren't they pushing back? Unbeknownst to us naïve folk, the PPP was financed by the very same high-rolling financiers who had funded the two major parties in the past. It was a clever shift away from what wasn't working to a system that would ensure the old system kept working—safeguard the affluent and mighty white class— and they were all in on it. The Peoples Cooperative Populist Party simply exploited the worst of humanity when we were at our most vulnerable. They dusted off that old slogan, 'Make America Great Again' with a slight twist—'Keep America Great Forever'. Before we could say, 'America is about to get royally screwed again', the American Peoples Populists Party's presidential candidate, a billionaire industrialist with no government experience other than the checks he used to write supporting his candidates, was swept into the White House along with control of both houses of Congress. They promised us the moon, but delivered Uranus, a planet with no solid surface."

"An interesting analogy."

"Their grab for the brass ring was about the preservation of the white race as the real power and to ensure their control of over the worlds assets. Would it surprise you to know they had the support of hate and militia groups, white nationalists, and the fringe malcontents? Not surprisingly, like-minded plutocrats around the world adopted the PPP's playbook winning high offices in country after country. Before we knew it, the PPP morphed into a worldwide political party. Smell the conspiracy yet?"

"Hard to miss, Jules. It sounds to me like that was the plan all along."

"Right you are, William, only we were too stupid to recognize it. The new world PPP party put forth a radical concept that caught everyone's attention—a world government to oversee all other governments. All military forces would be under their direct control on the premise that, if nations did not control their armed forces, there could be no wars. And Nuclear weapons were to be permanently banned. Who wouldn't fall for that bait? In full democratic fashion, every person throughout the world over the age of eighteen was given an opportunity to vote for or against the establishment of a World Government—they were that confident."

"That was risky, what if the people had voted no?

"The snakes behind the PPP knew we common folk were predictable and easily influenced as long as we believed whatever they were proposing was beneficial to us. A whopping seventy-two percent voted in favor of a world government—the people had spoken. It was and remains the most radical decision in the history of mankind. Once officially in power, the PPP reduced each country's military by a third and installed military generals loyal to the PPP to ensure no country stepped out of line. As promised, they decommissioned all nuclear weapons, which of course proved wildly popular. The PPP would also act as a world supreme court when arguments between countries arose. Every country had to cough up 5% of their yearly GDP for services provided. It's a hell of a lot more complicated than that, but that's the long and short of it, son—we were scammed and scammed good."

"This is beyond science fiction, Jules."

"If it were a movie plot, no one would believe it. But the people, God love 'em, bought it hook, line, and sinker. You gotta give the PPP credit for pulling it off."

"And now? What about resistance groups like this Apostolic Channel?"

"When you're talking about organized resistance, son, you better have a lot of sheep dogs herding the flock in the same direction—we didn't. The few resistance groups there are out there, like Apostolic Channel, are mostly hotheads who have no clue what the hell they're doing. There's a rumor of a well-funded and organized global movement, but it's just that, a rumor. If it does exist, Marseille will crush it like a cockroach. Listen, son, I promised you an abridged version, there it is, history lesson 101. If I understood it all, I'd be President for life instead of that narcissist French billionaire whose name I never can remember."

I'm so struck by the idea that what he's told me has merit, I'm too speechless to offer my own observations... Jules turns reflective.

"My father, God love him, passed at age ninety-two, Billy. The day before, when he could barely speak, he told me that what made his life worthwhile was the joy he received from mom, my older sister, and me. They're all gone now except for me. I don't believe in an afterlife, but just in case I'm wrong, my fondest wish is maybe there is and I will meet up with them again."

Sound familiar, Billy Boy?

"Okay, kiddo, let's head back, I'm getting a chill."

I'm elated to have gotten that much out of him... I won't press him further... he's ambling back toward the house but hesitates a beat and turns back.

"I could find myself in a fading, unwashed, loose-fitting orange jumpsuit for talking about this."

"Jules, my lips are sealed."

He's scanning the dark street like he's worried someone might be watching us. "What is it?"

"There's the camps."

"I've seen a local one at Moakley Park."

"No, not like those. Like the ones created by the Chinese that imprisoned over one-million ethnic Uighurs and other Turkic Muslims in order to wipe out their language, religion and culture, like the white European immigrants did to the indigenous Indians here, the Nazis to the Jews and others in World War Two, the North Koreans who sent thousands of their citizen to retraining labor camps."

He's scanning the street again before moving to my side.

"The vermin in Marseille are doing it again, rounding up homosexuals, the disabled, clergy, reporters, resistance fighters, and anyone who dares speak out against their policies. No one is ever labeled unfit to live among 'their' society. No, no, that would be racist and bring about a major backlash. Instead, people are charged with fabricated crimes, given a quick trial, found guilty, and off they go never to be heard from again. It's the government's ancillary program to those who aren't dying quick enough out here on the streets in what can only be described as a planned genocide. Jesus, they must believe we're all stupid."

"Where are these camps, Jules?"

"I suppose some know, but I don't. Okay, I've said enough, maybe too damn much."

He hands me his pack of cigarettes.

"Take these."

"No, I'm good."

"Don't argue, just take them."

Stop protesting, Billy, you know you want them, take them.

"Thanks, Jules."

He smiles and pats me on the arm and walks off again… but surprise, surprise, he turns back.

"Do you by any chance remember who Steven Hawking was?"

"He was a theoretical scientist, wasn't he?"

"One of the best to have ever lived. He summed up us

human beings this way. 'We are just an advanced breed of monkeys on a minor planet of a very average star. But we can understand the Universe. That makes us something very special.' Special at what, is what I ask? That's the one of the most important questions we have to answer before we all perish. As for you, young man, archaeologists discover remnants of ancient societies buried under many, many layers of time. When you're ready to peel back a few of yours and tell me why you don't know any of this stuff, I'm all ears."

"Maybe when you stop calling me, William."

His lips curl into a devilish grin.

"Okay, Billy."

And with that my history-loving energizer bunny landlord is heading back to the house at his usual quick-pace with me trying to keep up... when we've said our goodnights, and I'm safely back in my sparse but warm apartment, I pour the last remaining shot of Bourbon and ponder all that Jules had shared with me... how could we have allowed this to happen... had we learned nothing from our past fumbles? What does it take to protect ourselves from the evil that so frequently rises like ashes from a flame? I have way too many questions requiring way too many answers. And then there's the lingering stench of the horror that went down in that warehouse. Chernov, Wilson, Gustav, and Victor violated every code of morality that defines us as human... define human, Billy Boy... complicated, isn't it, huh? Give it a try again in the morning when your head's clear. With a cigarette dangling from my lips, I wash the dirty dishes and scrub the urine-stained bathroom floor while trying to come to grips with the implications of my missing years.

This sleepless night wins the prize *as one of my most distressful... along with Jules's dystopian world narrative, and the reprehensible executions in that barn, both play out in my head in an endless loop... I toss, I turn, I wake up, I sit up... the only way to stop it is to get out of bed a damn hour earlier*

than usual. Feeling s sleep deprived, a cup of coffee in hand, I sit on the sofa in a mental fog, unable to focus, staring blankly ahead as if the desk, TV, and the wall beyond were not there... an infinity of nothing. Hey, get your act together, Billy Boy, nobody gives a damn how you're going to deal with this... it falls on you to figure it out... remember when you took your last shower on Europa? You washed off the stink and grime of that insufferable planet... that's exactly what is needed now... find the courage within you to go forward, not sideways. I linger in the shower, my hands flat against the wall as the hot water streams over me. At 7:00, I wolf down a couple of eggs and toast... I'm out the door and on the sidewalk by 7:30... I'm met by two sixties-looking Hispanic men on the opposite side of the street pointing fingers and yelling at one another... they look like they're seconds away from a fistfight... one of them is poking the other in the chest with his finger.

"Hijo de puta, me robaste, tu vida baja!"

The other one steps back and gives him the finger.

"Era un pésimo pedazo de pan y queso"

My neighbors across the street, who I've never seen, let alone met, are watching this spectacle unfold from their windows... time for me to play cop.

"Hey you two!"

The aggressive one steps off the curb and advances in my direction.

"¿Hey que?"

"Do you speak English?"

"Yeah, do you speak Spanish?"

"Sorry, no. What's going on?"

"No Es asunto tuyo."

"No comprende, amigo."

"I said, amigo, it's none of your goddamn business."

Pushing my coat open, I expose my gun and badge...

"I'm making it my business."

He tosses his head back and laughs.

"Is that supposed to frighten me?"

"It will if you don't explain what you two are arguing about."

"This creep over here stole food from me."
I look to the other guy.
"Is that true?"
"I was hungry."
The first guy tosses up his hands and scoffs.
"You don't get to steal food, Maldito ladrón.
Okay, time to diffuse this situation before someone gets hurt.
"Senor, where's the food he says you stole?"
"I ate it... a lousy piece of moldy cheese and bread."
The aggressive one is wagging an accusing finger.
"It was my cheese and bread! I'm gonna beat your ass to a pulp!"
"Hold on there, that won't solve anything."
"Maybe not for you, but it will for me. He needs to pay for what he did."
"You two know each other?"
"He lives in the tent next to me in Moakley Park."
"Then you're friends?"
"Used to be before he stole my food."
"Okay, okay, let's settle this in a civilized manner. If I get you both something to eat, will you call a truce?"
The aggressive one hesitates... he looks to the other guy.
"Quiere darnos comida, Julio."
"¿Por qué tendría que hacer eso?"
"Julio wants to know why you would do that?"
"To keep you from harming one another over a piece of cheese and bread."
"¿Debemos confiar en él, Julio?
"Si."
"Julio says okay."
"Great. What's your name?"
"Domingo."
"Domingo, you and Julio wait right there."
When I turn to go back in, Jules is standing on the stoop in his robe... he's glaring at me.
"What are you doing, Billy?"
"Not now, Jules."

A quick trip upstairs, grab the open package of baloney and the rest of the sliced bread, a paper bag, and return to the street... Jules is still there.

"Big mistake, Billy."

"It won't be my first or last, Jules."

Crossing the street to the two men, I hold out the food.

"Take this, split it evenly between you—do it in front of me."

They eye me suspiciously like maybe they shouldn't trust this Gringo cop.

"Go on, take it."

Domingo snatches the food from my hand, takes his share, and passes the rest to Julio who stares at me with disbelief.

"Thank you, sir."

"You're welcome. Shake hands. Go on, do it."

Reluctantly, they do as I ask... and with that they're off down the street and around the corner... I smile and wave to my neighbors hiding behind the safety of their window blinds and return to Jules.

"Bad move, Billy. Like pigeons in the park, they'll be back for more."

"The situation was diffused with a package of baloney and some bread. How easy was that?"

"I'm just saying that—"

"Gotta go, Jules."

"You'll see that I'm right, Billy."

Okay, so I feel good about what I did... so what... it cost me a lousy package of baloney and bread... it's the first I've really felt halfway human since I got back. When I reach Broadway, I see that it has also been cleared of garbage... a major improvement. Weaving my way through too many Streetwalkers, I arrive at murder central a few minutes before 8:00 and risk flirting with Jade.

"Good morning, Jade."

She doesn't acknowledge me... her eyes are locked on whatever she's reading.

"And here I thought the sun only shined outside."

Hmm, that sounded a little juvenile, Billy Boy. She glances up unsmiling.

"Billy, if you're trying to cheer me up, this is not the morning to do it."

"It was worth a try."

"Yesterday is still too fresh in my mind."

"Yeah, sorry, for me too."

"Wilson's moving you to the desk between Hank and Gustav."

"Ah, the promotion."

"Go get settled."

"Yes, boss."

Best I zip my lip while I'm ahead... when I settle in at my new desk, the good German Gustav can't resist ragging on me.

"Welcome to the big boy's side of the room. Learn anything yesterday?"

"Call it what it was, Gustav... an execution."

"And for damn good reason."

"And that would be?"

"Es gibt mehr von inned als wir—there's more of them than us."

"Right, got it, I'll make note of that."

He smirks and turns away... I need a cup of coffee... I'm up and heading for the door... Jade stops me.

"You two sound like schoolboys."

"One of us is, one of us isn't."

"I'm having trouble telling which is which, Billy."

"The short one is, the tall one isn't. I'm headed to the break room, join me for coffee."

She graces me with a warm smile... probably because she blew me off when I arrived.

"Maybe later."

"Suit yourself."

She lied... I know she's coming... I could hear it in voice, see it in her eyes, those beautiful flashing, almond-shaped eyes... right, keep telling yourself these foolish lies, Billy, and they'll have you committed to a home for egomaniacs. The break room's empty... no sooner have I fixed a cup of coffee and settle at one of the tables, Jade waltzes in... score one for me. She fixes herself a cup and settles in a seat across from me.

"How's Antonina, Jade?"

"Luckily it was a flesh wound. She'll be out of the hospital tomorrow. Neither one of us believed we'd ever have to use our weapons, yesterday was a first, I pray it's the last."

She stares expressionless at her coffee. Slowly, her head comes up... I see the anguish in her eyes.

"I didn't hesitate, I just shot him."

"And for that reason you and Antonina are alive. Be thankful you didn't see what Chernov did to those two workers before Gustav and Victor executed them. It was inhumane. Chernov's one sick puppy."

"A word to the wise, Billy, be careful what you say to whom."

"You're right, I need to zip it."

"It's not always going to be like this, so keep the faith."

She picks up her coffee and stands.

"Where're you going, you just got here?"

"Remember what I said, keep the faith, Buckaroo."

"Buckaroo?"

"Gustav called you a cowboy. Buckaroo has a better ring."

Tossing me one of her heart-melting smiles, she saunters out.

Come Friday, it's quiet around Murder Central*... unless we're shooting one of the bad guys in an alley, or stacking bodies in an old warehouse to be reduced to ashes, there's little need for our services... I could pass the time reading more case files, but I'm not into fiction. All is not lost, however... Jade reminds me that it's the first of the month... three thousand big ones, minus my rent, were electronically deposited to my debit account... I'm looking to spend some of it, and a laptop computer is at the top of my list. Come noon, Hank and I head out for lunch... I invite Jade to go along... she has an errand to run... so she says.*

"It's payday, Hank, lunch is on me."

"Have any plans for the weekend, Billy?"

"My toenails need trimming."

"Ever been to the Kennedy Library?"

Yes, twenty or twenty-one years ago... but since he's kind enough to offer, I lie.

"No, never."

"How's tomorrow? I'll pick you up around ten."

"Great."

"There's to be no talk of the office. We get enough of that crap day in and day out."

"Hank, I'm looking to buy a laptop. Know of a place I can pick one up?"

"Sure, I'll take you there tomorrow."

At closing time, Wilson comes out of his hole long enough to remind us we're on call 24/7.

"Enjoy your weekend. Remember to keep your cell phones on in case something comes up."

On the way out I ask Jade how she plans to spend her weekend... if she doesn't come up with a good excuse, I'll invite her to join us on our outing tomorrow.

"Hank and I are going to the Kennedy Library in the morning, wanna join us?"

"Oh, would love to go, Billy, but I have way much to accomplish over the weekend."

My ego is sufficiently bruised yet again.

CHAPTER 17

A Time of Reflection

Saturday morning, Hank arrives at ten in his older and in bad
need of work Ford Taurus. The Kennedy Library turns out to
be the best two hours I've spent since returning from the single
biggest mistake in the Universe... but. hey, the world is
grateful for the ore, so I suppose we should be thankful for
that. Following the tour, Hank takes me to his favorite North
end Italian restaurant, Arico's, run by Italian immigrants
Carmela and Vincenzo Aricö. The place is small—twelve tables
and a minibar flanked by four tall stools... on this Saturday the
restaurant is a half full. A young-women greets Hank by name,
which confirms he comes here often.
   "Billy, say hello to Angie."
   "Nice to meet you, Angie."
   She leads us to a table and we settle in.
   "Carmela and Vincenzo run the kitchen, Angie the table
service. You're in for a treat, the food is the best."
   *Hanks insists on ordering for us... chopped tomatoes, olive
oil, fresh basil, capers and garlic simmered in a little red wine
with jumbo shrimp. He wasn't overstating the food... turns out
to be the best Italian food I've eaten, bar none... a major
improvement over mushy oatmeal.*
   "So, Hank, do you have a life outside the office?"
   "I play for the Boston Bruins and conduct the Boston Pops
on weekends. If you must know, I'm involved with a very nice
lady. To keep your sanity, I recommend you do the same."
   "Jade is on my radar."
   "Good luck with that, Jade's on every healthy male's
radar."

Following lunch, we're off to the computer store... I drop six-hundred and fifty-five dollars on a laptop... I hope there's not many speed bumps setting it up... I was never the most literate computer guy. When we return to my place, Hank pulls up to the curb and turns off the engine.

"Thanks, Hank, I enjoyed the day."

As I swing open the door to leave, he places a hand on my arm.

"Wait."

"What is it?"

He looks to the street with a plaintive expression... several ragged down and out souls come our way, glance briefly in our direction, then pass on.

"There isn't a day that goes by that I don't question how we got here, Billy. The villains in Marseille would have never allowed this to reach this state unless there was something sinister behind it."

"Well, there's a mouthful. Care to share?"

"How about the annihilation of what they perceive to be an undesirable segment of society?"

Whoa, wait a minute. Did he just confirm what Jules already laid on me? Don't let on, let him talk.

"That's a pretty damning accusation."

"How else to explain what's happening? A rigged economic disaster allows them to strip away the low hanging fruit without being accused of a planned mass extinction. A forced pandemic would have affected everyone, so that was out. So was an outright war since they control the military and could never justify an attack. They're reshaping society into their worldview, Billy. It's that simple, there's no other explanation."

"Why are you telling me this now, Hank?"

From his hip pocket, he rescues his wallet and removes a folded slip of paper and holds it out.

"Read it."

"What is it?"

"Just read it."

When I unfold the paper, I'm immediately taken aback by

what I see.

American democracy will fail when...

› When civil rights cease to be applied to all citizens equally.

› When the First Amendment crosses the line of dangerous rhetoric.

› When the Second Amendment is abused.

› When corporations are deemed to be "people."

› When partisanship in Congress trumps non-partisanship.

› When money rules Congress & State Legislatures.

› When citizens fail to engage in the issues.

› When there is voter suppression.

› When eligible citizens fail to vote.

› When whoever is running the government rules like an Autocrat.

"Why are you showing me this now, Hank?"

"In his infamous book, Mein Kampf, Adolph Hitler wrote the way to take control of people was to chip away at their freedom by a thousand tiny and imperceptible reductions. Those words ring truer today than ever before. What is on that paper is a stark reminder of what can happen if we take what we have for granted. We did and it brought us down."

"I had no idea that you—"

"That I what, Billy? That I have a soul, a conscience, maybe even a little empathy? What I'm forced to do against my will is the only way I know to stay alive and so will you. Turn it over, read what's on the other side."

On the flip side is written...

"I agree with the Constitution with all its faults... I believe, further, that this is likely to be well administered for a course of years, and can only end in despotism, as other forms have done before it, when the people shall be so corrupted as to need a despotic government, being incapable of any other." Benjamin Franklin.

"When I'm down, when I think there is little hope, I read what's on that paper."

When I hand the paper back, Hank fingers it lightly, folds it, and puts it away... his eyes go to the street again.

"They've turned me into what I'm not, Billy. They're gonna do the same to you."

"Not if I can find a way out, Hank."

"There is no out, not for me, not for you, not for any of us."

"Then I'll die trying."

Seconds tick away with neither of us speaking... what could I add that would make sense of the madness we find ourselves prisoners of. Hank turns pensive again gazing out the window as several lost, hungry, and wanting souls pass by, no doubt in search of food and a warm place to spend the oncoming cold night.

"They'll come a time when each of us will be asked to stand up and be counted. What will we do when that time comes, Billy?"

"I told you, I'm gonna find a way out."

"And if you do, where will you go?"

"The Arizona Desert."

He arcs his head back and laughs.

"That'll put you close to Base-Arizona again."

"Perish the thought."

He offers me his hand... we shake... I slip out, open the back door, and fetch the computer box.

"Hey Billy, it wasn't my intention to depress you."

"Not any more than I already am, my friend."

"Keep the faith, this too will pass."

"From your lips to God's ear, Hank—assuming she's listening."

I wave as he drives off... I can't help but wonder why he felt the need to show me that paper now. As I turn to go inside, Jules is coming out flanked by two men in dark suits... he's white as a ghost and he looks terrified... Jesus, he's handcuffed.

"Billy, find Frank Wilson."

"Wilson? What's going on, Jules, who are these men?"

"Don't make a scene, Billy, just find Wilson... tell him they're taking me in."

"Who is taking you in, to where?"

"Wilson will understand, find him."

The three begin descending the steps... I block their way... one of the men puts a hand on my chest.

"Step aside, sir."

"What's going on here?"

"I asked you to step aside."

"Who the hell are you guys?"

He whips out his credentials and sticks them in my face.

"That says I can arrest you if you don't mind your own business."

A frightened looking Jules pleads with me.

"Billy, let it be, just call Frank Wilson, please."

Reluctantly, I let them pass... Jules is led across the street and placed in the back seat of a black SUV... he presses his face to the window and mouths Wilson's name as they drive off. What the hell just happened? Rushing upstairs, I place the computer box on the desk and pace... what am I supposed to do, it's Sunday, how will I find Wilson? I have no idea where he lives nor do I have his personal cell number... Jade, I'll call Jade... damn it, I don't have her cell either... try the office, maybe one of the joy boys are there... after four rings I'm surprised to hear Jade's voice.

"Billy, what's up?"

"Thank God you're in the office."

"I'm home. The office number is transferred to my cell on weekends."

"Can you contact the Lieutenant?"

"Sure, why?"

"Tell him two guys hauled my landlord Jules off in handcuffs. He told me to contact Wilson."

"Who took him away?"

"I don't know. One of them showed me his credentials. I just remember big black letters at the top before he pulled it away."

"Do you remember what those initials were?"

"WMD."

"Oh, crap."

"Oh crap, what, Jade?"

"WMD... World Ministry Deputy. They round up people and haul them off to internment camps."

My heart skips a beat... the camps Jules told me about...

"Jade, what would they want with Jules and how does he know Wilson?"

"We're wasting time, Billy. Let me reach out to Wilson."

"Okay, call me if you find him."

"Will do."

The afternoon slips by with no further word from Jade... I should call her... no, wait for her to call... at 6:00 PM I'm in the middle of fixing a sandwich when the phone rings.

"Billy, it's Jade, I finally made contact with Wilson. He said he understood and he'd take care of it."

"He understood what, Jade?"

"He said he'd take care of it. That's all I know."

"All right, if you hear from him, call me."

"I will."

As the evening slips away and there's no further word from Jade, I assume the worst... in my short time here the old curmudgeon has ingratiated himself into my life in the best of ways... now I'm worried for his safety. Get your mind off it, Billy, do something else... the computer, unpack it... turns out it's thinner than the one I had before winging my way through the endless Cosmos to Planet Europa. Awe hell, I'm too upset to screw with a computer now, I'll leave it for later... for now my thoughts are for Jules and his safety.

Sunday morning, there's still no update from Jade. *After I shower and dress, I descend the stairs and knock on Jules'ss door... no response... okay, go for a walk and clear the cobwebs... I walk aimlessly for a couple of blocks... there're Streetwalkers about, but none bother me when they spy my gun and badge. My mind is on Jules. Why was he arrested? Maybe he's involved in one of those dissident groups... I wouldn't be surprised if he was, he's sure as hell no fan of that reckless bunch of bigots in Marseille. When I arrive back at the house, I knock on his door again.*

"Jules, it's Billy, you in there?"

Still no response... now I'm really worried.... maybe Wilson didn't find him, or if he did, was unable to intercede on his behalf. I skip lunch in favor of a nap... I'm up by 2:00, descend the stairs, and knock-on Jules's door again... if he's in there he's avoiding me... I head upstairs and turn on the TV... unable to find a program that holds my interests, I consider opening the computer box when there comes a loud knock at the door. With gun in hand just in case, I make my way across the room and peer through the peephole... dear God, it's Jules! Unlocking the door, I swing it open... his face is drawn... he looks crestfallen.

"Please, Billy, don't tell me you're out of booze."

"Sorry, I am."

With his shoulders hunched forward, he moves sluggishly across the room, settles on the sofa, and lights a cigarette.

"What the hell was that all about?"

"Whoa, slow down, Billy, give me a moment to breathe."

He sucking on the cigarette one puff after another like he's afraid someone's going to take it away from him... I pour an inch of water in a glass, light a cigarette, and we use it as an ashtray.

"Jules, you're killing me here, what happened?"

"Thanks to you, Wilson came to my rescue."

"Jade found him, not me."

"Then I owe the lady a debt of gratitude."

"Rescue you from what, how do you know Wilson?"

"I was Captain Frank Wilson's top dog in the Marines—Master Sargent Julius Sommers at your service. Our unit was part of a joint UN peacekeeping mission tracking down terrorists in Northern Sudan. Frank took a couple of shots in the hip during the skirmish that followed that caused him that limp. The Marines offered him a desk job, but he chose to retire and go into law enforcement. When he joined the drug enforcement unit here, he talked me into buying this place and dividing the upstairs into two apartments the government could use to house the likes of you."

"Gee, thanks. Now, are you gonna tell me what happened?"

He takes a long drag on the cigarette, holds it, and exhales slowly.

"I was arrested by the misanthropic Police."

"Who?"

"World Ministry Deputies... better known as Défenseurs de la société... French for 'Defenders of Society.' The sons of bitches round up undesirables and haul them off to one of those camps I told you about. Wilson secured my release in the nick of time before they could ship me to one."

He takes a deep breath... it comes out as a long sigh.

"What crime did you commit?"

"None by my standards, Billy..."

His eyes go the floor... several seconds pass before he looks to me again... his eyes have teared up.

"... My sexual orientation by theirs."

"Oh Jules, I'm sorry."

Dousing his cigarette in the glass, he's up on his feet wiping away tears.

"Look, uh, I'm gonna get some rest. I wanted you to know I was back."

"Yes, rest. Come back later if you need to talk."

"Yeah, I'd think I'd like that. Around 6:30, I'll bring a

pizza and beer."

"Okay, but only if you feel up to it."

He lingers by the door... the man never makes a clean exit.

"They interrogated me like I was a criminal not fit to live among them. Their day is coming, and when it does, I'll spit in their homophobic faces."

As promised, at 6:30 Jules shows up with a large cheese and pepperoni pizza and a six-pack of beer... his ordeal has left him looking drained and morose.

"I see you bought yourself a computer."

"Yes, which hookup is the house wi-fi?"

"First connection at the top of the list."

Without further chit-chat, we settle at the table, pop open a couple of beers, and begin eating. We talk about everything other than his arrest... the weather, the homeless, the oppression of the Marseille government. When we finish off the pizza and a second beer, he pops to his feet.

"I know you want the details, Billy, but I can't talk about it now."

"I understand, Jules."

"I'm gonna lay down again."

"Good idea. I'm here if you need me."

At the door, he stops and turns back.

"They're evil sons of bitches, Billy... every last one of them. If we ever get them in front of a firing squad, I want to be one of the ones with a rifle."

And with that, the Energizer Bunny is gone... I feel great compassion for the guy... all those many years back, we had taken major steps to curb discrimination, but prejudices are part of our DNA... how else to explain it? I finally turn my attention to the computer... as soon as I plug it in and turn it on, up comes **'Welcome to Microsoft 2.10.'** *Nice to see they're still in business. The screen changes to,* **'What would you like to do?'** *Below that are links...* **'Set up - Check Mail – Contact List - Google Search - Take a Photo – WORD,**

Write Something Brilliant.' *They've certainly made it easy, even for a computer dummy like me. I chose* **'Surf the Web'** *and set up the wi-fi connection... bingo, it works right off... like a kid in an ice cream parlor, I'm connected to the world, but have no idea where to begin... in* **'Google Search'** *I type in* **'Official PPP Website.'** *The PPP's home page comes up... there's the familiar eagle... underneath that,* **'The Peoples Cooperative Populist Party, One World in Unity—World Headquarters Marseille, France. In the name of the Creator, all citizens of the world are loyal and supportive.'** *Yeah, I just bet they are. Below is a series of links to various PPP information sites... okay, now I know where you vermin live... I'll be back to read more of your bullshit when I'm in a more solid frame of mind... not promising when that might be. Checking Twitter and Facebook, I'm dismayed to see posts are still pumping out unfiltered trash-talk by those too cowardly to spew insults to someone's face ... again, nothing much has changed. Opening the* **'Write'** *program, up comes Microsoft Word... at least I'm familiar with that... I type my name and address and find like riding a bike my typing skills, although minimal, are still there. Maybe I'll write a memoir... I have a bunch of really depressing stories I can tell... since I've never written much more than a DEA report, I'll attempt to document my experiences on Europa along with all that is happening now. Placing my fingers on the keyboard, I begin with my first day on Europa and my humiliating naked walk past leering, catcalling inmates. Next, I detail my encounter with the drug dealer in that alley, the barn raid step-by-step as it unfolded, as well as Colonel Chernov's bizarre, sickening, inhumane behavior... seeing my words on the monitor brings back the repugnance I feel over those cold-blooded executions. Naming the file 'Stuff", I save it, turn off the computer, and look forward to adding more later.*

CHAPTER 18

Life's a Bowl of Cherry Pits

On my way out Monday morning, I knock on Jules's door...
he answers in his robe... he looks tired... the loose folds under
his eyes are darker and puffier than usual.

"Billy, I'm fine, go save the world for the rest of us."

"I'll try, but I make no promises."

His lips curl in an impish smile.

"Then try harder."

"Yes, sir, Sergeant Sommers."

My next stop is Sully's for a cup of his dark roast brew...
it's a major improvement over the office breakroom coffee... a
sweet human being in his sixties, Sully and I are now on a first
name basis. When I arrive at the office, it's empty except for
Hank.

"Where is everyone, Hank?"

"Jade is in the ladies powdering her lovely nose, Wilson's
in his office trimming his fingernails, Gustav and Victor are off
on their latest assignments for Chernov."

Leaning over his desk, I whisper to him.

"If your theory about those two is correct, someone's going
to end up dead."

"News at eleven."

Wilson sticks his head out of his office door.

"Billy, a moment, please."

"Yes, Lieutenant."

When I enter his office, he closes the door and invites me
to sit.

"About that business with Jules. Thanks for having the
presence of mind to call the office and connect with Jade. They

152

won't be bothering him again. I saw to that."

"He's pretty distraught over the whole affair, Lieutenant."

"Jules is like family to me. I'd appreciate your keeping an eye on him."

"I will."

"Okay then, no more talk about it."

The next three days are quiet with no firm leads coming from Chernov's office, which means no imminent raids for which I'm grateful... I have no desire to be witness to, or participate in, the execution of anyone beyond what I did to that creep who took my wife from me. Why we're even briefed before one of these raids is a mystery, since all that's necessary is to point us in the right direction, we show up, shoot a few people, and our work is done... next case. When this fifth new guy shows up, I'll suggest we make him the designated executioner... my contribution to streamlining the operation. On the brighter side, flirting with Jade has become an enjoyable pastime... now and again she graces me with a smile, which only encourages me... I ask her again to join me for that cup of coffee outside the office, but she offers the same excuse... she has to feed her damn cat... well, Ms. Miro, until you tell me to screw off, I remain your ardent pursuer. To ease the boredom, Hank and I patrol the streets... it's basically a waste of time unless, god forbid, Hank drags me into another alley shootout... during this joy ride we spot a couple of small time street deals going down.

"The hell with them, let the WPF deal with it."

"That's not what you said when we came across that alley, Hank. It could have gotten both of us ventilated with a couple of well-placed shots."

"But it didn't."

"But it could have."

"But it didn't, Billy, get over it."

Thursday morning, Gustav and Victor are back from wherever they've been... not a word out of either regarding their cryptic travels... neither Hank nor I dare ask. At the end of the day, Hank and I have dinner at a Mexican joint on Athens Street around the corner from the office.

"An ex-member of South Africa's Parliament was assassinated at his Johannesburg home Tuesday."

"What was his sin, Hank?"

"From what I read on the Internet this afternoon, he made a public speech condemning the regime. Gustav and Victor were gone long enough to have assassinated him and be back here this morning."

"And if we could prove their itinerary took them there, what do we do about it?"

"Absolutely nothing."

"Hear no evil, see no evil. Click our heels and follow orders like the good brainwashed executioners we are."

"If we know what's good for us, Billy, yeah."

At the end of the day, Hank offers me a lift home... I decline... dangerous as these streets can be, I enjoy my walks... today, the sun is kissing the far Western horizon in a spectacular array of orange, blue, and purple, courtesy of the diffusing smog... two side-by-side drones sweep down low over the middle of Broadway... smile Billy, you're on camera, if not those drones, then one of the camera's mounted on the poles... why the gang in Marseille and the vast network of WPF feel they have to be watching us all the time is beyond me. Three homeless souls approach with outstretched hands begging for a handout... as usual, when they spot my gun and badge, they slink away like I have a communicable disease... bleeding heart that I am, I wish there was something I could do for them. As I near the grocery and clothing stores, I'm alerted to loud voices coming from the alley... keep walking, Billy, don't stick your nose in... but then I hear someone groan loudly... damn it, I have to investigate. Entering the alley, I make out three figures halfway down... two white men are standing over a black man face down flat on his stomach... they're taking turns kicking him... whoa, Billy, you can't let that go... taking out my weapon, I move further in.

"Hey, what's going on back there?"

I might as well be talking to myself... they ignore me.

"Are you hard of hearing? I asked what was going on."

Now I have their attention... one of them yells.

"Who the hell are you?"

"A cop, that's who."

The man on the ground lifts his head in my direction.

"Thank God, mister, they would have killed me!"

He begins to push himself up, but one of the men jambs a foot on the back of his neck and pushes him flat again.

"Don't move a black muscle, boy."

Now the other guy is moving in my direction... I raise my weapon a few inches higher.

"Stay where you are, show me some identification."

"Hey, flatfoot, why do you care what happens to this piece of shit?"

"The same way I'd care if the situation was reversed."

He laughs—it's more of a cackle.

"Ladies and gentlemen, boys and girls, what we have here is a white-ass liberal cop."

"Show me some identification, or this bleeding-heart cop will haul you into the station down the street."

"Okay, mister policeman, you win... this time... keep up the good work now, ya' hear."

Before I can react, both men are racing to the far end of the alley and disappearing around the corner.

"Hey, mister, are you all right?"

The man rolls over onto his back.

"My ribs hurt like hell, but I'm okay."

Stashing my gun in my holster, I help him to his feet... Jesus, he's just a kid, maybe in his mid-twenties.

"You know those two?"

"Yeah, I seen them scum around. They're members of a South Boston white boys' gang that goes around harassing people like me."

"You know where we might find them?"

"They're everywhere, can't miss them."

155

"Maybe we should have your ribs checked."

"No, no, I'll be okay. Say man, you got anything to eat? I haven't had anything since yesterday morning—hardly enough to keep me alive."

"Sorry, I don't."

"There's a store out there... you could buy me something."

My first reaction is to help him, but if I said yes to every lost soul I pass on these streets, I'd go broke.

"No, I can't do that."

"Why in the hell not?"

His eyes narrow... his look turns belligerent... taking a step closer, he wraps a hand around my left wrist and squeezes.

"Take your hand off me."

But he doesn't, he squeezes harder.

"What's a little food to you, huh?"

"I'm not going to tell you again... take your hand off me."

With a twisted grin, he pumps his fingers on my arm.

"What you gonna do, shoot me with that big gun, white boy? Come on, buy me a sandwich, that's all I'm asking."

I brush his hand away.

"Back off."

"Something to eat, that's all, man."

The fool makes the mistake of grabbing my arm again... maybe it was the fresh memories of violent inmates on Europa picking fights at the drop of a hat... maybe this kid on this day is pushing me one step too far... that's when I lose it... in one swift motion, I whack him up-side the head with a tight right fist... he howls and goes down and yells at me.

"Why'd you do that, man, why? Fuck you, man, fuck you!"

"I told you to stop, didn't I, Kid? Come on, let me help you up."

As I reach down to help him, he slaps my hand away and spits in the face... now I'm thoroughly pissed... in an instant, my slow burn turns into a rage... dropping to his side, I whack him across the face with an open hand... he gets off a quick punch that grazes the left side of my face.

"What the hell's wrong with you, kid, stop it!"

For the second time in my life, I've sunk into an

uncontrollable rage... my left hand goes to his throat... I squeeze hard... I pummel his face with my right fist until I draw blood... Jesus, Billy, stop, what are you doing? Breathing hard, I fall back on my butt staring in frightened disbelief at the kid's bleeding face.

"Jesus, I'm sorry, kid, but you pushed me."

Reaching into my hip pocket, I fetch my handkerchief.

"Here, put this to your face."

The kid looks stunned... he takes the handkerchief and presses it to his bloody face. Tears come to his eyes.

"I'm sorry, man, I shouldn't have pushed you like that."

"It's okay, kid, we were both wrong."

"They don't treat us like humans, man. We're nothing to them, you know, nothing. We're just disposable numbers."

"I understand. Look, you should have your face looked at."

"No, I'll be okay."

"You're sure?"

"Yeah. I'm sorry for what I did, Officer—?"

"Russell. And you?"

"Vance. Say, you got a cigarette?"

"Yes."

I take out one of the last that Jules gave me and hand it to him along with my lighter.

"Come on, I'll help you up."

"No, I'm gonna sit here and smoke this cigarette."

"Okay, but don't be sitting here too long, those guys might come back."

God Almighty, what possessed me to lose it like that? Time to get my ass home and off these streets.

"Get yourself to a walk-in clinic and have those ribs checked."

"Yeah, maybe I will, thanks."

And with that I leave him sitting there... stopping briefly under the corner light by Sully's, I examine my hand... my knuckles are bloodied and the hand is swelling... how will I explain that when I go to office tomorrow? I'm not within twenty-feet of the house when someone calls out my name.

"Mister Russell?"

Jesus, is there a full moon, what now? Across the street from the house someone's waving to me from the open driver's window of a shiny new black Lexus... now the door's swinging open... a man's slipping out and coming toward me at a slow pace like he's trying to look non-threatening... whoa, he's a big one... over six-feet, broad shoulders and maybe a good two-hundred and fifty pounds. Is this the guy Jules said was nosing around asking questions? Now a second guy is exiting the front passenger seat and leans against the car... instinctively, my right hand goes to my Smith and Wesson. The big one's within ten feet of me now... I can make out his face... it's round and beefy and he's smiling trying to look his friendly best.

"Mister Russell."

"Do I know you?"

"My name is Norman."

"I don't know any Norman."

His right hand is rising slowly... a glint of steel flashes... cripes, he's got a gun... who the hell are these guys?

"With your index finger and thumb, please remove your weapon and place it at your feet. Do as I ask and no harm will come to you, Mister Russell."

"I have nothing of value if that's what you're after."

"Please, your weapon, sir."

"I'm a police officer."

"I'm quite aware of that. Now, please remove your weapon."

My grip on the Smith and Wesson tightens... I hesitate... a shootout on this darkened street would be suicide for one or both of us... and there's that other one... I have to assume he's armed too. I've been back less than two weeks and I'm within a few feet of some guy I don't know and he's pointing a weapon at me... live another day, Billy, do what the man's telling you. Removing my gun, I place it at my feet.

"Please step back, Mister Russell."

As this Norman guy swoops up my weapon and slips it in his belt, the other guy is coming around to the street side of the Lexus.

"Thank you, now please walk to the vehicle."

"Look, uh, Norman, I—"

He raises his gun a few inches.

"Please, Mister Russell."

"Okay, okay, stop pointing that damn gun at me."

I get a better look at the second guy as I approach the Lexus... he's short and skinny with a thin face... reminds me of Harvey who shot the GPS in my arm, only this guy's shorter... his eyes are hiding behind thick dark-rimmed black framed glasses... he holding up something black.

"Please place this over your head."

"A hood? What for?"

Norman places his hand on my shoulder.

"We mean you no harm, Mister Russell. Please, put the hood on."

"Look, whoever you are, you must have me mixed up with someone else."

"No, sir. Now, do as we ask and we'll be on our way."

The skinny one hands me the hood... I balk.

"I'm not putting that on."

"Don't make this difficult, Mister Russell."

"Who me, Norman? Difficult? Never."

Easy, Billy Boy, you're not holding the cards here... do as you're told before this goes badly.... I slip the hood over my head... it's lights out for me... I assume it's Mister Skinny taking my arm.

"Turn around and place your hands behind your back."

The damn fool handcuffs me.

"How about ankle chains too?"

"I'll guide you into the back seat, sir, watch your head."

The interior of the car smells like new leather.

"How many miles you got on this beauty?"

Neither of these deadheads answer my attempt to lighten things up, so stop with the jokes, Billy Boy.

"Slide over, sir."

Mister Skinny slips in next to me and we're off.

We've been traveling for about twenty-minutes with five stops along the way... I'm guessing for traffic lights... when we stop a sixth time, Norman turns off the engine... Mister Skinny places a hand on my arm.

"I'll guide you out, Mister Russell."

"You two get an A-plus for politeness. How about one of you tell me what this is about?"

No answer from either... not that I expected one, but it was worth a try... Mister Skinny helps me out... with his hand securely gripping my left arm, he guides me a dozen steps before we stop... a door's being unlocked... as it's opened my nose is assaulted by a musty odor.

"Can't afford the high-rent district?"

"I beg your pardon, sir."

"Forget it, Norman."

As we enter the building, I begin counting steps on what sounds like a wooden floor... twenty before we make a left turn... another ten then a hard right... a few steps further and I'm eased into a chair... I hear footsteps ... someone else has joined the party... the hood is removed and a bright light hits me hard in the eyes... with my hands cuffed, I can't shield them... I blink several times... beyond the light, I can make out a figure standing next to a chair... the light's too damn bright, I can't make out a face.

"Thank you for coming, Mister Russell. My name is Gideon."

Whoever's back there speaks with a pronounced British accent.

"Yeah, at gunpoint with a hood over my head."

"My apologies. I assure you you're in no danger."

"I'll take your word for that. It's late, I'm tired, get to the point."

Well, that came out sounding like one of my better threats... not a time to be a smart ass, Billy Boy... in case you hadn't noticed, there are now three of them now and one of you.

"What's with the light? It's blinding me."

A few seconds of silence.

"Well?"

Another few second's pass.

"Norman, turn it off, please."

"Are you sure, sir?"

"Yes, yes, turn it off."

"But, sir."

"It's fine Norman, turn it off."

"While Norman's at it, these cuffs are cutting into my wrists."

"Those as well, Norman."

Well, that was easy... if points are given for politeness, all three of these circus clowns win hands down... Norman removes the handcuffs and turns off the light... the room goes dark until the skinny one switches on an overhead fluorescent. We're in a small stockroom... unmarked cardboard boxes are piled high along the back wall... this Gideon character is decked out in an expensive-looking gray pinstripe suit, matching vest, off-white shirt, two-tone blue striped tie, and a full head of white hair neatly combed to the last strand ... he looks to be in his sixties and smells of money.

"Your right hand is bleeding, Mister Russell."

There's dried blood on my knuckles.

"Caught it in a door leaving the office."

Gideon eyes me suspiciously.

"Hmm. Norman, can we find something to wrap Mister Russell's hand?"

"Maybe in the restroom, sir."

Norman disappears to wherever the restroom is... he returns with a tan wash cloth.

"I soaked it in cold water. It should help."

Wrapping the washcloth around my hand it feels good on my swollen knuckles.

"Would you like anything, Mister Russell, water, perhaps?"

"A Cappuccino would be nice, Mister Gideon."

The stoic-looking Gideon raises an eyebrow, a signal he doesn't appreciate my tepid attempt at humor... now he pacing... five steps one way, five steps back... I steal a look over my shoulder at Norman... he pays me no attention... his eyes are locked on Gideon like a well-trained service dog. When he finally stops pacing, Gideon lowers himself to the chair and stares... I know when someone's sizing me up, and he's sizing me up.

"If you see anything you like, let me know."

"You're quite direct, Mister Russell."

"That's me, mister direct."

He stares for a few seconds more... I stare back.

"Are you settled in?"

"What?"

"Have you experienced difficulty assimilating since your return?"

"My return from where?"

"Why, Europa, of course."

How the hell could he possibly know that?

"Where did you get that information?"

"We are not without resources, Mister Russell."

"Apparently not. Look, Mister Gideon—"

"Please, just Gideon."

"You know nothing about me, Gideon."

"On the contrary, we know all there is to know. Your DEA record in Providence was quite exemplary. You were on the fast track to becoming a section supervisor until your wife's tragic death followed by that regrettable incident in that closet."

Dear Mother of God, who is this guy... how does he know what he knows?

"First of all, let's be clear, I have no regrets about what happened in that closet. Second, I have no idea what that or anything else has to do with my being brought here. Since you seem to be well informed about my past, you should know I just left one hell behind, I'm not looking to enter another. So, whatever you're selling, I'm not buying."

"You're still in hell, Mister Russell, just a different location."

There's a snappy but less than happy thought... he stands, slips a hand into his breast pocket and out comes a long, fat cigar... pinching off the end, he rolls the tip over his lighter's flame until it glows red.

"Forgive me, would you care for one, Mister Russell?"

"Can we skip the niceties and cut to the chase?"

"Yes, yes, of course... cut to the chase as you Americans are fond of saying."

We're also fond of saying screw off... how might you react to that, Gideon? Don't, Billy, hold your smartass tongue long enough to hopefully get out of here.

"Now then, to the point. We each live within the comfortable bubble we created for ourselves, and all too often it is what holds us back from doing what is right. Would you agree, Mister Russell?"

"I went to college to study law enforcement I leave the deep thinking to philosophers."

"This time, history will record how we came together to bring to an end to this evil government's totalitarianism, brutality, and inhumanity."

"I wish you the very best in that effort, but what does it have to do with me?"

"It has to do with every man, woman and child on the face of the Earth if there is ever again to be a free and democratic society."

"I'll assume you have a plan, Gideon, but whatever it is it's a fool's errand since this World Government commands the only military force on the planet."

I wait for him to share further intimate details of just how they hope to accomplish their lofty goal, but he doesn't... he plows on with his speech.

"Following the Pakistan-India event, all of society was gripped by fear. It exposed like never before mankind's deep-rooted hatred and intolerance of one another, which made it possible for the PPP to offer a lifeline that people latched onto before they realized what was behind it. By then it was too late."

Thanks to Jules, I have a pretty good idea just how sucked in people were.

"Over time, there have been many observers who have examined political populism. One of them was author Robert Penn Warren. In 1946, he released his novel titled 'All the

Kings Men'. By chance have you had an opportunity to have read it?"

"As a matter of fact, Gideon, I have."

"Mister Warren painted a vivid picture of a populist leader and those he led. The novel's main character, as you will recall, was modeled on the life and political career of Huey Long, infamous Louisiana Governor and U.S. Senator. Even though it was just a novel, we should have learned from it. All too often fiction can mirror life itself, in this case, the scoundrels behind the Peoples Populist Party. They are the well-healed, the aristocracy, major corporations, banks, and elected officials looking to ensure the continuation of the wealth and power they enjoy. Their worldview, as warped as it is, calls for a reshaping of society in service to them. It is nothing new really, just a reinvention of what was. Why the masses did not see that remains one of life's mysteries."

"Forgive me for interrupting, Gideon, but long before I left, we were skating on thin ice within a morally bankrupt system. When we close our eyes to political malfeasance, we relinquish our rights. So, plain and simple, Gideon, we blew it and have no one to blame but ourselves."

"Well said, Mister Russell."

"I try."

Why the hell am I debating this guy? And why is he being so open with someone he just met?

"And yet, all is not lost, Mister Russell. The people put this government in power and they can remove it."

"Good luck with that, sir."

"Underestimating the resolve of the people when their backs are to the wall would be a grave mistake, Mister Russell."

"If the past is your touchstone for what people will or will not do, you're betting on a loser."

"Not this time, not this time. Be assured our movement will remove this oppressive den of thieves and cowards who use thuggery to achieve their vainglorious goals."

"Impressive words, but I don't trust the vast majority to get together on much of anything, let alone the overthrow of this government."

Gideon takes a deep drag on his cigar and blows perfect smoke circles... Jules would love this guy.

"Are you familiar with the term 'volte-face', Mister Russell?"

"Can't say that I am."

"It is French, meaning a reversal in policy, a change in direction... a rather benign moniker for a Byzantine task that will bring to an end the pestilence of tyranny by those who hold an entire civilization hostage. Make no mistake, we will purge these latet anguis in herba from the face of the Earth."

"The what?"

"Latet anguis in Herba'... Roman for 'Snakes in the Grass.'"

"Uh, I failed Italian class... or was it Latin, I forget?"

He ignores my acerbic remark and plows on.

"Allow me an abridged version of what occurred during your forced absence."

Save your breath, Gideon, Jules gave me an abridged version of our dreadful state of affairs... his version was enough to depress me for a lifetime.

"I would rather you get to the reason I was brought here."

He ignores me... he's pacing again... I've listened to enough of his bullshit.

"This one-sided gab fest is over. Norman, be a good man and take me home."

I try to stand, but Norman's baseball-sized mitt left-hand is on my shoulder pressing me down.

"Please remain seated until Gideon has finished."

"Are you threatening me, Norman?"

"No, Mister Russell, advising."

Since Norman's bigger than me by a third again, that settles that... Gideon moves on like nothing happened.

"Pakistan's iniquitous attack on India was humanity's red line in the sand, a spiritual awakening, at least for those capable of comprehending the ramifications of such an evil act. But as always, we resorted to praying, hoping The Almighty would take pity on us when in fact we should have found the courage to do something about it ourselves. If we had stepped back long enough and examined the PPP's populist pie-in-the-sky solutions, we might have concluded these snake oil salesmen's true goals were world domination, greater personal profits, and the preservation of the white race as the master of all races."

"Save your breath, I know the rest."

I shift in my chair... Norman thinks I'm getting up again and places his left claw on my shoulder... I glance up and smile... he doesn't... Gideon doesn't skip a beat.

"There is a French billionaire who played critical role in the PPP becoming a world political party. He and other like-minded men cleverly captured the desperation, acrimony, and bigotry of the masses. Jean Lumiere Laurent, President and controlling shareholder of MAXMinerai was..."

The name MAXMinerai stop me cold!

"Yes, Mister Russell, your former employer and jailer."

"Holy Christ."

"The PPP that began in this country was well-funded by Mister Laurent and others with the end goal of establishing a world party and then a world government. Once the world government became a reality, Laurent was promptly proclaimed President for life, not by a public election, but by the unanimous proclamation of his handpicked World Council. The elites had taken total ownership of the world without ever firing a shot. As for Mister Laurent, he is known as the shadow President because he never appears in public unless whatever he has to say is prerecorded. More often than not his henchmen do all the public speaking for him."

"Why is that?"

"He is an extremely private man to the extreme."

"Forgive me if I'm not impressed, Gideon. I've always lived by what my father drilled into me, that is, if a man or woman amass great wealth and power, it does not make them smart or a moral, just someone who tapped into a niche that made them wealthy and powerful. I've never understood what makes a person believe they are better than any other because of their wealth and leverage over others, but hey, that's just me."

Gideon's lips curl into a slight grin like maybe he knows stuff I don't... he inhales his cigar deeply, savoring the carcinogens that one day will curse him and the rest of us smokers with the lung disease that did in poor Leon Grover.

"Do you know who Commissioner Henry Dion is?"

"I heard his name on the news. Sounds like he's out of favor with the Marseille gang."

"Once a successful Boston trial attorney and political activist, Henry was an early supporter of the PPP. All else had failed, he reasoned, why not try something new. He ran for the United States Senate on the Populist ticket and won. When the PPP morphed into a world party and put forth the idea of a World Government and won, Henry supported it and was awarded a seat on the newly created World Council."

"Sound like Mister Dion was as naïve as all the others."

"Yes, he fell for it, at least for a time. But after Laurent was proclaimed President for life, Henry rightfully concluded he had made a terrible mistake, that President Laurent and his minions were nothing more than autocratic, megalomaniac, corporate charlatans playing a human chess game to satisfy their narcissistic appetites. He realized there was no way to defeat them through a public campaign, so he began organizing the Volte-face movement in secret. Today, millions upon millions the world over stand ready to cut off the head of the snake."

"What will they fight with, sticks, ball-bats, pitchforks?"

A smile crosses Gideon's lips as if once again he knows what I don't.

"Are you familiar with the term 'Black Swan Event?'"

"Can't say I am."

"It is a metaphor describing an incident that leaves an indelible mark on society. Although the PPP is guilty of many, it only takes one Black Swan Event to crumble their fragile house of cards. With the help of others, Henry has uncovered that one event, an abominable sin against humanity that the public is unaware of."

Gideon looks away and goes silent... his thoughts seem to have slipped elsewhere... I wait, but I've never been accused of being a patient man.

"I can't say this hasn't been fun, Gideon, even the high point of my evening. But you still haven't told me why I'm here."

This guy may know all about my past, but for the love of me, I can't understand why he's revealing this much to me.

"During a televised event, Henry will reveal to the world all that he has learned. While that telecast is in progress, he and others will require sentinels for a short period of time while—"

"Ah, finally, there it is. I qualify for your SWAT team because I took the life of a man in a closet, or that I work for an outfit that executes drug lords and their underlings."

No answer from Mister Gideon… I'm getting more pissed by the second.

"I wish you great success with this Volte-face thing, but I'm just a dumb cop with a GPS tracker embedded in my left forearm and strapped to a job I didn't seek and looking to get out of."

"Perhaps this is your way out, Mister Russell."

"So, I should cast my lot with you on the outside chance it could benefit me in some way? Give me a break."

He takes two quick steps toward me and points a finger.

"Do not tell me you were jumping for joy by the world that greeted you upon your return. Do not tell me you were not appalled by the brutal beating of a handcuffed man on your first day, or the drug dealer you and Officer Drummond confronted in that alley that was later executed by two of your own, or the cold-blooded execution of five men and a woman left to be cremated in a burning warehouse. Because if you do, Mister Russell, if you do, I will be forced to label you a liar."

Christ, where in hell does this man get his information?

"Have you considered that when I leave here I'll turn you and this Volte-face thing over to the authorities?"

"And for what reason, Mister Russell? To gain favor with a government that threatens to send you back to prison if you refuse to participate in their cold-blooded executions?"

"You think you know me, but you don't, Gideon."

"I know enough to trust that you are a decent and moral

man. Considering the circumstances, some might even forgive you for your crime of passion."

"Tell that to the jury who convicted me."

"Do you know who George Orwell was, Mister Russell?"

"I'm not illiterate. I read '1984'."

"In his insightful novel, Mister Orwell wrote. 'For if leisure and security were enjoyed by all alike, the great mass of human beings who are normally stupefied by poverty would become literate and would learn to think for themselves; and when once they had done this, they would sooner or later realize that the privileged minority had no function, and they would sweep it away. In the long run, a hierarchical society was only possible on a basis of poverty and ignorance.'"

"Bravo, Gideon, you have excellent memory recall. As for me, I don't expect the human race to come to their senses anytime time soon, nor do I have a burning desire to participate in some political movement that's doomed to failure before it gets off the ground."

"You're wrong, Mister Russell. The Volte-face movement will define mankind from this moment on. We will sweep away this government and create a democratic society that spans the entire globe."

He backs away from me a couple of feet... turns and strolls back to his chair and sits.

"I've taken far too much of your time, Mister Russell. If you decide not to join us, your decision will be respected. I ask only that you not reveal to anyone what took place here."

"I find it really surprising that you trust that I won't."

"Norman will provide you with a phone number."

"What am I supposed to do with it?"

"It is our hope that in the coming days, once you have searched your soul, you will offer your assistance. If you do, identify yourself only as 556. At that time, you will be provided further instructions."

Damn, he even knows 556 was my call sign on Europa... I can't help but smile at the irony.

"Thank you for coming, Mister Russell."

In a swirl of cigar smoke, Gideon is up on his feet and

abruptly makes an exit... Norman hands me a slip of paper...
without looking at it, I stuff it in my shirt pocket.

"We'll take you home now, Mister Russell."

I glance over at the skinny guy with a blank page for a
face.

"Norman, does your friend here have a name?"

"It's Jason."

"Jason, do I get to wear the hood again?"

"I'm afraid so, sir."

"Do I get to keep it?"

"If you like, Mister Russell, I have others."

"Uh, you brought more."

"A six-pack, actually."

At least Jason has a sense of humor... score one for him...
now I need to work on Norman.

CHAPTER 19

An Unexpected Visitor

For the ride back, I'm hooded but not handcuffed... I must have passed the threat test... I instruct Norman to drop me off at the corner newsstand... the last thing I need is for Jules questioning where I've been. When we arrive, Jason removes the hood.

"Good night, Mister Russell."

"Nothing much good about it, Jason."

"Be positive, Mister Russell, look on the bright side."

"Been trying for the past seventeen years without much success. But, hey, meeting you guys has given me hope."

"Are you being sarcastic, Mister Russell?"

"Yeah, Norman, I am. Good night, sleep tight."

As they pull away in their shiny black Lexus, they toss me a friendly wave like we're now best buds forever... humor them, Billy, wave back. What am I to make of this night's inexplicable meet and greet with Gideon the proper Englishman and his two trained Dalmatians? Wasn't Europa enough punishment for one lifetime? No sooner am I back on terra firma, I'm hijacked by some questionable dissident group with the whimsical name Volte-face they believe will save the world from a bunch of rich, lunatic, power hungry, greedy, autocrats, and in some cockamamie patriotic way, me, the son of Amelia and Alistair Russell from Orban, Scotland, would be willing to place his ass on the line to overthrow the government... it'll take more than a patriotic speech to get me to risk life and limb. And there's the question of where they got that information about me... maybe one of them is smart enough to have hacked into the office computer. So much for secrecy. Whatever this Volte-face is, it has zero chance of succeeding against the evil empire's armed forces, so best I stay clear of whatever they're doing. With any luck, of which I've had little to speak of, I'll never see Gideon, Norman or Jason again. Oh, crap, there's a man and a woman walking toward me... I'm in no mood to deal with panhandlers, not tonight... wait, it looks like the Asian couple I met my first night here... they must recognize me because they're backing away.

"Sorry, don't want any trouble, Officer."

"Me neither. Where are you headed?"

"Sometimes we spend nights in the alley between the clothing and grocery stores."

"Stay out of that alley, it's not safe. Are you two married?"

"Yes, sir."

"How long have you been living out here?"

The old man looks at the women like he's not sure... she answers.

"We ran a small tailor shop but had to close eight months ago."

"You have no place to go, no family that would take you in?"

"No, sir."

I know what I want to do, but I also know it's a bad idea... but suddenly I feel compelled to help these two... maybe because I didn't help that kid in the alley.

"Look, uh, tomorrow morning I'll be walking along Broadway around 7:30. If you're by the grocery store, I'll get you some food."

The old man's eyes light up.

"You would do that, sir?"

"Yes. Are either of you on drugs?"

"No, sir."

"Been arrested for anything?"

"No, sir."

"Okay then, if you're at the store when I pass by, I'll get you food."

They're staring at me no doubt wondering who this crazy man is offering his help.

"Goodnight. And remember what I said, that alley is not safe, stay out of there."

The old lady leans close to me and touches my arm lightly.

"Thank you, Officer. God be with you."

If God exists, Lady, you two need He, She, or It more than I do. When I reach the house, there's a fastback-Volkswagen Arteon parked in front behind that same blue Honda I saw leaving the other morning. Climbing the steps to the front door, I unlock it, step inside, and switch on the light at the top of the stairs... Jules's door swings open... he's in his robe.

"Jesus, Jules, you scared the crap out of me."

I stuff my swollen hand in my pocket.

"Where have you been?"

"I wasn't aware I needed your permission to go out after dark."

"I told you, it's dangerous out there."

"You forget I'm a cop with a gun full of real bullets. Whose cars are out front?"

"I have company and you've kept yours waiting—the female type—showed up ten minutes ago in that Volkswagen."

"What are you talking about?"

"That lady cop, Jade, the one who stocked your fridge, the one who located Wilson when they hauled me away. I thanked her and let her in."

My heart skips a beat... my eyes shoot to the top of the stairs.

"Oh, yeah, Jade."

"She's a damn good looker that one is."

"Yeah, she said she might bring over some files."

"Didn't see any files, just a brown paper bag."

"Okay, Jules, thanks."

"You're welcome. And stop roaming the damn streets after dark."

"You're, uh, you're okay now, right?"

"Fine, fine, Billy, stop asking. Go, don't keep the lady waiting."

As soon as Jules closes his door, I ascend the stairs two at a time when a disturbing thought hits me... if Jade was the one who stocked my fridge, might she know what only Wilson, Chernov, and now this Gideon guy knows about my past? Play it cool, Billy, don't bring it up unless she does. When I swing the door open, she's draped at one end of the sofa looking like a supermodel in a magazine ad for an expensive women's cologne... she's decked out in tan slacks that hug her long shapely legs like a glove... a light blue shirt hangs loosely to the top of her hips... neatly folded next to her is a waist-length black leather coat and a small brown paper bag... she doesn't smile... just stares with those penetrating eyes of hers.

"Been bowling, Billy?"

"A little fresh air, that's all."

"There's no fresh air anymore, just nitrogen gas, carbon dioxide, carbon monoxide, hydrocarbons, and nitrogen oxides."

"Don't say that out loud or everybody will want some. What are you doing here?

Without thinking, I remove my hand from my pocket... her eyes go to it.

"What happened to your hand?"

"Stupid me tripped and fell and scraped my hand on the sidewalk on the way home."

"Do you have anything to put on it?"

"Not really."

"Then wash it good."

"Give me a minute."

A quick wash of my swollen hand and I'm back wondering why she's paying me this unexpected visit.

"So, what brings you to my lavish penthouse pad?"

She scans the room... her sullen expression telegraphs her disapproval.

"Needs work."

"You're being kind. Want something? All I have is water and coffee. I don't recommend the water."

Reaching into the paper bag, she pulls out a bottle of Bourbon.

"I assume the first one was good to the last drop."

"What did I do to deserve this generous gesture, Jade?"

"Don't look a gift horse in the mouth, my friend."

174

"That's a cliché, young lady."

"Be quiet and pour us a drink."

"Yes, ma'am."

Okay, what's happening here, I'm getting mixed signals... draping my jacket on the back of a kitchen chair, I fetch a couple of glasses, join Jade on the sofa, and pour us shots... she raises her glass in a toast.

"To better times, Billy."

"And may I add, Jade Miro, may they come sooner than later."

She downs the shot in one gulp and holds out her glass.

"Two's my limit."

"Two it is then."

I pour her another... this one she sips.

"So, what it is that Billy Russell does for fun?"

"Dodging garbage cans, watching drones watching us. Entertaining stuff like that."

For the first time since I met her, she laughs.

"Forgive me, Billy, it's your sardonic sense of humor."

"Ah yes, my life's goal was to be a sardonic standup comic."

She smiles warmly and I melt... we sit quietly for a couple of beats... there's a rumble going in my head about bringing up the taboo subject... don't, Billy, you'll regret it... oh, hell, get it off your chest.

"You know, don't you?"

"Know what, Billy?"

Instantly, I regret bringing it up.

"Nothing, forget it."

"What is it that I know?"

The rule is, once you place a foot in your mouth, you're required to remove it and think fast.

"That I was once a bullfighter in Mexico City."

Her left eyebrow rises... if one can be visually spanked, I'm being spanked.

"What do I know, Billy?"

Now that I've opened the trap door, I have nowhere to go with this but down... okay, put it out there and see where it lands.

"Where I've spent my days and nights for the past seventeen years." *Her brow furrows.*

"Ah, that, well I, uh—"

She blows a breath... her eyes stray to the window pausing there for what feels like an eternity.

"I keep the office records, Billy, remember?"

"Well now, there's no putting that Jack back in the box, so we'll let it go at that and move on."

"Now you're angry with me."

"No, Jade, just curious why you didn't let me know right off."

She shrugs... it's almost as good as one of my practiced shrugs.

"Besides the booze, was there a reason for this visit, or is this be social to the new guy week?"

"Do you always pepper your conversation with cynicisms?"

"Come on, Ms. Miro, truth or dare, what brought you here this fine evening?"

"Were you born obtrusive, Billy, or do you have to work at it?"

"Answer my question."

She shakes her head and blows a hard breath.

"Okay. Maybe I see a wounded warrior that needs a lifeline."

"Wounded warrior? That's a good one. I assure you I can take care of myself."

"So far you haven't demonstrated that, Billy."

"If you mean that business with Gustav and Victor, it'll blow over."

"Those two are the last on the planet you want to be on the wrong side of. If you haven't noticed, they take their work seriously and—"

"Work? Is that what the hell we're calling it? Oh wait, I forgot, we provide a valuable service by reducing the population."

"I'm just saying, they don't take kindly to anyone calling

them out."

"Is that what I did?"

"Jesus, Billy, you're thick headed. Be forewarned, Gustav and Victor hold special status with Chernov. One word from them and you're gone."

"What makes you think I don't want to be gone? Besides, if they haven't canned me yet, I don't suspect they will."

"Don't cross them is all I'm saying, Billy."

"I already have, Jade."

Then comes one of those pregnant pauses that drive me nuts... I wait for her to pick it up, but she doesn't, so it's up to me... engage her Billy, seek more answers.

"Let's switch gears."

"To what?"

"What's really going on out there."

She leans back, crosses those lovely legs, and takes a long, slow breath.

"I assume you're up to speed on the Pakistan-India debacle?"

"Unfortunately, yes."

"Well, as the saying goes, we have met the enemy and he is us. For the first time since the atomic bomb was dropped on Hiroshima, Pakistan and India drove home the reality that we could wipe ourselves off the face of the planet if trigger happy idiots got into a worldwide pissing match. What it comes down to is our survival as a species. Pakistan and India drove that reality home with a six-inch spike."

"Jade, what I've seen on the streets isn't survival, it's desperation. There's no solution as long as these Fascists are holding all the cards."

"Don't be so sure, Billy."

"Hmm, an ambiguous answer at best."

I'm hoping she expands on that, but she doesn't.

"Okay, let's go for door number two. That big, fancy, flashing population billboard on Boston Harbor was destroyed by some dissident group calling themselves Apostolic Channel challenging the regime's population reduction policies. What exactly are the PPP's policies?"

"It's a slash and burn take no prisoners cleansing of the old, the sick, the poor, people of color, and anyone else who has fallen on hard times."

"Wow, I'm touched by their empathy."

"Or lack of. It's the age-old story, Billy, I have mine, you don't, we get to make the rules, you get to follow them. The only difference between what used to be and what is now is how this regime openly uses brutality to enforce their rules."

"What about children, I haven't seen one under ten or twelve years old."

"And you won't, either. It's zero births until further notice."

"You're kidding?"

"Until overpopulation is brought under control, if a woman becomes pregnant, she's forced to get an abortion. And if one slips through and discovered, the baby becomes a ward of the State and the parents taken away."

"To where?"

"One of their rehabilitation camps."

"My God, what have we become?"

"Try Nazi Germany circa 1933 on for size."

I pour myself another shot and offer Jade one, she declines... I still have more questions.

"How does this all work, how do sovereign countries interact with this World Government?"

"Nothing has changed except countries are now restricted to internal affairs only—the PPP makes the global rules. To ensure those rules are adhered to, countries are overseen by one of the regime's hand-picked generals. Here the top-dog is General Albert Joseph Natali, formerly of the defunct Joints Chiefs of Staff. For the love of me, I don't understand his loyalty to Marseille, but there it is. When those shiftless bastards took over, democracy became just another nine-letter word. First came censorship of the press. Then they tried shutting down social media sites other than those controlled by the government. Ha, nice try, the public wasn't buying that crap. So, Marseille settled for regulating what could and could not be posted. Keep it simple and never make mention of government policies unless you are in praise of them. These narcissistic villains have taken ownership of an entire civilization with the sole agenda of appropriating wealth and power for themselves and their cronies, and what happens to a wide swath of the world population is immaterial. Sorry to paint such a grim picture, but you asked, there's the reality."

"I fail to understand why people continue to put up with it. There was a time we stood up to political villains once we caught on to them."

"Accept these bad actors took it to the next level by consolidating the world under their authority. Now they're free to rape and pillage at will."

"In one of our conversations, my landlord, Jules, whipped out a twenty-dollar bill to make the point money controlled our lives. How right he was. Whoever has the gold, makes the rules."

"That will never change, Billy."

"What about this Commissioner Henry Dion? There was a story about him on the news."

"Henry Dion speaks to power, one of the few that dares. We need more like him."

"And they'll end up in a cell or worse just like Dion will."

"Don't be so sure."

"You know something I don't?"

"I never lose faith, Billy. Without it we have nothing."

"And then closer to home is this drug kingpin, Alvera. Chernov seems obsessed with him."

"Alvera, hmm, where do I begin with that ball of trouble. He's a dangerous dude who controlled the flow of drugs in and out of Columbia before the Police began closing in on him. That's when he fled the country and quietly reemerged on our East Coast. Hell, it was a year before the authorities even knew he was here. In that year he gained control of most of the manufacture and the flow of drugs throughout New England by eliminating much of his competition Mafia style. As for his product, make it cheap, sell it cheap, and make it addictive as hell. The problem is, those who don't have money to buy drugs prey on those who do, so it has led to a lot of petty crime and violence."

"How difficult can it be to find one man?"

"They don't call him 'Ghost Dog' for nothing."

She holds out her glass.

"Thought you said two was your limit?"

"Just pour, Mister Russell."

I do… she looks me in the eyes, grins, and downs it in a single gulp.

"You know they plan to test you next time out."

"I'll cross that bridge when I come to it."

"Cross your bridges carefully, Billy."

"I intend to. So, you know all about me, yet I know nothing about you. Where does Jade Miro fit in this out-of-focus black and white picture?"

"Not much to tell. I'm the only child of a Hawaiian mother and a Japanese father, both deceased, mom from cancer, dad from a heart attack. So much for my genes. I graduated with a degree in psychology from Boston University and took a position with the Boston PD treating cops suffering from psychological stress. Because police work is one of the most stressful careers anyone can choose, many burn-out sooner than later. After five years, their anxieties and stress began to become mine—I couldn't do it anymore. When the drug unit was being formed, this job became available. Since it was still law enforcement, I applied. Wilson liked my resume and hired me. That's the short and long of it."

"Were you aware of what the unit did when you signed on?"

"Hell no, Billy, otherwise I wouldn't have applied. I only knew the unit dealt with drug enforcement and that interested me."

"And yet, you stayed on. Why?"

"Were you given a choice to leave?"

"I wasn't offered a choice on anything in over seventeen years, remember?"

"Neither was I, neither were Hank or Rod. We're their prisoners as long as they're in power."

"And Gustav and Victor?"

"Different animals all together. Make no mistake, they answer to Chernov, not Wilson."

"So, what's the answer, Jade? What do we do?"

"We have no plans to punt, that's for sure."

I want to ask if she's knows anything about this movement called Volte-face, but that's risky... she'll want to know where I heard of it and I will have backed myself into a corner for a plausible answer... shift gears, time to get personal.

"You're what, Jade, thirty-six, thirty-seven? No rings, so I assumed there's no husband. Maybe a boyfriend waiting at home?"

"If you must know, Mister nosy, I was married to a Boston cop. It didn't work out. And I'm thirty-eight by the way, and no, no boyfriend waiting at home."

She glances at her watch and feigns a sigh.

"Show and tell is over, time to go."

"To feed your cat?" *Her head bobs back and she laughs.*

"I don't have a cat. Let's leave it at that. Oh, one last question before I go."

"Shoot?"

"Space, it must have been a mind-blower."

"That wouldn't come close to describing the incredible sights I was privileged to witness and the inevitable questions it left me with. It was a life-altering experience, but in a positive way."

"Another time you'll tell me all about it."

"Yeah, another time."

She's up slipping on her coat and moving to the door... her hand wraps around the doorknob... she lingers for a beat before turning back.

"We were raised to believe in American exceptionalism, that we were better than the rest of the world, that's what's happening now was never supposed to. We've survived wars, the race to the moon and beyond, the 9/11 attack in 2001, the COVID virus in 2020, the worldwide recession that followed, the Pakistan-India catastrophe, and now the biggest test of all —the soul of humanity is up for grabs. I believe with all my heart that this too shall pass one day soon. And when that day comes, each of us will be called upon to do our part."

"From your lips to God's ear… assuming She's listening."

She tosses her head back and laughs.

"The stuff that comes out of your mouth, Billy Russell. Okay, gotta go. Mum's the word I was here."

"Jade, about what happened at the warehouse."

"Ancient history, Billy, put it behind you."

"I meant you—you're okay?"

She smiles and nods reassuringly.

"Good night, Jade, thanks for the booze and the education."

"You're most welcome, Buckaroo."

CHAPTER 20

An Eye Opener

Old habits die hard... it's 5:30 in the morning and I'm awake... as usual, my dreams were in control of my sleep and I don't know how to stop them... last night was a mental mash-up of the encounter with that kid in the alley, my less than electrifying meeting with Gideon and his trained canines, Norman and Jason, and Jade's surprise, but welcome visit... I'm ready to shower the lady with words I haven't spoken in decades... slow down, Billy Boy, you're getting ahead of yourself... you hardly know her, she hardly knows you... don't smother her or you'll spook her for sure. Since I'm up, might as well have coffee and something to eat... scrambled eggs in lots of butter sounds pretty good... or maybe a nice bowl of oatmeal... perish the thought. Following breakfast, I fire up the computer and open my 'stuff' file. I'm going to keep making notes of my time on Europa... I have no idea why... maybe it'll help purge the memory of that hellhole as well as the closet encounter that ended my freedom. I have yet to feel the slightest twinge of remorse for what I did... an eye for an eye... that's what it came down to, end of story. Then there's the question of why I'm talking to myself. At 7:20, after making copious notes of my time on Europa, I'm down the stairs and out the door... Jules is there in his robe marching up and down the sidewalk with his trusty ball bat in hand.

"Good morning, Jules, what's going on?"

"Look over there, some lowlife pissed on my steps."

Sure enough, I had stepped over a puddle of yellow liquid on the bottom step.

"It must have been a dog since I haven't seen any moose

around?"

"Not funny, Billy. From my window, I saw the sub-human that did it. By the time I rushed out the son-of-a-bitch was gone."

"Jules, calm down, it'll wash off."

"Oh, gee, thanks, maybe you'll do it for me."

"Hold your breath, old man."

"I heard the foxy lady leave last night. Strike out, did we?"

"I told you, Jules, she was here on official business."

"Yeah, and I was a two-star general in the Marines."

"Bye, Jules, have a nice day."

Off I go up 4th Street while Jules is yelling and waving the bat above his head.

"Okay, you sons-of-bitches, the next one I see anyone hanging around my stoop, I'm going to beat their ass good with this bat!"

Go get them, Jules. Skipping coffee at Sully's, I move on down Broadway... there's the usual number of Streetwalkers... I see the Asian couple huddled by the grocery store.

"Good morning."

"Good morning, sir."

"Dare I ask where you spent the night?"

Neither replies.

"Okay, I have to get to the office, let's get you some food. Will they let you in the store?"

"No, sir, not unless we have money to spend and we don't."

"Okay, wait here. By the way, what are your names?"

"Mei, husband is Zen."

"I'm Billy. Do you have any preference for what food you'd like?"

"You choose, sir."

"Okay, I'll be right back."

Approaching the store's door, I pause and glance to the alley and hope the hell the kid was okay after I left. Inside, I pick up a loaf of sliced bread, sliced ham, sliced Swiss cheese, a couple of apples, and two one-gallon jugs of water... with my arms wrapped around two bags, I return to the old couple, but my attention is immediately drawn to the alley entrance with the arrival of an ambulance and WPF patrol car.

"What's going on over there, Zen?"

"Somebody said a dead man was found in the alley."

Oh, God, no, no! I left Vance sitting there having a cigarette. Okay, pull it together, Billy, give them the food and get out of here.

"Be careful, don't let anyone steal it from you."

I pass the lighter bag to Mei and the heavier one with the water jugs to Zen... he smiles, Mei's eyes tear up.

"Thank you for your kindness and generosity, Billy. May God bless you."

"And you also, Mei and Zen. Stay safe."

My attention goes back to the alley where a small crowd has gathered watching two EMS men rolling out a gurney carrying a black body bag.

I slip my swollen hand in my pocket before entering the office. Jade greets me with a smile... not a good morning smile, but an 'I'm glad I visited you last night' smile... at least that's the way my brain sees it.

"Good morning, Billy."

"Morning, Jade, Hank."

Hank smiles and nods... I make no attempt to acknowledge Gustav or Victor, nor do they me. Lieutenant Wilson pops his head out his door... he looks excited about something.

"Everybody in my office."

Gustav and Victor are first in and take the only two chairs... Hank, Jade and I stand by the window... Gustav shoots me a sideways glance and smirks... I smirk back... Wilson lights a cigarette... first time I've seen him smoke... and in the office yet... something's got him fired up.

"Colonel Chernov thinks he got a solid lead on Alvera's location. You know how bad the Colonel wants the big prize, so do I, so should you, so no screw ups if and when this comes down."

"What do we know?"

"No more than I've just told you, Gustav. Chernov's playing it close to the vest until he's got it nailed down tight. Until then, get out on the streets, make it a productive day, and bust some heads to stay in practice. If I get further word from Chernov, Jade will call you in. That's it. Billy, stay."

Wilson waits until the others have filed out before limping to the door and closing it... a sure sign I'm gonna get chewed on for something or other.

"Take a seat, Billy."

He looks miffed... like when he chewed on me for getting into it with Gustav and Victor on my first day... he raises the lid of his laptop, taps a few keys and stares at the monitor until whatever he's looking for comes up... his eyes come to me.

"Anything unusual happen on your way home last night?"

"No, nothing, why?"

"Uh huh. WPF's Captain Morris down the hall sent this to me this morning."

He's rotating the laptop so now we both can see the monitor... he taps a key... video begins... it's dark, but it's clearly the entrance to the alley on Broadway.

"A dead man was found in that alley this morning."

He turns back to the monitor as a figure comes out of the alley, turns left, and disappears.

"They found a dead black kid in there. Looks like he was beaten to death. Facial recognition identified you as the man coming out of the alley, Billy."

"Yeah, uh, well—"

"No bullshit, give it to me straight."

"Well, I, uh, I was on my way home and heard a commotion in the alley and went in to investigate. There was a young black man on the ground being attacked by two white guys. When they saw me, they turned and hauled ass out of there."

"And the victim?"

"His face was beat up and he thought a couple ribs might be broken. I offered to get him help, but he refused. He asked me for a cigarette, I gave him one and left him sitting there.

That's it. The two white guys must have come back after I left, Lieutenant."

"Somebody got to him."

Wilson turns back to the monitor, takes a breath and expels it slowly, then places a finger on the 'delete' button and presses down.

"That's the end of it. Next time stay the hell out of alleys or at least cover your ass and call it in."

Forgetting my bruised right hand, I take it from my pocket and stand... Wilson eyes go to it.

"Go on, get out of here. And you better have someone take a look of that hand."

I make it out of there without further comment. I'm not sure what that was all about or why he felt the need to show me that video. Was he telling me he thinks I killed the kid? If he does, since what we do around here is end people's lives, I take it he approves.

Hank and I are cruising the extreme end of South Boston, Gustav and Augier are off to the North end. I can't get that kid's death out of my mind... I could have insisted that he be checked out at a medical facility and that would have saved his life.

"Hey, Billy, are you in there?"

"What?"

"You seemed zoned out this morning."

"Just thinking, Hank."

"Anything you wanna share?"

"Nah, it was pornographic."

"In that case share, pal, share."

We come across a couple of street dealers plying their trade, but nothing Hank wants to risk life and limb for... that's fine with me. At 11:45 we arrive at Maggie's.

"What's the insult routine today, Hank?"

"Watch and learn, Billy, watch and learn."

As soon as we're settled in a booth, Maggie comes

trudging over with a long face that signals she in less than a stellar mood.

"Hey, Maggie baby, heard you won the Miss Bitchy Boston contest."

"Can it, Hank, not today."

"Bad night?"

"The wall police were here early this morning updating their spy cams. Nasty bunch they are... no sense of humor. Special today is Southwestern Chili with garlic toast."

"You mean you turned yesterday's rancid hamburger into today's special?"

"Hank, your sphincter muscle is hanging out your butthole."

"Wow, sphincter, big word. I may have to take your dictionary away."

Maggie waddles off mumbling to herself.

"She loves it."

"I don't know, Hank, today she seems upset."

"Trust me, it's an act, watch when she comes back."

I'm going to get into something that maybe I shouldn't, but here goes.

"In that barn, Chernov looked like he was ready to shoot that guy before Boris stepped in and took the gun away."

"What you saw wasn't all that unusual. I've never been on a raid when Chernov didn't take perverse pleasure in torturing people. The man's one dangerous mistake of a human being."

"He obsessed with catching this Alvera guy."

"Chernov's obsessed about everything, but particularly Alvera. Boris let it slip Chernov's up for a promotion with the International Drug Council in Marseille. Nabbing Alvera could snag him the job."

"After what he did in that warehouse, he should be locked away in a padded cell."

Maggie's back with our coffee looking more pissed-off than when we arrived.

"So, Hank, the word on the street is you're into bestiality."

Hank whips his head to me and feigns anger.

"Damn you, Billy, you been blabbing again?"

"Sorry, Hank, it slipped out."

Maggie sets the coffee cups down and frowns.

"Okay, you two, enough, you want the chili or what?"

"I'll give it a try, Maggie. You, Billy?"

"Sure."

"Made the stuff myself at six this morning, boys."

"Maggie, darling, the last time you were up at that hour, there was a full moon and you were running with wolves."

"Two of them were your parents, Hank."

Off she goes smiling like she nailed Hank good... Jerry the cook comes over with two bowls of chili and garlic toast... turns out to be damn good.

"Hank, I have yet to figure out Wilson. I get the feeling something's going on with him that I don't understand... like he's caught in the same vice we are."

"Don't let him pull the wool over your eyes because he acts semi-human sometimes. He's Chernov's man through and through. Both of them have ice water in their veins."

We fall silent for a few beats and begin eating.

"I saw a story on the news a couple of nights back that didn't compute."

"Nothing on the news computes, Billy, stop watching."

"No, listen. Two groups were protesting in a park somewhere in Brussels. One side carried placards demanding equal rights, the other was promoting white supremacy. The cops showed up, seized the equal rights placards, and arrested those carrying them. They took away the white supremacist signs, but none of them were arrested."

"So now you know the Fascist World Government denies equal rights to minorities while supporting white supremacy. What else do you want to know?"

"Does Maggie really run with wolves?"

We're all back in the office by 3:45*... Wilson bellows for us join him... again the joy boys take the chairs, leaving Jade, Hank, and me standing by the window again... one of them*

could have given Jade their chair, but that would require they show good manners... Wilson remains standing... he's pointing to the wall map.

"Colonel Chernov says it's game on. Alvera's camping out in a two-story oceanfront house on Old Orchard Beach, Maine."

"Maine? What the hell's he doing up there, Frank?"

"As opposed to where, Victor?"

"The Virgin Islands, Hawaii maybe?"

"It's Maine, and we're going up there tomorrow."

"Tomorrow? That's Saturday. Do we get double-time?"

"Victor, stop with the damn wisecracks long enough for me to get through this."

"Proceed like I never said a word, Lieutenant."

"Boris and Ivan are coordinating with SWAT and EMS to meet us there at one PM tomorrow behind the Blue Wave resort on Seaside Avenue in Old Orchard Beach. The resort is closed for the season."

Gustav's raising a hand.

"What about the local WPF?"

"They'll be notified in case we need backup, otherwise they'll stay away."

"Do we know how many of Alvera's henchmen are with him?"

"According to Chernov's snitch, several."

"How many is several?"

"More than one, Gustav. You and Victor ride with me. Billy, Jade, you'll go with Hank."

"We're driving? How about a nice helicopter ride?"

"That would be preferable, Victor, but Chernov's worried helicopters will draw too much attention. He wants Alvera alive, he plans to parade his ass around on the news. That means we drive in nice and quiet. Okay, that's it, we leave from here at 10:30 in the morning sharp."

Great, more fun and games that I would prefer not to be part of... tonight, Billy, tonight is the time you make a run for the Arizona desert... wishful thinking at best.

When I reach Playboy Mansion South, *I check on Jules again... a few seconds go by before I hear movement behind his door.*

"That you, Billy?"

"Yeah."

The door swings open... he's is in his robe looking tired and grumpy... he taps the door peephole six-inches over his head.

"Peephole's too high... I'll get it lowered one of these days. What's up?"

"Just checking on you."

"It's over; they won't bother me again. Wanna come in for a drink, I got a bottle of good whiskey?"

"Like you, I never turn down beverages laced with alcohol."

"Then get your sorry butt in here."

His apartment is not the Ritz, but it's not shabby either... a hell of a lot better than mine.

"Sit, Billy, be comfortable."

He shuffles off to the kitchen and returns with two glasses and two bottles.... one turns out to be Bourbon... he hands the Bourbon to me.

"I think I drank the last of yours."

"Thank you, but that wasn't necessary."

"A little gift for helping to save my old hide. You out of cigs?"

"I smoked the last you gave me."

He tosses me one... I have to buy a pack, that's all there is to it... can't keep smoking his... he pours two shots of the whiskey and sits across from me.

"That episode with the police represents the most humiliating moment of my life bar none. They mugshot and fingerprinted me like I was a common criminal and were ready to whisk me off to the nearest retraining camp. When Wilson's call came, the supervisor instructed the two cretins who arrested me to cut me loose. I smiled, told them to take a flying screw, and caught a cab home. Thank God for Wilson."

Sipping his whiskey, he turns pensive... he wants to talk.

"Jules, you don't owe me an explanation."

"Maybe I need to, Billy. Sometimes that's the only way to bury the pain. I was around fourteen or fifteen when I became aware of my feelings and it frightened me to death. I had no idea how to deal with it. After graduation, I joined the Marines. For the next twenty-two years no one knew other than those I became involved with. Wilson knew, but he never judged me, not once. All the years of progress and acceptance only to have it taken away by this homophobic government. To them we're freaks of nature."

I'm moved by his candidness... I know it can't be easy for him.

"I'm sorry, Jules, I don't know what to say."

"There's nothing to say, Billy, it's over, they won't bother me again, Wilson saw to that."

When we've both had too much whiskey, I bid Jules goodnight... I'm woozy from one too many whiskey shots, but not ready for bed... I turn on the government news channel... the announcer is droning on about the dangerous effects the Internet has on society.

"While the social and economic benefits of the internet are not to be denied, it is also responsible for the escalation of cyberbullying, cybertheft and a steady stream of misinformation. For that reason, the World Government is implementing tighter restrictions beginning—"

Turn it off, Billy... don't listen to anymore... sleep it off... you'll see things in a better light in the morning... like hell I will, tomorrow we're off on another hunting party.

CHAPTER 21

The Test That Almost Was

In the morning, I'm feeling the after effects of too much whiskey the night before... my head is throbbing, my mouth tastes like freshly picked unwashed cotton... man, can Jules put the booze away... make some coffee, take a shower, shake it off, Hank and Jade will be waiting at the office. When I finally hit the sidewalk it's cold... I wish I had accepted Hank's offer to pick me up, but no, not me, I prefer a brisk walk... this is not brisk, this is ice-water cold, dummy. Streetwalkers are scarce this morning... the temperature must be keeping them wherever they found warm refuge for the night... I wonder how many didn't make it through the night? I wonder if those lucky enough not to be targeted for this systematic government extinction agree with this cleansing of the unwanted... we do live in a class system, after all... not everyone cares what happens to those below them... thank goodness for those who do. When I arrive at the precinct, Hank and Jade are parked out front in a government vehicle... The Humvee is already gone... I slip in the back... thankfully, Hank has the heat on.

"Good morning." *Jade shoots me a sideways glance and grimaces.*

"Nothing good about it."

"I suppose not, Jade."

Maybe with Antonina recuperating she's apprehensive about handling things alone... best to leave it at that... I'm more than edgy about how this day will go myself... Wilson says Chernov wants Alvera alive... let's hope the morally bankrupt schizoid Colonel follows through with that. Wilson, Gustave and Victor pull up alongside and wave us on and we're off.

"Be prepared today, Billy."

"How does one prepare to be an executioner, Hank?"

Neither he nor Jade answer. A light snow has dusted our route in white powder... God, it's beautiful... how I missed it... how I've missed so many things I once took for granted. Little passes between us in the way of casual conversation, so we travel mostly in silence until I break it.

"Hank, what do we know about what we're in for?"

"I have no idea. Chernov's kept the details to himself."

"Why?"

"Afraid of a leak, I guess."

"From who, us?"

"He wants Alvera bad, so he's trusting no one."

After traveling north on I-95 for an hour and a half, Wilson exits to I-195 East until it turns into Temple Avenue in Old Orchard Beach, Maine... a few miles down we turn left on Seaside Avenue, which parallels Saco Bay... a short distance up Seaside, Ivan Oblansky, standing on the right side of the road next to a sprawling white oceanfront resort, waves us into the parking lot... the resort sign says the place is closed and will reopen in April. We proceed to the rear of the complex and spot Chernov standing by the Humvee with Boris... both looking sharp in their pressed fatigues and polished ankle-high brogans... they greet us with an unsmiling nod... Chernov points Northeast.

"The Spanish pig is camped out at the end of the Peninsula in a two-story gray house on River Sands Drive—third house in facing the ocean. It's a dead end, he has no way out."

"How many in there with him, Colonel?"

"Not sure, Lieutenant."

Jesus, what else do we not know besides the guy's address and the color of his house? Wilson's scanning the area.

"It's 12:25, where's SWAT and EMS?"

My eyes go to Chernov... his expression turn crusty... he shoots Wilson an unsettling look, but doesn't reply... he's strolling toward the ocean as we wait for his answer.

"Colonel?"

"They got the arrival time wrong by an hour, Lieutenant."

Wilson's brow furrows... he looks like he's going to blow a gasket.

"What? This was set for 1:00. How the hell could they get it wrong?"

"Because some asshole passed along the wrong arrival time."

We were on the road for several hours and Chernov failed to call Wilson with that information? This is loony-tunes time. Chernov blows a hard breath and checks his watch.

"Jade, check SWAT's ETA."

"Yes, sir."

All eyes are on Jade as she makes the call... she listens, her eyelids close halfway, then says something we don't hear, shakes her head and hangs up.

"SWAT leader says they're approximately fifty minutes out."

Angrily, Chernov tosses up his hands and groans.

"Chert by pobral, chert by pobral!"

Since none of us speak Russian besides Ivan and Boris, we have no idea what he said... he makes a fist and punches the air.

"We can't wait all bloody damn day—Idiocy!"

Now he's pacing, shoulders hunched forward, eyes to the pavement, his boots hitting the ground hard... he stops, his head comes up... he's staring at the ocean again.

"We'll move into position."

"Before SWAT arrives? That's against protocol."

Chernov pivots fast to Wilson.

"I say what protocol is, Lieutenant."

"But—"

"But nothing. We're not going to blow this because some desk jockey doesn't know how to tell time. My source provided me Alvera's cell number, I'll call him."

"Jesus, that'll give him a heads up that we're here."

"Zip it, Frank."

Whoa, a bit edgy today are we, Colonel?

"Andrei, if we move into position before SWAT arrives,

they'll be a shootout for sure."

"Then we'll give it to them back in spades."

Wilson steps to Chernov's side and wraps a hand around his left arm.

"Andrei, listen to me."

"Take your damn hand off me, Frank."

"I'm just concerned for everyone's safety."

"I've got it covered, Lieutenant. Boris, we're moving up."

What the hell is going on between Wilson and Chernov? Better question, what's going on with Chernov? After what we witnessed during the barn raid, I'm convinced he's mentally unstable... now would be a good time to mutiny and have him and hauled off to a padded cell before one or all of us gets killed. Ivan approaches with Kevlar vests, M4 rifles and communication headsets.

"We'll move up to the house using the Humvee for cover and—"

"Colonel, you're placing my people in jeopardy."

"My people, Lieutenant, everyone here answers to me. Don't ever forget that."

Okay, time out, this is getting sticky... if these two guys can't get it together, how are we supposed to pull this off? Chernov wraps himself in a Kevlar vest and grabs an M4 from Ivan.

"No more chitchat, load up, we're moving."

Hank edges close to me and whispers.

"Well, this is a first."

This could turn dicey real fast with or without SWAT... but Chernov's calling the shots, we salute and follow or end up in rusty leg irons. Once we're all suited up, we load into our vehicles and follow behind the Humvee up Seaside Avenue, turning onto Jones Creek Drive, then right on Avenue Five to the end of Pillsbury Drive stopping just short of River Sands Drive... a sign is posted at the entrance, 'No Exit.' *Chernov's out of the Humvee motioning for everyone to gather around.*

"Colonel, what about neighbors?"

"Gone for the season, Hank, that much we know. Gustav, you and Victor make your way around back of the house.

Anybody comes out, drop them. Go."

Hank and I exchange apprehensive glances… so far this operation smacks of amateur week in Dixie. Back in my old DEA days, an operation like this would have been planned down to the smallest detail with advance surveillance, aerial photos, and any other info that would give us an edge. River Sands Drive is a minefield just waiting for us to make our entrance… Hank sidle's up to me and whispers.

"Now would be a good time to bend over and kiss our asses goodbye."

If he meant that as a joke, his timing's off.

"What the hell gives here, Hank?"

"The Colonel Andrei Chernov one-act horror show."

"If this is how they do it in Russia, their operation manual is in need of rewriting."

Chernov's waving us over.

"Boris, drive the Humvee. Jade, ride with him, Ivan and me will hike it with the others."

Chernov's machismo is on scary display, which doesn't bode well for the rest of us… but like good little soldiers, or dumb ones, we're on the move looking like a ragged band of terrorists hunkered low on the right side of the Humvee as it rolls slowly past the first two houses… if one of Alvera's men spot us, in a matter of seconds this street becomes ground-zero with nothing more than the Humvee to protect us. We roll to a stop directly across from Alvera's house without incident, which I suspect will only last until someone in there wonders why a Humvee is parked across the street… over our headsets Gustav confirms he and Victor are in position.

"Do you have adequate cover?"

"We're behind bushes ten yards from the house, Colonel. Back door is in clear sight."

"Hold that position."

Chernov swings open the Humvee's rear door.

"Jade, Boris, give me the room. I'll call Alvera and give him the chance to end this without anyone getting killed."

Why in God's name would you move into position, Colonel, and tip your hand before the heavy troops arrive? Why? Jade and Boris slip out of the Humvee, Chernov slides in and closes the door behind him... I look to Wilson... he's rolling his eyes... he knows this operation is going down the rabbit hole fast. We wait in silence... five long minutes pass before Chernov slips out of the Humvee... his expression is grim... I look to Wilson... he's doing a slow burn.

"What did he say?"

Chernov shakes his head and grunts.

"On skazal mne trakhat'sya—he told me to take a flying fuck."

"Does the man have a death wish?"

"If he does, Lieutenant, we're here to accommodate him."

"But we still don't know how many we're up against."

Chernov ignores Wilson... we have no SWAT support, no EMS... we might as well be sitting ducks for all the cover this Humvee is gonna provide if—no, when—the shooting starts. Now Chernov's peeking at the house from the back of the Humvee. Go ahead, Colonel, sir, stick your head out there and see if anyone blows it off.

"Boris, come here and keep an eye on the windows."

Gee, Colonel Dick Head, you think we should be on alert after you gave them a courtesy call? Right about now they're loading and checking all the firepower they have with them? Now mad dog Chernov's pacing the length of the Humvee... once, twice, three times before stopping and glancing at his watch.

"Jade, call SWAT again."

Jade's standing by the front of the Humvee and makes the call... she's talking low out of range of the rest of us... thirty-seconds later she hangs up and moves to Chernov's side.

"Thirty to thirty-five minutes, sir."

"Goddamn it!"

"SWAT leader insisted we wait until they get here, sir."

"I'll give that brown bastard Alvera one last chance."

Hey, Russian guy, if Alvera told you to fuck off the first time, what do think he's going to tell you on your second call? You and your gang come on in for a cup of good Columbian coffee? Chernov's index finger is punching hard at his cell.

"Alvera, you son of a bitch, answer your goddamn phone!"
This is sheer madness... ten seconds, fifteen... it's clear Alvera isn't going to answer... Chernov grunts and terminates the call... in a forced whisper he curses the phone.

"Screw you, you immigrant son-of-a-bitch."

Atta boy, Colonel, let Alvera know you're a certified racist, and while you're at it, give the phone hell too... now the fool's barking orders at Boris and Ivan.

"Game on, tear gas the first and second floor windows."
His two aides exchange confused glances.

"Without SWAT, sir?"

"Goddamn it, Boris, did I stutter?"

"No, sir, but—"

"Then get it done."

"Ah, yes, sir."

I look to Wilson and catch his eye... grim-faced, he looks away. From the Humvee, Ivan retrieves two single-round riot tear gas guns, stuffs extra shells in his jacket pocket, and hands the same to Boris.

"Ready, sir."

"Well then shoot, goddamn it!"

No need to get snarky, Colonel. I was involved in enough of these operations in my previous life to know things can go South fast... this is beginning to smell like one of those times. Wilson, Hank, Jade and I huddle close to the Humvee. Boris and Ivan move to the rear, take aim, and fire their first rounds at two first-floor windows... glass shards fly off everywhere... guaranteed to rattle awake whoever's inside trying to take a nap... the second rounds shatter two second-floor windows. Chernov's pacing again, cell phone in hand, waiting, waiting... not a sound coming from inside Alvera castle by the sea... Chernov's dialing again.

"Alvera, you piece of shit-spic, answer your damn phone."

Wilson quicksteps to Chernov's side like maybe he's gonna take a swing at him.

"Colonel, listen to me."

But Chernov's not listening... his phone is to his ear... cursing under his breath, Wilson backs away.

"Son of a bitch!"

All eyes are glued on Chernov... abruptly, he terminates the call.

"Screw 'em. Boris, if they don't respond in the next five minutes, we're going in."

"Ah... yes, sir."

Is no one going to stand up to this out of control psychopath? Wilson's our only hope... I move to his side.

"Lieutenant, you have to do something."

"And what would that be?"

"Reason with him."

"Just do as you're told, Russell."

"But Lieutenant—

Hank grabs my arm and pulls me away.

"Best cool it, Billy."

Boris has retrieved his trusty launcher from the back of the Humvee... Colonel whiz-kid is pacing again constantly glancing at his watch.

"Screw it, time's up, open the damn door, Boris."

"You're sure, sir?"

Chernov glowers.

"Boris, open the goddamn door now!"

Boris and Ivan exchange apprehensive glances... I move to the front of the Humvee where I have a clear view of the front door... Boris lifts the launcher to his shoulder, steps clear of the Humvee, takes aim, fires and steps back... the shell travels faster than my eye can follow... the door and surrounding frame explode in a loud boom sending splintered pieces of wood flying in all directions as bright red and orange flames snake up to the second-floor and dissipate.

"Gustav, we're going in."

"Yeah, we heard, Colonel."

"Make sure no one makes it out that back door. Jade, stay in the Humvee. Boris, Ivan, lead the way. Go, damn it, go!"

Wilson's ready to explode... he moves quickly to Chernov's side.

"Colonel, take a step back, think this through."

"Who do you think you're talking to, Frank?"

"You, goddamn it!"

"Not another word out of you, Lieutenant. Stay in the Humvee with Jade if you like. Boris, Ivan, lead the way."

The next thing we know, we're leaving our only cover behind and dashing across the street behind Boris and Ivan like a high school basketball team not all that sure who has the ball... half way across the road shots ring out in the distance... we don't know where they're coming from or who they're directed at. Boris and Ivan stop dead in his tracks.

"Shots fired, sir!"

Chernov smacks Boris on the back.

"Keep moving you idiot!"

Just as we set foot on the sidewalk, there's a second burst of gunfire... sounds like it came from the second floor... dashing behind low hedges, we huddle against the house... Chernov's yelling into his mic.

"Who the hell is shooting at who? Gustav, Victor!"

Silence.

"Dammit, where the hell are you guys?"

No reply from Gustav or Victor... Chernov's pointing to the front door... Boris nods... he and Ivan approach the hole that was the entrance with us following close behind... we enter... the tear gas has mostly dissipated, but there's still enough to sting our eyes a little... a man with a gasmask on lies in pools of blood on the living room floor... Victor's voice comes over our headsets.

"All clear, come on up, Colonel, second floor last door on the right."

Chernov's eyes shoot to the second floor.

"What in the hell?"

Pushing past Boris and Ivan, he's bounding up the stairs like a stallion chasing a mare in heat with the rest of us on his heels having no idea what's happened... in the second floor hallway, a second body with a gasmask on lays in a pool of blood... stepping over him, we follow Chernov to the last door on the right... we enter a large bedroom... to our astonishment, Victor and Gustav, both smiling like the cat that snagged the mouse, are standing over two men down on their knees, hands cuffed behind him. They too have gasmasks on. Gustav removes the mask from one of the men and taps him on the head with barrel of his M4.

"Colonel, meet Mister Alvera."

"Yeah, I know who the prick is."

"After you busted out the front door, we rushed in through the back door, dropped the one in the living room, then the second one out there in the hall. These two were cowered in that closet over there like cornered rats.

"There was only three of them with him?"

"Looks that way."

Jade's voice comes over the headsets.

"Lieutenant, what's your status?"

"We're in—it's over."

"Everyone okay?"

"Yes."

"Alvera?"

"Got him."

"Alive?"

"Yes."

Not sure what I expected, but the infamous East Coast drug king kneeling before us is small in stature with an angular face, seventyish, dark complexion, brown eyes, receding hair and a neatly trimmed white mustache and goatee... he looks more like someone's kindly grandfather than a drug kingpin... a grinning Chernov approaches him.

"Nice to finally meet you, Matias Diego Alvera."

Alvera's head comes up slowly, studies Chernov for a beat and grins.

"Este mierda y muere."

Ivan's lips curl into a grin and translates.

"He said eat shit and die, sir."

"Did he now?

Chernov sets his M4 on the floor, takes out his Smith & Wesson, and approaches the second man.

"Take his mask off."

Ivan complies and removes the man's mask... Chernov approaches.

"What's your name?"

"Rubio."

"Ah, jackpot. Alejandro Rubio, Alvera's majordomo."

Rubio is taller and heavier than Alvera and maybe ten years younger. He looks Chernov in the eyes and sneers. Stepping closer, Chernoff swings his weapon in a wide ark striking Rubio on the left side of his head... Rubio cries out and tumbles to the floor... here we go again, a repeat of the torture that played out in that warehouse.

"Get the pig up."

Hank's closest... he lifts Rubio to his knees... Chernov squats and gets in Alvera's face.

"You know who I am, Matias Diego Alvera?"

Alvera's eyes narrow to slits his lips twisting in a crooked grin.

"Colonel Andrei shit-face Chernov."

Chernov switches his gun to his left hand... with his open right hand, he slaps Alvera hard across the face... Alvera's head whips right.

"Don't be disrespectful, Mathias."

"Colonel, we'll want to parade him around on the news without bruises."

"Duly noted, Lieutenant."

Alvera spits hitting the floor just in front of Chernov's feet.

"Pretty ballsy for a man who hides in a closet while his men go down in flames. "

"Says you, Senor Credo."

Ivan's trying to stifle a laugh.

"Uh, sir, he called you a pig."

Chernov tosses his head back and laughs.

"And here we were told you were a real tough guy. Last I heard, tough guys don't hide in closets. Okay, here's how this's going to play out, amigo. I'm going to provide pen and paper on which you'll write the location of your poison mills, top lieutenants, and the names of all your street peddlers. In exchange you two get to live. Oh, you'll end up in prison all right, but at least you'll be alive."

"Don't jerk me off, you pinchazos never take anyone in

alive. Mierda, idiota blanco."

"But in your case, I'm will to make an exception."

"Let me educate you, Colonel, just in case you don't get it. Rich or poor, people live for my drugs, and it'll go on long after I'm gone. You can take that to the bank, Cara de mierda, Chernov."

"Sir, he called you a—"

"Yeah, yeah, whatever, Boris."

Hard to decide who's more dangerous here, Alvera or Chernov... both are in serious need of Jade's psych services.

"How about you, Alejandro Rubio. I bet you know the answers I want."

Rubio makes uneasy eye contact with Alvera but quickly turns away.

"Colonel, let's take them in now."

Chernov's not listening to Wilson, he switches his gun back to his right hand and strikes the side of Rubio's head again... this time he draws blood... Rubio winches but remains upright.

"That's what happens when you don't cooperate."

Is no one going to step in and put an end to Chernov's barbarous cruelty? Chernov's up and circling Alvera like an animal circling its prey... he stops... ever so slowly, his eyes come to me.

"These sub-human minority bastards are invading our lands like ants, Officer Russell. They migrate from their decaying countries and bring their filth with."

He taps Alvera on the back of his head with the barrel of his weapon.

"Make no mistake, it's part of their master plan to use their drugs to one day rule over us. It's our responsibility to see that plan fails."

Boris, who seems to be the only one who has any real influence with Chernov, is looking damn nervous... his back stiffens... he senses something the rest of us don't... he takes a hesitant step forward.

"Colonel?"

Chernov, eyes laser-locked on the back of Alvera's head, his face twisted, moves his pistol closer to Alvera's head... his gaze comes to me.

"Officer Russell. In that closet, in that second when you decided to pull the trigger, you didn't hesitate."

I swallow hard.

"No."

"I thought not. It's the same here and now. It's my sworn duty to deliver justice to men like the scum knelling before us. I will not fail my duty."

He swings his gun around and shoots Rubio in the back of the head... everyone flinches ... Rubio's mouth opens wide, but nothing comes out, his eye sockets flood with blood as he slips forward to the floor... Chernov swings his hand back to within inches of Alvera's head... Wilson yells.

"Andrei, no!"

Chernov's second shot explodes Alvera's head spattering blood and brains on my pant legs and shoes... his body slams forward to the floor... Wilson wails again.

"Jesus Christ! Boris, get his goddamn gun."

Chernov's gun hand is oscillating... he looks muddled as if not aware he just executed two men... Boris rushes to him and wraps his hand around Chernov's gun.

"Colonel, let me have your weapon."

Chernov's staring blankly at Alvera's body.

"What?"

"Sir, I'm going to remove your weapon now."

Chernov looks dazed and confused, as if the reality of what just happened hasn't yet registered... Boris eases the gun from Chernov's still shaking hand.

"Come on, Colonel, time to go."

Chernov's head swivels slowly to Boris.

"Go? Go where, Boris?"

"Home sir, home."

Boris passes Chernov's gun to Ivan, then hooks an arm through Chernov's... Ivan takes the other arm and they lead Chernov from the room... Jade's voice comes over the headset.

"What's going on, Lieutenant, I heard shots?"

Wilson takes a deep breath and releases it.

"We're on the way, Jade."

"SWAT and the EMS just arrived."

"Okay."

Outside, Boris and Ivan lead an unresponsive Chernov to the Humvee and place him in the back seat... Jade comes over to me.

"Billy, what's going on, what's wrong with the Colonel?"

"I'll fill you when we get out of here, Jade."

The SWAT team leader, obviously clueless as to what's happened, approaches the Humvee.

"You went in without us, Lieutenant?"

"What gave you your first clue?"

"Hey, sorry, there was a screw up with dispatch."

"No, really? We would have never guessed."

"It looks like you guys have it under control. Say, what's wrong with the Colonel?"

"A bad headache. There are four recently departed in the house—get rid of them."

"What?"

"Did I stutter?"

"That's not our job, Lieutenant?"

"Today it damn well is."

"What are we supposed to do with them?"

"Donate them to medical science, bury them in the backyard, I really don't give a damn."

"But, Lieutenant—"

"But nothing, just do it.

Wilson pulls Hank and me aside.

"Hank, you guys head back. And not a word to anyone about what happened here."

"What about the Colonel?"

"I'll deal with him."

What happened here today is beyond madness... beyond anything that even comes close to reality... today was the last straw, my line in the sand... I have to find a way out of this nightmare... this hall of mirrors.

I can tell Hank and Jade are as revolted as I am, but not a word passes between us until we reach I-95.

"When Chernov tortured that man and woman in the warehouse, I wanted to beat him with my bare hands—Wilson too for allowing it to happen. Chernov's cold-blooded execution of Alvera and Rubio will live with me forever. I feel dirty and ashamed."

"Let it go, Billy, or it'll drive you nuts."

"Can't let it go, Jade, not now, not tomorrow, not ever. What kind of world are we living in where the government sanctions executions? No one has that right, ever."

"They have little regard for human life, Billy. That's their world and we live in it."

"Then I want no part of it, Jade."

CHAPTER 22

All is Not Lost… It just Feels That Way

Hank parks the government vehicle next to his Ford Taurus.
"I'll give you two a lift home."

"Thanks, Hank, I'm gonna walk."

"No, Billy, you have blood stains on your pants and shoes. Let me drop you off."

"It's dark, no one will notice."

"Billy, your emotions are on overdrive, don't walk home."

"I'll be fine, Jade, or I will after a couple of shots of booze and a hot shower."

"Suit yourself, but go straight home. And soak those clothes in cold water."

The sun has set, the street lights are on… better walk on the opposite of Broadway that's not as well lit… less chance of someone seeing the bloodstains… I need a cigarette… the drug store looks empty, so I slip in… thankfully, the cashier's reading a newspaper and hardly notices me. I buy a pack and quickly get out of there before another customer comes walking in. Back on the street, I light up and head for home… when I reach the house, I pause by the steps… I can't go in, not yet… I stroll aimlessly around the neighborhood for a half-hour trying to pull it together, but Chernov's unspeakable act of violence keeps playing over and over in my head. When I finally return to the house, Jade's Volkswagen is parked out front… didn't expect to see her again tonight… I unlock and swing the door open and switch on the light… my eyes shoot to the top of the stairs just as Jules pops out of his apartment in his robe.

"Ah, thought that was you."

His eyes go to my blood stain khakis.

"Jesus, Billy, who vomited on you?"

"It's not my blood."

"Whose is it?"

"Somebody else's."

"And?"

"Later, Jules, later."

"You've kept your company waiting again. That lady cop, Jade, she's upstairs. You hit the jackpot with that one. Why don't you give her a key, I have extras?"

"Goodnight, Jules."

"Blood's a bitch to get out. Soak those pants."

"I intend to. Goodnight, Jules."

When I enter the apartment, Jade's sitting on the sofa looking as beautiful as when I first saw her there... she's changed clothes... her right leg slung over her left in the same black slacks she was wearing when we first met... a gray long-sleeve sweater covers her top... her black leather hip-length coat by her side.

"I thought Hank took you home?"

"He did, now I'm here. Where have you been?"

"If you've come to cheer me up, please don't."

I toss my jacket on one of the dining table chairs.

"You need to soak those pants in cold water or you won't get those stains out."

"Give me a minute."

I retrieve another pair of khakis from the closet, head for the bathroom, fill the sink with cold water, slip off my shoes, soak the bloodstained trousers, and put on the clean pair... wiping my shoes with a wet washcloth, I leave them there and I return to the living room.

"I hope you don't mind, Billy, I took a tour of the place. It's small—needs work."

"An understatement. In the mood for a shot of Bourbon?"

"Sure."

Retrieving the Bourbon, I pour us both a shot.

"If you're here in your capacity as a psychologist to restore my crumbling state of mind, save your time because I—"

"I thought you might like company."

Lighting a cigarette, I sit beside her on the sofa.

"What would you like to talk about?"

"To begin with, your state of mind."

"Huh, little hope there, Jade. What Chernov did in the warehouse and again today isn't drug enforcement, it's sadistic torture and cold-blooded execution. Both are acts of a psychopath. He should be in a padded cell in a psych ward in a straightjacket. How else do we stop him?"

"We don't. Marseille condones and encourages that behavior hoping it sends a message to others who chose drug manufacture and distribution as a career. On the other hand, if it became public that Chernov, or any of the drug enforcement commanders partake in the actual killings, Marseille would give them cover and one of you guys would be tossed under the bus. Keep that in mind. And you're going to lose your ash."

"What?"

"Your cigarette."

"Oh, right."

In the kitchen I grab a glass to use as an ashtray and join her on the sofa.

"When are you going to quit those things?"

"When the moon turns green."

"By the way, Billy, for the record, I don't have a cat."

"Yeah, you said that. Why did you say you did?"

"Female defense mechanism."

"Against?"

"You've been circling me from day one. I can is was offended by the attention."

"Then what?"

"I wasn't sure where you were going with it so soon after we met."

She's stringing me out like a rubber band.

"Life is short, say what you mean and mean what you say."

She takes a deep breath, exhales slowly, and locks those lovely eyes of hers on mine.

"I told you, Billy, my marriage didn't go well. So maybe

I'm skittish, especially with another cop."

"Are you planning on going through life being skittish?"

"It sounds silly when you say it."

We laugh... it feels good if only in the moment... she looks away... something's on her mind... whatever it is I wish she'd get to it.

"Where are we going with this, Billy?"

"Us?"

"Yeah."

"Wherever it leads—the ball's in your court."

Again, she goes silent and looks away... seconds feel like minutes while I wait for her to pick up the conversation.

"We live in strange times."

"That's an understatement, Jade. If it gets any stranger it'll —"

"That bed in there looks kind of small for two."

What? Did I hear right? Did she just give me the green light to go past go?

"Did I interpret that right?"

"If you didn't, your dense."

"This isn't a mercy mission, is it?"

"You should scrub your tongue with soap for even suggesting it."

Can't get any clearer than that, Billy Boy... now would be the time to dig deep into the recesses of my memory bank and recall how this is supposed to go. Come on, no more idle chit chat, don't keep the lady waiting... either this is it, or it's not.

"Are you sure of this?"

"Kiss me before I get cold feet."

Okay, Billy Boy, you've been given permission, what are you waiting for? Placing the glass I'm using as an ashtray on the coffee table, I stand and lift her to her feet, place my arms around her waist, and kiss her... her arms go around me... the kiss advances from gentle to intense until she breaks it off, pulls her sweater up over her head, and drops it to the sofa... off comes my shirt... I drop it to the floor... my arms are around her again... we're moving unhurriedly to the bedroom, body to body like a well-rehearsed ballet... removing her remaining clothes, she lays down on her back... God, she's stunningly beautiful, everything I imagined and more when I first followed her down the hallway to the break room... off my pants and shorts come... I slide into the bed... it's barely big enough for both of us.

"Don't rush it."

Is she kidding? Count on it to be slow, beautiful, very slow... let's make this last into the afterlife. What happens next is what I imagine it might be like traveling to heaven on the wings of an angel, wherever the hell that is. My whole being is aflame with primal desire... I'm not sure where to put my hands first... I kiss her without touching... a long kiss, one of those wet, open-mouth kisses that go on forever... my right hand is on the move now... to her shoulder, down to her waist, up to her firm right breast... I'm dizzy with passion, floating, floating, ascending on a white puffy cloud on my way to that heaven on the wings of angels.

An hour later we're laying quietly in each other's arms... I've experienced what it has taken over seventeen long years to reclaim... I feel whole again... good sex will do that... wrong, this wasn't good sex, this was skyrocketing sex with fireworks, strings, loud horns, and crashing cymbals accompanied by a chorus of heavenly voices... she was into me one-hundred percent... I know that... I felt it. And yet, she knows nothing about me other than what's in my file... I want her to know everything... I want to bare it all and put it behind me forever.

"My wife's name was Diedre."

"Billy, you don't have to talk about this."

"I want to, I need to. It's the only way I'll be able to box it up and bury it."

She takes my hand in hers and squeezes.

"I met Diedre on a blind date arranged by a friend who was dating a friend of hers. After a whirlwind eight months, we were married."

Swallowing hard, my eyes well up.

"Two years later, she was taken from me. The coroner said she died of strangulation most likely while the creep was—"

"Oh God, Billy."

"What happened next wouldn't have if I hadn't heard the Boston PD had found fingerprints on the headboard and were about to make an arrest. I wrangled out of a friend the suspect's name and looked up his address. I had motive so I knew upfront I'd be a suspect right off. But I had worn gloves, got rid of my clothes, cleaned my shoes, and tossed them in the back of a closet. During the search of my place to either charge me or eliminate me as a suspect, they found traces of the guy's blood on the heel of my right shoe. That's it, that's the whole story. I paid for it with seventeen years of my life."

There follows an awkward silence... there wasn't much more to be said on that subject. She squeezes my hand and smiles.

"You promised to tell me about space."

Now, there's a nice pivot away from a subject I had no further interest in pursuing.

"Yeah, that. Well, to begin with, from the moment I stepped in front of that portal I was in absolute awe. What I witnessed was so far beyond anything I could have imagined, it left me questioning where we and our little blue dot of a planet fit in, if at all. A spiritual change came over me, not in a religious way, but in a life-changing way. I gained a new respect for the short time we're given here. It forces you to think about why we waste so much of it. I came away wondering, if everyone could see and experience what I was privileged to see through that portal, would we finally treat our lives as the precious gift it is along with the respect it deserves. Does that make me naïve?"

"No, it places you a few steps ahead of the rest of us."

"Huh, for all the good that does."

I kiss her gently on her forehead.

"How about you stay the night?"

"Maybe next time."

"Is there going to be a next time, Jade?"

"I hope so, Billy, I really do."

213

A short time later we're standing by the door in each other's arms sharing one hell of a great goodnight kiss. When we part, she smiles and her eyes sparkle.

"Sleep well, Billy Russell."

"Tonight, I will, Jade Miro."

I'm still struggling to explain my deep emotional attachment to this woman... there was an unexplainable magnetic draw from the moment I first saw her... I admit at first glance it was her stunning looks and my carnal desire that I had been deprived of for so many years... but I realized early on my feelings for her were beyond just physical attraction. She wouldn't have come tonight if she didn't feel the same. I'm too wired to sleep now... I'll try documenting the bloodbath I witness this day. Cranking up the computer and opening my file, I begin typing.

"Today, I watched in horror as Colonel Andrei Chernov executed two men in cold blood before witnesses. He was not in control of himself, not even close. Hank Drummond told me that although he's witnessed Chernov's cruelty time and again, Chernov's never participated in or for that matter remained in the room for an execution—this was a first. We have a blood-thirsty madman running the show and I will find a way out of the quagmire if it's the last thing I do.

Enough, find something to watch on the boob-tube before you go nuts thinking about what's to be done about Chernov... he's Marseille's guy so I suspect nothing will be done. The government channel comes up... the on-camera guy is right out of central casting... young, movie star handsome... he's droning on about how many citizens have passed on and how it is contributing to population reduction... yeah, man, keep those crematoriums working 24/7. The announcer stops mid-sentence and his face slackens... his hand cups his right ear.

"I'm being informed by control there has been an incident at a large gathering in central Paris. We go live now to world news correspondent Alexander Charbonneau."

The shot cuts to the reporter Charbonneau standing in a

deserted park... he's speaking in English, but with a thick French accent.

"I'm standing in Square Suzanne Buisson at 7 bis rue Girardon in front of the reflection pool beneath the statue of Saint Denis where a short time ago World Council Commissioner Henry Dion was addressing a crowd of approximately two-hundred."

The name Henry Dion jumps out at me.

"Several men and women in the crowd began booing Mister Dion for his continued attacks against the very government in which he serves. A scuffle broke out. Twelve people received minor injuries and nine were arrested. Mister Dion is reported to be unharmed."

Hey Gideon, if they can get to him this easily, you need to find your boy better security. Screw this crap, they're all out of their frigging minds, every last one of them... go to bed, Billy, shut out the world because you ain't gonna change it... shedding my clothes, I crawl into the sack... Jade's sweet scent lingers... I hug her pillow... what a nice way to fall asleep for a change.

CHAPTER 23

Déjà Vu All Over Again

This night my dreams are about Jade and her exquisite body lying next to mine... a major improvement over the distressing images that normally stampede through my head each night... but soon my thoughts segue to Rubio's and Alvera's heads exploding and his blood splashing on me. There's only way to stop it and that's to get my ass out of bed... my watch shows 6:30, my bladder's calling for relief anyway... the bloody pants are still soaking in the sink... the dark red blood has turned light purple... I rinse them and hope the rest washes out... it's Sunday, a perfect day to wash clothes. At 9:00, I hustle down to Jules's door... as always, he greets me in his robe.

"Do you know what time it is?"

"Sorry, Jules, I thought you'd be up."

"As you can see, I am."

"Then why are you harassing me?"

He grins wide.

"It's what I do best, Billy."

"I was hoping to wash these clothes."

"I was wondering how long you'd be recycling underwear and socks."

"Are you going to chew on my ass or show me how to use the machines?"

"Where's your soap?"

"Don't have any."

"Come on, you can use mine. I trust you slept well."

"I did, Jules, thank you."

"And well you should, considering how late your company stayed."

"Mind your own business, old man."

"I'm too old to start now, son."

The basement is dark and musty with a half-dozen dust-covered boxes piled up in one corner.

"Saving canned goods?"

"Years of my old military stuff. Don't know why I keep it."

"For when you open the Julius Sommers military museum."

"With the Marine band in attendance. Okay, pay attention. Never mix these black socks with colors."

"That much I know, Jules."

He provides a quick tutorial on the workings of the washer, but none of it sticks, it'll take a second lesson for sure... he takes pity on me and gets this load going.

"Come down in about thirty minutes or so, I'll show you how to use the dryer."

The trip to Jules's dark, dank basement turns out to be the highlight of an otherwise boring Sunday. After finishing with the laundry, I spend an hour switching channels watching badly written, badly directed, and badly performed episodes of bad TV series... I want to call Jade, but idiot that I am, I neglected to get her number. It's Sunday, I could call the office and it would be forwarded to her... no, don't, she'll think you're a love-sick schoolboy... I'll go for a walk... no, bad idea, too cold... with nothing further on my dance card, I opt for a nap. When I awake at 6:00, my mood is in the shitter... for the love of me, I still can't get Chernov's cold-blooded, maniacal killing of Alvera and Rubio out of my head... I need company and Jules is the only human within range... he answers the door in his robe.

"It's only 6:30, going to bed?"

"What's wrong with being comfortable? What's up?"

"I'm cooking."

"Good for you."

"I feel like company."

"Are you inviting me?"

"Yes."

"What's on the menu?"

"Ham steak."

"Where did you come across a ham steak?"

"At the grocery store like everyone else in search of a ham steak. Bring that extra key you offered. Fifteen minutes."

I'm in the middle of frying the ham when Jules shows up waving a key chain with two keys dangling from it.

"Can't imagine what the lady sees in you?"

"Good looks, charm, charisma and—"

"Don't oversell it, Mister Russell."

"Sit, dinner's almost ready."

"By the way, you have a new neighbor across the hall. He moved in around five."

"Does he have a name?"

"It's, uh, uh—damn it, what's his name?"

"I asked you first, Jules."

He scratches at the back of his head.

"Shit, I can't remember."

"First signs of dementia, old man."

"Hold on, it'll come to me soon enough."

"Have a shot of Bourbon, it's good for a failing memory."

"Then pour."

I pour two shots and set them on the table.

"Food's ready. Ham steak, stale brown bread, a side of mushy oatmeal, and all the water you can drink."

"What?"

"Never mind, let's eat."

Food must be good because Jules has gone silent... until he gets this eureka look on his face and his right hand shoots up over his head.

"Henley!"

"What?"

"The new guy, his name is, uh, Henley, Chris Henley."

Jesus, what? Can't be.

"Seems like a nice enough fella."

Could it really be Chris? No, no way... probably some guy with the same name... as soon as Jules leaves, I'll slip across the hall and check him out for myself... I count the minutes until Jules finishes eating.

"Was there something else on your mind, Billy, or were you trying to impress me with your culinary skills?"

"Neither."

"In that case, I'll thank you for the meal and the Bourbon. Time for me to get back in my robe. My best to the Asian lady."

"Jade."

"Yeah, Jade. You're one lucky son-of-a-bitch."

"Put your tongue back in your mouth, old man."

When I hear Jules's door close, I slip out and listen at the door across from mine... if this turns out not to be Chris, I'll introduce myself and welcome whoever it is to the building... the TV's on... I knock but there's no answer... I knock louder... the TV goes off.

"Yeah, who's there?"

"Your neighbor across the hall—just wanted to say hello."

The door swings open... hot damn if it's not Chris Henley in the flesh... the look on his face is pure astonishment as if he just came face-to-face with the ghost of Billy Russell... my reaction is the same.

"Billy Russell!"

"Chris Henley!

"What in God's name are you doing here, Billy?"

"I could ask you the same."

We fly into each other's arms like long lost siblings separated at birth.

"I live three feet away through that open door."

"No way."

"Come on, I'll show you."

Grabbing his arm, I drag him into my place.

"Welcome to chateau Russell."

He sniffs the air.

"Whoa, this place smells better than mine."

"Another story for another time. What happened, Chris? Where'd you go?"

"You're not going to believe this. I expected we'd meet up on the bus, maybe spend time at the airport before going our separate ways."

"I was hoping the same."

"The guy processing me gets this daunting look when he pulls up my file. My assignment check-in wasn't for the next day, it was for tomorrow—a typo, it seems, at Colonel Maks' end. The guy says he had no authority to change my orders, so he completes the paperwork, another guy shoots a GPS tracker in my arm, and they bunked me on the base until this morning."

"And you sat around for a week?"

"I hooked up with this delicious looking, sex-starved, unattached, staff sergeant lady who worked in base administration. Told you I'd get laid— several times to be exact."

"I never doubted it. Come, sit, make yourself at home."

Retrieving two glasses and the Bourbon from its hiding place, I join Chris on the sofa, pour two shots, and set the bottle on the coffee table.

"Never in a million years did I imagine we'd end up in the same city in the same boarding house."

"It must be kismet, Billy Boy."

His eyes go to the bottle of Bourbon... a quizzical look comes over his face.

"Where did you get that?"

"What?"

"The Bourbon."

"A gift from my new employer, why?"

"I got one too, same brand."

"From who?"

"The landlord said the booze along with some food in the frig was from my new employer. That's all I know."

"Where are you assigned, Chris?"

"A drug enforcement unit. What the hell do I know about drug enforcement—nada."

"Unit 513?"

"Yeah, yeah, that's it. Why?"

With a crooked smile, I'm up on my feet crossing to the kitchen and reaching into the cabinet where I keep my gun and badge... grabbing the badge, I march back and hold it up to his face.

"It appears, Sir Chris, we'll be working together. How weird is that?"

"Jesus, Billy, weird as weird gets since I know dick about drug enforcement. Fill me in."

Best I don't offer a blow by blow of what goes on at unit 513... that'll spook him for sure... he'll learn soon enough from Wilson and Chernov... assuming the Colonel hasn't been institutionalized since I last saw him sitting in the back of the Humvee looking like he had been given a full-body shot of Novocain.

"You'll meet first with our immediate supervisor, Lieutenant Frank Wilson, he'll give you the rundown. How much did processing tell you about what's going on in the world these days?"

"The guy told me a lot had changed. They gave me a book to read and—"

"The RedBook."

"Yeah, haven't opened it yet."

"Don't bother, it's all bullshit. Here's a crash course before you hit the street in the morning."

Painting a pretty glum picture, I leave nothing out about the condition of the world we've returned to... at least as much and I know... the look on Chris' face is one of disbelief.

"Take it slow. It's gonna feel like you landed in a parallel universe for a while. On your way to the precinct tomorrow, you'll—"

"You're not going with me?"

"Maybe we shouldn't let on that we know one another."

"We returned on the same ship. Surely they'll make the connection."

"Let's see if they do first. You know how to get there?"

"The landlord gave me directions."

"On your way in you'll pass a lot of homeless. Don't engage with them, tell them you're a cop and they'll leave you alone. You're gonna want new clothes. There's a store on Broadway. I'll take you there at lunch if you want."

"Sounds like a plan, can't wait to ditch this brown uniform.

Jeez, Billy, I'm still can't believe we're together again walking around like free men."

"As long as we have those GPS trackers in our arms, Chris, we're not free."

CHAPTER 24

What's Normal, What's not.

Glancing out the front window Monday morning, the sky is clear, the sun's doing its best to shine through the haze of pollution... what's left of the snow is melting. If I run into Chernov today, I just might knock him on his sick Russian ass. No sooner am I out on the street, a disheveled man and women with a young girl in tow approach... the kid looks to be her early teens... I see it coming, they're gonna hit me up for money, but they spot my badge and gun and scurry off in the opposite direction. Further up 4th, another poor soul is weaving and talking to himself... he's clearly high on something or other... this could be trouble... get rid of him... I push my jacket open so my gun and badge are visible.

"Whoa, a cop? Am I supposed to be impressed?"

His speech is slurred.

"No, other than I can haul you in."

"Hell-of-an idea, go ahead. At least they'll feed me and give me a warm place to sleep."

"Just move on."

"Yes, sir, I'll do just that since no one gives a shit whether I live or die."

He growls like a dog and walks off mumbling to himself. When I arrive at the office, I find Jade and Hank alone in the office... no sign of Gustav, Victor, or Wilson.

"Good morning you two, where's Frick and Frack?"

"Off on an assignment for Chernov."

"Any word on the Colonel this morning, Jade?"

"I checked. Boris said Chernov took the day off. If he knows more, he's not saying."

"Hopefully, he's resting comfortably in a sanatorium somewhere."

"Hey, Billy, the walls have ears."

"Thank you for that timely reminder, Hank. I'm in of a cup of coffee."

On my way to the door and test my luck with Jade.

"How about you, Jade?"

"Yeah, sure. Hank, watch the phones."

Hank playfully lowers his face within inches of his phone.

"She means only if it rings, Hank."

"Oh, right, got it."

In the breakroom, I fix Jade and me a cup of coffee and join her at the table.

"I'm still coming to grips with Chernov's unforgivable actions, Jade. For the love of me, I'll never understand our propensity for human-to-human cruelty."

"Men like Chernov are just what Marseille's wants, cruel men with no filter when it comes to violence and human life. By the way, the new guy is scheduled to show up this morning. He won't be meeting with Chernov according to the note Wilson left me."

"I wonder why?"

"You know him?"

"Who?"

"The new guy, Chris Henley."

"I, uh—"

"I keep the records, remember? You both returned on the same ship. But for a blip on his transfer papers, you were supposed to check in together on the same day. Plan on Wilson bringing it up."

"On a more suitable subject, my life took a turn for the better Saturday night. How about an encore, come by tonight?"

"Love to. I'll come bearing pizza and a six pack of beer."

"Hey, before I forget."

Digging in my pocket, I pull out the extra set of keys Jules gave me.

"Your own keys to the castle."

She smiles and slips them in the pocket of her white, hip-

hugging jeans. We head back to the office. At 9:45 Wilson shows up and heads for his office without saying a word... he looks pissed... Hank leans to my desk.

"He looks like he was off dealing with the Chernov mess."

Chris arrives at 9:50... neither Hank nor I acknowledge him... after her initial remarks, Jade sends him in to meet with Wilson... twenty minutes later he and Wilson emerge... Wilson's still wearing a grim expression... he introduces Chris to us, but makes no mention that Chris and I know one another.

"You'll meet Heinz and Augier when they return, Chris. Sit with Jade, she'll get you up to speed."

"Thanks, Lieutenant."

Off Chris goes to get the skinny from Jade. When she finishes, she instructs him to take up residence at my old desk between the interrogation room and the men's room... lucky him, he gets to wade through those phony case files.

Come 11:45 Wilson calls me into his office... his expression is grim.

"You're not to let on to the others that you and Henley know one another."

"Lieutenant, I had no idea he was assigned here until he showed up yesterday."

"If I had been my decision or the Colonel's, the two of you would not have received the same assignment—that was Marseille's call. If it was up to me, I'd have one of you moved out of there."

"How about I volunteer?"

"Not funny, Billy. That'll be all."

Come lunch time, I take Chris to lunch and then we're going the clothing store.

"Did Wilson spell it out for you?"

"I'm not dense, Billy, the message was loud and clear. I took men's lives in war because if we didn't kill them, they'd have killed us, war is that simple. This is a whole different bag of tricks. What have we got ourselves into?"

"A hornet's nest, Chris, a hornet's nest."

"How do we get out?"

"I'm working on that."

We hit the Mexican place around the corner and settle in. I make no mention of what Chernov did to Alvera and Rubio, but I think it best I level with him about my evolving relationship with Jade on the chance he sees her coming and goings at the apartment.

"Whoa, Billy, you didn't let any grass grow under your feet. She's a stunner."

"And a warm, wonderful, lady."

"So, it's more than—"

"Sex? Yeah, you could say that."

"Lucky you, Billy."

"Come on, let's get you some new clothes in any color other than brown."

At 7:30 that evening, Jade arrives with a pizza and a six-pack of beer. As soon as we've eaten, we move on to more primal nourishment. The dessert course that follows lasts far longer than the pizza... it's 9:30 before we roll out of bed.

"Jade, I need to level with you."

"Sounds ominous."

"The first opportunity I get, I'm out of here."

"Out of here where?"

"Away from here, away from this madness and the violence. I'm not leaving without you."

"Then you're not going anywhere, Billy."

"Why?"

"Because the WPF will track us down and execute us on sight."

"There's always the chance they won't catch us."

"Billy, listen to me, that's a chance I'm not willing to take. The world isn't going to stand still for what's happening much longer, we need to hang in there."

"From your lips to God's ear, assuming She's listening."

"Yeah, well, maybe this time She is."

She's up on her feet heading for the door.

"Where're are you going? Stay the night."

"Soon, Billy, soon. Until then, keep your powder dry and stay put."

*And with that, the lady I now hold dear to my heart leaves me wondering what she might know that I don't, because I don't see the madness ending anytime soon. Once men seize power, they're not likely to go gently into the good night without a fight... assuming it could even come to that anytime soon. Jade's right of course, if we made a run for it, they'd find us and that would be the end of that. I'm tired but not ready for bed yet, let's see what TV is spewing at this hour. I punch in channel twenty-three... it's a nature program about a pride of lions on the vast Serengeti... happy to see there're still some left. As I'm gathering up the empty pizza box and beer cans, the program is interrupted by four loud beeps... the lion program is replaced with a one-word graphic—***BULLETIN***.*

"We interrupt this program to bring you this special report. A short while ago, World Council member Henry Dion was shot to death in New York's Central Park."

The pizza box and beer cans slip from my hands to the floor.

"Jesus, what?"

A headshot of Dion fills the screen.

"Commissioner Dion was struck twice in the chest at a gathering of approximately three-hundred supporters at Central Park's Bethesda Fountain. He was pronounced dead at the scene. The attack was caught on a bystander's cell phone. Warning, the footage you are about to see contains graphic images."

The scene changes to video of Dion addressing the gathering... he has a bullhorn to his mouth, but there's no audio... suddenly he jerks back... the bullhorn slips from his hand... he's clutches his chest, recoils a second time, wobbles back two more steps and collapses. The video swings wildly, swishing one way, then the other until it comes to rest on Dion's motionless body, then backs up as several in the crowd rush to his aid... the images blur again as the cell phone swings to the crowd scattering for safety. Wait! There! Holy shit, if I had blinked, I would have missed it. The announcer returns.

"We will update this tragic event as further details become available."

The lion program returns. With stunned disbelief, I turn off the TV... now I'm pacing... if I'm right about what I think I saw, I can't keep it to myself... Gideon, I have to call Gideon... what did I do with his number? Think, damn it, think... the desk, I tossed it in the drawer. If I do this, I'm committing myself to who knows what... think, damn it, Billy, think... make a command decision... do it, do it now... I dial Gideon's number, but get cold feet and disconnect before the first ring... screw it, let the madness not be mine... let the human race destroy itself if that's our destiny... God knows we've been trying to get it right for centuries only to have failed time and again. Go to bed, Billy Russell, pull the covers over your head and shut it all out, this is not your problem to solve. I'm back under the covers, but sleep eludes me... I can't get the image of Dion lying dead out of my head. At 1:20, unable to sleep, I sit up and stare into the darkness... you know what you should do, Billy, what you have to do, so get your dumb ass out of bed and do it... I'm up dialing Gideon's number again, hoping against hope I'm not making the biggest mistake of my life... four rings, five rings... come on, answer the damn phone... an automated voice comes on.

"Leave a message, I'll get back to you."

Jesus, an answering machine?

"This is 556. Call me as soon as you receive this."

I'm pacing the living room hoping Gideon calls back before I get cold feet again. I go back to bed... an hour goes by... still no call from Gideon... enough time for me to question my decision... but then the phone's ringing and it jolts me... I'm up following the sound of the rings... it's coming from the living room, but where's the bloody phone? There, it's peeking out from between the sofa cushions.

"Hello!"

"You called?"

"Gideon?"

"No names."

"I saw the news."

I'm expecting Gideon to express sorrow over Dion's death, but there's no response.

"Are you there?"

"Yes."

"I saw something."

Silence again.

"Did you hear what I said?

Silence again... damn it, I can hear him breathing.

"Be out front in thirty minutes."

"Make it the newsstand on the corner of 4th and Broadway."

The line goes dead... now to sneak out without alerting my first-floor guardian angel. The last thing I need is to explain to Jules where I'm going at this hour... it's 2:10 AM when I make my way down the steps and slip out as quietly as I can locking the door behind me... I trot to the newsstand... the Lexus is waiting... Norman's driving, Jason's riding shotgun.

"Good morning, Mister Russell."

"Nothing much good about it, Norman."

"No, nothing, nothing at all. Dog-shit villains have silenced Mister Dion. May their black hearts rot in hell."

I slip into the back seat... Jason passes me the black hood.

"Not again."

"I'm afraid so, sir."

As soon as the hood is on, Norman speeds off... for the next twenty-minutes not a word passes between us... either he's run every red-light or he's hit them all green... we don't stop until we reach our destination. Once inside, Norman sits me down in my favorite chair and removes the hood... Gideon is sitting across from me looking drawn and washed out.

"I'm sorry about Commissioner Dion."

"He leaves behind his wife, daughter and two grandchildren."

"After the Paris attack why didn't he go into hiding for a

229

few days?"

"Unable to get a direct flight to Boston, he flew from Marseille to New York planning to catch a connection to Logan Airport. Instead, he insisted on staying in New York and asked us to arrange that rally in Central Park. We had to scramble to make it happen."

"I saw two men fleeing with the crowd and—"

"Chernov's attack dogs, Heinz and Augier."

"You know?"

"I saw the same footage you did."

"It was so brief I almost missed it."

"You can be certain the video was taken by a government official—they wanted it out there for the whole world to see, to send a message to anyone who dared challenge Marseille's authority. Evidently, they failed to see what we saw before releasing the video. No one will ever accuse Marseille of being smart, Billy, just vicious."

"So, what happens now?"

"Nothing changes. Henry will unveil the Black Swan event to the world as planned."

"Dead men don't speak, Gideon."

"In this case they do. As planned, Henry taped his message before leaving Paris just in case. A few hours ago, one of his aides delivered it to me. Now, it's our job to broadcast it to the world."

"How you gonna pull that off?"

"You will know soon enough."

"You still don't trust me?"

"It is not a question of trust, Billy, it is simply a precaution. If you know nothing, they can't get anything out of you."

"Uh, a wonderful thought. Should I be worried?"

"I'm simply answering your question."

"This taped speech of Henry's better be bullet proof."

"I assure you, Billy it is."

"Then you know what's on it?"

"I do."

My life is in dire need of a refresher course... let's hope this is it... Gideon's on his feet... from his breast pocket he takes out one of his fat cigars and lights it, take a draw, and blows smoke circles.

"Many, many years ago, back in the early 90's, the United States Senate Chaplain spoke these insightful words: 'We now demand freedom without restraint, rights without responsibility, choice without consequences, leisure without pain. In our narcissistic, hedonistic, masochistic, valueless preoccupation, we've allowed ourselves to become dominated by lust, avarice, greed, and violence.' Society failed to heed the chaplain's words. Now, all these years later, here we are firmly under the thumb of this Marseille mob of impassionate, money grubbing thieves. In their never-ending quest for more power and wealth, we—Volte face—have united the masses to take action against them. And you, Billy, will have a front row seat."

"You seem cocksure you'll be able to pull this off."

"From across the globe, people will come together as one for the good of all.

"But surely Marseille knows something's up."

"Perhaps. But, as tragic as Henry's death is, they are too late—the wheels of freedom are in full motion and will not be denied."

"When is this supposed to happen?"

Gideon takes a drag on his cigar and looks away.

"Well?"

"Soon, Billy, there are still details that need to be locked down. By your presence here, I assume you are with us?"

"Yes."

"Excellent."

"I ah, I might know someone who may want to join us."

"Might that be Christopher Henley?"

"Jeez, is there anything you don't know?"

"Do you trust him?"

"We became close on the trip back. Yeah, I trust him."

"Have you spoken to him about this matter?"

"I had no reason to until now."

"Very well, proceed with caution. I will be in touch with further instructions. Good night, Billy."

"Wait."

"Yes, what is it?"

"This dissent group that calls themselves Apostolic Channel?"

He looks away followed by a long pause.

"It's a simple enough question, Gideon."

"They are a diversion."

"For what, from whom?"

"Those men and women are members of Volte-face and have placed themselves at risk to give us cover. So far, it has worked, so far as we know. I will leave you now. Goodnight, Billy."

"Whoa, hold on, big guy."

"Yes?"

"You know everything about me, I know nothing about you. I'd like to know who I'm putting life and limb on the line for."

"For Henry Dion, for the people of the world."

"For Billy Russell's peace of mind, answer the question."

Gideon pops to his feet, takes a drag on the cigar and walks off.

"I will be in touch soon. Thank you for coming."

"Trust, Gideon, remember, trust."

He stops, sucks on that damn cigar again before turning to me in a cloud of smoke.

"If you insist."

"I do."

He pulls another long drag on his cigar followed by a swirling cloud of white smoke.

"I first met Henry Dion at a U.N legal symposium in New York when I was chief solicitor to the British Ambassador and Henry was a prominent Boston attorney. After he became a U.S. Senator, we met at several social events. Although I was diametrically opposed to the PPP when it was introduced, Henry and I hit it off personally and our friendship grew. When he gained a seat on the World Council, he offered me the position of his chief of staff. I accepted. That's the long and short of it."

"Your name, your real name."

"Goodnight, Billy."

"Your name."

"Is this really necessary, Billy?"

"For me it is."

"All right, it's Oliver Neville."

And with that, Oliver Neville, the proper English gentleman, saunters off in a cloud of cigar smoke. Norman is at my side handing me the hood.

"We'll take you home now, Mister Russell."

"The hood again?"

"Hopefully for the last time, sir."

During the drive back, I tray engaging Norman and Jason in conversation to see if I can learn more, but all I get is an occasional grunt... beyond that, nothing. It's 6:28 AM by the time they drop me off at the newsstand... if I return to the apartment, Jules might be up and grill me to no end. The newsstand is open... I grab a newspaper and Sully pours me a cup of black coffee. Arriving at the office at 7:00, I'm surprised to find Jade at her desk.

"What are you doing here so early, Jade?"

"Couldn't sleep, so I came in. You heard the news?"

"Just before I left my apartment. Tragic, Billy, tragic. They'll stop at nothing against anyone who dares speaks out against them."

I want to take her into my confidence about Gideon, as well as what I saw in that video footage, but I hesitate involving her... on the other hand, if she saw the footage, she may have seen what I saw and not tell me.

"The world is spinning at a faster rate than I can catch up."

She takes my hand and cradles it in hers.

"The good guys will win, you'll see, Billy."

"Are we the good guys, Jade?"

She smiles warmly.

"Damn right, Buckaroo, damn right."

Bending to her, I kiss her lightly.

"Look, uh, Jade, too much is happening all at once. I'm overwhelmed and wound tighter than a drum. I need time to figure out a few things. Tell Wilson I called in with a touch of food poisoning and I'm spending the day bent over the commode."

"You're not planning anything, are you, Billy?"

"I told you, I won't leave without you. You stay, I stay."

"Go home, do whatever, put the rest out of your mind."

"Easier said than done, Jade."

"Tomorrow night around 7:00? I'll bring Chinese this time."

"Haven't had any Chinese food in—"

"Seventeen years—got it."

I'm strolling along Broadway one foot in front of the other at a snail's pace in no hurry to return to my meager surroundings. At least Henley is there now... I have someone to talk to who shared cold sleeping quarters, dust swirling, lung-destroying mine shafts, bad food, brutal guards, and all the rest of the crap that went with subterranean life. When I reach the house, I stand and stare at the building for a few seconds, then turn and keep walking... a block down I spot Zen and Mei... we exchange glances, Zen nods... I would like to speak with them, to learn more about the personal circumstances that put them out here on the streets. There're other Streetwalkers in the area... Zen and Mei slink away not wanting to be seen talking to a cop... can't blame them. After walking aimlessly for almost an hour, I head back to the house.

At noon I open a can of Chef Boyardee's SpaghettiOs © with little meatballs that was part of my welcome package eating it cold right out of the can as I used to as a kid over my mother's stern objections. Following my gourmet lunch, I turn on the computer. In my 'stuff' file, I document my meeting with Gideon. I just hope the hell he can deliver what he's promising... to get most of the world's population on the same page at the same time requires a minor miracle... I don't believe in miracles. Next, I add to the notes of my time on

Europa... today, it's about Quasi and the guards, trained gorillas on Colonel Maks short leash, men without morals who placed little or no value on human life. Before I know it, it's 5:45... I hear a door close in the hall... Chris must be home... I want to rush over and fill him in about my meeting with Neville and this Volte-face movement and how, if successful, we could find ourselves free of this new hell we're in. I better be cautious, Chris might place a greater value on his new found freedom, such as it is, and tell me to leave him out of it... until the day comes when he's ordered to do what is inhumane, immoral, and every other word in the English lexicon that describes an executioner. Screw it, I have to trust he trusts me... he has a stake in this too whether he realizes yet or not... only one way to find out... I'll go over there, and as Hank once said to me, put our cards face up. Or maybe not, maybe this is a mistake to involve him so soon after he's returned... he barely has his feet on solid ground yet. Oh, hell, I'll just tell him all that's going on and let him make his own decision. When I knock on his door, he answers in his underwear.

"Hey Billy, Jade said you weren't feeling well."

"Can you come over?"

"Not if you're sick, man."

"I'm not."

"Then what?"

"Put your pants on and I'll explain. I'll leave my door ajar."

"What's going on?"

"Just come over."

I return to my place and wait... five minutes later, Chris waltzes in wearing his new clothes... a dark-blue T-shirt and blue jeans.

"Whatta think?"

"Never saw you looking better, my man. Want a beer?"

"Yeah, sure, Billy, love one."

Grabbing two cold ones left from Jade's visit, we settle on the sofa... go slow and easy, Billy, don't hit him over the head with this.

"I think often of poor Leon. It was a horrible way to go."

"Yes, it was."

"Every time I went to the John, I wondered if his body was still in that closet."

"Same here, Billy. But something tells me you didn't call me over to talk about Leon."

"All right, to the point. Now that you know what's really going on at 513, where is your head at?"

"If I had known, I would have never gotten on that plane to come here. Having said that, I'm a free man, with my own apartment, a salary, I walk the streets freely and—"

"Chris, Chris, I told you, we are anything but free men. We may have broken the bonds of Europa, but there was a reason we were chosen to do what they ask of us."

"And your theory would be?"

"What was it that got you a reserved bunk on Europa?"

"Why do you need to know?"

"It'll all become clear."

"You're turning out to be a pain in the ass, Russell."

"I hear that a lot. Now tell me why you were sent to Europa and I'll tell you my story."

He shoots me a grim look… he's pissed with me for asking.

"You need to trust me on this one, Chris."

"If you must know, I was a Marine sniper."

He goes silent for a few beats.

"That accounts for that rifle tattoo on your arm."

"Yeah. What's that in your shirt pocket?"

"Cigarettes."

"Toss me one."

"I've never seen you smoke, Chris."

"You gonna preach or toss me one?"

He sounds like Jules. I pass him a cigarette and lighter… he lights up, takes a long drag exhales the smoke slowly.

"We were in Syria trying to help those people keep the peace after their government was overthrown."

He goes silent again and takes another drag on the cigarette.

"I took down two Libyan dudes who weren't on the official kill list."

"You shot them by accident?"

"Billy, I never took anyone out by accident."

"Then what?"

"Me and Brad Stone, my spotter, we're on a small hill overlooking the Syrian town of Suwayda, just north of the Jordanian Border. Jamal Hassan, a known maker of IEDs, was our target. We had tracked him to one of four houses on an isolated street at the southern end of the village. We see two screaming teenage girls being dragged out of the nearest house by two men followed by the girl's mother and father. We recognized the two men right off—Karam Samaan and Mahdi Yousef—paid informants for our side, so we thought. Yousef shouted something at the father, then he and Samaan executed the four of them right there in the street."

"Jesus."

"Brad and I were enraged. With his high-powered rifle-mounted scope, he provided me the range. I didn't hesitate for a second. I dropped Samaan and Yousef each with a shot to the head."

Chris turns away and washes a hand over his face.

"Turns out Samaan and Yousef were taking money from both sides. The brass knew it, but for whatever reason that information was never shared with us on the ground. Fearing a backlash, Command needed a scapegoat. I was accused of going rogue and taking down two civilians without authority. To save his ass, that son of a bitch Brad Stone testified against me, said he tried to stop me, which was a lie, he didn't. I was court martialed and sent to Europa."

"I'm sorry, Chris."

"Not near as sorry as I am. Okay, your turn."

I proceed to give up the details of what I did in that closet and why... he's speechless and doesn't know what to say. When I finished, I round up the two remaining beers and hand him one.

"You better have another—there's more."

I fill him in on all that Jules shared with me, beginning with the Pakistan-India episode, the fear that followed, the creation of a World Government... everything I had learned about the upside-down world we found ourselves trapped in capping it off with Chernov's erratic behavior and his execution of Alvera and his top gun, Rubio.

"You executed those two Afghani's for the same reason I executed my wife's murderer. We both served up justice when we believed the system wouldn't or couldn't."

"And we both paid dearly for it, Billy."

"Yes, we did."

What I have in mind next could go either way ... here goes nothing.

"You're aware a man by the name of Henry Dion was assassinated in Central Park yesterday?"

"It was all over the news this morning. He was some big shot in the government, wasn't he?"

"An outspoken member of the World Council who made the mistake of openly challenging the Marseilles regimes policies. It's what happens to everyone who crosses the line against Marseille. That video they ran on the news, you saw it?"

"Yeah."

"I saw something that could crack this wide open."

"Like what?"

"Gustav Heinz and Victor Augier were in the crowd."

"The two guys I haven't met yet?"

"Yeah."

"What would they be doing in New York?"

"Unit 513 is their cover."

"Cover? Cover for what?"

I roll out the details of Gustav and Augier's suspected extra-curricular activities ... as much as Hank told me ... Chris's expression changes to disbelief.

"They take their orders not from Wilson, but Colonel Andrei Chernov, who reports directly to Marseille. Every time they're off on an assignment for Chernov, someone who had the balls to speak out against Marseille dies. That video footage confirms it."

"Holy shit, man."

"Now for chapter two. There's an underground movement

238

planning to overthrow the World Government, and—"

"What?"

"… and Dion is—was—the force behind it."

"And you know this how?"

"I've met twice with the man running the show for Dion."

"Why in the hell would you do that, Billy?"

"Initially, I didn't, at least not voluntarily. They chose me."

"To do what?"

"If you'll let me finish it'll all become clear. First, they knew everything about me—Europa and all the rest. They know everything about you too."

"How?"

"Good question, I don't know how they get their information, but they do. Anyway, I told them to screw off, that I wasn't interested. But that changed when I saw that video."

"Wait a minute, back up. Who are these people?"

"The movement's called Volte-face and—"

"Volte what?"

"Volte face."

"Have you lost your marbles, man? We finally escape the Europa iceberg and you wanna jump into the fire. Why the hell would you do that?"

"Because I have nothing to lose. If this movement is successful, I'm a free man, so are you."

"Or we could be dead men."

"Dion taped his message. When hits the airwaves, it's game over."

"What's it got to do with me?"

"I was hoping you'd sign on to—"

"Me? To do what?"

"I'm trying to explain."

"Let me educate you, Billy. This is how it really works. When the alarm sounds, first comes bravado, then fear, followed by a need for self-preservation, then no one shows up, and those of us who volunteered are left standing there wondering where all are the others. Besides, the government controls the military—end of the revolution. What was it you called it?"

"Volte-face. It means 'change' in French."

"I've heard enough."

Chris sets his beer on the coffee table, pops to his feet, and heads for the door.

"Where're you going?"

"As far away from this as I can get, pal."

"Chris, listen to me, I've been assured that Henry Dion's message will—"

"Get a good night's sleep, Billy. You'll come to your senses in the morning."

His hand encircles the doorknob... he's turning it. My phone rings once, twice, three times.

"Answer your phone."

And then he leaves... I sweep up the phone and listen.

"556?"

It's Norman's voice.

"Yes."

"Day after tomorrow, 4:00 AM at the newsstand."

"I'll be there along with the other gentleman I spoke of."

"Goodnight."

The line goes dead... tossing the phone on the sofa. Determine to get Chris involved, I march across the hall to his door... it's slightly ajar.

"Chris?"

"You gonna talk to me through the door or come in?"

I push the door open, but don't enter... he's sitting in a chair sipping Bourbon and looking quite pissed.

"I'm sorry, Chris. I'm not trying to talk you into anything."

"You could have fooled me."

"That call was to let me know it's going down day after tomorrow. I told them you might be with me."

"You were that sure of me?"

"If you don't want any part of this, say so and I'll be gone."

"Goddamn you, Billy Russell."

"Yes, goddamn me, Chris Henley. Look, do what you think is right for you."

"You never told me what they're asking you to do?"

240

I explain the role I agreed to play... as least as much as I know... Chris blows a hard breath... he's thinking.

"I suppose if I let you go alone, you'll get yourself killed."

"Is that your way of telling me you're in?"

Grim-faced, his head bobs up and down.

"I'm proud of you, brother Henley."

"Yeah, that's me, patriotic brother Henley. Don't stand there, come in and have a drink. On the other hand, maybe we should take that Shepherd's advice when he saw the storm rolling in."

"Or maybe not."

"Get your ass in here before I change my mind."

CHAPTER 25

There but For the Grace of God

As I'm preparing to leave the house Tuesday morning, my cell rings… it's Jimmy Oliveri, my parents' attorney. With all that's happened, I had completely forgotten about him. He's happy to hear I'm back safe and sound, then apologizes… seems my message fell through the cracks and he just came across it. Yes, he drew up my parents' will… I am the sole beneficiary… as soon as the estate makes it through final probate, the assets will be turned over to me. I don't want any material stuff … the memories would be too painful. He agreed to have his office handle the liquidation of all assets and turn the proceeds over to me. For now, I think I'll just keep this news to myself.

Chris and I walk to the office together, stopping on the way for a cup of coffee at Sully's. Chris is taken aback by the number of homeless walking about aimlessly.

"It wasn't near this bad yesterday."

"It's worse at the tent cities. You won't believe the conditions people are forced to endure."

When we arrive at the office, Gustav and Victor are still missing in action… Jade's nowhere to be seen.

"Hank, where's Jade?"

"Ladies."

Wilson comes out of his hole long enough to instruct Hank and me to take Chris out for a taste of the streets, turns around and goes back without ever so much as a good morning… ah, there she is, Jade's back.

"Good morning. We're taking Chris out for a joy ride through paradise. The office is all yours."

"I'll do my best not to burn it down. Be careful out there."

Once out on the streets, Chris is shocked at what he sees.

"Hank, how do these people survive?"

"Many of them don't, Chris. Those who do are hooked on cheap drugs, which leads to petty crime, increased violence, or worse, death. If the government believes we drug units are going to stop the madness, they're smoking funny cigarettes. There's no solution as long as they stay in power. It'll take a worldwide uprising to bring those lying, cheating bastards to their knees before we can really address the problem, because the problem is them."

Chris shoots me a knowing look.

"Hank, let's take Chris by Moakley Park."

When we arrive, Chris stares in disbelief and sighs.

"My God."

"This is just one of several encampments."

"Hank, I could have gone all day without seeing this."

"It's our reality, Chris, get used to it."

At 11:45 we end up at Maggie's for lunch... the insult routine between her and Hank amuses Chris.

"She seems to enjoy the jabbing, Hank."

"That she does, Chris, and she dishes it out pretty good too."

By 4:45, after covering most of the South end *without incident, we're back in the office... I smile my usual flirting smile.*

"Where's the troops, Jade?"

"Gustav and Victor are back. They're down the hall huddled with Boris and Ivan getting an update on Chernov. Wilson's with them."

"What's with the good Colonel?"

"Still missing in action is all I know, Billy. You guys should call it a day too."

Hank is on his feet heading for the door.
"Billy, Chris, you guys want a lift?"
"I'll walk, Hank."
"Chris?"
"Thanks, Hank, I'll walk with Billy."
As we reach the door, Jade stops me.
"Hey, almost forgot, the Lieutenant left a note in your in basket."
"Chris, I'll meet you downstairs."
In my in-basket is an envelope with my name scribbled on it... inside, I find a short-handwritten note from Wilson... he wants to meet with me first thing in the morning.
"Jade, do you know what this is about?"
"What is it?"
"Wilson wants to meet with me in the morning."
"No, I have no idea, Billy."
Crumpling the note, I toss it to the basket next to Gustav's desk and miss... scooping it up, I drop it in the basket when I notice one word in the middle of Gustav's computer monitor— **EMAIL.** *I glance over to Jade... she's busy typing. With my left hand, I hit the space-bar and up comes his email in box. The most recent message contains two words all in caps,* **"Neville ASAP.** *" The return address is listed as WG... has to be World Government... I check his outgoing emails... there's his two-word response.* **"On it."** *Closing the screen, I look to Jade... she's still typing... act casual, make a lame joke, then get out of here fast, Billy.*
"Hey, need a bucket of water?"
"What?"
"You're gonna set that keyboard on fire."
She stops typing and swivels to me.
"Very funny. I'll see you later for Chinese?"
"I'm running on two cylinders, how about a rain check?"
"You're not coming down with something, are you?"
"I don't know, I just feel punk."
"Come here."
She places a hand on my forehead.
"No fever. Go home and get some rest."

"I will."

I'm out the door, rushing down the stairs two at a time... Chris is waiting on the sidewalk.

"Come on, we need to get to the house."

"What's the rush?"

"Someone's going to die."

"Who?"

"I'll explain when we get to the house, come on."

As soon as we're in the door at my place, Chris is all over me.

"Now will you tell me why we rushed back here and who's going to die?"

"In a minute, Chris."

I find Oliver's number and dial it.

"Who are you calling?"

"Shh, Chris, wait!"

Four rings later someone answers... it's Norman.

"This is 556."

"Yes."

"Where's the man?"

"He's not available at the moment."

"Where is he?"

"Home resting, I'm covering his calls."

"Call him now, tell him to turn off his lights, pull the shades, and lock his doors."

There's no response.

"Norman?"

"Why would he do that, Billy?"

"Because he's in danger."

"What sort of danger?"

"Norman, for God's sake, stop talking, get in your damn car, and pick me up right after you call the man."

The damn fool doesn't answer.

"Did you hear what the hell I said?"

"What sort of danger is he in?"

"Damn you, man, you can keep asking questions or can get to his place ASAP. What's it going to be?"

"Um, okay, but it'll take me twenty minutes to get to you."

"Call the man first, then pick me up at the newsstand."

I hang up and bark to Chris.

"Chris, get your gun."

"Now what?"

I quickly fill him in on the email I found on Gustav's computer.

"It can only mean one thing—they're gonna take out Oliver Neville."

"Who is Oliver Neville?"

"I'll explain on the way. Get your gun and let's get to the newsstand.

By the time we get to the closed newsstand, *it's dark and the temperature has dropped several degrees.*

"That note can only mean one thing. Marseille knows something's about to happen and it's Oliver Neville leading the charge."

Norman arrives none too soon... we're freezing our asses off out here... I slip in the front seat, Chris in the back.

"Norman, Chris Henley, Chris, Norman. I don't know Norman's last name."

"It's Wagoner. Nice to meet you, Chris."

"Same here, Norman."

"Did you contact the man?"

"I called, but he failed to pick up, Billy."

"Damn it, damn it. How long to get to Oliver's place?"

"He resides in Beacon Hill. It'll take us thirty minutes."

"Drive, Norman, drive."

As Norman navigates traffic, I fill him in on what I found on Gustav's computer.

"Dear God, no."

"Dear God, yes, Norman."

Norman makes it to Beacon Street in twenty minutes flat pulling up short of a high-rise condominium identified by a black plaque with gold letters as **'Lederman Tower'**.

"Mister Neville resides on the seventh floor. There's a

doorman in the lobby 24/7."

"Do they know you?"

"Yes, I'm in and out regularly."

"Let's go."

We enter the lobby... it's empty except for the doorman who greets Norman with a hesitant smile.

"Good evening, Mister Wagoner."

"Hi Walter."

"Is everything okay?"

"Why do you ask?"

"Two policemen are up with Mister Neville."

Damn it, damn it, Gustav and Victor are already here!

"They said it was an official matter and insisted on going up unannounced. Is there a problem, Mister Wagoner?"

"A misunderstanding. These officers are here to straighten it out."

"Can I see their identification, please."

Chris and I reveal our belt-mounted badges.

"Thank you. I'll call up and let Mister Neville know you're on the way up."

"That's not necessary, I'll escort them up, Walter."

"Well, okay, if you say so, Mister Wagoner."

"Thank you, Walter."

Norman leads us down the marble floor hallway, then left to two elevators... one to our right, one to our left.

"The one on the right stops at each apartment on the East side, the other on the West—Mister Neville's is on the West side. We should use the service elevator in the garage. That will take us to the back entrance to Mister Neville's apartment."

"We could have driven in?"

"Sorry, Billy, I should have thought of that."

"Never mind, let's go."

Norman leads the way to a door at the far end of the hallway that leads to the ground floor parking garage... around the corner to the right is the Westside service elevator... Norman punches in a four-digit code... the doors open and we load in... he taps 007 for the seventh floor and we're on the move... fifteen seconds later we arrive... the doors open to a small lobby... Norman points forward and whispers.

"Mister Neville's apartment is through that door."

He approaches the door... I reach for his arm.

"Wait."

Placing an ear to the door, I listen.

"I hear voices, but I can't make out what's being said."

Norman points to a keypad mounted on the wall to the left of the door and whispers.

"I have the code, Billy."

"Do it."

He punches in a four-digit code... the door lock slides open... let's hope they didn't hear that... Chris and I take out our guns.

"Norman, do you have a weapon?"

He pulls back his coat revealing a stainless-steel Walther PPK.380 tucked in his belt.

"Okay, open the door."

Slowly, Norman slides the door open about halfway... off in the distance, we hear Victor's voice.

"Our patience is running thin, Mister Neville."

"I told you a half-dozen times, I have no idea why you are here or what you're talking about."

"Save yourself the pain of having to pry it from you."

There's no answer from Oliver. Then comes the unmistakable sound of him being slapped... Norman bolts forward... I grab his arm.

"Wait. Where are they?"

"The living room straight ahead at the far end of the apartment."

Gustav's talking again.

"It would pain me to ruin this beautiful Persian rug with your blood, Mister Neville. We can avoid that if you cooperate."

There's no answer from Oliver... he's slapped again... he groans... with our weapons raised, we move cautiously down a darkened hall past two bedrooms, one to the left, one to the right... we enter the kitchen and then the dining room beyond where Norman stops us and points forward... ever so slowly we advance... the living room comes into view... Gustav and Victor's backs are to us... Oliver's sitting in a chair facing us with his hands secured behind his back... he spots us... his eyes widen... damn it, don't give us away, Oliver... I raise my weapon to eye level and move quickly toward them.

"Either of you even twitches, you're dead men."

Gustav and Victor spin around to find three guns pointed their way.

"Russell, what the hell are you doing here?"

"Making sure you don't screw up the world more than you already have. Oliver, are you okay?"

"Yes, except these handcuffs are cutting into my wrists."

"We'll take care of that. Gustav and Victor, remove your weapons, place them on the floor and kick them to me. Do it slowly, do it now."

Gustav glances sideways to Victor and nods... they remove their weapons, drop them to the floor, and kick them toward me.

"Which one of you clowns has the key to the handcuffs?"

Gustav nods.

"Reach in your pocket and hand it to Norman. Do it slowly."

Gustav hands the key to Norman who quickly frees Oliver.

"Norman, cuff Gustav. Chris, do the same to Victor."

Oliver's pops to his feet and moves to my side.

"Billy, how in God's creation did you know?"

"German sloppiness. Mister Heinz, in his haste to get here, left his computer open to his email. The most recent one said, **'Neville ASAP.'**"

Victor's face goes pale, his head whips to Gustav.

"De quoi parle-t-il?"

"Oliver, do you speak French?"

"Mister Augier is quite upset with Mister Heinz."

"And well he should be. Chris, watch them."

I reach down to pick up their weapons... growling like a dog, Gustave thrusts his body toward me... I strike the left side of his head with the barrel of my gun... he yelps and goes down... blood's seeping from his cheek.

"Jesus, Heinz, you're even more stupid than I gave you credit for."

"The cleansing is well underway, Russell, and nothing you do will stop it."

"The cleansing? Is that what we're calling it?"

"Whatever you're planning, Marseille will shut you down."
He tosses his head back and laughs.

"Wir werden uns durchsetzen, wir sind die Meisterrasse."

"Anyone speak German?"

"I do."

"Norman, you're full of surprises."

"My parents were German immigrants. German was my first language. He said, we are the master race and we will prevail."

"Gustav, you and Victor have been eating too much oatmeal and washing it down with Cool Aid spiked with propaganda. Oliver, call your doorman. Tell him all's well, that it was all a misunderstanding and we're leaving on the service elevator."

"What will you do with them?"

"Not sure yet. Oliver, does this change your plans in any way?"

"No, we go on as planned."

"Are you okay staying here alone?"

"Yes, Billy, I'll be fine."

As we ride the elevator to the garage, I'm arguing with myself as to what to do with Heinz and Augier... listen to your gut, Billy Boy, you know what you have to do, so get on with it.

"Norman, where's the nearest body of water?"

"The Charles River bordering Lederman Park a couple of blocks from here."

"Lederman Park it is. Get the car, meet us here in the garage."

"We'll have to leave the car in the Vesta garage across the

street from the park—it's pedestrians only."

"Better yet, Norm."

"What are you thinking, Billy?"

"Nothing good, Chris, nothing good."

When Norman arrives with the car, I place Victor in the front seat, Gustav's between Chris and me in the back... Chris's gun is pointed at Gustav's head, mine at Victor's... not a word is spoken as Norman drives to the nearby Vesta garage, then we're off on foot crossing the street to Lederman Park... we get a break, there's not a soul in sight at this hour.

"Norman, is there a boat ramp?"

"Down by Fielder Field."

"Take us there."

"Billy, what the hell are we doing?"

"Reinstating the rule of law, Chris... kind of."

"Huh?"

It's a five-minute walk down the esplanade to the boat ramp where we cross over the short walkway to the break-wall.

"Norman, set them on their knees on the edge."

"Billy, think this through, let's not do something we'll regret."

"I've done all the thinking and regretting I'm going to, Chris. Norman, down on their knees."

Chris grabs my arm.

"For Christ's sake, Billy, think this through."

Gustav tosses his head back and laughs.

"Yeah, Billy Baby, think this through."

"Chris, did you think it through when you took those two guys out?"

"That was different."

"No, no it wasn't. These two traveled the world assassinating people who had the courage to speak out against an evil empire. What we do now is for them in their memory."

"Du bist ein totaler ideio, Russell."

"Norman?"

"Mister Heinz called you a fool, said you have no insight into human stupidity."

Gustav laughs again and spits at my feet.

"Nicht alle Männer sind gleich geschaffen, etwas, das du noch lernen musst.

"If I interpreted correctly, Billy, he said, 'You have yet to learn that all men are not created equal.'"

"And therein, Mister Heinz, lies the reason we must bring down this government starting here and now. The color of a man's skin is not the measure of a man, the amount of money a man makes is not the measure of a man, nor is the power he might hold over others. What a shame you don't understand that."

Gustav sneers.

"What a shame you don't understand how this world works, mister bleeding heart."

"I understand it all too well, Gustav. I pity you because you don't. Enough chit-chat, let's get on with the main event."

I place my weapon to the back of Gustav's head... Norman grabs my arm.

"Wait, Billy."

Norman doesn't hesitate, he places his gun against the back of Gustav's head and squeezes the trigger... there's a loud 'Oh, shit!' from Chris... Gustav's skull explodes and he topples forward into the icy waters of the St. Charles River. Norman steps behind Victor and pulls the trigger again... the impact drives Victor forward into the water next to Gustav's floating body... Norman's smiling.

"That was for Oliver Neville."

CHAPTER 26

Failure Is Not an Option

When we return to the newsstand, Norman *turns off the engine.*

"If we hadn't arrived when we did, they would have—"

"It's done, Norman. Go home, indulge in several stiff drinks. We'll meet you back here at 4:00 AM as planned."

Norman is grinning from ear-to-ear.

"Not sure why I should feel good about taking a life, but in the case of Heinz and Augier, I do."

"Thank goodness we were able to stop them, Norman."

He shakes our hands and drives off... Chris and I linger on the corner under the street light... I light a cigarette.

"Give me one of those."

"Chris, even though cigs were free, you never smoked on Europa."

"I never participated in an execution on Europa either."

We stroll slowly down 4th... not a word passes between us... we enter the house as quietly as we can so as not to arouse the Energizer Bunny.

"Let's try to get some sleep before we meet up with Norman again."

"I make no promises, Billy, I'm wired tight."

"Ditto. I feel contaminated and dirty, like I've been wallowing with pigs... I need a hot shower and time to reflect."

"Me too."

The first thing I do upon entering my apartment is to get me first a shot of booze, which turns into a second one followed by a hot steaming shower. Not for a second do I regret what happened to the joy boys... I only regret Chernov wasn't there to have joined them in the cold waters of the St. Charles river.

At 3:50 AM, Chris and I are pacing *under the streetlight by the newsstand again.*

"Did you get any sleep, Chris?"

"No, you?"

"No much."

"Billy old friend, it would be nice to know where we're going and why?"

Before I can respond, six male Streetwalkers are headed our way... more than a couple is a gang and should be treated as a threat.

"Hand on gun, Chris."

They're coming directly toward us... as they get closer, they spot our badges and our hands resting on our weapons... pretending they never saw us, they cut across the street disappearing into the dark cold night. Norman arrives... I assume the other guy with him is Jason. Chris goes around to the street side and slips into the back... I slide in from curb side and close the door.

"Good evening, gentlemen."

"It's early morning, Norman, I could use more sleep."

"Is that a complaint?"

That voice... are my ears deceiving me?

"Hank?"

"In the flesh."

"What are you doing here?"

"What, you think you're special or something? Oliver recruited me months ago. You two are late comers to the game."

"You never said a word, you could have at least—"

"That day in the car, when I showed you that paper, I was ready to tell you."

"Why didn't you?"

"You had not committed to the movement yet."

"Jesus, Hank, so you're the office mole?"

"Welcome aboard, Chris."

"Hank, answer my question."

"What was it again?"

"Stop playing games, you're the office mole."

"Not me, man, not me. Gentleman, expect lots of fireworks before this day is over. By the way, Norman told me about Gustav and Victor's fate. My only regret is I wasn't there to see the look on their faces when you guys showed up. That was one hell of an indoctrination for you, Chris."

"One I hope to never repeat."

Norman catches I-93 North, crosses Boston Harbor, turns Southwest on Edwin H. Land Blvd., while Hank fills us in on his involvement in Volte-face.

"The choice was clear. It was either this or live in servitude for the rest of our lives."

Norman turns West on Main Street, Southwest on Vassar, past the Massachusetts Institute of Technology, then right on Massachusetts Avenue. At the corner of Massachusetts and Albany Streets, he slows and glides up a wide driveway to the right, stopping at a high double-wide metal gate attached to a cement block wall that surrounds a large compound... he flashes his headlight three times, pauses for a second, then flashes them twice more... the gate begins to slowly swings inward... we move forward into a dimly lit parking lot... three vehicles are parked in front of a large two-story building... the first and second floor windows are boarded over and painted the same off-white as the building.

"What is this place, Norman?"

"It was a local TV station, Billy. The government took it over and turned it into a regional relay station that covers all of the East Coast."

In the center of the first floor are solid double steel doors... in a grassy area off to the right of the building are three satellite dishes... one large and two smaller ones.

"Okay gentlemen, game on."

We follow Norman to the steel doors... he presses a wall-mounted buzzer on the wall next to the right door... a slot in the door slides open and a pair of eyes peer out... the slot closes... we hear several security bolts being released and the door swings open... none other than Norman's partner in crime, Jason, greets us.

"Gentlemen, come in."

Jason closes and bolts the door... Norman makes the introductions.

"Jason, you know Hank and Billy. This gentleman is Chris Henley."

"Welcome, Chris, glad you could join us. Follow me, please."

Jason leads us down a semi-dark hallway passing several empty offices on either side to a double-wide high-ceiling hallway that goes left and right... to the right it dead ends at an overhead garage door... Jason turns left to double doors that are the same height and width as the hallway... he swings the right door open... the room is the size of a basketball court... the front and left walls are wrapped in an L-shaped white Cyclorama... a table laden with refreshments runs along the left side of the Cyc... an overhead lighting grid with a few lights still hanging illuminate the space... at one time this had to have been a production studio... a large television monitor is mounted on two stands several feet in front of the Cyc... the screen is filled with a photo of Henry Dion... facing the TV are a dozen or more folding chairs.

"What's with the chairs and food, Norman, movie night?

"Mister Neville will explain, Hank."

"That's what you always say, Norman."

Oliver is standing by the refreshment table speaking with two men... he spots us and comes over with one of them.

"Gentleman, good morning."

"Is it, Oliver?"

"Trust me, Billy, it will be. May I introduce Brian Adams, the facility's engineer."

Brian is middle aged, tall with receding brown hair and pleasant smile.

"Brian, these are our friends Billy, Chris and Hank. I'm pleased you could join us, gentlemen. I'm sure you have many questions concerning the role you'll play. Brian will take you to the engineering room and answer all of your questions. Grab some coffee food if you like and we'll chat again when you return."

Oliver motions for me to wait while Hank, Chris, and Norman move to the refreshment table.

"I'm left to wonder my fate if you hadn't arrived when you did. For that, I will be forever in your debt."

"I was afraid we'd be too late, Oliver."

"Ten minutes more and you would have. Norman informed me of how Heinz and Augier were dispatched. There is nothing to be gained by sharing that with anyone here."

"I understand."

Taking my hand, he shakes it vigorously.

"When this is over, Billy, I owe you one."

"If we all survive whatever is about to happen."

"We will be victorious. Now help yourself to breakfast. We'll talk when you return."

He smiles, shakes my hand again, and strolls across the room rejoining the other man he had been speaking with. The refreshment table is loaded from one end to the other with juices, coffee, bagels, croissants and fresh cut fruits.

"Expecting a big crowd, Brian?"

"Yes, there will be others joining us."

I grab a coffee and off we go with Brian out of the studio and down a dimly lit hallway to an elevator that takes us to the second floor... the doors slide open... directly ahead is a steel door... Brian unlocks it... we enter a cold, brightly lit room... as bright as Donald P. Costigan's white-on-white office. Six metal racks line the left wall filled with monitors and blinking electronic equipment... Brian stops at the third rack.

"First, a bit of background to clarify what the plan was and how it has changed. Mister Dion was to deliver his message live from the studio. However, the plan called for him to record his presentation in case something went wrong, which of course it tragically did. Now it's up to us to ensure his message is broadcast."

"Sounds complicated and risky."

"Not as difficult as you might think, Hank. Relay stations like this one are totally automated and require but a single engineer to keep them humming along. At this facility, it's yours truly. Programming from all commercial sources is first beamed to Menwith Station in England, then to government-controlled broadcast satellites that download content to regional relay stations like this one throughout the world."

"Why the extra steps?"

"Government censors scrutinize all content region by region before any programming is allowed to be broadcast."

"Everything?"

"Everything down to the commercials, Chris."

"How about local newscasts? They're usually live."

"They are restricted to thirty minutes at seven AM and six PM in the different time zones around the world. Network news in each country is allowed one-hour following the nightly local news. The only international news comes from the government channel, which, as you know, is 24/7."

"And the cable news networks?"

"Gone."

"And just how do you plan to send Dion's message?"

"I didn't get a pedigree in broadcast engineering just to play mechanic to a bunch of blinking electronic lights, Billy."

With a couple of twists of a Philips screwdriver, Brian removes a blank faceplate in the middle of the third rack exposing a square gray box with a small lock attached to an eye loop at the bottom... on its cover is stenciled **'Caution, Electrical Box.'** *A yellow wire runs out the lower left side and disappears behind the rack... Brian unlocks the box and raises the cover. Whoa, what have we here? A laptop computer with the 'HP' logo on its cover is mounted flat against the back of the box. Running out of the left side of it is that same yellow wire.*

"I wired this computer directly to the large satellite."

"Come on, Brian, it can't be that simple."

"Oh, but it was, Billy."

Brian snakes a hand around the left side of the box and retrieves a white box no bigger than a bar of soap and opens it... inside is a single UBS stick... he holds it up.

"This contains Mister Dion's recorded message. I copied it to this computer."

"So, you know what's on it."

"I do, Billy."

"Oliver described it as a Black Swan event. Does it live up to that?"

"Per Oliver's instructions, I'm not at liberty to reveal its contents. Everyone will see and hear it together when it's broadcast."

Nice try, Billy Boy, but loyal soldier as Brian is, he's not about to clue us in.

"Menwith's control room is manned 24/7 by three teams of three engineers. They are the only ones allowed inside other than security that comes around five-minutes past each hour to ensure all is running smoothly. This morning, at 8:50 our time, three security officers will enter the control room. Along with the engineers on duty, all are members of Volte-face. They will secure the door from the inside. When the real security guy's shows up, it'll be too late—by then we'll be on the air. At 8:59:59, Menwith's primary and backup satellite will be cut and replaced with the signal we'll beam to them from here. That's the good news. The bad news is, there was no way to test it without being discovered. Since we only have one shot, I've scrutinized every detail a thousand times."

"I don't understand. Wouldn't it have been simpler to provide your people at Menwith with the thumb drive?"

"A reasonable, question, Billy, but security at Menwith is tight as a drum, it would have never gotten through the door. The question is can we stay on the air for twelve minutes—the length of Mister Dion's speech—without this facility or Menwith control being breached. If either was to happen, the you-know-what hits the fan, and it's game over."

My mind's eye is flashing unsettling images of the firefight that would take place if this facility is pinpointed and breached before the broadcast is over... how would we hold off a full-on attack?

"What are the odds of either one or both those scenarios

happening?"

"Menwith's control room is a bunker that can withstand a nuclear attack. The door alone is several inches of solid steel. The chances of anyone getting in once it's locked from the inside is near impossible."

"That leaves this place."

"There is a very good likelihood they'll pinpoint our signal."

"Sounds like we volunteered for a possible suicide mission."

"It's the only chance we have, Hank, and we're taking it."

I can think of a hundred more questions, none of which I'll ask... this caper either works or it doesn't... it's a Hail Mary pass if ever there was one. Brian replaces the flash drive in the box and returns it to its hiding place, then screws on the rack faceplate.

"Norman, give me a hand."

Brian and Norman disappear around the back of the racks... when they emerge, they're each carrying three AR-15 rifles with 100-round drum magazines attached.

"There's an additional magazine for each weapon. Let's hope we don't need them. Okay, gentleman, that it's for now. We'll stash our weapons in the hall closet downstairs until we return."

I look at Chris, his brow furrows, and he rolls his eyes.

"Billy, my friend, remind me to thank you for getting me into this."

As soon as the elevator reaches the first floor and the doors open, we hear a cacophony of voices coming from the studio... Chris whistles low.

"Well, now, sounds like the office party has begun without us."

In the hallway, we place our weapons inside a closet and head for the studio that was all but empty when we arrived... to our surprise, it's now populated by a dozen or more people milling about.

"Norman, who are all these people?"

"Mister Neville will explain, Billy."

I'm left to wonder what role this group is here to play... hell, I'm not that sure what ours will be if this place is invaded... how would we hold off a well-armed military unit? Oliver's standing by the refreshment table, spots us and heads in our direction... he looks as apprehensive as we do... with him is the second man he was speaking with when we arrived.

"I trust Brian brought you up to speed?"

"He double-double brought us up to speed."

"Good, Billy, good. May I introduce Joe Natali."

Natali, Natali, I've heard that name before. He's bald, stocky with a round, likable, friendly face... we shake hands all-around.

"Your name is familiar, Mister Natali."

"Until last night it was General Joseph Natali, Commander of the North American-Caribbean World Government Forces. Today, it's just plain Joe Natali."

Whoa, what? Marseille's top dog in the region is involved with this movement? The plot thickens... Oliver turns to the gathering.

"I dare say you would find the pedigree of the men and women gathered here quite impressive. There's two of Henry Dion's World Council colleagues, a Harvard constitutional scholar, a United States Supreme Court Justice, ambassadors to the U.S. from England, Germany and Brazil, as well as former Directors of the CIA, NSA, FBI, and Interpol. All had a hand in assisting Henry in the creation of Volte-face."

Hank and Chris look as perplexed as I do.

"I had no idea."

"Billy, is it?

"Yes, General, Billy Russell."

"Well, Billy, the goal of the military has always been first and foremost to keep the peace. The military doesn't start wars, civilians who run governments do. So, when the Populist Party morphed into a world political force, I liked their ideas and supported them, as did most all who wore the uniform. The very idea the PPP would control military forces and ban nuclear weapons was the first sensible idea to ending wars. Little did any of us suspect the Marseille government's true intentions of becoming selfish, oppressive, Fascist dictators. Once they controlled the military, there was nothing standing in their way to achieve their goal of complete world domination. That's when they lost my support."

Oliver glances at the gathering before turning back to us.

"It is worth remembering that in 1878 Albert Einstein said, 'The world will not be destroyed by those who do evil, but by those who watch them without them doing anything.' Today, we the people take the steps that we should have taken long ago that should, if successful, save democracy for all mankind. Today we will reignite a world where intellect and science lead the way to a better future. Thanks to Henry Dion, today we take back the freedom that has been stolen from us."

I can't help worrying if government forces were to breach this place before we pull this off, all would have been for naught... I pose that possibility to Neville.

"Oliver, what happens if it all goes wrong and they storm this place?"

"A good question, Billy. General, would you like to answer?"

"Happy to. As soon as we are on the air, General Couture will order the military to stand down."

"Couture?"

"Yes, Hank, the very same General Couture that commands the world military."

"Wow, is there anyone who's not involved in this?"

"Before this is over, you'll learn just how committed the world is to removing these devils."

"Oliver, these people gathered here, what role are they here to play?"

"You'll understand the role they're here to play following Henry's presentation, Billy. Now, please help yourselves to the refreshments."

I was hoping Oliver had shared at least something, anything, that would give us confidence that what's recorded on that computer will succeed in bringing about an uprising on the scale he promises... it damn well better or we're all burnt toast. There's quite a spread on the refreshment table... I settle for a cup of black brew and a sesame bagel smeared with cream cheese... Hank's chewing on a croissant... Chris settles for a cup of coffee. Hank's looking over my shoulder and smiling.

"What are you smiling at?"

Before he answers, someone taps my arm.

"Be careful, don't choke on that bagel."

For one of the rare moments in my life, I'm at a total loss for words.

"Jade!"

"So good to see you, Buckaroo. Hey Hank, Chris."

"How you doing beautiful?"

"Anxious to see this over and done with, Hank."

"Will one of you please tell me what's going on?"

Hank pats me on the shoulder and grins.

"Best to ask the lady, Billy."

Jade glances to her left, then to her right.

"Not here, let's find a quiet spot."

"But—"

"No buts, Buckaroo, follow me."

Placing my coffee and bagel on the table, I follow her behind the mounted television screen out of sight of the others.

"You are the last person I expected to see here."

"Why is that, Billy?"

"Because, I, uh, I just never suspected that you too were involved."

"Well then, my cover worked."

It takes a millisecond for my brain to connect the dots.

"It's you, not Hank, you're Neville's mole."

Her face scrunches.

"Jeez, Billy, you make it sound like I committed a felony."

"Sorry, that came out wrong."

"I sure hope so."

"Hank knows about this?"

"Yes."

"And you didn't tell me?"

"If you hadn't taken your sweet time committing to the cause, I would have. So now you're angry with me?"

"No."

"Then stop sulking."

"I'm not."

"Then unscrew that look on your face and I'll tell you what you want to know."

"I'm just—stupefied?"

"Hmm, stupefied—strong word. Okay, here goes. When I was with the Boston PD, I would on occasion spout off about this retched regime. All I was doing was expressing out loud what others were thinking in private. The brass warned me I should hold my tongue unless I was looking to spend time in a women's prison or worse. Chad Cunningham, head of the Boston detective division—he's the tall one over there talking with Oliver and Natali—invited me to lunch one day. Rule number one, when divorced, never turn down a free lunch. I thought he was hitting on me, but he was actually scouting me out. He made no bones about his personal feelings—the regime was evil and they had to go one way or another. I assured him I shared those feelings. He asked if he could introduce me to a man he was involved with, someone who thought like he and I, a well-known Boston attorney by the name of Oliver Neville. To make a long story short, Oliver must have felt comfortable with me, because he told me right-off he was involved in a group planning to do something about the Marseille gang, but he held back on providing details. It was only after I signed on would he tell me that Commissioner Henry Dion was spearheading an underground movement called Volte-face, a term I had never heard before."

"Your position with the unit, how did that come about?"

"When Marseille announced the creation of the worldwide Drug Enforcement Bureau, Colonel Andrei Chernov, a former official with the defunct Russian Federal Counterintelligence Service, was placed in command of the New England unit that was to be located here in Boston. Why, Oliver asked, would they send a full-bird Colonel to do a Captain's job? With Chernov came Boris Tangenev, Ivan Oblansky and Antonina Lebedev, also former WPF officers who worked for Chernov in Marseille. Both Dion and Oliver suspected something else was going on beside drug enforcement. As it turned out, their suspicions were right on target."

"And the Lieutenant?"

"Frank was a retired Marine who commanded the New Hampshire Police Department who made no bones about his anti-establishment feelings. That made him perfect to head up our office. Then came Heinz and Augier who, Like Chernov, held top security positions in Marseille. That sealed it for Henry and Oliver. Something was going on with this unit beyond drug control, and they wanted to know what it was. When Oliver found out the unit had an opening for an administrative assistant with police experience, he suggested I apply on the outside chance the movement could get someone on the inside to nose around. Wilson was impressed with my credentials as a psychiatrist and I was hired. Even though Oliver had no idea how that might prove useful, at least he now had someone on the inside. It wasn't long before we discovered Chernov's real job was getting rid of dissidents using the talents of his attack dogs, Heinz and Augier. Once I discovered the unit's real mission, I regretted signing on, but by then it was too late to get out."

"And where do Hank, Chis and me fit in?"

"You can thank Oliver for that. He targeted you guys because he thought it was a good way for you to get out if today's efforts succeed. As for Marseille, they must have gotten wind something was imminent. Why else would Heinz and Augier assassinate Dion and pay Oliver a late-night visit?"

"You know about the visit to Oliver?"

"Oliver filled me in."

"Enough said."

"Yes."

How can I be angry that she left me out of the loop? She had placed herself in the mouth of the lion and stood tall for her beliefs, her principles, knowing that if discovered, she would have paid with her life.

"So, here we are, a band of would-be hero's attempting to overthrow an entrenched government that could easily squash us in a millisecond. And that, boys and girls, remains a real possibility."

At 7:16, tension in the studio is at a fever pitch, especially those of us armed with AR-15's, hoping like hell we don't have to use them. While Jade mingles with Oliver and two other ladies, I take the opportunity to speak with several of those in attendance whose credentials not only impress, but inspire... the former US Supreme Court Justice, the lady philosophy professor who still teaches the subject at a Pennsylvania university, two former World Council Commissioners who secretly supported Dion's efforts, and former General Joseph Natali who I get another chance to speak with.

"General Natali, I—"

"Please, call me Joe."

"Mind if I ask why you supported the idea of a World Government?"

"Like millions of others, Billy, I thought the idea of a world government, as radical as it sounded, could be the answer to restoring balance and a lasting peace in the world. As it turned out, we were wrong. Within a year of taking over, the devils running the PPP were stuffing their pockets with the spoils at the expense of the less fortunate. Hate groups and white nationalists were on the rise along with enough conspiracy theories to fill a small book, and the government was openly supporting them. There was one lingering problem that had to be addressed—overpopulation. Some nine billion plus humans were roaming the planet—The government had to bring it under control if they were ever to achieve their goal of complete domination over people, the world economy, and Mother Nature's assets. Their solution was to force-feed a series of complex economic policies meant to fail."

"I've heard this before, but it doesn't make sense. It would hurt them too."

"It makes perfect sense when you consider overpopulation continues to add pollution to an already polluted planet whose natural resources are being exhausted faster than they can replenish them. Then there's the problem of wide-spread drug use. It's impossible for Marseille to achieve their goal of total economic domination if the drug problem continues to escalate. You can't rape and pillage what's not there. Marseille's solution was to crash the economy forcing the undesirables—minorities and the poor—out of work and on the streets without them being accused of causing the death of millions. Next time you're out take note—the Streetwalkers are brown, black, yellow and poor whites. Marseille promises they'll fix the economy. They'll fix it all right, but not before they've achieved their goal of reorganizing society by systematically removing a swath of those they deem as disposable."

"But, Joe, everyone is suffering, not just the working and the poor."

"Those who don't fall into the undesirable category and can weather the storm turn a blind eye out of self-preservation and fear. And don't forget, there are millions of angry, disappointed fringe thinkers and malcontents displeased with their own lives who support this vile government despite the government having done nothing to help them. We must shut down these thieving crooks and liars for good."

Let's hope the hell you're right, General. If this doesn't work as planned, we're all off to one of those internment camps... or worse, a firing squad... that is, if we make it out of this building alive.

At 8 AM, Oliver is standing in from the TV screen calling for everyone to take their seats... he looks tired and apprehensive.

"First, I thank each of you for your willingness to place yourselves in harm's way. All mankind owes you a debt of gratitude. Now, at 8:30, Volte-face regional directors around the world will receive confirmation the event is a go as planned. In turn, they will instruct millions upon millions of Volte-face supporters to tune into the government news channel at 9:00 AM eastern standard time when the world will learn just how far the PPP is willing to go to ensure their domination now and in the future. Hopefully, we'll witness the largest uprising the human race has ever experienced. If there is one lesson we have learned, to preserve freedom, to protect democracy, we have to continually work at it. There is an old but appropriate Italian saying. 'You wanted a bicycle, you got one, now you have to peddle.' Today, we peddle and peddle hard to bring this oppressive regime to an end, not out of fear, but with courage and conviction that what we do this day will free all humanity. There are factions out there that will continue to fight us, that's a given. But from this day forward, we will squash them whenever and wherever their warped ideology rises."

Spontaneous applause breaks out. Oliver sounds pretty damn sure that this is going to work. What does he know that we don't? I suspect the answer is what Henry Dion has to say on that recording... Oliver takes a deep breath and continues.

"At 8:58 make your assigned connections and begin relaying information as you receive it. Does anyone have a question?"

A distinguished white-hair woman in the fourth row stands.
"Yes, Gloria."

"I just want to say, God bless Henry Dion."

The room breaks out in resounding applause again.

"Lastly, but perhaps most importantly, General Andre Couture, head of the World Military, will direct all military and WPF forces to stand down. There will be resistance from within their ranks from those who support this wretched government. General Couture assures me they are prepared to shut down any resistance quickly."

That's reassuring, Oliver, but I'd rather have Couture's faithful troops here defending this place instead of the six of us? We'd never be able to hold off an attack from troops loyal to Marseille if it comes to that... okay, Billy, enough negative thoughts, you're here and that's that... if there is a fight, remember to shoot straight and shoot to kill.

*At 8:30 **our gang of six retrieve out weapons** and return to the*

engineering room. Brian lays out a play-by-play of how this will go down... he's holding a satellite phone.

"At precisely 8:59, the control room at Menwith will ping us once on this secure phone. If all is going as planned, five-seconds later there will be three additional pings—that's the final go signal. At nine I'll press play and Henry's presentation will begin."

"What if those final three pings fail to come?"

"Perish the thought, Hank, perish the thought."

Chris sidles up to me.

"That's when we do what that wise shepherd did."

"Chris, if we survive this, you are never to utter that joke again."

"Good luck with that, pal."

The tension in the room is electric as the clock ticks away... no one is talking. At 8:55, Brian has the computer ready to roll Dion's message.... four minutes to go... four very long minutes before we're supposed to receive those pings... all eyes are on the clock... turn away, Billy, watching that clock won't make it go faster... closing my eyes, I wait until I hear what we've been waiting for... the satellite phone pings once... I'm holding my breath... five long seconds later the phone pings once, twice, three times... Brian throws up his hands.

"Praise the Lord."

Everything feels like it's moving in slow motion except my heart... my pulse is doing double duty... all eyes are on the clock's sweeping hand as it approaches 8:59:58... Brian rolls Dion's message and the screen comes alive... hallelujah, we're on the air... the late Henry Dion stands tall against a nondescript blue wall... his expression is contemplative... at least I think it is... let's hope it's not foreboding.

"Greetings to all people of the world. My name is Henry Dion. I was born seventy-one years ago in the State of Massachusetts in the United States of America. Over those many years, I, like most, failed to raise the alarm as nefarious forces of the economic elite and the body politic unashamedly placed their aspirations to enrich themselves at the expense of all others. It has led to an intentional dismantling of democracy that has left us in the enslaved world we live in today. If not for the mortal sin that we have uncovered, they may have gotten away with it. Despite all the damage this government has already done, it is difficult to imagine that what you are about to witness is happening yet again."

Dion pauses and looks away thoughtfully... come on, Henry, we don't have all day here.

"Deep within the wildlife refuge of PARC Naturel Regional de Millevaches en Limousin, Southwest of the town of Claremont-Terrand, France, a high-ranking member of the Military, at great risk to himself, recorded the images you are about to see using a hidden mini-camera. Be forewarned, the video is not only difficult to watch, but repulsive and egregious to even imagine something so horrible could be happening once again."

The screen dips to black for a couple of heart-pounding seconds before an image appears of two windowless, single-story forest green wooden buildings resembling military barracks ... they're separated by a narrow dirt road... a tall stand of trees hug the outer edges of both structures... two armed sentries in WPF uniforms walk the dirt road between the buildings, two more are stationed by the entry doors to each building. The person taking the video approaches the building to the left and stops... apparently, he's speaking to the guard, but there's no audio... the guard says something, then opens the door... the camera swings left and enters the building... the interior is dark, the images turn grainy... the video taker is on the move down the center aisle swaying first to the left then slowly to the right. There are simultaneous gasps from each of us at what we see. Single beds line either side of the aisle... each is occupied by young women dressed in identical white nightgowns... as the camera moves slowly down the aisle, Henry Dion begins narrating again.

"The Marseille government has committed countless sins, but this is their most repulsive. One-hundred young white women, deemed ethically pure, are housed here—fifty in each building. All were brought here for the sole purpose of bearing offspring sired by men chosen by the regime."

Chris puts a hand to his mouth and takes a step back.

"Jesus Christ! Is this real?"

Brian whispers.

"All too real, Chris."

Dion's narration continues.

"The children born to these women will be taken from and raised by the government. They will be educated and groomed to become future world leaders who will spread Arianism first taught by Alexandrian Priest Arius—a plan later adapted and implemented by the Nazi's in World War Two."

As the camera reaches three-quarters of the way down the aisle, a door on the far back wall opens... light spills out... a middle-aged man in a military uniform walks out tightening his belt and buttoning his open shirt... he's followed by a young blond woman, head bent, eyes to the floor... she looks to be in her early twenties... she's being led from the room by an older woman in a white nurse's uniform... the man whispers something to the young girl as she passes... she doesn't respond... she's led to a nearby bed, lies down, pulls her knees up into a fetal position, and begins to cry... the older woman is comforting her. Another young woman is led into the backroom by a different nurse followed close behind by an older man in a business suit... he exchanges words with the military man... they both smile... the second man enters the room and closes the door... the video goes to black for a beat before Dion is back on screen.

"We would do well to remember that in 1925, Adolf Hitler wrote in Mein Kampf, 'Everything we admire on this Earth today—science and art, technology and inventions—is only the creative product of a few peoples and originally perhaps one race...the 'Aryans'. On them depends the existence of this whole culture. If they perish, the beauty of this Earth will sink into the grave with them'. The Third Reich's sinister plan to preserve the 'master race' left behind an ugly legacy, one the current Marseille regime has revived to ensure the white race remains the master over all others, not in their numbers, but in positions of power."

Come on, Henry, wrap it up... the longer this goes on, the better the chance we'll be discovered.

"As I speak, a paramilitary squadron is making their way to this camp to liberate these young women. Now, it is our turn. Together we will reclaim our birthright to live and prosper in peace and harmony. I leave you with the words of the eighteenth-century French economist, Frederic Bastiat, who wrote, 'When plunder becomes a way of life for men, they create for themselves in the course of time a legal system that authorizes it and a moral code that glorifies it.' People of Earth, let us not be guilty of ignoring this warning yet again. Rise up without fear, for we are safe within in our numbers. Thank you, be safe, and may God bless you all."

The screen goes black... we stand speechless... what we have just witnessed was unspeakably abhorrent and beyond belief that human beings would do this to other humans... again. Brian's cell is ringing... he answers and listens.

"Yes, got it, thanks."

He ends the call, but he's not smiling.

"Natali wants us in the studio."

"Is there a problem?"

"No, Billy, so far so good. Bring your weapons."

I was fully expecting the door to this room to be stormed before the video ended... ye' of little faith, Billy Boy. When we enter the studio, there is a hush... like us, everyone's shaken to the core by what they've seen... Oliver is standing before the TV screen.

"We still have work to do, so let's get to it."

The atmosphere in the room is filled with anticipation as we await whatever is supposed to happen next... Oliver's pacing... as I recall, he likes to pace... Jade, God love her, crosses the studio and stands by me, takes my hand, and smiles her warm smile.

"My heart's pounding."

"Mine is threatening to explode, Jade."

"Still angry with me, Buckaroo?"

"If we get out of here you can make it up with that Chinese dinner you promised."

The gathering is dead silent as we wait... five long, silent minutes pass when Joseph Natali waves his phone above his head and lets out a loud hoot.

"I just spoke to General Couture in Marseille. The military has been ordered to stand down."

A cheer goes up... now it's a matter of waiting to see what the world will do. There is dead silence in the studio... then, excitedly, a woman on the far side of the studio with her phone to her ear jumps to her feet.

"London is reporting thousands streaming into the streets."

She's followed by a man in the middle of the group who whoops.

"Moscow Square is jammed with people."

And then, one after another, a chorus of frenzied voices follows.

"Traffic in New York is at a standstill!"

"Same in Miami!"

"Chicago reports thousands pouring into the streets!"

"Los Angeles too!"

"Pretoria, South Africa!"

"Ditto Berlin!"

"Same in Toronto!"

"Sydney, Australia!"

"Beijing!"

"Los Angeles as well!"

"Paris!"

It's happening exactly the way Oliver predicted it would... the jubilant voices continue until major populations around the world have been accounted for. Natali is waving his phone again.

"General Couture reports the Government headquarters in Marseille has been invaded by citizens after a skirmish with a few diehard members of the military! Laurent and his gang were nowhere to be found... they must have run like rats in a flood when Dion hit the airwaves."

The cries of joy are suddenly interrupted by a loud crash coming from outside... my head whips to the door.

"What the hell was that?"

"Brian, the front door."

"I'm on it, Mister Natali."

Natali quick-paces to the center of the room.

"Listen up, everyone. Follow Oliver behind the Cyc. Norman, Jason, post yourselves at each end of it."

This can only mean we've been discovered... I squeeze then release Jade's hand.

"Go with the others, Jade."

"Be safe, Billy."

When she reaches the Cyc, she turns and blows me a kiss... I blow one back... from his jacket pocket, Natali takes out a pistol.

"Come on, let's see what the ruckus is about."

We follow him down the hall to the front door... Brian is there peering out the peep hole... a second crash is heard... with a look of dread, he turns to us.

"It appears not everyone got the message, Joe. An M1130 armored vehicle with a battering ram just broke through the front gate. Ten or so men in riot gear are on foot with it. These doors are reinforced steel, but they won't stand up to a ramming from that vehicle. And the rear door is bricked over, so this is the only way in or out."

"Come on, Brian, stand back over here with us?"

"What?"

"Come on."

Natali's acting pretty cool for what we're about to face... Leaning close to Hank, I hiss.

"What's Natali looking so smug about?"

"I'm wondering the same, Billy."

It becomes eerily quiet except for the sound of the armored vehicle engine as it moves closer to the doors... it stops... its engine is idling... what's sweeping through my head are the times as a young DEA Officer, I charged headlong into the pit of danger with fearless arrogance... yet here and now I feel helpless, not fearless... my tingling hands are wrapped tightly around the AR-15... it feels like it weighs a hundred pounds... is this where my role in the video game of life ends along with the others? Is this that train speeding through the dark tunnel ready to crush us like diseased-spreading bugs? The sound of the armored vehicle's engine revving up snaps me back.

"They're closing in on the door, Joe."

"I hear them, Brian. Close the slot and come over here."

The vehicle's engine sounds like the roar of a jet engine as it approaches... then comes a burst of gunfire... PING, PING, PING... bullets are hitting the metal doors... all of us except Natali take a step back... the gunfire is increasing... I'd swear it's coming from two different directions.

"General, what's happening?"

"Hold fast, Brian."

Now Natali's moving to the door... he slides open the peep hole... he's watching... we wait... then silence... the gunfire stops as quickly as it had begun.

"Okay, Brian, unlock this baby."

What? Is this a deception... has Natali betrayed us?

"It's okay, Brian, unlock it."

"But, Joe?"

"Go ahead, unlock it."

Hesitantly, Brian approaches the doors and pulls back the deadbolts... sucking in a deep breath, he swings the left door open... a man in a WPF uniform sporting Captain bars is standing just a few feet away... we all look to Natali's... damn him, he's grinning.

"John, you are one hell of a welcome sight."

The Captain salutes and smiles.

"Same here, General."

"Gentlemen, this is Captain John Crawford. He and his special WPF ops team were stationed in that building across the street just in case something like this were to happen."

"With all due respect, General, did it ever cross your mind to share this information with us?"

"Not for a millisecond second, Hank. Good work, Captain."

"All in a day's work, sir—like shooting fish in a barrel."

"I'll be in touch. Until then, pass the word, keep an eye out for government loyalists."

"Will do, sir."

I'm more than a little pissed off... I don't know whether we should pat Natali on the back, or kick his ass for not letting us in on his backup plan... he's grinning from ear to ear.

"Okay, guys, let's go tell the others it's over."

We're about to turn back when we hear loud rumblings coming from the street just outside the busted gates... Natali moves back to the door and peers.

"What have we here, Captain?"

"I think you better come take a look, General."

Filing out the door behind Natali, we pass dead men sprawled around the ramming vehicle... two more are slumped in the front seat of the vehicle... as we cross the parking lot, a throng of human bodies begin to fill the gaping hole that was the front gate... the street is now jammed with throngs of cheering people... Natali whispering to no one in particular.

"If there's a heaven, I know where Henry Dion is."

Oliver comes running up behind us with Norman and Jason in tow... he's excited about something.

"Great news. I was just informed by former United Nations Secretary General Arturo Cordozar he has taken charge of the government headquarters in Marseille as planned. The long overdue recovery from injustice and suffering begins."

Let us hope, Oliver, let us hope. I want to share these moments with Jade... turning back, I see her standing in the doorway and quick-pace across the parking lot.

"What's on your mind, Buckaroo?"

This moment in time, this moment that history will enshrine forever, must not be wasted... sweeping Jade into my arms, I kiss her long and hard.

CHAPTER 27

Closure and Renewal

Never had a world-change of this magnitude *taken place with such celerity... less than an hour after Henry Dion's presentation, the Marseille regime had crumbled like a fragile house of cards. With great courage and conviction, the majority of citizens around the world had delivered the coup de grace by taking to the streets in an organized revolt against the radical elites and their feloniously gained privileges... it was a boisterous, unified message to President Laurent and his supporters... domination and oppression would never again be tolerated... period, full stop, repeat. But freedom from oppression was only the beginning... as expected, there was high anxiety of what was to come next... now more than any time in the history of mankind it was paramount that people across the globe be reassured their world had not gone from the fire into the frying pan... that process was to begin at three that afternoon when former Secretary General of the United Nations, Arturo Cordozar, would make a televised address to the world. Like everyone, I was drained mentally, exhausted physically, and anxious to get home... but the streets of Boston were clogged with revelers, making it impossible to maneuver in a vehicle... it was 12:30 before Norman was finally able to give me, Chris and Hank a lift home... Jade stayed behind huddled with Oliver, Joseph Natali and others, no doubt discussing plans already in place to take this victory to the next level... Oliver had not shared those plans with me, so I remain in the dark along with the others. As we're cruising down 4th street, we find it still crowded like all the others streets... on this brisk February day, it resembles a 4th of July celebration.*

When we finally reach the house, Hank twists in his seat and flashes a devilish grin.

"Well, boys and girl, it's been one hell of an interesting day. Let's catch up with one another somewhere in the aftermath."

I pat him on the shoulder.

"Whatever the hell that's gonna look like. Norman, it's been fun."

"That's not exactly how I would describe it, Billy, but all's well that ends well." *There're handshakes all around... Chris and I slip out... There Uncle Jules standing at the top of the stairs grinning from ear to ear.*

"Where have you two been?"

"Cooped up in the office waiting for the streets to clear. It appears there's been a revolution of sorts."

Jules laughs, his belly jiggles and his key chain jangles.

"Thank God for small favors."

"Oh, so now you've found religion?"

"Just covering all the bases, Billy."

"Catch you later, Mister Summers."

"Later, Mister Russell, Mister Henley."

When Chris and I make it to our doors, we stand silently for a moment... he shakes my hand.

"It was fate that first brought us together on that evil planet, Billy, and it was fate that brought us together here. Friends forever."

"As long as you promise never to tell that damn shepherd joke again."

He laughs and enters his apartment. Once in mine, I head straight for the Bourbon and down a shot, then it's off to a hot soaking in the shower that lasts ten minutes... after dressing in clean clothes, I turn on the government news channel... patriotic music is playing over video footage of millions around the world celebrating in the streets... moving to the kitchen, I'm contemplating lunch when there comes a knock at the door... I assume it's either Chris or Jules.

"It's unlocked."

To my surprise in walks the ever-lovely Jade Miro carrying a white paper bag.

"Hey, gorgeous, thought you stayed behind with Oliver and company?"

She smiles wide and raises the bag.

"The Chinese we never got around to eating."

She's moving toward me, those long, lovely legs floating across the room like they're walking on air... she sets the food on the table and kisses me.

"Any discussion of the past twelve or so hours are strictly verboten. I make a motion we partake in this savory Chinese food and move on to you know what."

"Then set the table, Big Boy. Arturo Cordozar's address comes on at three."

"Anything going on with Oliver that I should know about?"

"No, is all up to Cordozar and his team now."

Setting out two plates, silverware and napkins, we dig in to the food. Lunch is immediately followed by a triple X-rated roll in the sack... we're like two kids in a candy store overwhelmed at the variety of goodies available to us... our gymnastics continue until shortly before it's time for Cordozar's broadcast... we're in front of the TV... me in my underwear, Jade's covered in one of my shirts... at three minutes to three, I turn on the TV... A tranquil nature scene fills the screen... super imposed at the top is a graphic.

At 3 pm EST, Former United Nations Secretary-General Arturo Cordozar will address the world live from Marseille, France. His address will be repeated hourly on this channel.

The background video switches to scenes of the millions upon millions who had taken to the streets in the largest peaceful protest in recorded history... an incredible sight to behold, one that we hope we'll never again have cause to repeat. New music begins, the chyron text at the bottom of the screen identifies it as **"We are the World'** *sung by someone named Michael Jackson... not familiar with the singer or the song, but the lyrics couldn't be more appropriate and uplifting... mankind had defeated the evil empire... except for* *the fight outside the relay station, and some of Laurent's diehards at government headquarters in Marseille, the entire uprising went off without a single citizen injured, which would have been impossible if the military and the WPF had not obeyed Couture's order to stand down. At precisely 3:00 the music concludes... the screen dissolves to Arturo Cordozar sitting behind a large wooden desk... his name appears at the bottom of the screen... Marseille's palatial Museum d'histoire naturelle de Marseille is superimposed behind him.*

"I don't know anything about this guy, Jade."

"Cordozar was Spain's ambassador to the United Nations before he was chosen as United Nations Secretary-General. The UN under the PPP was not much more than a puppet organization. Eight months ago, Cordozar resigned. Lucky for all of us, Marseille didn't have him arrested."

Cordozar folds his hands, places them on the desk, and leans forward.

"Greeting to all citizens of the world. Today we celebrate our triumph over the men who have held the world in bondage. The courage and conviction that transpired this momentous day occurred with lightning-speed because of the heroic efforts of Commissioner Henry Dion and the millions upon millions who found the courage to rise up with a unified voice condemning tyranny. If there is a lesson to be learned from this painful period, it is that we must demand future leaders be of solid character, placing the highest value on truth, opportunity and equality, and must be applied to all mankind regardless of race, color, creed or economic standing. Without the highest respect for these values, we are nothing more than a nomadic civilization akin to our earliest cave-dwelling ancestors. Some months ago, Commissioner Dion asked if all went as planned this day, would I accept the temporary role of World Administrator. I readily accepted. No doubt there will be many challenges ahead, but unified we can and will meet them head on. Over the past year, a Volte-face committee of volunteers drafted in secret a plan of renewal that is to be enacted immediately. To begin the process, three distinguished scientists, academics, and religious leaders from each of the six continents will serve in temporary positions on a newly established World Council. For the moment, that is the quickest mechanism and fairest way to ensure that all voices across the globe are heard equally. The task ahead will begin with our most urgent needs. All countries with food storage depositories will release their stores to food distribution outlets throughout the world. Hospitals, medical centers, and drug rehabilitation facilities are open to all requiring assistance. Housing will be assigned to the homeless as it becomes available, and a return to common sense economic policies will begin to repair the world's ailing economy. One month from now, a world referendum will be held to determine whether a World Government will be retained or sovereign nations are to return to total self-governing. Until then, General Andre Couture will continue as Commander of world military forces and the WMP. Finally, and sadly, we stand on the cliff of a climate disaster. This must remain a priority if we have any chance of saving our planet for current and future generations. We must never allow ourselves to forget for even a moment all that we are capable of accomplishing if we work together as one for the good of all. I will keep you informed as we work our way back to a healthy, safe, and prosperous society. I promise you, those responsible for perpetrating this travesty upon society will be found and charged with their crimes. Thank you. I bid everyone peace and safety."

The screen changes to a striking sunrise over a vast body of water... the song 'We Are the World' is repeated.

"He hit all the bullet points that were needed. Question is, can we pull it off?"

"You have doubts, Billy?"

"Trust me, as factions grapple for control like they always do, it'll be political warfare all over again."

"Not this time."

"Yeah, well, I hope you're right. My father was fond of saying there's right, there's wrong, and there's negotiated compromise, which inevitably leads to watered down solutions to appease the negotiators. Money, power, and politics, that's what has always been the engine that made this world tick, and

I don't expect it will change any time soon."

"You'll see, Billy, this time it will work."

"I would like nothing better, Jade. But keep in mind mankind has always existed in three worlds, those at the top, those in the middle, and those at the bottom. The billionaire doesn't embrace the millionaire as a coequal, the millionaire doesn't embrace the middle class as equals, and the middle class doesn't embrace the poor as equals. Like it or not, that's the way it's been. This time, if we fail to address and resolve these issues, what took place today will have been an exercise in futility. And don't for a second believe the factions that supported Laurent's Government have magically disappeared. Their odious dogma will rise again and we'll be forced to deal with it again."

"Don't be negative, Billy, it doesn't become you."

"Where I've been for the past seventeen years, Jade, negativity was an attribute."

"Well, you're not there anymore, Buckaroo."

Sauntering to the window, I gaze out... a large crowd of revelers lingers on the street below. Do they understand what has taken place, or are they living in the moment, joyful to be free again, but unsure or incapable of comprehending how what has occurred affects the whole and not just their tiny corner of the world? Can we, will we, come together for the benefit of all mankind, or in time will we revert to our old tribal ways? Life is filled with boundaries, most of which we chose to ignore... we lie, cheat, steal, we're greedy and selfish, we're the only mammals in the animal kingdom that murder each other in large numbers... mankind is the real endangered species, we just haven't accepted it yet. Can we, will we, choose promise over hostility, faith over fear, empathy and understanding over confrontation? It can only happen if we stop taking three-steps forward and one back every time we hit a speed bump in the road.

"Hey, Billy, where are you?"

"Huh? Right here, Beautiful."

It's now or never, Billy Boy, don't let this moment that you thought would never come your way again slip from your grasp... take a deep breath and do it now.

"I once told you, say what you mean and mean what you say."

"I remember it well, Billy."

"That applies to me as well. So here goes. I want to spend the rest of my life with you, Jade."

"If you think I'm going to make this easy on you, you're are mistaken. Down on one knee and do it right, Buckaroo."

I cross the room, kneel on one knee and take her hand in mine.

"Jade Miro, I, William Evan Russell, love you and want to marry you."

"And I, Jade Amaya Miro, accept your proposal."

Damn it, her phone's ringing in the middle of my proposal.

"Hold that thought, Billy."

She digs the phone out from her purse and answers.

"Hey, what's up?"

As she listens, her face tightens.

"Okay, yeah, got it. Thanks for calling."

She hangs up... she looks disturbed.

"What's wrong?"

"That was Norman. General Couture directed all drug enforcement units to be immediately shut down and those who commanded them arrested. Wilson, Boris, Ivan, and Antonina have already been taken into custody."

"And Chernov?"

"They found him in his apartment dead of a gunshot wound to the head. He committed suicide."

"A coward to the end."

"Authorities are still looking for Heinz and Augier."

"Ha, good luck, they're someplace in the Charles River. That leaves us. Are they going to arrest us too?"

"I didn't kill anyone, neither did you, Billy."

"Yeah, well Hank did."

On day one following the revolution, *Hank comes by for me*

and Chris and the three of us pay a visit to South Boston Community Health Center to have our GPS trackers removed. We celebrate by feasting on fish tacos and Tequila at Loco Taqueria & Oyster Bar on Broadway with way too much tequila.

"Don't know about you two, but I feel like a heavy weight has been lifted."

"Me to, Billy. The only question now is who's sober enough to drive us home."

"Hank, it's your car."

"Oh, yeah, right. Just one more shot before we go."

***Things were moving fast, and although** there was great joy and celebration across the world, it was overshadowed by mankind's greatest enemy... fear. We had won the battle, but could we, would we, win the war... we have no one to blame but ourselves if we fail again. Each day at 6:00 PM, Arturo Cordozar took to the airwaves to update the world of the progress being made... on the fourth day, and with great fanfare, Cordozar announced the Cape Town South African police had arrested former President Jean Lumiere Laurent. He and his cronies had arrived there on phony passports. Arrangement were being made to return them to Marseille to face charges. The temporary World Council proposed a Nuremberg-type tribunal that would charge them with crimes against humanity. Then came the day we were dreading... the four of us... me, Jade, Hank and Chris... were in a courtroom facing a judge. Oliver represented us elucidating in great detail how each of us had been forced to participate in the unit's heinous activities under threat of incarceration or death. Following Oliver's presentation, the judge returned to his chambers to consider our situation... it was the longest thirty minutes of our lives. When the judge returned, he said he had considered all the circumstances that had forced us into our positions of servitude. He also took into consideration how we had risked our lives participating in the overthrow of the*

regime. Then came the words we had hoped for... he ordered us cleared of all charges... we were free to get on with our lives without further fear of prosecution. As promised, a month following the fall of the World Government, a worldwide referendum took place to determine if that type of governing was to be retained... the answer was an eighty-five percent resounding 'Yes', but only if the world government was to retain control of the military ensuring no country would ever again have the capacity to start a war, and the nuclear ban was to remain in force. The world government would also act as the arbiter in all disputes arising between countries. The WPF was to be disbanded... local police forces would be reactivated. Finally, every citizen on the face of the Earth would participate in the election of new world government officials. For all intents and purposes, the world was pretty much back too normal... only time will tell if it all works as we hope.

Early one morning, while working on my notes of my time on Europa, *I received a call from Norman. Would I be available to join Chris, Jade, and Hank for lunch with Oliver at his condo the following day?*

"Yeah, sure, what's it about, Norman?"

"Mister Neville will explain."

"Yes, Norman, got it."

He laughed and hung up leaving me wondering what might be on Oliver's mind this time.

The following Day, Hank came by for Chris and me *and we were off to Oliver's... when we arrive, Jade and Joseph Natali were already there... we assumed it was to be a celebratory lunch, a way of thanking us for our support and participation... a lady Oliver introduced as his housekeeper, June, was in the process of setting the table with bangers and mash, onion gravy, steamed broccoli, and oven-baked crescent roles... very British indeed. Following lunch, we repaired to*

the living room. Turning pensive, Oliver meandered to the window lingering there for several moment.

"I see the wheels turning, Oliver."

"Yes, Billy, they are. To fully restore the damage done by Laurent and his supporters will not be accomplished in a week, a month, or even a year. It will take time to educate the public that we have entered a new era, one that demands we make basic structural changes to society, changes not to be feared, but to be embraced for the good of all mankind. One of our ongoing challenges will be to bring the drug problem under control. It is destructive not only to the addicted, but to society as a whole. These damn drug lords are too well entrenched and local police departments are ill-equipped for the task. So, with that in mind, the World Council is reactivating the drug enforcement units."

"Using different tactics, one hopes."

"Yes, Hank, of course. I'm pleased to announce that our friend here, Joe Natali, will not only assume the role of director of U.S. drug enforcement operations, but will assist other countries in setting up their programs. He'll be operating from your old offices."

"Congratulations, General."

"Thank you, Billy."

Oliver hesitates... his eyes go to each of us individually.

"I'm offering you the opportunity to join him."

"Us? What role would we play?"

"Hear me out, Hank. Along with Billy's training as a DEA officer, the four of you would be a great asset to Joe's team."

Hank, Chris and I exchange glances.

"The three drug enforcement units in the U.S. will be manned by trained SWAT teams that will conduct all field operations. The fate of those involved in illicit drug production and distribution will be decided by a court of law, not an execution squad... that is, if the SWAT teams do not encounter resistance when making arrests."

Total silence... I look to Hank then to Chris...none of us knows know how to react.

"Are you guys ready for desk jobs?"

Again, we exchange hesitant glances, but no one answers. Considering we're all presently unemployed, we're not only surprised, but grateful... a smile crosses Oliver's lips.

"I'll take your silence as a yes? Tea anyone?"

Five days later, we were gainfully employed *again busily setting up shop in our old offices... Jade, appointed administrative director, took up residence in Wilson's office... Hank, me, and Chris at our old desks... the infamous interrogation room was turned into records storage... Natali and his two new administrative assistants have taken over Chernov's offices. The Commander of the newly created New England drug enforcement now occupies the old WPF space down the hall.*

CHAPTER 28

There Is Reason to Hope

The room is pitch-black... *my eyes strain to see through the fog of sleep*... *there's a warm body lying beside me*... *come on Billy, this isn't brain surgery, it's Jade, dummy, it's Jade*... *don't wake her. Making my way to the bathroom and switching on the light, I stare in the mirror*... *I'm smiling from ear to ear. Turning on the cold water, I splash my face twice before heading off to the kitchen for coffee*... *when it's ready I slump to the sofa, set the coffee down, and stare blankly at the opposite wall for a few seconds before my eyes drift to my left forearm where the GPS tracker had documented my every move*... *my right hand covers the spot.*

"Contemplating your future?"

Jade's standing in the bedroom doorway wearing one of my long-sleeved shirts that comes down to the middle of her thighs.

"Sorry if I woke you, beautiful."

"You didn't, I smelled the coffee."

"Madam, how do you get up looking so damn sexy in nothing but one of my shirts?"

She's floating toward me... *I can't take my eyes from her*... *she settles in my lap and kisses me.*

"You taste good, Mister Russell."

"So do you, Ms. Miro."

"You do remember what day it is?"

"Enough to remember Hank will be picking us up in an hour. You want the shower first, or should I?"

"You go first, I need coffee."

And then we engage in one of those long, delicious, wet

kisses before we part.

"I have a wedding present for you."

"Really, what?"

"When we get back from our honeymoon, you'll hire a realtor and buy us a house."

"And what will we use for money?"

With a broad smile, I fill her in on my inheritance... her eyes turn misty... her arms encircle me, and then we engage in another one of those long, wet, kisses.

"Go, take your shower, William, or we'll be late for our own wedding."

An hour later, Jade appears from the bedroom in a stunning off the shoulder off-white dress that drops to the top of her white shoes... my God, she looks absolutely stunning... I'm decked out in a newly purchased dark blue suit, pale blue shirt, and red and white striped tie.

"We have to be the best-looking couple on the planet."

"One of us is, one of us isn't, Billy."

She laughs, then twirls in place to show off that beautiful dress. "The first time you came to visit, I found you draped on this couch looking like a supermodel—you still do."

"You know exactly what to say to a lady on her wedding day, Mister Russell."

"Hey, my mother didn't raise no dummy."

At 9:30, Hank shows up with Stephanie Gosling, his live-in squeeze... and a lovely lady she is. When we reach our destination on North Tremont Street, Hank parks on the eastern side of the Boston Common in sight of the Parkman Bandstand... according to Jade, who chose the location, the small, round, pillared structure, used for concerts, rallies, and speeches, was built in 1908 and named for George F. Parkman in honor of a five-million donation he willed for the care of the Boston Common and other city parks. Chris, Jules, Oliver, Norman, Jason and Joe Natali and his wife are already there... Chris is to be my best man... Hank's lady Stephanie will be

Jade's Maid of Honor. On this clear, sunny day, with the temperature hovering around an unusual seventy-two for this time of year, we are to be married by Oliver Neville. In Massachusetts anyone can perform a wedding for family or friends by obtaining a special one-time permit from the Secretary of State's office. Who knew? As the ceremony began, passers-by out for a stroll stop and watch... by the time Oliver pronounces us man and wife, about a dozen people have stopped and join in the applause. Following the ceremony, Oliver hosts a reception at Yvonne's, a refined supper club a block East of the Boston Common. All was well in Boston that day.

CHAPTER 29

That was then, this is now

My head is still swimming with all that has happened with such lightning speed in the short time since my return. It's said that things come in three's... I always thought that was an old wives' tale. Well, I've proven that old wife's tale wrong... in my case there would be five. First was my freedom from the bowels of Europa... then I was the luckiest man in the world to have met and married Jade, and then there's my inheritance, which has given me financial independence... there were two more to come. After a two-week search, Jade found a lovely three-bedroom house on an Oak-tree-lined street in the Boston suburb of Brookline. A few days later, Jules announced he was selling the house and moving back to his hometown of Springfield, Massachusetts.

"We're going to miss you, Jules."

"It's an hour and a half drive, you'll come visit."

"Yes, I promise."

I go silent, but Jules knows me well enough to know something's on my mind.

"What is it, William?"

"How do I thank you for accepting me into your life?"

"You don't. Just be damn thankful I did, young man."

"Wise ass to the end, aren't you?"

"Why would I change now at my age, William? Shut up and give me a hug."

"Only if you'll stop calling me William."

It is thirteen months since the wedding... soon Jade will give

birth to our first child... we've learned it is to be a girl... Jade has suggested we name her in honor of my mother, so Amelia it will be. During my darkest days on Europa, I would never have believed that I, William Evan Russell, son of Amelia and Alistair Russell from Orban, Scotland, would be blessed with a loving wife again and the impending arrival of our first child. Although I still question why we are here on Earth in the first place, I have to admit my attitude has flipped from how I once dismissed life out of hand as nothing more than a waste of time, until feeble and diseased we faced death, the supreme equalizer. I now accept that every moment of life is a precious moment.

When I had made my final entry in my notes, *which had grown to over three-hundred pages, I worked up enough courage to ask Oliver if he would read it, which he did. Without telling me, he thought it was good enough to send it off to a New York based publisher friend of his. To my surprise, the publisher liked what they saw and agreed to publish it... pinch me once, pinch me twice. Oliver negotiated a publishing deal and we were off and running. Since I haven't the slightest idea how to write a book, let alone how to assemble one, the publisher assigned their top editor to help me shape the final version. She asked me to give the book a title... I came up with "The Devil Came to Visit."*

Europa continues to be a penal colony, *but now inmates are paid a fair wage for their labor, medical services are provided, and inmates are required to remain on Europa no longer than five-years of their total sentence, their remaining time is to be served back on Earth. Since MAXMinerai folded, the mining of Phostoirore is now controlled by a world government oversight committee that ensures all one-hundred and ninety-five countries are treated equally in its distribution. Oh, yeah, almost forgot... the trial of President Laurent and his*

henchmen is underway back in France. Needless to say, everyone is anxious to see how that comes out. As for my book, I ended it with these words.

"Many years ago, the Protect Democracy Project, a non-partisan, non-profit organization dedicated to fighting efforts at home and abroad to undermine our right to free, fair, and fully informed self-government, argued that the onset of authoritarianism would not come suddenly, but with the gradual taking away of long-standing norms we had come to expect.

The growth and spread of democracies that defined the 20th century peaked in the early days of the 21st century— one in six democracies had failed. In countries around the world—Hungary, Poland, Turkey, and Venezuela— autocrats had slowly dismantled democratic systems, leaving governments that were for the most part democracies in name only. Larry Diamond, one of the world's foremost scholars on democracy, wrote, "The death of democracy is now typically administered in a thousand cuts. In one country after another, elected leaders have gradually attacked the deep tissues of democracy—the independence of the courts, the business community, the media, civil society, universities, and sensitive state institutions like the civil service, the intelligence agencies, and the police."

Once they were in power, what Protect Democracy Project [1] had predicted, was the exact game plan put into play by The Peoples Populist Party. Hopefully, we have learned that we the people are the ultimate check on power; the downfall of the PPP proved that. We now know we must combat nefarious forces wherever we find them, for they are highly skilled in their ability to pull us apart and keep us divided.

Following the revolution, we were consumed with restoring our broken lives. Yes, we were now free of the evil empire, but the age-old question loomed like a category five hurricane; could we, would we come together for the benefit of all mankind or revert to our old ways? If we fail this time, we are not the victims, but the perpetrators.

Each of us is obligated to answer this question: what is our passion and what are our goals? How are each of us using the time we are given on Earth? Arturo Cordozar's initial address to the world made it clear that mankind's quest for the good we seek in ourselves must be based on placing the highest value on truth, fairness, equality, and above all, total respect for all life and the rule of law. This will only be achieved if we put aside our biases and tribalism, and accept that we have always been, and will always be, a global community.

When I arrived at Base-Arizona at the beginning on my dark journey to Europa, all I could see was doom and gloom... my life was over. Now, for any number of reasons, I've come to believe that within all of us there is integrity, humanity, and morality. We just require the courage to do what is right, not just for ourselves, but for all mankind. Anything less will eventually hasten our extinction, leaving the planet to the bugs and animals.

A major turning point for me came when my friend Jules Sommers introduced me to the writings of theoretical physicist Steven Hawking. Hawking summed up life this way... "We have this one life to appreciate the grand design of the universe, and for that I am extremely grateful." With those words of wisdom forever edged in my memory, mere words, no matter how colorful and descriptive, will never accurately describe what I witnessed in space. I am left to wonder; if every living soul on Earth could spend just a few moments gazing out that portal on Europa Two, what would they see?

[1] Source: https://protectdemocracy.org/the-threat

The end... or might it be the beginning.

"The world will not be destroyed by those who do evil, but by those
who watch without them doing anything."
Albert Einstein
German-born theoretical physicist who developed the
theory of relativity

Author Robert J. Emery
Affiliations:
The Directors Guild of America
The Alliance of Independent Authors
The Association of Editors and Writers.

Robert J. Emery writes non-fiction under his real name and fiction under the pen name R.J. Eastwood. Over his long career as a member of the Directors Guild of America, he has written, produced, and directed both feature films and television programming and everything in between. Over his career, his film work garnered him over seventy-five industry awards. This release of the revised and expanded version of **MIDNIGHT BLACK** marks the publication of Mr. Emery ninth book, five of which were nonfiction.

When not writing, Bob can be found in the kitchen creating and preparing sumptuous Italian meals. He credits his culinary expertise to his Sicilian mother, Angelina Carmela Arico Emery, who taught him and his siblings to cook. They had to pay close attention because she never measured ingredients. It was all by taste.

Visit Mister Emery's author website to learn more about his work as a writer/director in the entertainment industry as well as his current writing projects. He enjoys hearing from readers and encourages them to connect with him on his social-media sites.

http://www.facebook.com/robertjemeryauthor.
http://twitter.com/bobemery
http://www.goodreads.com/author/show/1169565.Robert_
J_Emery

What Reviewers Wrote About Eastwood's Previous Novel.

THE AUTOPSY OF PLANET EARTH

Winner of the 2018 Readers' Favorite in Fiction

The 2018 Book Talk Radio Book of the Year

The 2017 Author's Circle Novel of Excellence Award for Fiction

The 2018 Pub Den Award for fiction

The 2019 International Review of Books Bronze Award

"Eastwood does an excellent job of taking what is familiar and crafting new worlds that are relatable allowing readers to logically suspend disbelief."

"Eastwood is Robert Heinlein on speed—a concept around every corner, an event around every page. This one is a page turner."

"His writing reads like 'The West Wing', with zingy dialogue and a strong authoritarian stance."

"Eastwood outstrips Dan Brown novels by miles. His writing provokes thought about concepts we seldom think about."

"Eastwood has panache in his style of writing reminiscent of Michael Crichton: crisp prose, intelligently humorous dialogue, and a structure that provides just enough momentum for a steamrolling pace to feel dangerously comfortable."

"Highly recommend to everyone interested in an intelligent, well-crafted novel written with a keen perception and cleverly apt expression of ideas that awaken the senses."

"Eastwood's short chapters and constant shifts in the storyline will create a powerful sense of suspense in readers and keep them turning pages, eager to discover what comes next."

"Brilliantly plotted and accomplished with a master's touch. A great read, indeed."

"Eastwood is creative and inspirational with a great imagination. Take the time to read this one!"

"I wish I had read this one with a Book Club because there were a lot of ideas and areas I would have liked to discuss as a group."